PRAISE FOR FO1

Phenomenal swoons, next-level heat, and a gorgeous exploration of taboo done right--not to mention characters so richly and sensitively drawn that I dare any reader to walk away not inspired to love themselves and their fellow humans better after they've finished reading Starla and Lowry's story.

— USA TODAY BESTSELLING AUTHOR SIERRA SIMONE

My favourite kind of erotic romance...deeply intimate, shockingly honest, and bravely kinky. For Her Own Good is one of my top reads of 2019.

— AINSLEY BOOTH, USA TODAY BESTSELLING AUTHOR OF HATE F*@K AND PRIME MINISTER

Come for the daddy kink, but stay for the rich character development and nuanced depictions of the human condition. I loved this book. *For Her Own Good* is classic Tamsen Parker.

— RITA AWARD WINNING AND USA TODAY BESTSELLING AUTHOR MOLLY O'KEEFE

A masterful crafting of kink, romance and love. It's been a very long time since I was so moved and engrossed by an erotic novel. My top erotic pick for 2019.

A deeply emotional and seriously sexy romance that flirts with the taboo, in the best way possible. Not many authors could make a kinky romance with daddy play between an older psychiatrist and his former patient work so well. But Parker absolutely can and does.

I have never been captivated by a story more quickly than I was with this one. This book is next level greatness and I cannot recommend it enough.

FOR HER OWN GOOD

TAMSEN PARKER

For my Fempire

$\mathcal{L}$owry

COULD'VE CALLED AN AMBULANCE. Probably should've. Couldn't bring myself to, and now I regret it. My hands are shaking so hard the steering wheel feels as though it's going to vibrate right off the drive shaft and I'm going to go careening into one of the perfectly groomed trees that line this far-too-long driveway. Starla and her rich friends. Though this boy, I can't call him a friend of hers. He never would have let her do this if he were a true friend. Fucking teenagers, thinking they know better than everyone else.

I'm even angrier at Starla, because of all people, she should know better. But the anger is a handful of dust scattered over a mountain of panic, concern, dread, and guilt. She's got to be okay. Even this shit-for-brains man-child should know enough to call 911 if she were truly in danger. But then again, look at me, screeching to a halt in front of this house. If you can call it that. More like some kind of monstrosity. I grew up in Scotland, I

1

know from castles, and this isn't one. It's trying so very hard, though.

I don't bother parking in any semblance of order, just vault up the few stairs before I pound on the door, ring the doorbell. Is it loud enough? Is there a humanly possible way in which I could be louder? My assault on the house echoes. The enormous door is locked and it feels too long until I hear the fall of footsteps. Long enough that I begin to consider breaking a window.

Finally, the door's pulled open and I nearly bowl over the person who answers it. He's a child. Tall and built like an athlete, but not a man yet. I wouldn't trust him with the keys to my car, never mind…

"Where is she?"

"She's in my bathroom. What the hell is wrong with her, anyway?"

If I didn't need his help finding Starla, I'd do him physical harm. What's *wrong* with her? Nothing he didn't encourage, nothing that couldn't have been prevented.

I get why Starla is angry and resentful. I get why she'd rebel like this. What I absolutely don't understand is how anyone who claims to love her could let it get this far.

I talked to her a month ago, when she skipped her appointment. She never skips her appointments. Because she's too smart, she's worked too hard, she's too mature—

But there's the rub. No matter how grown-up she may seem, she's not an adult. Which I am having to remind myself of with greater and greater frequency, to the extent that it's almost a chant in my head during our sessions.

She's a child, she's your patient, she needs your help.

Perhaps this will serve as the mallet to the brain I clearly need to banish any other kinds of thoughts about Starla Patrick from my mind. She still has some of that wild optimism and recklessness that teenagers do, and perhaps that's enough to quell my wildly inappropriate thoughts about my turned-eighteen-two-months-ago patient.

Or not.

"I feel good," she said when I called after she didn't show.

"You feel good because you've been doing what you're supposed to do. You don't feel as good as you did a week ago, do you?"

"I feel fine."

Lies. I could hear it in her voice. She's always been shite at lying to me. So I tried to coax her, talk her out of doing something at best ill-advised and at worst flat-out dangerous.

"Come into the office and we can talk about this. I don't want to see this get out of hand. You've got everything under control."

"I know I do! So maybe I'm fine now, maybe I don't need your help anymore."

Rage. Embarrassment. Indignation. These are the things that had colored her voice, and I pinched the bridge of my nose, held my breath, sent up prayers to long-forgotten saints that I would be able to fix this before…before…

Then panic gripped me hard, because I couldn't stop myself from thinking the unthinkable, the thing that makes my stomach riot.

I've lost patients before. Not as many as my colleagues battling in the ER, or the ones fighting the good fight in cancer wards. But I've failed them all the same, and they've ended up just as dead; lives taken by diseases that forced their hands. I cannot, *will not,* lose Starla. Period, end of story.

Sheer terror scrambled my brain, though, and I said the absolute last thing I should've.

"Was this Milo's idea?"

"No!"

Then she hung up on me. Turned off her phone altogether because no matter how many times I tried calling, the hospital tried calling, her father tried calling, it always went straight to voicemail. I resorted to having my admin call local hospitals and police stations to see if she'd shown up there. Her father went looking for her as well, but the thing about rich kids is that they have too many resources at their disposal and are well-practiced at going to ground for some fucking privacy.

Here we are a month later because it finally occurred to Milo that Starla is in fact *not* fine, that she does actually need help, and no matter what he thought he could offer her, it wasn't enough to keep her demons at bay. She's probably scared him to death, and I hope he's taking some of the blame on himself because she never would've been able to hide away for so long if she hadn't had someone to help her. Worse, someone whispering bullshit into her head. Someone probably making her feel ashamed for the things she needs in order to be a functional human being. I loathe this boy.

This house is too goddamn big and it takes forever for Milo to lead me to a bedroom plastered with posters of snowboarding and concerts with laundry strewn about, including on the queen-sized bed, and into an en suite.

There she is. Everything else melts away because she's here. In rough shape, yes. But alive. I can see her breathing, narrow shoulders heaving while she's curled into herself on the bottom of the tub. Her dark hair is soaking wet, stringy and sticking to her face and neck; her skin is pale and goose-pimpled, and she's clutching a towel while her entire body shivers.

The momentary relief I experienced at seeing her alive is eclipsed by rage, and the only thing stopping me from ripping a towel bar out of the wall and beating Milo to death with it is that I'd lose my license and go to prison. No way to look after Starla then.

Instead, I start digging through the linens on the floor to find a dry towel, and speak to Milo in a tone I'm sure he doesn't realize is a knife's blade on the edge of slitting his throat for being an irresponsible, negligent dilettante.

"Why is she in your bathtub?"

He wrinkles his nose as if I'm the blockhead here. "That's where she was when I got home. Look, I turned off the water and gave her a towel, okay? But she wouldn't get out."

"You didn't move her? You didn't dress her? She's not violent."

"I don't know what the fuck to do with her. Look at her!"

I am and it's killing me. Milo can fuck off and go to hell. He's not my concern. Starla is. With the towels I grabbed, I get down on my knees beside the tub. As much as I want to touch her, I don't. Can't.

"Starla?"

She clutches the towel tighter beneath her chin and doesn't look at me. I can only imagine she's scared, but also mortified, and because she's so damn hard on herself, likely disappointed and angry at herself. And depending on how firmly Milo's opinions have taken root in her head, she's probably wondering what is so very wrong with her that she can't be like other girls. She's said these things before in sessions, and I try my best to help her understand that the fact her brain chemistry isn't the same as other people's doesn't make her broken, doesn't make her less than in any way.

It's been so long too, since her last ECT that her depression is probably drowning her. Making it hard to get out of bed—Christ, she'd probably been proud that she'd made it into the shower at all—yelling at her that she's useless and pathetic and no one wants her or loves her. She's wrong about all of that. But that's the kind of shit depression pulls, and it's my job to make it quiet enough that she can hear the good and true things over it. And to never, ever mention the unseemly thoughts I have about her.

"Starla, come on. Look at me."

She shakes her head, though, and my heart crumbles. It's not the first time she's refused to look at me, but it's usually out of bullheaded intransigence, not anguish and embarrassment. I've got to do something, got to fix this. No matter what it takes.

"Hey. If you're worried I'm mad, I'm not. I've been worried because I was concerned something had happened to you. I'm happy you're okay, and your father will be so relieved. No one is angry and no one thinks you're a failure. I know it's hard to hear, so let me make it easier. You know it can be better. It wasn't so long ago that you did feel better. If you come with me, we can make it better again. Together. I promise."

The slightest turn of her head lets her peek out between the lank strands of hair plastered to her face. "Promise?"

Her whisper reaches deep into me, twists my gut until I can barely breathe. I rarely make promises to my patients. I don't bullshit them, I don't lie. Mental illness is really fucking hard, and it's a crapshoot seeing what will work and what won't. If, in fact, anything *will* work, and then how well, and at what cost. But in this case, I know what works for Starla, and there's no reason it shouldn't work again. Even if it doesn't? I will be there to help her figure out something that does, if it takes the rest of my life.

"Promise."

CHAPTER 1

owry

"You know you didn't have to bring me to the airport. Even married people don't bring each other to the airport. 'Take a Lyft —no way in hell I'm going to O'Hare at that time of day. Are you completely daft?'"

Maeve gives me the same kind of look she's been leveling at me for the past decade which translates directly to "Shut up, Lowry."

"I know I don't have to, but it's a nice thing to do and I can do it. You never let me do enough nice things for you. I'm surprised you said yes to this."

I scratch at my jaw. "Well, I would rather spend an hour in a car with you than with a chatty cab driver. And at least I know Denny obeys traffic laws."

Maeve's chauffeur gives me a salute in the rearview mirror. I've always liked that guy. Made me feel better during the split knowing he'd be around. Not that Maeve's ever needed much in the way of help, but you never know what'll come up.

"I'm flattered you think so highly of us both," she responds archly. "But I also wanted to see you before you took off. I wasn't sure when you'd be back. If you'll be back."

I shrug. "Truth be told, I don't know either. It's not like I've got anything against Chicago, I just feel more at home in Boston. I'll ring you up if I'm in town for a conference or something. And if you'll be in Boston, drop me a line. I'll make room in my busy social calendar."

"For your favorite ex-wife? I'd hope so."

She arches one of those perfect dark brows of hers as Denny guides the car up to the curb in front of the terminal.

"Eh, you're my favorite wife I've ever had too." I lean over to give her a kiss on the cheek and she accepts it regally, like most things she does, no doubt refraining from rolling her eyes because she's been my only wife. "Don't be a stranger, and don't get into too much trouble. At least that you can't get yourself out of again, aye?"

I climb out of the car, grabbing my briefcase from the floor, and she calls after me, "As long as you agree to take care of yourself. Not just everyone else, but actually yourself."

Ducking into the doorframe, I give her a half smile, because we both know I'll be fine-ish. After all, if I don't put my oxygen mask on first, how can I help anyone else's with theirs? I could examine *that* logic more closely but I'd rather not, so instead, I'll deflect.

"What are you, a doctor or something?"

"No, I was just married to one. But really, be careful, okay? I know you don't think you're going to Boston for her—"

"Because I'm not."

"Mm-hmm. You could've gotten a job anywhere and that's the one you took? The exact same place you left fifteen years ago? You don't fool me, Lowry Harrison Campbell."

Nor do I fool myself. Maeve and I both know about the impromptu trip I took a few months ago. And who I definitely did not take it for. It's just that I always like to make a trip to Boston in August, sure. When the humidity is so thick you feel as though you're swimming through the city instead of walking through it. The oppressive heat that makes a person break into a sweat as soon as they step outside, plus the bugs? Yes, it is chef-kiss perfection, precisely what I enjoy. *Sure you do, Campbell. You wouldn't believe that steaming heap of bullshit from any of your patients either.*

"Never could."

We exchange wan smiles, years of being friends, lovers, spouses, and then friends again between us. Why could things not have worked out with Maeve? She's intelligent, lovely with her sharply bobbed deep auburn hair and dark brown eyes, and I like her very much. And yet. We turned out to be pieces of a puzzle who fit together, just not the way we'd hoped.

Without another word, I close the car door and take my carry-on from Denny who's retrieved it from the boot. Everything else has been shipped ahead to the apartment I've rented sight-unseen, so I'm traveling light.

"You look after her as much as she'll let you, aye?"

"Always."

I shake his hand, and then it's time to make my way through the bustling airport to head back to Boston. A city I fled fifteen ago and at the time, never thought I'd go back to. But there's been a hole in my heart since then, and I'm hoping it will be filled by going back to this old New England city. If you can call it *old*, at any rate. Americans have no sense of history.

It's ridiculous, really, to be going back. There's no reason to think—

Well, as I told Maeve. It's about the job. I wanted the job. I loved that job—though I'll be working with adults and not children and adolescents as I had before. But most of what I loved is the same: the colleagues, the culture of constant learning and improvement via the latest research, the bucolic campus of the hospital. That's all there is to it. A job.

STARLA

Airports are not my favorite. The people, the bustle, the announcements you can't understand but are probably trying to tell you something important? Yeah, not my jam. It's better now that I'm settled in my seat in the last row of first class and don't have to worry about missing my flight, or it being delayed without me knowing. All the things that, while fundamentally insignificant, really cheese people about air travel. I can breathe easier now.

Traveling for work isn't my idea of a good time. But when a client like Rafa Cabrero asks me to come to Chicago to help set up his brand-new eight-million-dollar condo, I don't say no. Not that I need the money, but I do like my business to run in the black. Also, Rafa really does need me and it makes me feel good to be part of his secret to success.

We struggle with different things—anxiety is his primary issue whereas mine's depression—but we both find keeping tabs on our physical space to be helpful in managing our shit. So, he took a few days out of his busy finance industry schedule so we could set up systems big and small to help him be successful and in control, which in turn lowers his anxiety, which leads to being more successful and feeling more in control and well, you see how this works. It's not magic, but it does take attention to detail, and an understanding of how mental illness can fuck with people's heads.

These cycles we get ourselves involved in don't always have to be bad, and that's what I'd been here to help with: setting up this incredibly talented and brilliant man whose brain glitches when faced with certain stimuli to spend less time glitching and more time doing the things he's awesome at. Those things he's awesome at? They helped him buy that prime piece of real estate in the first place. Yes, Rafa had been very grateful, and I'm headed home feeling satisfied with a job well done.

Besides, it's good for me to get out of Boston on occasion. I don't often—what's this "vacation" some people speak of?—but I had enjoyed the couple of extra days I'd taken to do some sight-seeing. The museums, the aquarium—I even braved Navy Pier—they'd all kept me busy, my mind engaged with things other than the issues constantly gnawing at me lately.

It's been rough for the past three months to be at home, ghosts around every corner. I miss my father. So much. But I've also got Tad Harding breathing down my neck and not the way he used to when we were together—that was, if ultimately a fail-ure, still the sweaty, sexy, orgasm-inducing kind of being on top of me. This is none of that, except maybe the sweaty part because anxiety is fantastic like that.

I've inherited a controlling interest in Patrick Enterprises and I need to make some decisions. But I'm not ready yet. Aside from it feeling like a very final goodbye to my father that I can't bear to make, even thinking about it spikes my anxiety.

If managing my own shit is like rolling a boulder up a hill on my best days like a modern-day Sisyphus, then holding tens of thousands of people's livelihoods in my hands is like having a rockslide behind the boulder. But even knowing what I'm headed back to—and as much as I don't like planes because strangers are all up in your shit and honestly, air travel brings out the worst in humanity—I'm glad to be on my way home. Traveling makes my anxiety kick up too, and it's getting closer to the six-week mark of my ECT cycle so everything's getting more difficult because of the depression that's started tiptoeing around again.

Getting out of bed. Getting dressed. All the things most

people take for granted are tasks that start to make me feel accomplished when I check them off my list. So, more difficult, yes, but not anywhere near impossible. I never get anywhere close to impossible these days. Which is perhaps part of the reason my father felt it was wise to direct that rockslide in my direction.

I don't need to think about that yet, though. What I should do is take this opportunity to relax, breathe, and enjoy the last few hours before I'm on the ground at Logan—Boston, you're my home.

Compared to the flat, wide-open spaces of Chicago, this space is cramped. I'm hoping the aisle seat next to me—which is technically mine, but I prefer the window so I've occupied it—will remain empty, although the flight attendants have been telling everyone the flight is full and given the overstuffed overheads, I believe them. Nothing I can do about it though, so I may as well read my book while I wait for takeoff.

I'm perhaps more tired than I thought after spending two full days with Rafa and then two more wandering around Chicago, taking advantage of the city's excellent culinary scene when I wasn't walking or riding the "L" between tourist sites.

The words on my Kindle start to blur and swim, and I catch my chin dropping to my chest a few times but try to shake myself awake to read more of *The Devil in the White City*, which I started on my way out here.

I wake with a start to someone dropping into the seat next to me. I crack a crabby eye to see who's disturbed me and instead of some standard road warrior in a Brooks Brothers skirt suit or a guy coming home from a bachelor party weekend with his buddies, I get hit with a bolt of lightning. It's like a kick to the chest, and my lungs empty in a choking rush. It's not possible.

But from the way he's looking at me—blue eyes blown wide, ginger brows crunched, and his mouth slightly open—he feels the same way, which is what confirms it. It's him. It's really him.

After not having seen him for fifteen years, I have the... misfortune? Tough break? Devil's own luck—yes, that seems most apt—to find myself trapped next to the only man I've ever really loved, the one who abandoned me when I needed him most, the one who alternately haunted and blessed my dreams even before he'd gone. And oh yeah, the man who saved my life and kept me from destroying myself when it was so, so tempting to end it all.

Lowry goddamn Campbell.

Or should I say *Doctor* Campbell, since I only ever called him Lowry in whispers at night in the dark, half the time with my hand between my legs.

LOWRY

I'd wondered when I first saw the woman in the window seat. Her long, chestnut-dark hair, the slope of her shoulder. I couldn't see her face since it had been turned to the window, neck unnaturally bent in sleep, but those similarities alone had brought on a fond pang in my chest. That pang has turned into a riot of some sort, like the lads down at the football pitch, because it's not an apparition. Or if it is, it is the most realistic one I've ever seen. Disturbingly so. If she is indeed a doppelganger, she's going to haunt my dreams.

She's glaring at me with those hazel eyes of hers rimmed with dark lashes.

"What the fuck are you doing here?"

So it is Starla. If I'd had any doubts left knocking around in my head, they'd be cleared by the way she snaps out the question. She always did have a tongue like a whip, except when things were at their worst and I could barely get her to look at me, never mind speak. It shouldn't please me, the way she cusses and looks like she's going to dig my eyeballs out with her nails—wouldn't please many people, that's for sure—but a good portion of what I'm feeling is delight. Relief. She's doing well. Looks tired, sure, since I woke her, but on the whole, very good. Healthy, vibrant, and very much alive.

I would've known if she'd died. If she'd... Well. But it's not as easy to know from afar how a person is faring otherwise. Google alerts only tell a person so much, although more in the past three months than in the last fifteen years altogether. I suppose that's when the fact she's an heiress to a massive corporate conglomerate became much more relevant—since she's not an heiress anymore. Simply one of the wealthiest people on the Eastern seaboard. She's still just Starla to me.

"I..." *You're a smooth one, you are, Campbell.* "My ticket's actually for the window."

She looks at me as though I'm rather daft with those forest-floor hazel eyes of hers and then shakes her head, muttering what I'm certain are more curses, and reaches for her seat belt.

"No, no. It's fine. You don't have to, I prefer the aisle actually. I just..."

Didn't know what to say. It's been fifteen years and I've seen photos of her, but had resigned myself to never seeing her in the flesh ever again.

She's had an expressive face ever since I've known her, at least when she wasn't drowning, and it's remarkable how I can still read her, how the clues on her face have remained so similar, though her features have become concentrated somehow. Sharper. She was lovely then, and she's beautiful now, her cheekbones and jawline more defined, making her wide mouth and her round eyes more prominent. She's truly gorgeous, the fact that she wants to murder me not detracting from her appeal in the least.

"Whatever."

She looks me over again, and if it were possible to send

daggers through one's eyes, I would be dead as a doornail right now.

"So are you going to answer my question?"

Question? Ah, right. What the fuck am I doing here?

"I live in Chicago. Well, lived, I suppose. I…I'm moving back to Boston."

"You're…you're moving back to Boston? You left fifteen years ago without a goddamn word and now you're back? You're not supposed to come back. You're supposed to be gone. Forever."

Not exactly a hero's welcome, but I'm pretty far from a hero. I do wish this had gone some other way but this is how it's going and I scramble to make it a tad less awkward and, well, less likely to result in my death.

"I, uh, am sorry to disappoint you." Not as sorry as I'd been fifteen years ago, but now I can tell her I'm sorry. "I hope you know I really am truly sorry about—"

She puts a hand in my face, the universal symbol for stop, and my mouth snaps shut. The fury in her eyes is still burning hot and even if it weren't, I'd honor her request for silence. It is literally the least I can do.

"No. Absolutely not. I don't accept your apology and I never will. You're the one who taught me that I am not required to give anyone my forgiveness, that sometimes there are hurts too deep to be forgiven. That's how much you hurt me when you left, and you don't deserve my forgiveness so, no. You can shut your face and you can find yourself a new seat on this plane because I would rather sit next to a rathtar than you."

Girl still loves *Star Wars*. Not girl—woman. She's thirty-three years old and a grown, mature, elegantly dressed woman.

Who still uses *Star Wars* references. I knew she'd see the new ones; had wondered as I watched them if she'd enjoyed them. I'd ask, but she's punching the button to summon the flight attendant.

One bustles over, the red, white, and blue kerchief at her neck fluttering as she makes her way to us.

"Yes? We'll be taking off shortly, so unless it's an emergency—"

"Could you switch this man to a different seat? Any seat will do. I can see there are no free seats left in first class, but seriously, even something on the wings or in the cargo bay would do. You don't need to worry about his comfort. At all."

The woman's gaze flicks between me and Starla, and I give her a pleasant, innocent smile.

"I'm sorry, the flight is completely full and there are no open seats. And federal regulations prohibit—"

"Fuck my life," Starla mutters, burying her head in her hands.

"Is he... Is this man bothering you? If he's assaulted you or is harassing you, I can have them delay takeoff and get security onboard, but..."

Her mouth wrenches to the side, clearly unable to decide which of us to believe. I'm calm, Starla is livid, but if I'd done something truly awful to Starla—now, not fifteen years ago—I'm glad the attendant is willing to shut this whole thing down to fix it. As things are...

Starla's head snaps up and she levels me with a calculating glare before clearing her throat and putting on a forced smile to turn on the flight attendant.

"No, he hasn't done anything like that. Or committed any kind of crime. He deserves to have his heart cut out with a rusty spoon and fed to him, but he's not violent, he's not a threat to anyone. He can see if someone will switch after takeoff."

I suppose I could, but I don't want to. Boundaries, though. She's allowed to have them, as are we all, and it would be unforgivably hypocritical of me to insist that she dispose of hers. She needs them more than most people, and I helped her build them.

～

STARLA

Never has three hours seemed so long. It is absolute torture to sit this close to Lowry, burning with questions—where have you been? What have you been doing? Who have you been doing it with? Are you happy? Did you miss me? Did you think of me at all?—and determined not to say a single word. Because if I open the floodgates, I doubt I'll be able to close them. And I cannot subject myself to that again. To feel anything but anger toward this man who abandoned me at the worst possible time.

Yet I feel the other impulses creeping in and I hate myself for them. Fifteen years didn't do anything to dull the attraction I feel for him. It's still as sharp as a knife that could gut me, leave my entrails spilling into my hands. If anything, he's gotten more handsome. How is that a thing men can do? Some women too, I suppose, but it's mostly a guy thing.

He's always had a line bisecting his brows, one I thought of as the mark of him being a psychiatrist because it would deepen when he had his listening face on, which was most of the time. The past decade and a half has also given him brackets around his mouth—I hope from the broad smiles that always made me feel like the sun had come out—lines on his forehead, plus some crow's feet and red fading into strawberry blond and gold at his temples for good measure. It pokes at a part of me that doesn't need poking, especially not around Doctor Lowry goddamn Campbell anyway.

He is, after all, the one I blame for my daddy kink. Well, not so much *blame*, because I suspect I would've had an eye for older men no matter what. Would've wanted to be cosseted and doted upon, instructed and corrected even as I'm cherished, regardless of whether or not I had been his patient and foisted my adolescent affections upon him. But I feel like he's the one who confirmed those feelings for me. Distilled them into something so strong, I could no longer ignore it or think this was how

17

everyone felt toward their puppy love crushes. No, the urges and fantasies I had—and annoyingly, still have—about this man weren't the same as the ones I heard the girls in high school and in college repeat.

I am definitely not sneaking glances at him whenever humanly possible. Certainly not taking the opportunity to stare when his back is turned as he gets up to use the restroom. He still seems tall. Still dresses in a way that pushes my buttons real hard; shawl-collared sweater with a button-down underneath that should make him look ridiculous, but he gets away with it in his neatly tailored wool trousers and—someone must've gotten ahold of him because he's upgraded his shoe game considerably. I ought to know; I spent a lot of time staring at his feet throughout my latter years of high school.

Goddammit. Goddammit all to hell. Because when he sits back down, our forearms brush and I barely keep from whimpering at the electric charge. Same fucking one that would always hit me whenever I had the—rare—opportunity to touch him. Then humiliation surges through me remembering the last time I touched him. Or rather, was touched by him. No wonder he left. Which doesn't make any sense. I'm sure he'd tell me so himself. He always was telling me not to take on too much, and this is something I can't—or at least shouldn't—blame myself for.

Him leaving had nothing to do with the fact that he'd had to pry me out of a bathtub, soaking wet and naked save for a towel, only to dress me and braid my hair because he knows—knew—I hate hair in my face, and then take me to the hospital so I could do what I should've done over a month before. Because that's what happened—we both knew it would, and I did it anyway. Skipped my ECT because I wanted to be a "real girl"—whatever the hell that is—and be able to live my life without being anesthetized and have electricity run through my brain every six weeks.

Haven't skipped it again since because that disaster left me scarred. The greatest humiliation of my life. And while I often have some memory issues from the day before and the two after my treatments, that particular episode is forever seared into my brain. Because I'm lucky like that.

It's a wonder he didn't request to switch seats himself. He can't have fond memories of the calamity I was, how much work he poured into me—and how did I show my gratitude? By trashing it all for a month of living with my boyfriend at the time, which resulted in the inevitable breakdown because as much as I'd like it to, my depression won't quit, and there's only one thing I've ever found that can keep it at bay. And it ain't tepid teenage sex and other adolescent indulgences like eating cookies for breakfast. Lowry knew better, and I should've too.

Is there enough room beneath this seat to crawl under? No, which is unfortunate.

At least he doesn't talk to me for the rest of the flight. The rage has faded and I doubt his lilting accent would do anything to reignite it. If anything, it would crank up my steadfast lust for him and I don't think I could deal.

We land without incident, and as the plane makes its way to the gate, I feel him turn to me and I steel myself. *Don't. Just don't. Get up and leave and don't talk to me because hearing you speak hurts me too much. Reminds me of when you carried me out to your car, tucked me into the front seat, and spoke to me the whole way to Harbinson.*

He must've known given the state I was in that I could barely hear him, but he did it nonetheless. Stayed with me until the anesthetic took effect, and I can only imagine after that as well, though my memories of him being there are solely of when I woke up.

Yes, Lowry. Please leave and don't force me to endure your presence any further.

He clears his throat and I close my eyes. *Don't fucking do it.*

And yet.

"Starla. I—"

I turn away because having him say my name is a stab to the heart. It is physically painful, an intensified version of how my body starts to ache from the depression that's bogging it down. It's all exhausting, it all hurts.

"I'm sorry. I'm sorry to ask this of you. But could you look at me so I know you're hearing me?"

Ah yes, up to his old tricks. He used to ask me for this when I didn't have anything to give. I could always look at him, though. For the most part, enjoyed it even when I couldn't feel much of anything else. An animal reflex, that feeling of comfort and safety when I saw his face. I don't feel that way now, but my body apparently doesn't realize that, so before I can consciously stop myself, I'm glaring at him. At least there's that. Let him know I'll do it but I am not happy about it. Not at all.

"I wanted you to know I'll be back on staff at Harbinson. You might see me. If you're still—"

"I am."

For fuck's sake.

"Then you might see me there. I didn't want to surprise you."

"Well, you're doing a bang-up job so far, Doctor Campbell."

He has the good grace to look abashed. I don't love going to Harbinson anyway—who would?—but it's at least a place I associate with feeling better. I'm not as resentful as I was as a teenager, but all things being equal, I'd rather not be a regular at a psychiatric hospital. Which I know is ridiculous, and I allow other people far more grace than I do myself. The shame and embarrassment about being "defective" is deeply ingrained. Even knowing that's not true. Brains can be shitty sometimes.

He nods once, the motion crisp, and I turn away. He doesn't insist I look at him again so I gaze out the window until everyone —including the good doctor—has deplaned and then I try to get on with my life. As if that's going to be possible knowing that Doctor Lowry Campbell is back.

owry

I'VE BEEN in town for over a month, back at Harbinson, settled in a new apartment nearby though still in the city, whereas the hospital complex is at the inner suburban edge. I've seen some old colleagues and met new ones. Joined a gym, established a schedule. Been asked out on a date but didn't go.

Everything is falling into place, and it turns out that yes, I did miss Boston. There's something to be said for the haphazard and cramped streets of the city, and knowing the chill that radiates from most of the people here covers up a deep and abiding loyalty—and not just to the Red Sox.

My slate of clients filled up almost immediately, which is good. I like to be busy. From dawn to dusk, and sometimes later if I go out with colleagues, my days are full. I have everything a man could want. And yet…

I haven't seen Starla since I walked away from her on the plane. Which she's most likely fine with but I am…not. I won't do anything about it because she made it clear that I'm not welcome in her space and I understand why. Even if I didn't, I would respect her request.

I'm reminded of her presence not through anything particular in the office—though I know she sees Doctor Gendron regularly because it's on the office schedule—but because I can't be here without thinking of her. She's a clear, clean note at the back of my brain I want to silence—mostly for her sake—but I can't help returning to it again and again.

Like now, when I'm lying in bed, waiting for my alarm to go off. I went to bed early last night because there was nothing else I wanted to do, and now I'm staring at the blank ceiling in my bachelor's apartment. Maeve would be disgusted. Perhaps I'll ask her to visit. She'd decorate the place whether I wanted her to or not. But if I do end up dating and someone compliments me on the decor, do I really want to say my ex-wife did it? Probably not. So the walls will mostly stay bare. Maeve at least ensured my closet's full of decent clothes and nominally fashionable shoes.

But as kindly as I think of Maeve, she's not at the forefront of my mind. No, that would be Starla. Starla with the fury sparking in her eyes and the way she gave me a very thorough tongue-lashing. *Christ, Campbell, you can't think of her tongue.* Or her lips, or her wide eyes, or the gloss of her hair. Does she still hate to have it in her face? She always did. It was one of the signs she was feeling truly awful: she'd let it hang in her face, not bother to get it out of her eyes, off her forehead.

What I do know is despite her best efforts to ignore me, she snuck glances in my direction. Is she as curious about me as I am about her? I know some things—what the most basic search on the internet would tell me—but not the most important things.

Is she happy? Is she at peace? Does she like her job? I'm assuming so, because it would be easy enough for her to drop it if she didn't. It's not as though she needs the money.

As for what she's doing, well. She set up shop as a consultant to help people with mental health issues arrange their schedules and living/working spaces in a way that fits their needs better, which is admirable. Clinicians don't always have time to do that granular work, but it can make huge improvements in patients' quality of life. I'd think she'd be very good at it, and the flexibility of running her own business must be a boon as well, though a lot of pressure. Or perhaps she can handle those elements in her sleep given her father taught her how to run an empire.

These are the things I'd like to know but have no way of asking her. I won't violate her privacy by asking Lacey—Doctor Gendron to her, I suppose—either.

And I definitely need to stop thinking about how goddamn good she looked even as she scowled at me on that plane.

My alarm goes off, rescuing me from my sad attempts to shove Starla Patrick from my mind and not—definitely not—daydream about her while I'm in my bed. Saved from perving on my ex-patient by the bell. Again.

STARLA

As much as I'd like to focus on the reminder system I'm setting up for one of my clients with ADHD, I'm thinking a lot more about a certain ginger psychiatrist than I am about sticky notes, white boards, and planners. It's annoying.

It's annoying to have a man who abandoned me in reality haunt my dreams where I can't tell him to fuck off. I could, I suppose—lucid dreaming is a thing and I've made use of it before —but I maybe enjoy it. Especially since the only way I'm regularly getting off these days is by my own hand. Yes, I see my play partner Jade sometimes, though not since my father's death. And if Dream Lowry wants to help me obtain orgasms, then perhaps it's the least he can do. He owes me that much, right? *Right?*

That's my story and I'm sticking to it, because I don't want to have a guilt complex about how I perhaps woke up this morning with my hand in my underwear and didn't remove it until after I'd rubbed one out while transmuting my dream into a much more conscious fantasy. A fantasy which involved the good doctor bending me over his knee and taking his belt to my upturned bottom and then fucking me into next week while telling me he's wanted this for years, and how happy he is that I can finally be his good little girl.

Yeah, it was definitely one of the most explosive, toe-curling, back-arching, moan-inducing climaxes I've had in some time. I mean, prior to the past month at any rate, because they're a somewhat regular happening now that Doctor Lowry Campbell is back in town.

We had a chance run-in on a plane, yes, but also knowing he walks the same halls I do at Harbinson makes dread and anticipation—two sides of the same anxious coin—war inside me. Alongside the low buzz of wanting to find out what it would be like for it to be him getting me off with his thick, blunt fingers while he croons to me in that dreamy voice of his, or even better, for him to be pounding into me with his cock, instead of me making use of one of my favorite dildos while I imagine all the filthy things we could do together.

How the fuck am I supposed to think about Kanban boards now? Not that I don't find organization and office supplies sexy, but do they really compare to a somewhat-taboo crush—complete with masturbatory fantasies—on my ex-psychiatrist? Frankly, I don't think they do. There is little in this world that does.

Thank fuck my phone rings because I've got to get this man out of my head. Hell, I'd even be less than ragey at the prospect of talking to Tad right now if I could only get Lowry to vacate the premises of my mind. As if he hasn't spent enough years sifting around in there. But it's not Tad, it's the main line at Harbinson, perhaps Lacey's admin calling to reschedule or something like that. Whatever it is, bring on the distraction.

"Hello, this is Starla."

"Starla, it's—"

Goddammit. Goddammit all to hell. He doesn't need to say his name. I know who it is. Yes, there's a thrill that runs through me at the sound of his voice, but all he needs to know about is the fit of pique.

"What do you want, Doctor Campbell?"

"You could start by not calling me Doctor Campbell. We're both adults, you're not my patient anymore. You can call me Lowry."

If he only knew how many times I'd called him that in my mind, while I had incredibly inappropriate fantasies about him when I was in fact his patient...and also a couple of hours ago. Which is less scandalous, but no less mortifying. My face burns hot thinking about it. Thank god he can't see me and the shade of scarlet my cheeks have no doubt turned given the heat warming my entire face.

"What can I do for you, Doctor Campbell?"

Yes, I have all sorts of feelings about Lowry Campbell and a whole bunch of them involve wanting to make all those dreams I had come true, but I'm still a child to him. So, to remind myself, "Doctor Campbell" and a crisp, no-nonsense address it is.

"This is a purely professional call. I was wondering if you were taking on new clients."

That brings me up short. I wasn't aware Lowry knew what I do for a living. It's not as though the information isn't readily available, but why would he have looked? A spike of that same exhilaration goes through me. He thought of me? I wasn't merely a passing—and super angry—thing flitting by like an enraged wasp? But clearly not in the same way I've thought of him. *Professional.* I can be professional as fuck.

"I have a couple of openings, yes. Why?"

Now that Rafa is settled in Chicago, my workload for my own business has been comparatively light. It's of course more than made up for by all the time I spend doing things for my father's business and I'm still not doing enough. I'll never be able to do enough because... It doesn't matter. The point is that I'd be more than happy to wedge another client into my schedule and be able to make excuses about why I can't be on yet another interminable conference call or some other meeting because I'm expected to make decisions about everything, all the time. Yes, please, for the love of god, give me something to do that I'm competent at.

"I have a patient I think you might be able to help. She deals with some anxiety, but her primary diagnosis is ADHD which isn't my area of expertise. I've been seeing her weekly for the last month and while we talk through some of the ways she could organize her space and her workload, we also have a lot of other issues to address. Given that it would take more time than I can devote to her, and also that it's not precisely in my wheelhouse, I mentioned you to her but didn't want to make any promises. May I send her your way?"

Oh. Lowry thinks enough of me, my professional acumen, to refer a patient to me? He believes I'm stable enough to help others? Which I fucking am, thankyouverymuch, but still. It's... it's really nice. It makes the fire that lit on my face moments ago settle into a crackling warmth in my belly. Approval, from a nurturing man I respect and find attractive. It's basically my daddy kink kryptonite and I could... I don't know, whatever happens to Superman when he gets exposed to kryptonite. I'm a *Star Wars* nerd, not a DC Comics geek.

I try to focus on the pride of it, which makes sense. Anyone would be proud their former psychiatrist who saw them through 90 percent of the worst shit of their lives thinks they're good enough to be trusted with their own patients. Not everyone would be getting turned on by that, though. Not everyone would want to be told that while sitting, cradled, on Lowry's lap and then squirming with delight until he issued a mild threat to spank me if I didn't stop. And would I?

Doesn't matter. What does matter is that Lowry has a patient he thinks I can help. Even though potentially working with Lowry to help this client to the best of my abilities pokes at some vulnerable places, I won't pass up work or refuse to offer my services to someone because I'm still bruised from Lowry's abrupt departure over a decade ago. Especially since I already told him I had time. I'm awkward enough already, thanks.

"Yes, of course. You, uh, obviously have my number. Or she can email me if she prefers. I assume you have that as well."

He makes a noncommittal noise that I'll take as agreement.

"Have her mention she's your patient, and we'll see how it goes."

"Brilliant. Thank you."

Lowry thanking me? That's something I never expected. I always figured I'd be the one forever being grateful to him. Which I am. I doubt I would be here on this earth if it weren't for him, never mind being a successful professional to whom he feels comfortable referring his own patients. Yes, that is a flattering turn of the tables, and it's perfectly reasonable to have to swipe at the corners of my eyes. Perhaps allergy season has started? But fucking A, it's November, so that's bullshit. Steaming heap of it. Feelings it is, then. Worst.

I don't need Lowry knowing he's got me choked up, but I suppose I should respond. At least somewhat politely. Manners— I have those, right?

"You're welcome." Damn it felt good to say that. And I should say something else as well. "Thank you for thinking of me… That means a lot."

And then because a human being can only take so many feelings in a day, I hang up on him.

~

LOWRY

The feisty little thing hung up on me. I take the phone from my ear and stare at it in case that's not actually what happened, but it definitely is. I wasn't finished yet. Although perhaps this is better since I did tell her it was a purely professional call.

It wasn't. I mean, I do have a patient who I think could benefit immensely from Starla's particular services, that wasn't a lie. I wouldn't do that to Starla. She sounded so innocently pleased that I would refer someone to her, but honestly, how could I not? I looked around her website, read the testimonials, and it surprises me not at all that she's excellent at what she's chosen to do. There was never any doubt in my mind about her intelligence or drive, only whether she could manage her depression well enough to let the rest of her shine. And it seems she's been able to. I couldn't be prouder.

I'd been pacing my office while talking to her, and now I drop into one of my office chairs. My desk looks odd from this angle since I never sit over here. Mostly my patients don't either. We're usually in the sitting area, which is more comfortable. It's a different office than the one I had before, when Starla was my patient, but the things I have in here—my books, my diplomas, the photographs I took on a trip to the Isle of Skye—they're all the same.

My office phone rests in my hand and I fiddle with it.

If she hung up on me, does that mean she doesn't want to talk to me? Or does she want to talk to me but doesn't think she should? You'd think spending ten years studying psychiatry and figuring out how the human mind works would prepare one for dealing with real people. That's less true than I would've hoped.

When she was a girl, on her good days, Starla wasn't great about hiding how she felt about me. I'd known she had a bit of a crush. Which, honestly, was to be expected. I was young, she trusted me, I talked to her like she was a responsible and intelligent person—because she was—and I like to think I helped her. It's not at all unusual for patients to develop crushes on their therapists.

These days, getting a read on her is more complicated. She seems to want to gouge my eyes out with whatever might be handy, but I could swear there's something else there as well. Maybe nothing more than a residual curiosity or fondness from all those years ago. But if I'm not completely deluding myself that she could be interested in a man eighteen years her senior—my God, I'm a fossil—then possibly more than that. Of course, for all I know, she could be in a serious relationship. Although anyone she might be dating wasn't mentioned in the press recently, and I'd guess she would've volunteered that on the plane and didn't. Maybe not, though, in her fury.

What do I care if she's got a boyfriend, anyhow? Or a girl-friend? Or whomever? It's not as though I'd be asking her on a date. Any romantic interest I may or may not have in her is not why I'd like to have dinner with her. Entirely. But I would like to know that she's safe. Happy. Satisfied. Is that really so bad?

Yes, Lowry, you git. That is bad. She was your patient. You shouldn't be asking her to dinner, even fifteen years later. She has every right to want your head on a stake, your balls on a platter, and your entrails roasting over an open flame.

Given that, I shouldn't be doing anything with the phone in my hand other than returning it to its cradle on my desk. And yet, my fingers seem to be connected to a far more animal part of my brain, the part that would like to talk more to the beautiful, sharp, and challenging woman. The part that had been stewing in the back of my mind, putting these ideas in my head about, how, perhaps after I'd been in town for a bit, I could casually ask one of my former colleagues about her. And…I don't know. Is there a good way to run into your former patient on purpose? I'm fairly certain that's called stalking. So, though the urge is there, I won't act on it. I'll give her an opportunity to turn me down and then that will be that. One more phone call and then I'll force myself to stop, because if anyone deserves peace, it's Starla.

Before I can think better of it, I press redial because even having to press each of the digits would give me time to think better of this. Even though I know it's a terrible idea and anyone would tell me so, I don't *want* to be talked out of it. Because I'm terrible. Or human. Perhaps there's more overlap in that Venn diagram than I'd like to think, particularly when it comes to myself. Saint Lowry, my brothers used to call me. If they could see me now...

"Hi, this is Starla."

"Starla, this is—"

"Did you forget something, Doctor Campbell?"

Ach, the archness in her tone makes my balls ache. *Not good, Campbell. Not good at all.*

"Ah, no."

Forget? No. Not exactly. Wasn't given a chance to make any kind of chitchat that might've more naturally led up to this invitation? Yes.

"Then you're calling because...?"

"Because that last call was purely professional."

There's a pause, and I check my phone screen to make sure she hasn't hung up on me again. But no, the connection is still live.

"And what's this one?"

"Well, I...I'm new in town, and—"

"You're not new. You went to med school and did your residency and fellowship here, in addition to practicing here for four years after that. That's sixteen years, if I'm not mistaken. You've been gone a long time, but you're not new. I'm sure you've kept in touch with friends and colleagues and old classmates who are happy you're back and would like to spend time with you, so don't give me that."

I hadn't realized she'd paid any attention to where I'd gone to school or done my residency, though all that's true. I ought to have come up with a better excuse. Though given that much time, I might've come to my senses and decided not to call her at all, and I like the sound of her voice in my ear—rimy though it may be. So, continued fumbling will have to do. "Okay, that's true, but I don't know the hot spots these days. Half my haunts are probably closed."

"And that's my problem because?"

Ice cold. Well, I do deserve an icicle through the heart for having left when and how I did. I saw her through the acute, inpatient time after that unfortunate episode but when I wasn't tending to her and my other patients during her stay, I was doing my utmost to find other employ and it didn't take long to succeed. Then I was gone, without a word of warning to Starla because I couldn't stomach it. Left Lacey to do it, which was a— what do the kids say, a dick move? That, definitely that. Since dissembling isn't going to work, perhaps I could try honesty? Churns my gut, but what have I got to lose? Nothing, as far as I can tell, since that's what I have right now.

"It's not, at all. I am in no way your responsibility and you are in no way, shape, or form obligated to me. If you say so, I will never have any communications with you outside of a professional context if this referral works out, and I swear to keep those to a minimum. But…"

But what? What am I doing? Why am I rebelling against every professional bone in my body to speak with her? What do I have to offer?

"But I've thought of you often since I left. And I would like it very much if you would have dinner or coffee with me and tell me about your life now. From what I've seen, you're flourishing, and I'm so glad for it. Selfishly, I'd like to know more. And this is wildly unprofessional to say, but I always enjoyed talking to you. So, what do you say?"

It's done then. I have shot my shot and it's no longer up to me.

31

It's been a while since I asked a woman on a date and despite not being a date, this—whatever "this" is—is even more fraught than that ever was. I don't remember being breathless after I'd asked Maeve out after the cocktail party where we'd been introduced. But this isn't the same as that at all, now is it? This wouldn't be a date, nor would it be a therapy session. Uncharted territory for both of us. I don't actually have a word for what Starla Patrick is to me, nor do I have a word for what she ever was to me, which quickly became more than an average patient.

Which is perhaps why I feel like I've had an artery severed when she says no and hangs up. Again.

CHAPTER 3

 tarla

It's been a week. A week since Lowry called me. No, not just called me. Called me twice. And I cannot stop thinking about it. The first call would have been enough to distract me for days. The second call...short-circuited my brain. And my brain doesn't need any more of that, thanks.

As much as I would've liked to take him up on his offer to...I don't even know what that was. There's no way he was asking me out on a date. Was there? Of course not. He would never do that.

I don't know what the rules or ethics or whatever are about dating your ex-patients—especially when you're a psychiatrist, and they were a *minor* for most of the time—but I can't believe that would be okay. Even if it technically were, Lowry strikes me as the kind of man who takes his professional responsibilities even more seriously than he's required to. He loves his job, cares very deeply for his patients, and to throw that away on... anything? No, I don't think so.

Definitely not a date. He was being nice. Because he's always nice. Which is what I tell myself as I drive out to Harbinson. It's a pretty drive. I could've switched to the other hospital in metro Boston that does ECT, which is closer to my apartment downtown, but… Whatever, I didn't. And now I like the drive because I get to see more trees, and green things, or as is the case at the moment, heaps of fallen leaves and skeletal trees. Come on, snow. This is perhaps my least favorite time of year here. After the foliage and before the white magic of snowfall.

I'm doing okay, though, considering. My next ECT is coming up on Friday and I suppose I could've skipped seeing Lacey this week, but I have my routine and I like to stick to it. I see Lacey every Wednesday at ten thirty in the morning, and I have ECT every six weeks. You could set a clock to it.

I find a parking spot and head into the building. This place is almost as familiar to me as my childhood home, which shouldn't be surprising given I've been coming here regularly since I was eleven. Wow. Twenty-two years of my life. I suppose it could've been worse, which is what Lowry always reminded me of when I got to be a grumpy asshole about doing ECT. "Better than the alternative," he'd say, and yeah. Doing ECT and being alive and functional is way better than…doing none of that stuff, which is almost certainly where I would've ended up. Where I was headed by the time I turned fourteen.

Which is when I met Lowry. Who was definitely Doctor Campbell then. I remember in vivid detail my father yelling at Lacey when she told him she thought I might do well with this young, brand-new doctor.

"What the fuck, Lacey? You're going to send my child to your junior varsity squad? Have you given up on her? Because I can't think of any other reason you'd hand my seriously ill daughter's care over to some goddamn Doogie Howser type."

He'd gotten so loud, and more furious than I'd ever heard him. Even though I'd felt half-dead at the time, I remember thinking he shouldn't yell. Doctor Gendron really did do her best, had tried all the things with me. Any kind of psychotherapy you can think of, I'd done it. Acupuncture. Yoga. Meditation. Drugs, all the drugs: SSRIs, SNRIs, TCAs, MAOIs. Herbs: St. John's wort, gingko. Diet: gluten-free, dairy-free, caffeine-free. Seriously, if it was a thing, I'd done it. It wasn't her fault nothing worked.

Wouldn't it be easier if it all stopped? Wouldn't it be easier if they let me go? So much time and money and effort and stress and for what? I still had only a lukewarm interest in being alive on my best day.

I'd sat outside Lacey's office pretending not to hear, pretending I wasn't feeling increasingly guilty for being the source of the yelling, pretending I wasn't feeling like an even bigger disaster because even Doctor Gendron—the head of the whole department at the best psych hospital in metro Boston, of course, because my father insisted on the best—couldn't help me. What the hell kind of fucked-up mess was I if even *she* couldn't help me? If she was, in fact, sloughing me off to one of her Triple-A players for... I couldn't even think of for what. Learning experience? *This is what a hopeless patient looks like. Good luck!* Or maybe it was meant as a hard lesson: how to cope when one of your patients—inevitably—kills themselves.

And then a man had come by, looking like he worked there. Barely. Disorderly reddish-copper hair, five o'clock shadow at ten thirty in the morning. But he had one of those ID tags all the staff wore. He plopped himself into the seat next to me and leaned over like we were kids waiting outside the principal's office.

"What are they fighting about, do you know?"

He'd had a nice voice. Some kind of accent. Not English, but I couldn't tell then whether it was Irish or Scottish. I'd given him a sidelong look, which was a vast improvement over the reaction most people could pull out of me in those days, but I didn't answer his question. Seemed, frankly, like a lot of work. And for who? Some rando? Not worth it.

"Aye, no, you're right. Nonna my business."

Sat back in the chair, crossed his arms over his chest, and my gaze followed.

"But if you do know, it'd be grand if you shared, because that's my boss in there. I'm new here and I'm hoping this isn't about me, that I'm not going to get sacked. You'd tell me if that were it, right?"

I had liked the look of his face, the way he talked to me like he assumed he would get an answer because clearly I was a person capable of holding a normal conversation. I didn't get a whole lot of that in those days. It didn't feel as though anyone saw *me* then. I was a problem to be fixed, something fragile teetering on the edge, and everyone was convinced I was going to fall and break. Why should I bother trying to hang on if that was the outcome they were banking on? And it was so fucking hard. To get out of bed. To get dressed. To do any goddamn thing. So, I wasn't sure what to tell this man but I appreciated, at least a tiny bit, that he was asking.

"It'd probably help if I introduced myself. Then you could nod if it was me they're caterwauling about."

We both looked toward the door because something crashed. Wow. I'd never known my father to throw things, but I couldn't honestly say I was surprised. He could lose his temper sometimes. And when you're one of the richest men in Boston, in the country, it must've been very frustrating to not be able to get your way. Perhaps I'd been sent to him as a lesson in humility.

"I'm Lowry Campbell. Doctor Campbell," he amended. Arms still crossed, he tilted his head, again insinuating that we were in on some conspiracy together. "So, this is about me. Isn't it? Can you give me even one wee hint?"

I should've been disgusted. Or insulted. Or something other than what I was. I felt bad for him, trying so hard, but also grateful he was trying so hard when it seemed like everyone else around me had about given up. What would be the harm? Letting a word or three out? Would I be giving my father false hope if I did? Should I walk into a pond with rocks in my pocket, or out into the woods like a dog who knows it's going to die? I was going to hurt him anyway. What did it matter if I took pity on this man—who smelled good, I realized—and answered him? It wouldn't.

"Me. They're yelling about me."

～

LOWRY

"Tony."

He looks at me, and something about his expression sends chills up my spine. My patients all look very different—God knows mental illness comes in all shapes and sizes. But there's something the ones with the worst depression have in common. I can't say what it is precisely, but there's a look, a tone, *something*, that pings a wary part of my brain, makes the hair on my arms and the back of my neck rise. It's the most disturbing sensation and I'm having it now.

"Tony. I know things are bad right now. I know you're hurting, and you've had a time of it lately. I know you're in a dark place and you can't see the light, but you know there's always light. There is. You have a wife and two daughters who you love and who love you back, and I know you don't want to hurt them. Emily and Portia and Clara would be devastated if anything happened to you."

Tony doesn't say anything, just turns so he's not looking at me anymore. Not good, this isn't good. I can practically hear the arguments in his brain because other patients have made them to me out loud. *Things would be easier for them if I was gone. They'll be sad for a minute but ultimately better off because I'm worthless and a drag on them. Better to take myself out of the equation than to have them realize how unlovable and useless I actually am and they leave.* Oh, I've heard it, and I'm going to do my damnedest to be louder than all that. I can be pretty fucking loud.

"If you think there's a chance you might harm yourself or someone else, let's get you checked in so you can take a break and get the help you need. There's no shame in it and it's better than the alternative. You haven't tried TMS or ECT yet. Let's give those a go before you do anything rash and in the meantime, Harbinson might be a good place for you. I'll make the call right now, handle everything. Please, let us help if that's what you need. That is literally what we're here for."

His gaze flicks to the clock, and he pushes off the couch. "Time's up, doc."

Son of a bitch. I don't want him walking out of this office, but I've got nothing to go on other than a feeling, and I can't commit him based solely on my gut. God, I wish I could.

"You're right. But I want your word that you'll be in my office this time next week and if there's anything that's going to keep you from that"—like you killing yourself, or God forbid, going murder-suicide as some of these men are apt to do, though Tony's never struck me as the type—"you'll call me straight away. I don't care what hour it is. You want to talk about the Bruins game at three o'clock in the morning? Ring me up."

I'm not really a hockey fan. Not a sports fan in general, truth be told, except for football. Soccer, as the Americans call it. But I've started keeping up with the Bs so I can talk to Tony about them. He's a huge fan. Maybe that would be a reason to keep living if nothing else has a strong enough pull—they have a real chance at the Stanley Cup this year. I'll bring it up next time.

He shakes out the sleeves of his hockey sweater, heads for the door, and my brain feels as though it's been flipped to a channel that's all static. Helpless. I don't like feeling this way, and hopefully it won't last long. Perhaps Tony will come in next week complaining about the Bruins' goalie or perhaps I'll get a call from Emily in a few days saying she's convinced him to check in to Harbinson for a bit, or maybe he'll phone me later and tell me to schedule a course of TMS.

While I wait, I'll check in with Lacey and some of my other colleagues to see if there's not some other thing I ought to be doing. Sometimes they can offer suggestions, and if not, at least empathy for how difficult this job can be.

"I'll walk you out, I need some more coffee. Stayed up too late watching the Sharks get their fins handed to them."

Nothing from Tony who's headed down the hall without a glance back. Not that my jokes are hilarious—though some of them are, and that was pretty good—but it was about hockey. Really hope I'm reading this wrong because severe depression manifests differently in everyone, but in my experience, not even being able to fake a reaction when it would be in your best interest to do so isn't a good sign. A lot of my patients are very bright, very good at faking because they don't want to go through the hassle that results when I know how they truly feel. When they don't bother…

I continue to chatter at him until we reach the exit. Tony at least gives me a half-wave, his standard "see ya, doc," and a sort of grimace I'll take as an effort at a smile as he walks out the door and toward his SUV. Okay, that's something. At this point, I'll take anything. And some caffeine.

Water would probably be a better idea than coffee, but sometimes water is not going to cut it. It's sure as hell not going to cut it at the end of this day—I know that already and I've only seen two patients. Whisky will be required. Good thing Maeve is a love and had a local liquor store send me a stock of some of my favorites. I think full-on bog petrol is called for this evening, and I can already taste the Laphroaig 30 on the back of my tongue. It'll burn my throat and send miasmatic fumes through my nasal channels. What better to accompany my ruminating about Tony while I attempt to pay attention to the game.

At least putting together a cup of coffee is a task I can complete on autopilot because I can't clear Tony from my mind to focus on my next patient, and I need to. She deserves my complete attention, but my brain is fixated on Tony's plight, cogitating on how I can fix this. Or if not fix it, nudge it far enough toward better that disaster doesn't feel so imminent. But sunk I am, and I'll be able to focus better on Shreya once I have her in front of me. Plus, the SNRI we've got her on now seems to be kicking in and making a difference in her anxiety without the shite side effects she'd been struggling with on the SSRI she'd been taking.

Back to my office then. I take a deep breath before leaving the staff lounge, and nearly run into Starla, who is walking smack toward me down the hallway.

Bollocks.

How is it that I run into her now after managing to avoid seeing Starla for over a month? I'd been carefully remaining in my office during the times she might be coming or going because she's made it clear she doesn't want to see me and would mark it as an unfortunate event if she did. *Bang-up job so far, Doctor Campbell*, and two separate hang-ups. Must be I was so occupied with my concern about Tony that I forgot this is around the time she comes in every week. I'd been trying to be respectful, and one moment of absent-mindedness has hurt a person I care about very much.

Indeed, her mouth drops open and she flinches. Aside from the vague distress though, she looks marvelous. Slim-fitting jeans hug her thighs, and they peek out from between brown leather knee-high boots and a dark green angular coat that's belted around her waist. Her hair's down but pushed behind her ears and it's all I can do not to smile. But I won't. I will interact with her in the mildest, most neutral way possible. Not rude, but not anything that demands any response from her either.

So, as we're passing by, I dip my head in her direction, offer brief eye contact, state a low "good morning," and keep walking, closing my eyes with regret, goddamn *craving* crowding my chest and making it hard to breathe.

~

STARLA

Lowry goes into his office and closes the door behind him, and I'm left standing in the hallway like some sort of nerf-herder. I *never* see him here. I've half-hoped and half-dreaded that I would, played over what I would do a million times in my head, which has ranged anywhere from taking one of the paintings off the wall and smashing it over his ginger head to giving the ice-queen cold shoulder, to maybe being a little flirty to see if I could tell if he had asked me on a date—he didn't, I know—to, in my dreams, accosting him to grab his tie and stroke my hand down his button-down-clad chest all the way to the placket of his pants where he'd be hard for me. Imagining the groan that would result from me palming him through his pants, well, that's making me tug at my collar.

The way he looked at me... His jaw had flexed momentarily and his expression had been the one I'd seen a million times as his patient. The one that said he was threading a needle. That regardless of how calm he seemed, he was working so very hard. Of course, I hadn't noticed that at first. Had been too mired in my depression to notice much of anything that wasn't smacking me in the face.

It was only after my suicide attempt and my first course of ECT that I could see it. That I could see so many things. It was like I'd been living life behind a windshield caked with dirt and muck and insect carcasses and someone had finally started to wipe it clean.

Don't get me wrong; ECT isn't perfect. It's not some magic elixir that made me 100 percent better. And I know I'm lucky my side effects are mild—not everyone is so fortunate. But for me? Totally worth it to lose a few days every six weeks to fuzzy memory and perhaps some nausea or a headache in exchange for functioning at a high level for the rest of the time. I still struggle, my windshield gets dirtier the further out I am from having had a treatment—hence my being here—but it's so much better.

And lets me obsess over the clenching of my ex-psychiatrist's jaw. Perfect.

What was he trying so hard for? Was it difficult for him to see me? And why? Lowry's never struck me as the kind of man to get worked up over a rejection. Pretty sure he's handsome enough to have a fairly easy time getting laid whenever he feels like it. I know he's kind and considerate enough to have a partner if he'd like one. He wasn't asking me on a date anyhow so that doesn't even apply.

Maybe he... Did I hurt his feelings? By not wanting to spend time with him? And if so, what the hell did I do that for? Yeah, I'm still pretty fucking mad at him, but wouldn't it be fulfilling a lot of my fantasies to see him outside of a clinical setting? Isn't that something I've wanted for years? Am I so stubborn to prevent myself from having that so he knows I'm angry? I mean, yes, clearly, but more to the point, *should* I be? Who am I punishing with my refusal?

Having a meal with him might be a disaster, but it also might be enjoyable. Perhaps we could be friends. I don't have many of those. Being a trust fund baby certainly has its perks, but it also makes a person somewhat paranoid about why people want to be friends with you. Do they actually like you or do they like your money? The number of people who started acting weird after they found out who my father was and what that meant… Let's just say it was close to 100 percent awkward sauce.

Things get even worse when you add mental illness to the picture. I didn't have any friends when I was at my lowest. It didn't get much better when I was recovering because ECT scares the living shit out of people. They've watched *One Flew Over the Cuckoo's Nest* one too many times. God, I fucking hate that movie. Besides them being freaked out by the very thing that saved me, depression can be rough. I bowed out of plans because I couldn't imagine getting off the couch, never mind being personable. Sometimes I'd be optimistic about going to a game or a movie and I'd genuinely want to go, but I couldn't actually get out the door. The idea of socializing was too tiring, forget *actual* socializing. Lowry's not going to be surprised by any of that. And he's not going to be surprised by my money; he knows all about it.

Maybe I could have a drink with him. And if it goes badly—I almost hope it will so this nearly two-decades-long infatuation can die the ignoble death it deserves—then it does, and I can move on. We'll have nothing to talk about and that's fine. He won't be rude. Or a creeper. And after that, we can exchange pleasantries in the hallways here and that will be it. How is it I haven't seen him before? Maybe he usually has a patient during this block.

Or maybe he's been hiding from me? No, he gave me a heads-up that I might see him here, I can't imagine he'd go out of his way to avoid me like I have the plague after that. Another possibility occurs to me, which is that he knows when I'll be here and he's done his best to not be in public areas when I'd be coming or going because I told him I didn't want to see him ever again. Something about that rings true, like that perfect last note of a tuning orchestra. Yes, that is precisely something he'd do.

My urge to see his somewhat unruly ginger hair emerge from the ripped canvas of a painting I'd brought down upon his head is all but extinguished. The desire to talk with him across a dinner table and have a conversation because he knows my history and isn't afraid of or disgusted with me because of it is ignited instead. Perhaps I'd like that. Very much.

I could certainly use more pleasure in my life given how much of it is taken up by corporate bullshit I never wanted but that I've been saddled with, and I had—have—a very complicated relationship with my father which makes it impossible for me to simply slough off like most of the other things I find unpleasant.

"Starla? What are you doing out here? I tried calling because you're never late."

That's embarrassing. Having Doctor Gendron catch me in the hallway mulling this over. But now that I've arrived at this conclusion, I should follow through before I talk myself out of it. Which will be in approximately twelve parsecs. Even though that famous line doesn't make any sense because parsecs are a unit of distance not time, but it's the best I've got. I'd count myself lucky to have Chewbacca at my back, too, but no Wookiees in sight. It's all up to me.

"I will, uh, be right there. Give me a minute?"

Doctor Gendron regards me as though I'm a specimen she thought she was intimately familiar with, but instead of what she was expecting, she got something entirely different, perhaps a whole new species.

"Sure," she metes out, and then walks deliberately back to her office and over the threshold. I'm not fortunate enough to have her close the door, but this will have to do.

It's only a few steps for me to get to Lowry's door. I know it's his because I've seen the nameplate every time I've come and gone from Doctor Gendron's office. This is the closest I've gotten, though, and my heart beats harder, faster, knowing he's on the other side. Also that he's alone—he wouldn't have grabbed a coffee if he had a patient scheduled for now.

I hold up a fist to knock and my stomach twists. It feels as though my face twists in a similar fashion and I take a deep breath while I try to smooth it out. No bigs, whatevs, I can totes do this. No problem. At all. Plus, the longer it takes, the more curious Doctor Gendron is going to be, and I don't need that in my life.

So I do it. Rap my knuckles against the wood and don't breathe until the door swings open. Shit. I thought he'd say "come in" from behind his desk. Not be standing like a foot away. So much for that whole friends thing because at the first whiff of him—he still smells the same—I want to climb him like a squirrel up an acorn-laden tree. Fuck my life.

"Starla? Everything okay?"

Yes, he looks downright concerned. As well he might since I'm seeking him out when I've essentially told him to fuck off. Repeatedly.

"Is Lacey not there? I saw her earlier…" He pokes his head through the doorframe, looking in the direction of Doctor Gendron's office and he's even closer to me. I'm going to die.

Everyone thought depression would kill me, but no, it's lust for my ex-psychiatrist that will do the trick, and I won't even have to sleep with him to do it, just have his hands brush me and… Oh, Christ, can't think about that without contributing to the bonfire that's been set alight on my face.

"No, she's there. Waiting for me. I—"

His brows go up in the middle, wrinkling his forehead, and I swear if he opens his mouth to say anything, I won't be able to finish this sentence, so I barrel on before he has the chance.

"I've thought further about your invitation. And yes, we could, um, have dinner. Or something. Sometime. Whenever. I don't care. But you'll have to call me because I don't have your number and I don't want to call you at work because I know everyone here and I…"

I trail off as though I've lost my train of thought, but really I've lost my nerve and now I want to sink into the rug, never to be seen again. This was a terrible idea. I should've allowed my more practical self to reason with my more impulsive self because she's fucking right. Mortifying.

Except that he's smiling. A subtle but genuine smile that reaches into my body and squeezes my heart because it's so very kind and approving. Makes me feel like I have been the very best girl and that he'd like to reward me for it. Thoroughly.

"I'd like that. And yes, I can call you. But you should go see Lacey." He leans down like he did the first time I met him, and his breath ghosts over my ear as he says in a near whisper, "You know she gets grumpy when she's kept waiting. And she's still my boss, might sack me any day."

Then he's standing upright again and I'm trying not to collapse or spontaneously combust. I can barely stammer, "Okay," and then try not to trip over my own feet as I head toward Doctor Gendron's office.

CHAPTER 4

 tarla

I'M WORKING on a daily checklist for one of my clients when the phone rings. Nora is a wildly successful comic book artist, but she forgets to do things like take a shower for days at a time. Which is less of a problem than it would be if she had to go into an office every day, but she still needs to brush and floss her teeth so she doesn't get cavities and have to make an unexpected trip to the dentist because who the hell knows how long it would take her to make *that* appointment. Which is another thing I need to add to her checklist.

She's got a backlog of bills to pay, calls to make, emails to send —all that daily stuff most of us take in stride, but for Nora it's literally easier to pull an all-nighter to bang out several pages of incredibly detailed and gorgeous work than it is to call to make a grooming appointment for her beloved Shih Tzu, Barney. So we'll put one thing a day like that on her schedule and then put something she enjoys doing right after it. Like taking Barney for his walk.

While I'm not a fan of the phone either, I've learned to think of it as a tool. A tool that is sometimes more expedient than sending a zillion emails back and forth. Unfortunately for me, this call will not be quick, nor will it be easy, likely not even useful. What would be worse is not answering and then having to deal with a fracking voicemail. I hate that shit.

"What do you want, Tad?"

"Good thing your father isn't alive to hear you talk to me like that."

Tad is arrogant. Can be obtuse. I would go so far as to say he can be inconsiderate, but I wouldn't have called him cruel. That statement, however, is going to force me to reconsider.

"*You're* lucky my father isn't alive. He'd fire you for being so callous."

"Hey, Starla. Don't be like that. I'm sorry. You're right, that was over the line and I apologize."

I'd still deck him if he were here, but I appreciate the apology. Tad was always good with apologies. We dated for two years, so I would know. I think my father hoped we'd get married and rule over his empire when he decided to retire, but clearly, none of that worked out: my father never had the chance to retire, Tad and I are over and have been for a couple of years now. Doesn't stop him from being overly familiar with me. I guess what's what happens when men stick their dick in someone; they think they own them, are entitled to them. Fuck that.

"Fine. But my question remains the same. What do you want?"

"You know what I want."

For fuck's sake, not this again. I do know what he wants and I also know I don't want to give it to him.

"I do and you can't have it. I haven't decided what I'm doing with my shares, and you calling me every three days to chat about it isn't going to speed up the process."

There's a grunt of frustration and it sounds unpleasantly like when we used to fuck. Didn't need a reminder of that either.

"Then what will it take? You're not fulfilling your fiduciary duty as the person who holds a controlling interest in Patrick Enterprises. You have a controlling interest and while I know topping isn't your thing, you have to fucking do something."

The truth is I *don't* like making these decisions. They feel overwhelming and too huge and it's easy to start catastrophizing. When you have a controlling interest in a Fortune 500 company, it's not actually exaggeration to say that decisions you make could ruin people's lives. Tens of thousands of people's lives. Which makes me feel queasy. And unworthy. Whose fucking idea was it to leave me with all this? My father's, which on the one hand was an incredible vote of confidence. After all we'd been through together, he believed I'm stable enough, strong enough, to be trusted with his life's work.

After years of acting like I couldn't be trusted to handle anything, he'd started to treat me as though there was a possibility of handing me the reins someday. I couldn't bring myself to tell him I didn't want the wild stallion he was trying to get me to take on. I'd done everything he asked like attend meetings and look over reams of reports and keep up with all of the market fluctuations and what that meant for Patrick Enterprises because I wanted so desperately to win his approval. I was so proud that he saw me as potentially worthy after half a lifetime of being a disappointment.

On the other hand of what I feel was an enormous compliment, I don't want this, and god, I feel the weight of it. It's so heavy and makes the tide of my depression come in faster.

I find myself wishing a dozen times a day he hadn't left this all up to me. I cannot handle it and maintain my hard-won mental health. It's too much stress, too much pressure, too many hours, too many moving parts...too much. And I wish to fuck Tad didn't know that so well.

Yes, I hate it. But would I also have been mortified and insulted if my father had taken the choice away from me entirely? I'd like to think no because I'm aware of my own capabilities and capacity, but if anyone knows brains aren't always rational, it's me.

The point now, though, is to get Tad to back all the way up because whether I like it or not, I'm the one who's been charged with this responsibility, not him. And while I've never had reason to believe he'd act against my father's wishes, I've also not had much experience with him without my father's guiding hand. I do know Tad wishes my father would've been more aggressive in his business decisions and that alone gives me pause. So, he wants me to make a choice?

"I will, once I figure out what is in the best interest of my father's legacy and the people who rely on Patrick Enterprises for their livelihoods."

"Legacy? What the fuck is that? Maybe you should care more about the living than the dead."

"I do, and so did my father. Which is why I'm going to take my time, do my homework, and figure this out. You bullying me is not going to help your case. If you'll excuse me, I also have a responsibility to my clients and I need to get back to my work. I'll see you at the next board meeting."

Hanging up on Tad is not quite as satisfying when there's only a button on a screen to press instead of a handset to slam down onto a cradle, but it's satisfying nonetheless, perhaps because of how little effort it takes to shut him up, at least in this medium. Except his call has riled me and it's going to take a bit to center myself enough to silence the thoughts now stampeding through my mind instead of concentrating on what will work best for Nora.

I close my eyes to do one of my meditation exercises, since outright telling my mind to shush has never worked for me. I need something to focus on and my breath isn't going to cut it.

On my worst days, it made me think about how much oxygen I was taking up and maybe it would be better used by someone else who wasn't such a waste of space. So, no, breathing isn't going to work. I have a catalog full of meditations I can guide myself through, but the one I reach for most frequently is one Lowry taught me.

I thought for a while that I had a fondness for it because he'd been the one who gave it to me to store in my mental toolbox. But even when I was at peak fury with him, I would still reach for it because it plays nicely with my brain.

Colors.

Taking a deep breath, I start with yellow because it's my favorite color. Summon images of all the best things of that hue. Daffodils. Roses. Fat fuzzy bumblebees, their round bodies defying physics as they trundle through the air. The warmth of the sun on my face. A favorite rain slicker I had in elementary school before my brain went haywire. Lemons. Fluffy Easter Peeps, tomatoes, sunflowers, perfectly ripe and spotless bananas. The tart-sweet flesh of pineapples, lilies in full bloom. Yellow.

My breath and heartbeat have already slowed and I haven't even finished with yellow. That's why I love this. By the time I come around to orange, I'll be thoroughly grounded and able to do my best work for Nora. Except my fucking phone rings again, and I swear to Christ, if it's Tad again, I'm going to march over to his penthouse and push him off the balcony. Can he not take a hint? It wasn't even a hint, it was a smack in the face. *Go away.*

But the name flashing on my screen isn't Tad. It's one I haven't seen for years. Fifteen years to be exact. Lowry Campbell. My heart doesn't slow, it skips a beat and then goes double time to make up for it. That's cool, just going to have a cardiac event right here at my desk.

Lowry. I did tell him to call me yesterday, but I didn't expect... Well, I did have his number. Because why would he have changed his cell? He wouldn't have. Didn't. And that didn't occur to me, why? The man impairs my cognitive abilities. Which is probably why I'm still staring at his name flashing on my phone instead of answering his call. I'd better pick it up because I don't know if I'll be able to work up the nerve to call him back. Though I wouldn't mind having a voice message from him that I could listen to whenever I pleased. That would be beyond satisfactory. But the risk is too high and I already used up my moxie speaking with him yesterday. Best to pick up now. Now. *Now, you foolish girl.*

I try not to choke as I greet him with what I hope is an airy, nonchalant, "Hello?"

∼

LOWRY

She picked up.

It's only now I realize I've so thoroughly convinced myself she wouldn't that I haven't actually prepared anything to say. Basics work.

"Starla. It's Lowry."

"Hi."

Great. Off to a brilliant start. A-plus for the lot of us. Good thing neither of us make our livings from talking...

"You asked that I call you. So, unless you've changed your mind—which is always your prerogative"—*please don't have changed your mind*—"I was calling to arrange a time for dinner. Or coffee. Or whatever you'd prefer. If anything at all."

Jesus, Campbell, how many times are you going to tell her she doesn't have to see you? Which she doesn't, but she's a capable adult who's proved herself able and willing to say no to me. Repeatedly. Don't give her an excuse. It's okay to want to see her and to let her know. Hell, she knows already. So perhaps I ought to tell her so.

"I'd like very much to see you, so if you let me know when you're free and what you'd like to do, I can take care of the details. If you'd like."

It's up to her because I already know that I would, in fact, very much like to take care of the details. Those types of things wear on her. She likes routine, schedules, so she doesn't have to make decisions over and over again. It's far easier to do things that have already been decided than to have to do all the work to set them up in the first place. Or at least it was. Perhaps she's changed. And I know most women like to dictate the terms when they're meeting a strange man. We're not precisely strangers, and I hope she trusts me not to lure her into a dark alley or my laboratory, but I'm not going to be offended if she wants to pick someplace where she'll likely see a familiar face. Does she go out enough to have a favorite haunt? Perhaps.

There's a pause and I'm about to offer an apology, say she's surely busy and she can call me back at her convenience, if ever, because I ought not to be doing this, but I couldn't help myself, and smelling her hair when I leaned down to speak low in her ear over the threshold of my office at Harbinson... Let's just say it didn't do anything to quell my desire for her.

"I need to eat dinner on Thursday. I mean, I need to eat dinner every night, but I don't have plans for Thursday yet. And I haven't for a while. So sometimes I forget. Or eat tuna fish salad scooped out of the bowl with Doritos." She curses under her breath. "No, I don't. Who does that? It's disgusting."

I have to smother a laugh behind a hand, because that's a very detailed description of something she *doesn't* do. Slipping my hand into my pocket, I walk the length of my office and back because sometimes it's easier to think literally on my feet. Since she's not here to be disturbed or amused by my pacing, I let myself.

"Aye, well, wouldn't want you to resort to some fictional,

revolting, and not terribly nutritious sustenance. I'm also free on Thursday. How's six thirty?"

"Is seven thirty too late? I work eleven to seven on Thursdays."

"Seven thirty's fine. Might actually get to the gym that day."

Brilliant, Campbell. She already knows you're a damn sight too old for her, you should definitely make sure she knows you're out of shape as well. I pinch the bridge of my nose because clearly that inane gesture will fix everything. That not working, I press on.

"Anyplace you'd like to meet up or shall I choose?"

"You can choose. I should be able to get anywhere in the Back Bay, Beacon Hill, North End, Downtown Crossing, Leather District, or Chinatown by then."

That's plenty of options and I should be able to find something suitable.

"Brilliant. I'll make a reservation and text you the details, shall I? You're one of those young people who prefers texts, aye?"

She snorts which is adorable and also makes me scrub a hand over my eyes. *You'll be in the grave soon enough, no need make yourself sound like a moldy old geezer.*

"You realize I'm an adult, right? Like in my thirties and everything. But yes, texting is good. Much less disruptive than a phone call. But you know, feel free to use emojis. I hear the kids these days are totes into them."

She's mocking me and I don't mind. In fact, I rather like it. Far better than her hanging up on me, and I'm not going to look a gift horse in the mouth, particularly when it's gifted me with time spent with Starla.

"I, uh, totes will."

Her laugh is a tinkling light thing that I'd like to hear again and again no matter how much a fool I need to make of myself to have it. I would throw all the pride I have at Starla's feet for her to tread on if it would make a difference.

"I won't keep you, then. But I'll see you Thursday."

"Looking forward to it," she says, and something like hope surges inside me. Yes, hope, not anything more sinister or lascivious than that.

What does it matter that I have to moderate my tone when I respond, "I am as well. Good night, Starla."

CHAPTER 5

 tarla

NOT A DATE. This isn't a date. This is a psychiatrist wanting to catch up with his former patient and make sure all the work he did with me didn't go to waste. That's all it is.

Except that when he'd called the first time—okay, the second time—he said he'd always enjoyed talking to me. Which was somehow wildly unprofessional? I mean, I'd entertained feverishly inappropriate thoughts of him for sure, but I can't imagine they were anywhere near the same. I mean, doctors must have favorite patients, right? Much as parents have favorites among their children even if they would never admit it? Perhaps despite being a hard case, I was one of Lowry's. That's nice. I guess.

And for this definitely-not-a-date I definitely didn't carefully select my clothes. I work from home most of the time and while I get dressed in professional clothes every morning because it helps me get in a work mind-set and keeps me from crawling back into my bed or collapsing on the couch when I'm having a hard day, I don't usually look quite this nice. Perhaps I don't pay as much attention to how flattering the cut of my shirt is or whether my butt looks good in this skirt. It does, by the way. Thank the heavens or the witches or whoever blessed us with pencil skirts and peplum sweaters. They at least give the illusion of being effortlessly chic.

Are there people for whom being alive is *actually* effortless? Given that I've got a pretty heavy diagnosis and it's been made clear to me for almost as long as I can remember exactly how dire, how serious, my situation is, I suppose I'm not at a great point in the bell curve to judge. At least I can afford to hire a stylist to find me clothes and put them into outfits I have only to pluck from my closet and not put together myself. Toward the end of my ECT cycles, that might be too much to bear.

Lowry's chosen a newish place in the Back Bay for us to eat, and I have to dodge some slush puddles in these shoes, even though it hasn't rained or snowed for days. I like walking down the wide, straight streets of the Back Bay—it's one of the few places in Boston where cow paths didn't determine how the roads were laid out—they're soothing and pretty.

When I get to the brick front of the restaurant, I take a deep breath, smooth my skirt down my thighs, and square my shoulders. Two professional people having dinner. As...friends? Whatever it is, it doesn't matter because it's not a date.

Except that when I give the waitress Lowry's name and she shows me to the table, it sure as hell pushes all my date buttons. Candlelight at an intimate table by a window, the way Lowry's face lights up when he sees me, how he stands to greet me. I expect him to offer a handshake, because that's what I've prepared myself for, except that he goes in for a hug and I'm only too happy to oblige. And I'm sure my face turns as red as the roses in the centerpiece when he pecks my cheek; a brief but deliberate brush of his lips, enough contact for his scruff to scrape deliciously against my skin.

I've also made the mistake of inhaling while he's so close, and I'm guessing he did make it to the gym because he smells freshly showered, like sea salt soap, and some kind of piney aftershave or cologne. I can picture the forest by the sea so vividly I can hear the waves tumbling into shore and my shoulders drop a couple of inches.

Even if it is awkward to sit across a table from my high school (and apparently current) crush, Lowry's a good man. A kind man who is intelligent, has a good sense of humor, and won't be a self-centered dinner companion. This evening will be far more pleasurable than many I've spent, especially as of late, so I should enjoy myself.

It's likely wishful thinking on my part, but our hug feels like it lasts longer than your standard greeting, and his smile is perhaps wider than he'd give a stranger. Or a patient, for that matter.

He's still smiling when he says, "I'm glad you made it. Nice to see you."

I duck my head and flush some more when he pulls out my chair. Men don't do that anymore, and why not? It's charming. It's the kind of chivalrous gesture that makes me feel cared for but not condescended to.

My gaze perhaps grazes his butt and his thighs in the wool trousers he's sporting. I mean, I think they're wool. I'd have to touch them to be sure. *Jesus, Starla, don't think about getting into your ex-psychiatrist's pants.* But it's kinda hard not to when he's got an ass like that…

He settles into the seat across the table and regards me with those blue eyes of his. They ought to be cold, with the crisp shade of them, but they're not. Everything about him is warm. Maybe it's the ginger hair, streaked with a grey-blond. Or maybe it's his hand with its veined back and thick fingers resting on the tablecloth. Dammit, god*dammit*.

His eyes narrow slightly as he seems to drink me up with those eyes. "You know I wasn't entirely sure you'd show up."

"I told you I would. I always show up."

He smiles again, and it makes me feel fuzzy, warm, seen. Yes, he remembers. There was only one time I failed to do so, and I don't want to talk about that, think about it now. It still mortifies me to have been that foolish. To have put myself in that much danger and to have caused the people I care about so much worry.

"Aye, you did. But that was before we'd had a few conversations where you told me to go away, leave you alone, or you'd hung up on me. Twice. So you can't blame a man for wondering."

His response is easy, but it reminds me that I don't want to be easy. When I think about why I responded that way, fuck yeah, I had the right to be churlish. Still have, and he should know that. "Yes, well, I was pretty angry with you for a long time. Not all of that has gone away."

His features darken, taking away some of the warmth. Maybe I shouldn't have said anything, but he deserves to know. Besides, he was the one who brought it up.

"You've made that clear, rightfully so. And I apologize again. If you'd like to throw a drink in my face or yell at me, I wouldn't argue. But you've never seemed like the type of person who would cause a scene. You simply wouldn't have come. It's obvious you're more than capable of saying no to things you don't want to do, so I'm going to assume you're here because even though I hurt you and you've been deservedly angry at me because you trusted me and I…I left, that you want to be here. You were curious, if nothing else. Or perhaps you just wanted me to pay for dinner."

I can't help but crack a smile and shake my head. I don't need anyone to pay for anything. Hell, I could buy this restaurant at the drop of a hat. I wouldn't because restaurants are risky ventures, but I could and he knows it. He's teasing me and I like it. Want him to do it more.

I also can't help but appreciate his faith in me to say no. Not something that I've been particularly adept at over the past few months, though I've tried to hold the boundaries where I can. No, I will not fly to New York for a meeting with a potential partner. Yes, I will attend the board meeting. Of course, I will review the quarterly earnings report, but fuck no will I be playing golf with a visiting dignitary from a country where we have some of our manufacturing plants. I want to tell him about all of it so he can tell me I'm doing a good job, but I can't bring myself to.

"Fine, your treat. And you're right. I am curious. It's been a long time and I could never really ask you all the things I wanted to when..." When I was your patient. When it was your job to crack my head open and sift around to make sure there wasn't anything life-threatening in there. When I was a teenager and you were very much an adult. He's well aware of all of that and I don't want to remind him so I go with, "Back then."

The waitress comes and takes our drink orders, and when she's departed, Lowry takes a sip of his water.

"So, what do you want to know?"

"What have you been doing for the past fifteen years?"

"Ah, is that all?" He sits back, his brow furrowing. "I worked at the same clinic in Chicago the entire time I was there. Made the switch to adult psychiatry from children and adolescents. Mostly worked with patients who were dealing with severe depression and anxiety."

"Still your specialty."

He nods, and folds his hands across his midsection. "I was married for a time there too."

Something inside me lurches, which is ridiculous. I had no claim on Lowry then, and I have none now. Of course he was married. I will do my best to ignore the satisfaction that accompanies the "was."

"Was?"

"Yes. Maeve and I were married for six years, but then we split up. Nothing dramatic, it was about as amicable as these things can be. She's a lovely woman, I think you'd like her."

"And you split up, why?"

It's not really any of my business, but if he wanted me to back off, he would say. He is, after all, the person who taught me about boundaries. He shrugs and takes a swig of his Bourbon and Blood that the server brought by, along with my Fabiola.

"I thought Maeve would be happier with someone who wasn't me, and she's not the adulterous or polyamorous type. It wasn't a bad marriage, but I thought she deserved better."

"What about you?" I take a sip of my drink before I say anything else, like "Are you dating anyone?" Lowry looks at the flatware on the table, and the crease between his brows deepens.

"I don't know that I could ask for anyone better than Maeve."

That's a kick in the teeth, which is, again, ridiculous and not at all fair. *Not a date.* He's not interested in me romantically. He's not saying these things to make it clear that he'd never want to be with me, he's saying them because it's never even occurred to him that we *could* be.

"You must have loved her very much."

"I did. I do. We still talk often. She had some opinions about me coming back to Boston."

"And what were those?"

He looks at me, and there's a... I can't quite put my finger on what it might be. It's not a sheen or glimmer or anything poetic like that, but there is an intensity that makes my heart beat faster, makes a certain kind of feeling crop up in my breasts, my pelvis. Men have looked at me like this before, or at least I think they have. This feels like when they want me.

In my fantasy life, Lowry would let the brogue fly, his voice going low and gravelly when he'd say, "First and foremost that I was foolish for coming back for a woman I had no reason to believe wanted me. You. I came back for you."

And then he'd rush my side of the table to heft me up on the white-linen-covered surface before laying me out like I was his dinner, like I would be better sustenance than anything a chef's tasting menu could offer.

My disturbingly vivid erotic daydream is interrupted by what Lowry *actually* says: "That it was foolish for me to come back here. That I had a good life and a good career in Chicago and moving halfway across the country seemed impulsive and ill-advised."

I suppose someone could have said that about him moving to Chicago in the first place, but I won't poke him with that. At the moment. "Those sound like pretty good reasons to stay put. Why did you come back?"

There it is again, that look. That look that gives me sillier ideas than I've ever dared to have about him.

"I…"

The waitress chooses that extremely inconvenient moment to set down our salads in front of us. When she's departed with our dinner orders and a request for a bottle of wine since both Lowry and I are nearly through with our cocktails, I search his face again. Is he going to—

"And how's your romantic life?"

Apparently not.

~

LOWRY

Maeve was right. I'm a fool. And I swear I didn't ask Starla to dinner as a date. I was genuinely curious about how she is and it's my own goddamn fault I find her utterly captivating. She's been beautiful the times I've seen her lately, but the way that skirt hugs her round bum and her lush thighs… Well, it's a wonder I haven't had to use my napkin to wipe away the drool. The sweater with the little ruffle at the waist shows off her slight hourglass shape and how bountiful her breasts are is icing on this lust-worthy cake.

I've dug myself into a deep hole by letting her ask whatever she'd like, and by it taking a turn toward my love life, which I suppose is to be expected. I did after all volunteer that I'd been married and that usually leads to some questions. Now I've gone and turned the tables on her because I couldn't tell her that I *am* here for her. Not that I had any intention of letting it get this far. At all. I could've been in the same city and if we'd happened to run into each other at Harbinson, then we would have. If she'd continued to give me a hard pass on spending time together, I would have respected that. Did.

But I don't think I can explain to her—or anyone else for that matter—why precisely I felt compelled to return here. All I know is that after I'd come here four months ago when her father had died, it felt right to return. To be in the city she loves, calls home, to be near her even if I didn't see her, even if I never talked to her. I would be here if she *did* ever need me and that would be enough.

It's rather daft, I know, and I would urge a patient who came to me with this kind of—such an ugly word but I suppose it's deserved—*obsession* to examine their motivations and try their best to get over it and move on. The inconvenient thing is that I thought I had and then all of my willpower, all of my good sense, crumbled when Jameson Patrick died.

Starla blinks at my abrupt question. "My romantic life? Pretty much nonexistent. I date occasionally, but nothing's been serious for years. It's more trouble than it's worth. Partners take up time and energy, and I know probably sooner rather than later they're going to make me feel like shit, so why bother?"

That's rather harsh and my heart aches for her. Would I be happy if she were doe-eyed in love with some dashing fellow who fulfilled her every need? No, I'd be jealous as the day is long. But I'd also be happy for her. She deserves that.

"And I swear to god if you say Not All Men, I'm going to kick your shin under the table."

Fair. Sure, not all men, but enough of them to have convinced her it's not worth it. And I don't relish being kicked. I bruise easily.

"We don't need to discuss those losers, then. Unless you want to?" A quick and decisive shake of her head tells me no in no uncertain terms and I'm relieved. I'd listen to Starla talk about her exes, but I'd rather not. Jealousy would no doubt rear its ugly head and that's not a good look for friends. "How's business, then? Lois has been singing your praises, so I know personally you have at least one superfan."

Unlike when I asked about her love life, Starla's face lights up. "Lois is great. And she's the kind of client I can really make a difference for. We've been focusing on the structure of her workday and how she can be more efficient while also giving herself breaks. And unlike a lot of my clients, she was quickly onboard with the idea that taking breaks could actually make her more productive. Sometimes I have to practically beg them to take a time out. Work smarter, not harder. But some of them are used to working so hard to make up for the things they're not great at. They burn themselves out trying to run a marathon when they're sprinters."

"You know, I'd never thought of it like that, but that makes all the sense in the world now that you put it that way. Take advantage of that hyperfocus and don't let them bang their heads against a wall when their brains need to run wild for a bit. I can see why you're good at this. And I don't mean that to sound condescending, I'm sorry if it does."

"It doesn't."

She shrugs, swallows the last of her cocktail, and her cheeks might pink a bit. Maybe it's from the Fabiola, or maybe it's because she values my opinion and it makes her happy to know I've a good one of her. Very good—I think she's incredible.

I rub the skin between my brows, trying to ameliorate the headache gathering there.

"Do you ever work with people who don't have mental health issues?"

"Not really. I've had a few people sign on with me who didn't have diagnoses when they started, but after I worked with them for a while, it became clear—to me anyway—that they did actually have something going on, but no one had ever identified it or addressed it. Especially women. We're really good at compensating for shit, which can be great—part of my job is teaching people coping mechanisms and they've already got a lot of them —but it can also be a problem. I had one client who got a diagnosis of ADHD, started on meds, and it made a huge difference for her. What would her life have been like if she'd been diagnosed earlier? It's so frustrating to see people whose potential is wasted."

"That's a—"

"Oh, no, I know that can be a huge trigger phrase for people. I mean that society as a whole is wasting all this brain power because it insists on everyone fitting into round holes. Well, a lot of my clients are squares. They're fucking awesome at being squares and can accomplish so many incredible things, and just because they can't fit into these round holes, people think they're lazy. It's infuriating. I love getting to talk to my clients' coworkers or partners or bosses. Because I can hammer the point home in ways my clients aren't always able to. But anyway, you were asking about whether I take on clients without mental health issues. Why, you need some help, doc?"

I like the way she says "doc." It's teasing and familiar, not like when she called me Doctor Campbell. Not as good as if she called me Lowry, but I'll take it.

"I might. But I don't want to take advantage of your professional acumen. It's like asking your massage therapist friend if they could work out the knot you've got in your shoulder when you're supposed to be meeting up to watch a match at the pub, or if your friend who's an accountant could take a quick peek at your taxes during the previews at the movies. Kind of rotten to ask them to do their job for free."

"I heard you were paying for dinner."

Hell, that mischievous smile is going to get me into trouble. Makes my heart squeeze and something low in my belly get tight. Have to be careful though, because this isn't a date. Friendly, yes, but the objective here is not to charm Starla Patrick back to my place for a nightcap and a good fuck—though that might exorcise some demons for the both of us. It's to be a pleasant companion, and if I'm pleasant enough, perhaps we can be friends, and I won't have to go another fifteen years craving her company, wanting to know how she's actually doing.

"It's a deal," I offer.

"So, what seems to be the trouble?"

She takes a bite of her salad, but doesn't take her eyes off me. Starla's in professional mode now, a sharp cast to her features. I can almost feel her concentration alighting on me. I have all of her attention and it's a heady sensation. I'd like to be at the center of her attention more often. Far, far more often. Probably more often than would be healthy for either of us.

"Not so much a trouble, really—"

She shakes her head, sending her high ponytail shaking behind her head. "Don't do that. It's bothering you enough to bring it up with me, so it's obviously bothering you. And it's okay to not be perfect. To need help. Doesn't make you a bad person or a failure, or bad at your job." She points her fork at me, a sly look in her eyes. "You taught me that. Listen to your own good advice."

Busted. "Aye, you're right. Thing is, I'd like to be better at my job, and better at being, well, human."

"Wouldn't we all?"

"I think I mentioned I don't get to the gym as much as I'd like.

I did tonight, because I knew I was meeting you afterward. If I'm going home, I often just go home. Because I'm tired, it's been a long day, and would it really be so bad to have a break?"

She nods and chomps down on another forkful of kale. "You're allowed to have a break. But it sounds like you're frustrated by this, so maybe we can figure out an alternative. How do you feel in the afternoons? Like two to four or so? Do you feel like you're at your best with your patients or do you feel like you're dragging a bit?"

She's a witch. Or has cameras in my office.

"How did you know that?"

The waitress clears our now-empty salad plates and sets down our entrees. We both ordered the sole, and it looks delightful. Smells delicious too. I can't wait to dig in. And I do as she answers my question.

"You said it yourself, I'm good at my job." She smirks, looking extraordinarily pleased with herself. So pleased. It's goddamn adorable. "It's a hard time during the day for a lot of people."

"Okay, so what do I do about it, Little Miss Expert?"

Ugh, Campbell, if you're trying not to be a condescending numpty, Little Miss followed by anything—even if it's expert—probably isn't the way to go. But Starla doesn't look irritated. To the contrary, she looks smugly delighted. And tips her head in a way that... Och, I don't know how to explain how changing the tilt of her head could make her look sweetly charming, but it has. Innocent but up to something, perhaps her coyness is hiding... No, definitely not. *Knock those filthy thoughts right out of your head, Campbell.*

"If you have some flexibility with your schedule, I'd recommend you use that less-than-optimal-productivity time to go work out. A lot of people find that actually energizes them to finish out the rest of their days. You have a gym on-site at Harbinson, right? Or you could take a run around the neighborhood when the roads are finally clear. If you'd rather. I don't know what you do when you're at the gym."

She seems flustered, and I don't know why. Whatever it is, she shoves another bite of green beans into her mouth.

"Hmm. At present, everyone in the office keeps the same hours. Not sure I'd be able to find an admin who'd want to deal with that split schedule."

Starla shakes off whatever had ruffled her feathers and gets back to business. "You might be able to if someone wanted the same break that works for you. That's pretty likely, actually. Or you might be able to find someone who wants to start a few hours later who could work straight through. Or you can keep doing what you're doing if it's too much of a trial to change. But I think it'd be worth it to try. At least make the effort to ask. You asked me to do a lot more back in the day. Whether I could actually make it happen or not, I always did try."

I know she did. Starla couldn't always do what I asked of her. Sometimes it was too much and she literally couldn't. The point of my asking wasn't to make her fail, but so often to offer the chance to succeed. And I always made sure to praise her for whatever she *had* done. She was always so apologetic, but she needn't have been.

"I know. I asked you for the impossible sometimes and you delivered with alarming frequency. I see you're as tenacious as ever. So, yes, I promise to at least investigate the possibility."

"Good. I expect you to report back next time."

She seems to realize what she's said—her eyes get wide and she immediately studies her plate rather closely. It's a good-looking piece of fish, but not worth that much of her attention.

"I mean, whatever. You can call me. Or text. Texting's good."

"Or we could have dinner again next week," I offer, trying to take the most casual bite of sole meunière that's ever been taken. Because I don't have strong feelings about wanting to see Starla again. Nor has a thrill run up my spine at the idea that she'd like to see me again too. That would be wildly inappropriate and would certainly mean I should head my growing attachment off at the pass.

But when she blinks those wide hazel eyes up at me, I know it's hopeless. Now that I've made the offer there's no way I'll rescind it. And if she asks me for anything—anything at all—it's hers. No question in my mind.

"Yeah?"

I nod, trying to ignore the tightness in my chest, no doubt from the tenterhooks I'm on, waiting for her to say yes. Despite the fact that it's probably not a good idea. For either of us. At all. Too late. It is far too late. "Yeah. I'd…I'd like that, actually."

She looks down again, pokes her fork at her fish, dislodging another flake that she spears and raises before looking at me. "This isn't some kind of pity date, is it? Since I told you how pathetic my love life is? Not that it would be a date. At all. Just…"

"No, no pity here. You can pick up the check next time if it'll make you feel better. It's been nice, is all."

She nods, her head bobbing thoughtfully. "Fine. Then I'll see you same time next week. Different place. You pick."

"Yes, ma'am."

The fish tastes more buttery, the wine cleaner and crisper. I have another not-date with Starla Patrick.

$\mathscr{L}$owry

EVERY TIME I have a not-date with Starla, dread gathers around my heart as I wait for her at whatever restaurant I've picked. Surely this will be the time that she realizes what a pervy old man I am, what I really think about as I sit across the table from her.

I fantasize about her. About what it would be like to go on a date with her, what it would be like to ask her to come home with me afterward. To strip her out of the pretty outfits she wears and see if the understated elegance but also, dare I say, cuteness persists to the layer of her underthings.

She has this way of dressing that's mostly what one might expect from a very wealthy young woman, with clothes I can only imagine cost more than my rent, but there's always a detail that's almost…childish. A bracelet with a charm, a pattern on her sweater that recalls Alice in Wonderland or Peter Pan, the shoes that are yes, heels, but also have rounded toes with buckles and sometimes she pairs them with lacy socks with a fold-over frill. Does it speak to my depravity that I notice these things?

Things I have tried my best not to think at all ever for reasons that are ancient history yet still trouble my soul, but especially not within a hundred yards of Starla. It's not right. No, it's not right at all.

Once again, though, she silences the fear in my heart by showing up on time, her hair in a high ponytail with these sweet wild strands curling around her face and droplets scattered over her crown. My heart cannot take these things; it cannot take her.

But I can't imagine not seeing her anymore. Perhaps it will always be a friendly dinner and I can live with that. Probably. Unless she keeps showing up looking as gorgeous as she does and then my heart may give out. It's hers to do with as she likes, anyhow. Doddering old infatuated man, that's me. I'm glad Maeve isn't here to see how besotted I am. I don't think it would hurt her feelings because I didn't feel that way about her, but I would get mocked. Mercilessly. Deservedly.

I stand and greet Starla with a brief embrace, a brushed buss against her soft cheek. One of two times this evening I'll allow myself the pleasure of touching her. She smells of rain, though it had only been cloudy on my way here.

"Sorry, I'm soaking wet. I didn't grab an umbrella on my way out and by the time I realized it was going to rain, I would've been late if I went back to get one. Don't get yourself drenched. Ugh."

Despite her words, she doesn't shy away from me but lingers and I take an extra breath of her. The sweet scent of her skin overlaid with the freshness of rain on asphalt. Intoxicating.

I'm well aware as we sit that people are looking at us, likely trying to determine what our relationship is. Father and daughter? Lovers? I'm sure psychiatrist and ex-patient never crosses their minds, which is just as well. I'm getting some dirty looks as it is.

We both sit, me smoothing my tie down my chest and her dropping into her chair with a sigh. She does look harried, which may be the wetness, but still, she needn't look that way on my account. The words are out of my mouth before I can stop them.

"Next time you'll get your umbrella. I don't mind if you're late if you arrive in one dry piece."

Her eyebrows go up and my collar feels tight. I'm going to brazen this one out, though, act as though it's not at all odd that I've gone and given her instructions like she's a schoolgirl. She's not. She can tell me where to shove my umbrella if she feels like it, and I half wish that she will.

A smile dances around her lips, though, and every curse word I ever learned pings around my head.

"You wouldn't be worried if I was late?"

"I would, because you're never late and I'd assume something was wrong. But that's what cell phones are for, aye?"

The cocktail menu in front of me has become very, very interesting all of a sudden.

"I meant that you always look faintly relieved when I show up. That could be more overactive imagination than reality, though."

I glance up and the bottom half of her face is covered with her own menu, but her eyes say she's smiling behind there. What a wretched little tease. Noticed that, has she? The only response I can come up with is a very eloquent grunt. Scotsmen are legend for our ability to speak an entire sentence with a single grunt.

"Whatever the case, I don't want you making yourself sick being out in bad weather. I'll live if you're a bit late."

"Okay," she says, a lilt of mockery in her voice. "Next time I'll go back for my umbrella."

Next time. This seems to be an indefinite standing date. Though when she's not sassing me, she sometimes seems like she's off-balance. I could ask her about it, but perhaps I've been paternalistic enough for one evening already. Perhaps she thinks so as well because she sets her menu down and starts to fiddle with a ring she wears on her left middle finger.

We don't speak for a minute and as I always do when something interrupts our patter, I fear the easiness between us is over, that we've both come to the conclusion that this is far too bizarre to continue, and make excuses about next time for long enough we forget we ever had a standing date. I'm about to dredge up something to say, ask her an inane question about her day, anything but sit in awkward silence, when Starla reaches into the enormous sack she calls a bag. "This is for you."

The thing she shoves at me from across the table is a water bottle. "Thank you?"

I don't mean for it to come out as a question, but I'm a bit perplexed as to why she's given me a water bottle. I'm not a billionaire like her, certainly, but I've got a reusable water bottle or two knocking around my apartment.

She rolls her eyes and slumps before giving me the eye of the devil. "It's not just a water bottle, laser brain. It's special."

I mean, it is, because she gave it to me—I'd treasure a worm carcass she picked off the ground and put in my hand—but I don't think that's what she meant. I look at the thing to puzzle out what's special about it. It's green; that's nice. It's tall, so I won't run out quickly, also good since I don't always have time to go to the kitchen between patients. It has lines on the sides, which, fine, most of them do, but... Ah. That's it. It doesn't just have the amount of water written next to the lines, it's printed with times.

"I give these to my clients all the time. Most people are dehydrated but they don't realize it, and it's a pain to keep track. With some of my clients, we can set alarms, but since you're with patients all the time, that's not a good strategy for you. This way, when you're in between clients, you can look at your bottle and see how much you should've had to drink by that point in the day."

"That's very clever, thank you." I smile, not giving in to the grin that's tugging at the corners of my mouth. If I make too big a deal out of it, she'll be embarrassed and won't do anything like it again. But the smile on her own face doesn't escape my notice. She always did like to be praised and it seems that hasn't changed.

"You're welcome," she sniffs, trying to cover up her pleasure at my words, but that smile doesn't lie, nor does the pink blooming on her cheeks. "Hopefully that will help with your headaches."

"Headaches?" I mean, yes, I do regularly get headaches, but...

"You rub your temples, pinch the bridge of your nose frequently. You keep asking me to dinner, so I'm assuming it's not because you find my company tedious."

Sassy britches.

"I don't find you tedious at all. This is the best part of my week."

The pink on her cheeks gets darker, and she gulps down some water without looking at me. "Well, you know you should drink more than that if you're working out or if you've been having a lot of caffeine. I can't do anything about that."

"I'll do my best to remember, but I can't promise anything. I'm a bit of a wreck, can barely dress myself as you can see."

She scoffs, and I watch as her gaze skims over my tie, my blazer, my shirt. I don't want to say that I spent a lot of time selecting them with her in mind, but I absolutely did. She likes blue, so I'm wearing a blue and white checkered shirt with a blue and silver paisley tie, and then my one grey houndstooth blazer. Not bad, I don't think. And it's possible I texted Maeve a picture to make sure mixing those prints wouldn't make me look like an arse. Either she was lying, or I really do look okay.

"Well, I can't help you with that either, but it seems to me you're doing fine."

She looks down in her lap again and fiddles with her napkin. I need a new topic before she gets skittish or starts to wonder what the hell she's doing here with me. Again. After she'd said no —emphatically, repeatedly—not all that long ago.

"Ah, I meant to tell you my new schedule starts Monday next."

She blinks but then it must occur to her what I mean.

"Oh yeah? You found someone to work late?"

"No. One of our admins volunteered to work a split shift with me so she can pick her son up from school and drive him to his gran's house. His after-school program's closing and she wasn't sure how she was going to make this work, but having those two hours free will be perfect with time left over to run an errand or two."

"Hey, that's so great. I look forward to your report about how it's going once you're in the habit. The start might be a little rough because change, but I bet it'll be a good fit for you."

"I think so. A very smart woman suggested it, so I've great confidence."

I offer my glass for a clink and she obliges, the flush growing in her cheeks. She's so lovely. Always, but especially when she blushes. Must stop thinking about her and her blush. Must stop wondering if her bottom would become the same shade if I took her over my knee. Have got to stop picturing that, otherwise I'm going to get hard in my trousers and I won't be able to carry on a conversation at all. Which is why I blurt out the first thing that comes to mind.

"And how are you doing? Work is okay?"

STARLA

"Yes, work is fine."

Work *is* fine, in fact. Well, mostly. I have a client who's becoming agitated that my services haven't completely changed his life. Which is never what I promise in the first place. Nor does it help that he doesn't actually do most of what I suggest.

I'm on the verge of dismissing him as a client, because I don't need the irritation and I have other people who could benefit more from my help. Though Kirk isn't my real problem. That distinction goes to Tad as per usual.

Fucker will not leave me alone about making a call on my shares of Patrick Enterprises and I continue to try to swim in this ocean I didn't want to jump in in the first place. It's taxing and enervating and I hate it, plus though I'd like to think I'm doing a serviceable free style, it more likely seems that I'm doing a third-rate doggy paddle. My father had faith I wouldn't drown, though, and I can't stand the idea of disappointing him so I will do my best to at least keep treading water no matter what it costs me.

And while I'm sure Lowry would listen to my fretting and offer any counsel he was able to, I don't want to talk to him about it.

First, he seems to think me quite competent and I don't want to disabuse him of that notion. Second, I don't want to talk about this any more than I absolutely have to and I already spend far more time than I'd like to talking with board members, Patrick Enterprises' C-suite, my father's former advisors, my attorneys, all the goddamn people about it.

It's tedious and a gnawing worry, and I don't want to think about it when I'm with Lowry. I want to think about nicer things, like how he always looks happy to see me, and how I can fool myself into thinking he might have a bit of a thing for me. Of course he'd never admit it because it would be wildly inappropriate but that doesn't stop me from wanting him to. Doesn't prevent me from dreaming up what it might be like if he did in fact want me and acted on it.

What would it be like to sit on Lowry's lap while I told him about my day? Have him stroke my hair and kiss below my ear? Hear him threaten Tad's life in that soft burr of his?—even though I know he'd do no such thing because it would cost him his license and besides, Lowry's not a fundamentally violent man. Would he like that? Would he like it if I called him *daddy* as I snuggled against his chest and told him my troubles?

No, I doubt he would. He might say it didn't bother him with that impenetrable therapist neutrality that sometimes makes me want to swear and throw things, but he wouldn't mean it. He'd likely find it disturbing since he did know my father, he did know me when I was young, and technically speaking, he is in fact old enough to be my father. You can't erase that. Even if he were into daddy kink, he probably wouldn't want that with me because it would hit too close to home.

I'll have to content myself with what I can have and use these things he says offhandedly as fodder for my masturbatory fantasies—*Next time you'll get your umbrella.* Jesus, I almost orgasmed right here at the damn table. It wasn't a request, it was an order, and given so nonchalantly at that. I need to not think about it anymore before I get uncomfortably wet between my legs.

"Work is fine, but I'm a little tired. Could probably use a vacation or at least a weekend away, but that's not really a thing I do," I shrug.

Especially not while I'm trying to hold down my father's empire alongside tending my own small corner of the world. I shouldn't have said anything because his head, which had been angled down, studying the menu, snaps up.

"Tired? Are you all right?"

"Yes, I'm fine. Just tired, like a normal human being. It doesn't have anything to do with…"

I wave my hand, indicating the severe depression that's dogged my heels for most of my life.

"Then you should take a vacation. When's the last time you took a vacation?"

"Does the two extra days I spent in Chicago count?"

"No."

"Why not?"

I know why not, but I want to hear him argue with me. Coax me, convince me. Childish to want, perhaps, but I'll take what I can get.

"Two days in the freezing cold going to a few museums does not a vacation make."

Yep, that stern tone and that disapproving glare. Perhaps he'll drum his fingertips on the tabletop and scold me.

I shrug. "I don't really vacation. It's work to arrange things and my clients need me, and I don't relish being a woman vacationing alone. Do you know what that's like? It's not restful, it's more like an invitation for harassment and men trying to get in my pants even if I have sunglasses on, am wearing headphones, and have my nose buried in a book. Does that sound like fun to you?"

He wrinkles his nose. "Men are utter shite."

"Basically."

Then he looks like he might say something else but thinks better of it. Then opens his mouth before shutting it again. It would be funny if I weren't so desperate to find out what he was going to say. He shakes his head, though, determined to foil me, and then the waiter is here, taking our dinner and wine orders.

This is what we do, every time. It's familiar but still exciting, and I can't help but pretend in my head that we're a married couple who does this all the time: date night, to keep things fresh. Well, no wonder things are fresh because we're not dating, never mind married. Lowry was married, though. I bet he and Maeve took vacations together. And thinking of Lowry walking on a beach in swim trunks and aviators makes me whimper internally. That is a thing I would like to see very much.

I am perhaps dwelling on that image when Lowry speaks.

"Why don't we go together?"

"What?"

He shrugs, looking oddly disconcerted. He's almost always certain, confident, so it's odd to see him...not.

"I could use a vacation too. Not like I've anyone to go with either. Come on, why not? Or are you worried you can tolerate me for a couple of hours over dinner but a long weekend would be a bridge too far?"

That is hardly my concern. More like I would tolerate him far too well and my fixation would become even more unhealthy. No way in hell I'm copping to that, though. I do have other excuses.

"It's too much time. I have clients, you have patients. Besides, I already lose at least four days every six weeks."

"Having ECT isn't a vacation."

Don't I know it.

Lowry must see me getting stuck, because he volunteers, "Why don't you use the days you can't do anything else to travel?"

I have briefly considered that. But along with having to spend the energy figuring out where I want to go, for how long, and all those other things my personal assistant can't simply choose for me—Holden's wonderful, but he's not a mindreader—it's a bit of a terrifying prospect. The idea that I wouldn't remember most of it is a shrug. It's not as though I don't have the money to spend and I'd enjoy it in the moment, so why the hell not. The idea of being out in the world when I'm not at my best is a significant deterrent.

Some people I would tell to leave it, I don't want to discuss it, end of conversation. Because this is Lowry, though, I explain it to him.

"Look, I feel very comfortable at home, in my routine, with all of my things around me, with everything I need to do written out ahead of time. But out there? That's a recipe for anxiety and completely losing my shit, which defeats the purpose of a vacation, wouldn't you say?"

"Well, that's what I'd be there for."

So simple, so easy, obviously that's the solution. I want to roll my eyes because oh yes, sure, why didn't I think of that. Easy-peasy, bring my ex-psychiatrist who I'm madly in love with along. I do allow myself to level a glare at him while downing the last of my cocktail.

"Shepherding me through an airport and around some vacation destination doesn't sound like much of a break for you."

"Unless things have changed drastically, you're perfectly functional after the anesthesia wears off, not some invalid who couldn't navigate an airport. I'd be there merely as backup."

"And what if I get a headache? A bad one?"

"I assume you'd have your meds on hand. You can take them as well on a plane as on your couch. Or if it's truly horrific, we'll postpone. Come on, you could use a break. It would be good for you to relax."

He's leaning back in his chair, his big hands spread wide on the table, looking so very sure of everything. What must that be like? To walk through life instead of wading through it? To not feel the creep of your own brain trying to destroy itself? Unless something miraculous happens in the next fifty years or so, like science starting to give a shit about women's mental health, I'll probably never know.

As much as I'd like to take him up on his kind and enticing offer, I can't. Can't. I wouldn't be able to survive being in such close quarters with this man and come out with my heart intact. It's not possible.

"Lowry, I…"

Oh god.

I have been oh so careful to not say his name. Because it feels like there's no coming back if I say his name out loud, to his face. Not doc, not Doctor Campbell. Not nerf-herder or laser brain. And this is why. All of this has become so much more real. The fact that we are adults who enjoy spending time together and have some kind of chemistry that might be sexual and what the hell would be so wrong with that? Everything. *Everything* would be wrong with that.

I don't think it's my imagination that he feels the same. His lips have parted and there's that fucking look again. The one I would take to mean he *likes me* likes me from anyone else. A look that confuses the hell out of me and I can't deal with right now on top of everything else because it's going to end badly and I can't take that. No, not from him, not right now, and let's be real, not ever. So, before he can say anything else, I spit words out. Any words.

"That's so nice of you to offer, really, but I couldn't possibly take you up on it. That feels like it would be…inappropriate. And I can't…I just can't, okay? Please drop it."

Which is precisely the opposite of what I want. I want him to coax and cajole me, make me give in because he knows what's best, and he can tell I'm exhausted. That work is taking its usual toll, which I can handle, but all this with my father's empire is wearing me down.

He would understand, not think I was lazy, insist I take care of myself, and if I refuse, do it for me. Which, yeah, as a modern independent woman doesn't seem okay to want, but in my heart of hearts, I would cry with relief if he was willing to shoulder that responsibility.

The fucked-up thing is that I think he would, but I don't want them from Lowry my friend, or from Doctor Campbell my former psychiatrist. I want that from my daddy who would expect me to follow his rules and reward me when I did. Who would truly have my best interests at heart and I would believe him because I would have so much respect for him and he would know how to navigate the world far better than I do.

The thing is, while I trusted Lowry that way when I was his patient, it was in an amorphous way. It was in the air I breathed, the water I drank. It was a feeling I had, but I couldn't put a finger on it because it was so pervasive. It took a while for it to build up to that concentration in the atmosphere, but it was eventually a thing I took for granted. That no matter what else might go wrong, he would always be there.

On the day he came to Milo's house, something crystalized. I can't say if it was when he lifted me out of the bathtub in his strong arms, when he toweled me off, when he got me dressed, or when he braided my hair. Perhaps it was the way he spoke to me tenderly and without judgment the entire time. I don't know. It was the precious experience of a need being fulfilled, of someone seeing what I required and handing it to me without making me feel like I was broken, even though that was one of my lowest points.

Or so I thought. Because despite him always being there for me, no matter what shape I was in, doing his best to provide for me, convincing me it was not foolhardy to put my trust in him… once I had placed my life in his hands and felt relieved to be doing it, he left. Abandoned me. Took that precious gift I held sacrosanct in my cupped palms and smashed it. Years and years of carefully cultivated belief in not only him, but also in my ability to be loved. Yes, loved. Because there was something more than a professional obligation there. And then there was nothing.

I was not lovable, I was not even tolerable. The one person who had successfully convinced me I was couldn't stand to be around me anymore. The weight of my issues was too heavy, I had asked for too much, been so needy and desperate that I sickened him, forced him to leave.

He broke my heart and I believed it was my fault. That I deserved it, that I could expect nothing more from anyone. I was a failure and would continue to be one for the rest of my life.

I'm not sure why that didn't result in another suicide attempt. Given the circumstances and the fragility of my mental health, that would have perhaps been predictable. But the combination of a full course of ECT and Lowry's success in convincing me that killing myself wasn't an option meant I didn't. It was perhaps too all the therapy I'd done that helped me recognize the difference between rightful sadness and depression. What I felt when Lowry left was abandonment, grief, heartbreak, anguish, and desolation. Not the insidious whisper of depression, so I'm the girl who lived. Who is alive. And, despite the loss of my father and the other hardships I've endured since, will continue to live.

Having dinner with Lowry has become one of the best parts of my week. I enjoy his company very much and have allowed myself to enjoy it, to trust him this far. But while my fantasy life of handing him every delicate part of me yet again and having him cherish and keep it is very much alive, that's what it is. A fantasy. While I enjoy daydreaming about Lowry—and yes, getting myself off to the many episodes I've crafted of *Lowry Loves Starla* in my mind—I cannot risk even imagining that could be a reality.

So, to be given a chance to effectively play house with him? To have so many parts of my fantasy come true, to be so tempted to disclose the rest of it? To believe in him and place myself in the hands I once believed would treasure and nurture me, hand him every fragile part of myself? I don't think so.

I can't stomach the possibility of floating that offer to Lowry only to have it sink like a paper boat in a hailstorm. Again. This time it would be worse too. A rejection so thorough it would not only split me down to my core, but likely crumble that part of me as well. A girl can only take so much. And apparently, so can a man, because Lowry looks like I've slapped him in the face.

CHAPTER 7

*L*owry

THE LOOK on Starla's face when I suggested we go on vacation...
How quickly it went from the purest wishful delight to the most
profound horror.

And here I am on a rowing machine at the gym on Harbinson's campus at three o'clock in the afternoon, rehashing the
whole thing in my head. I am here because of her wise counsel,
and she... I don't honestly know where she is, what she's doing,
or who she might be doing it with, and it seems as though she
would like to keep those things true.

The rest of our dinner had been eaten in near silence and we
hadn't said anything about next time. Me because I wanted her to
be the one to initiate our next meeting since I wanted to know if
she wanted there to be a next time. And her...apparently because
she didn't want there to be a next time.

I overstepped my bounds. Asked far too much of her. Asked
her to trust me with her safety after a handful of dinners. What

was I thinking? Oh, I know very well what I was thinking. That I could have more time with her, that I could provide a sense of security so she could run about and make her world bigger without a care, that perhaps being together like that would let her see me in the way I see her: as a possibility. The brightest, boldest possibility, one I am terrified of, because of how perfect it has the potential to be.

Yes, it feels dangerous. I don't like the implications of what I want from her. But I do know I want her. It's been two full weeks without her and I feel like one of those trees that's rotted from the inside—the only thing holding me up is an exoskeleton of bark. Without the structure of how I've arranged my life, the fact my patients need me, I would have collapsed because I miss her so. Miss her smile, miss her sass, miss her darling outfits, and how she gives me no quarter, challenges me all the time.

It feels eerily similar to when I'd left for Chicago, a darkness I never thought I'd have to endure again. Does she feel anywhere near the same? Or is she glad to have left me behind?

Though I've already exceeded my usual speed on the rowing machine, I push harder with my quads and calves, pull with my arms, shoulders, all the way through my back until my muscles burn and scream for relief. But I will not give in. Not when the sweat courses down my forehead and stings my eyes, not when my shirt is plastered to me with the truly excessive amount of perspiration this workout has engendered. Not even when my stomach has started threatening a revolt—it doesn't scare me because it's got nothing to throw up. Which is what finally makes me slow and then come to a stop, slip my trainers from the toeholds and try not to stumble when I push to my feet. I'm not keen on the idea of fainting in front of my colleagues.

I have thought about texting or calling Starla many times over the past two weeks, but haven't because I don't want to be pushy. Perhaps if I stand very still and hold my hand out, she will nudge against it. But I can't bear the idea that she might not. Besides, I remember how much effort it took for her to knock on my door at Harbinson. It might take even more if she wants to see me now.

It's freezing outside but I still consider ducking out without showering first because now that I've decided on a course of action, I want to get on that as soon as possible. But Starla believes me to be a practical and responsible man, and if she did the same, I'd be tempted to scold her. If I were too distracted to think better of it, I probably would. Far better to wash the grime away and outfit myself properly for the cold than to go out in weather like this and end up a sweatcicle. As if Starla would be able to sense such a thing. She's clearly no mind reader, but better safe.

STARLA

I know on Wednesdays we smash the patriarchy. Would it be possible to arrange to *stab* the patriarchy on Thursdays? Because the only weapon I have right now is a really nice fountain pen my father gave me. I'd be loath to ruin it on these fuckfaces, but it would be worth it.

While my daddy kink for sure extends outside the bedroom, it does not extend into the boardroom and it makes my blood boil that these people still treat me as little Starla Patrick. As if at any moment, I'm going to take a doll from my satchel or perhaps crayons and a coloring book to camp out under the boardroom table. Have I done those things in the past? Of course, as a child when my father toted me around as his kindergarten-age protégé. Would I perhaps participate in those activities even now? Yes, but not in a boardroom where I am functioning as a major stockholder in an international conglomerate. For fuck's sake.

I am however, verging on hangry, and am definitely wound tight from the stress of managing never-ending statistics and balance sheets, real estate agreements, legal matters… everything. I have a sneaking suspicion this doesn't have to be so onerous except Tad wants me to feel overwhelmed. Is in fact using his knowledge of my shortcomings against me. He wants me get rid of my shares. I suspect he would like it if I sold enough directly to him—or whatever partnership he put together to actually come up with that much money—that he would have a controlling interest in Patrick Enterprises, and that leaves a bad taste in my mouth. I don't trust him. And I like him even less when he clears his throat and levels me with a look that says he doesn't think I'm very bright.

"Could we all flip to page eighty-three of the quarterly report? I think Ms. Patrick could use yet another review of our cash flow."

Seriously. Violence has never been a symptom of the mental health issues I have, and given the expressions on the faces of the other board members in the room, it appears that most rational people would love to shiv this asshat through an eye. Annoyingly, I know they're making a judgment about *me* and not that annoying sack of shit Tad.

I'm about to say so, when my phone buzzes in front of me on the table. It's Lowry.

Thrill and dread run up my spine in equal levels. I've wanted to speak with him. Have missed him since we last spoke, have clutched tightly to my daydreams about him even as I've tried to shove them from my mind. Is the universe trying to tell me something by having him call at the very moment I would most like to escape this godforsaken room? No matter if it is or not, I'll take advantage of the excuse to get the heck out of Dodge.

"I don't need to go over those cash flow numbers again, Tad. What I need to do is think about what I'd like to do with the information those numbers are giving me and I don't need the board sitting around this table and staring at me while I work it out. Also, I'm getting a phone call from Harbinson which I ought to take. Excuse me."

There's a murmur of surprise from the room and I barely refrain from rolling my eyes as I push back my seat. They all know I have serious mental health issues, so I'm not sure why that ripple went through the room at the mention of Harbinson. Wouldn't they rather I seek treatment and manage my depression as well as I can than not? Though it occurs to me like a punch to the gut that perhaps Tad would *not* prefer that. He'd be able to sue for control by citing my instability. The thought makes me sick to my stomach. Yes, better to be transparent about the fact that I receive the finest psychiatric care in metro Boston and not leave any room for doubt about my competency.

I leave nineteen pairs of staring eyes behind as I stalk to the door, answering my phone as I do.

"Hello, this is Starla."

"Starla, it's Lowry. I'm so glad you've picked up. I thought…"

The air still feels stifling in the fiftieth floor hallway of what I will always think of as the John Hancock building, so I head to the elevator and slip open the first two buttons on my blouse.

"You thought what?" *That I would like to be your darling little girl and the idea of you rejecting me makes me want to hide in my bathroom forever so I've been avoiding you? Correct!*

"Ah, perhaps we could talk about it later," he offers. Or never, which would be my preference. "But I wanted to ask if you were free this evening. Or perhaps you've already rebooked your Thursday evenings?"

Maybe I should get a cat. A cat wouldn't judge me for scooping tuna salad out of the bowl with Doritos. They'd probably want to share. I could move into my father's house, get a shit ton of cats, go all *Grey Gardens* on the place, and let's be real— very few people would be surprised.

Or I could have dinner with Lowry and be a functional adult. I do enjoy giving the finger to the haters...

"I haven't rebooked. What did you have in mind?"

I'm expecting him to give me the option of several cuisines or perhaps say he'll text me with the name and address of the restaurant, but instead, he surprises me by asking, "What do you say instead of dinner, we go ice skating?"

"I say I'm terrible at skating." I only ever went a few times as a kid, and mostly I remember the bruises I got from falling on my ass repeatedly.

"I didn't ask if you wanted to try out for the Olympics. I asked if you wanted to go skating. I used to go pond skating with my brothers near our house and it was always a good time. Course, mostly we ended up having a snowball fight."

Ugh. Picturing little ginger Lowry out on a picturesque pond in some scuffed up skates taking a snowball to the face is... Goddamn the man. And it does sound nice. If I couldn't let myself go on vacation with him, I could at least let myself have this, couldn't I? Indulge that little part of me, which he'd never have to know.

Of course, it could turn out to be one of those things that looks fun in the movies and then is quite terrible in reality. But at least if he asks me to go skating again, I can say no without him being all reasonable and asking, "How do you even know you won't like it if you haven't done it in twenty-five years?"

His presence is twisted so deeply into my grey matter I make arguments for him. I'll save my fighting for a battle I want to actually win, like the one against Tad and company, the people who have no faith in me and are likely rooting for me to fail.

"Fine. I'll see you at the Frog Pond at seven thirty."

LOWRY

It's darling what a terrible skater Starla is. I mean, really, truly terrible. She said she'd be bad, but I didn't expect this. The woman can't keep her feet under her to save her life. Of course, in addition to being adorable, it has the perk of her clinging to me as though I'm a life preserver on a frozen sea. My arm's getting a bit sore from where her fingers are digging in hard even through the layers I put on so I wouldn't freeze to death, but I don't mind. Means I get to be close to her, feel her pressed up against me, and also smell her.

She smells like sweet almond cookies, like butter and sugar and all the good things. I could eat her up, but I won't. That's not our relationship, and though she's given me far more than I could've ever expected from the way she reacted to seeing me on the plane, I won't push for more. Especially after what happened when I suggested she could have it. So I will enjoy what I can, the way she swears under her breath as she inches along on the ice and clutches my arm, her chest snug against my biceps.

"When is time for hot cocoa? I was promised cocoa."

She's looking up at me, eyes round, tip of her nose red, and her cheeks rosy. This has got to be at once the best and worst idea I've ever had.

"Are your feet frozen blocks of ice? Do your toes feel as though they could snap right off? Because that's when it's time for cocoa, not before."

"I feel like my nose hairs are frozen, is that good enough?"

I snort, and yeah, my nose hairs are feeling like tiny icicles too.

"I suppose. Let's try to get you off the ice without a tumble, shall we?"

She glares at me, and if I were frozen all the way to my heart, that one wrinkled-nose glower would thaw me. Starla is like a bunny. An incredibly rich and powerful bunny who could have her henchbunnies end a person in a second, but with me, she seems only to want her ears stroked. "Oh, shut it. I haven't fallen at all. I'm pretty impressed with myself."

I am smart enough and fond enough of my own hide not to return that she's been using me as a crutch the entire time and it would take a truly cursed skater to fall whilst doing that. And indeed, after another couple of minutes of shuffling, we do make it off the ice and onto a wooden bench.

It's probably not comfortable, but my arse is so cold I can't honestly say if that's the case. Starla's cheeks are a pretty shade of pink above the scarf she's got wound round her neck, and there's a glisten of perspiration at her temples and on her forehead.

"How is it possible," she mutters, "to be so cold and yet sweaty at the same time?"

"Talent?"

She elbows me, but it doesn't hurt since we both look like marshmallows in all our layers. When we'd exited the rink, she'd let go of my arm—much to my dismay—but now she's leaning against my shoulder and gazing at me with imploring eyes.

"Can I be done now, please? If you get me some hot cocoa, I'll sit and watch you skate if you want to go out without an anchor holding you back, but I'm dying here."

I am in the worst shit if Starla's going to start asking my permission to do or not do things. Makes my voice come out all gruff and stodgy. I suppose that's better than cracking which is the other possibility, given how I feel so light inside. I may as well be stuffed with helium.

"Aye, you can be done." I tip my head in the direction of the concession stand where there's a bit of a line but it's not awful. "I'll get your chocolate while you take your skates off."

She has the prettiest smile when she says thank you, and it makes me glad I'm walking away from her. Because I can hear her saying, "Thank you, Daddy," and I could collapse from horniness right here. Which... What in God's name is that about?

Never did I wish for Maeve to call me that. Nor want for her to be the type of woman who would. I liked her toughness, her self-sufficiency, her cutting intelligence and wit. Not that those qualities are incompatible with wanting to call your lover *daddy*, but...

Christ almighty. That vivid, thrilling sound bite is playing on repeat in my head. It pokes at all of my worst fears about who I am, the things I want, wishes I keep in my darkest heart. Despite all that—and I'm not proud of it—I know what I'll be jerking off to later.

When I come back from getting her cocoa, she's sitting prettily on the bench, rubbing her hands together, stomping her feet. The fur-topped boots she's wearing complete the picture, and I'm glad she's given me the excuse to go exert myself and also freeze my arse off again because she's so darling, I'd otherwise have trouble keeping my hands to myself. I would, but I wouldn't want to.

Once her hands are wrapped around the waxed paper cup, she smirks up at me.

"All right, Campbell. Show me what you've got when you don't have me slowing you down."

Her teasing challenge makes the foolishly masculine part of me perk up, the part that wants to preen and strut, like a peacock spreading its feathers to attract a mate. I'm not going to make it to the Olympics either, but I can at least pick up some speed and I can skate backwards and come to one of those showy, ice-spraying stops. For her, I will.

"As you like."

tarla

AN HOUR and three cups of hot chocolate later, Lowry is making a last few loops around the perimeter of the makeshift rink. He's fast and graceful, and I feel guilty for having held him back, but only a little. It's fun to watch him now, but I'm glad I tried. He probably knew I'd be glad I tried.

When I haven't been warming my hands around a cup of cocoa, I've offered him high fives and fist bumps, cheered his fancy hockey stops that send particles of shaved ice spraying into the air. He's not the best skater out there, but he's not far behind. And despite there being people with better moves, more speed, I can't take my eyes off him. It's not as though I can see his body through the many layers he has on; it's a competence porn thing. He's good at this, as he's good at so many other things. And while I can sometimes be jealous of the ease with which people walk the earth, I'm not jealous of Lowry. I enjoy him.

Soon enough there's an announcement that it's closing time

and all skaters need to exit the rink. I meet him at the gate in the boards that line the ice and somewhat overcome by—I don't know, I guess this is joy I'm feeling? Secondhand elation from the way he's been zipping around? Something comes over me and I hug him, arms thrown about his neck, bodies pressed together from chest to pelvis and wow, that's a terrible idea. Truly, truly terrible. I don't want to let go.

But anxiety brain is watching out for me—after a split second of contact, it starts hissing that this is weird and I should stop. When I've stepped back, red-faced from embarrassment and not the cocoa or the cold, he's standing there with his mouth open. Whatever he's got to say, I don't want to hear it.

"Get your skates off, I'll grab you a hot chocolate before they close."

And then I promptly run away because that's what grown women do.

By the time I'm back, he's packed up his skates—because of course he has his own skates—and is thumbing through his phone.

"Everything okay?"

The furrow between his brows smooths out a bit but doesn't go away entirely because it never does. "Everything's fine, just Maeve checking in. She's glad you got me outside."

Telling his ex-wife about me? He did say they were friends still so I guess it's not surprising. But still, I'm not sure whether to feel self-conscious or pleased. "Did you tell her this was your idea?"

"Course."

His lopsided smile kills me, and I can barely stand how much I like this man, how good he makes me feel. I hand him his cocoa and he takes a sip. He's cute, and offers me a one-sided cheers since I think if I have any more I will explode. Or be awake all night from the caffeine, which may be piddly if you've had one cup, but I've had three. So.

Lowry stands, slings his skate bag over his shoulder. "I know you're perfectly capable of walking home by yourself and that you do it all the time, but do me a favor and allow me to walk you back to your building?"

Now it's my turn to half smile.

"Next time we meet up, are you going to ask me to text when I get home?"

He grimaces and it occurs to me that it's probably because he would have liked to ask me for that and didn't. I don't know quite what to make of that. It's that same feeling of knowing I'm not supposed to like him being overly protective, but I do. While I still don't think he would be okay with the extent I wished that were true, I don't want to discourage him. I'll take these bits and pieces and make what use of them I can. Before he backpedals, I volunteer, "I could do that. Next time. And I wouldn't mind company on the walk."

There. That wasn't so bad. Very mature. And I've had about enough of acting my age.

It's snowing, pretty flakes drifting from the sky and Beacon Hill with its gas streetlamps and picturesque purple-windowed town houses as the background. It's like we're in a snow globe and it's so pretty I can't stand it.

I'm pretty sure my mother loved the snow, maybe because they didn't get much of it in Southern Italy where she was born. I am very sure my father was completely smitten with her. It's in every picture of the two of them; he's almost never looking at the camera because he's looking at her.

I don't have any memories of my mother. Not real ones. I was only two when…when I didn't have a mother anymore. There are a lot of pictures from when I was a baby, though, and my mind has elaborated on those moments frozen in time. Has made movies out of stills, written novels from a single word scribbled on a scrap of paper.

Anyway, this weather reminds me of her, and one photo in

particular, when she was holding me in a snowsuit that was so poufy I looked like a star. She was swinging me around, my little body nearly parallel to the ground. I like to imagine I remember her laugh.

My eyes water and surely it's the cold breeze that's kicked up, sending the flakes into delicate cyclones. Whatever it is, it makes me want to run. Skip. Lowry got the opportunity to soar around the rink and now I want a chance to fly.

LOWRY

Starla's taken off with a whoop that nearly makes me drop my hot chocolate. Truth is, I don't care for the stuff. It's too sweet and I'd rather have coffee or a hot toddy. But I wasn't about to say so when Starla had done something thoughtful. I'm also aware that she can be—has always been—self-conscious about some of the things she enjoys because other people have insinuated or outright stated they were immature. Fuck that. If it's not hurting anyone, we should all take pleasure wherever we can find it.

Starla has apparently found it whirling like a dervish through the storybook paths of the Common. But she could very well injure herself because it looks beautiful, but is in fact treacherous.

"Starla, careful. It's icy in some spots. I saw someone slip on my way over."

Yes, there's an undercurrent of worry as I watch her skip and spin, but it's overcome by something more than fondness. Something that has been building, shifting since the day I met her.

When she was my patient, Starla was a serious girl. Big eyes, rarely a smile on her face, especially when I first started seeing her. Most of that, I know, was the monster she's always carrying on her back, but some of it was something else and it took me a while to crack it.

She came into my office one day when she was fifteen, looking absolutely miserable. Which was worrisome, but honestly, less so than when she looked blank. That flat affect would send ice flooding my veins, because when she was so numb she wasn't feeling anything at all, that's when things got the most dangerous. When she was most likely to tell me she'd been thinking about hurting herself or worse. So misery, I'd take. Misery I could work with.

"Some boys at school were being assholes."

My hackles went up like a hyena's when someone's trying to drag away a tasty carcass it'd claimed. Despite having a lot of experience keeping a neutral look on my face, I had struggled to keep my voice level because I wanted to kill those fuckers.

"Are you okay?"

"Yeah, I'm fine. If this fucking depression hasn't killed me yet, no way am I going to let some shit-talking pubescent dickheads do it."

Shite, it was hard to keep from cracking up when she said things like that. But somehow I managed to only let the corners of my mouth turn up instead of full-on cracking up.

"That's fair, although you know just because something doesn't kill you doesn't mean it can't bother you. Whatever these boys did obviously bothered you."

And I obviously wanted to rip their faces off.

She shrugged. "Just their normal taunts, which are sucky. But the worst part…" She shook her head, not looking at me. "Never mind."

"Ah, but you know I do. Mind, that is. Come on, let's have it."

The look she gave me then made me feel it—the heaviness she always had pressing down on her, as though this seemingly average high school sophomore had the weight of the world on her shoulders. Then she shook her head and pursed her lips slightly.

"I told my father about it."

"That seems sensible, if it upset you. That's what he's there for."

Her full mouth wrenched to the side, and she looked down at her hands wringing in her lap. "Not really. I mean, he's already got all this to deal with, so anything on top of that actually seems unreasonable."

"What do you mean by 'all this'?"

I was met with one of her trademark withering glares, and she waved a hand in front of her face. "You know, this. Me. I'm… I take up a lot of time. I know he feels bad and that it tires him out. All the doctors, the appointments, me being in and out of the hospital. He's had to put up with a lot, so on top of all that, I guess normal kid stuff seems like the last straw."

I'm not in the habit of yelling at my patients, or shaking them senseless, but that's what I'd wanted to do with Starla.

Tell her it wasn't her responsibility to fret over her father, that he was a grown man with effectively unlimited resources, so if he wanted help, hell, if he wanted anything, he could have it. Except of course a cure for his daughter's depression. No amount of money was likely to ever "fix" her. It was her father's job to care for her, and that should include letting her be a regular kid. How awful must it have been for Starla when her father made her feel as though she wasn't allowed to express normal teenage frustrations because it was too much for him to bear? I had suspected it wasn't limited to boys at school, but any complaint she might have, any risk she might take.

"I don't think that's true, but let's say for the sake of argument it is. What would be the worst thing that could possibly happen?"

She looked at me with those big, heavy eyes of her, and I swear, I don't know how she hadn't been crushed into dust by everything that was weighing on her.

"He could kill himself like my mother did."

Ah, Christ. I'd known this since before I ever met Starla. But I'd also been told in no uncertain terms that I was never to mention it to Starla because she didn't know. Her father had never told her when she was smaller, and by the time he thought she could handle it, she was depressed herself and he didn't want to give her any ideas. I'd lobbied for telling her because knowledge is power, and perhaps knowing her mother also struggled would make her feel not so alone. Perhaps, too, make her more determined to not give in because she might be able to see how people missed her mother even if she couldn't see how she would be missed. But no, Jameson refused and I'd kept my word.

"You—"

"Aren't supposed to know about that? Well, I do. Why does everyone think kids are so fucking stupid?"

Anger's better than blankness, though I resented her father for putting me in this position. This didn't have to be the way we talked about her mother's suicide, but there we were, and I'd do the best I could.

"I certainly don't think you're stupid. You're one of the smartest people I know, and that includes grown-ups. And your father doesn't think you're stupid. He's constantly going on about how bright you are"—and how frustrating it was that depression was sapping so much of that from her.

"I can't speak for everyone else, obviously," I continued, which got me a well-deserved Nerf ball to the face. "No one thinks you're stupid. What we do think is that it's our job to protect you, and you've got a hard enough road to hoe already. No one wants to make it any harder, that's all. Especially since your father has spent so much time making your mother into some sort of fallen angel as far as I can tell. Vittoria was a saint, the prettiest, kindest, most beautiful woman to walk the earth, to hear him tell it. And all of that might be true, but she also suffered from really severe depression, like you. So, you understand that her suicide—"

"Wasn't my fault? Yeah, whatever."

Except that she clearly didn't. Now if only I could *Good Will Hunting* her into believing it…

I'm not sure I ever succeeded at that. One thing about clever patients is that many of them can fool you, tell you what you want to hear, or hide the things they're embarrassed about. Starla's always been fairly good at that, even as a kid. But never mind that. Never mind the past. She's better now, has her depression under control.

At the moment, Starla's skipping and spinning down the wide pathways of the Common, graceful in a way she most definitely wasn't on skates. And more than her grace, it's her joy I'm loving. She looks happy, carefree, like she can fully breathe.

She heads toward a set of steps that leads up to Beacon Hill, and I think about calling out my caution again, but I doubt it will stop her, and she's a grown woman. I don't relish being the overbearing, paternalistic arsehole who makes her feel as though I don't trust her. If I could look after her in a way that wouldn't make me a domineering, egotistic bawheid, I'd be only too glad to.

She dances on the stairs, up three and down two—she looks like she could be in one of those old musicals my mum used to love, and she'd scream at us boys to pipe down because she was trying to listen and of course, there wasn't any OnDemand or TiVo or what have you back then. If you missed it, you were shite out of luck. If Starla were truly on one of those soundstage monstrosities though, she'd probably have an umbrella for this scene.

Nearing the top, she makes a few more jubilant leaps and I'm half expecting her to slide down the metal banister that bisects the steps. But then her foot goes wrong, and she's not dancing anymore. She's more flailing than anything else, and then, then… she's falling.

CHAPTER 9

 tarla

THERE'S A SECOND that seems to last much longer than that, after my foot slips on a patch of ice I didn't notice while doing my best Rockette impression. It's that weightless sensation you get when you take a hill too fast in a car. I've heard roller coasters can cause that stomach-dropping-while-the-rest-of-you-floats feeling too, but I wouldn't know. Never been on one. All too soon, though, that weightlessness is gone and I am meeting the stone stairs, hard.

My hip takes the brunt of it, a teeth-chattering jar that's so stunning I lose my breath. It doesn't hurt, not yet, just feels like an impact when flesh and bone meet granite steps. But then my ribs, my elbow, and yeah, the back of my head make contact with the stone also and...ow. *Ow.* Motherfuck, that hurts.

Everything hurts and to add to the ignominy, there are a ton of people on the Common right now and they all fucking saw that. I curl up onto my side and try to catch my breath and do my best not to cry. Yeah, I'm going to have some bruises, not fun ones, and I feel incredibly foolish after Lowry warned me—

"Starla, love, are you okay? Are you hurt?"

Lowry's head blocks the light from an overhead streetlamp, the ends of his ginger hair set on fire by the glow. And he looks worried, oh so worried. Which he shouldn't be. It does warm me some, though. *Starla, love?* I know it's a Scottish thing, it doesn't mean anything, but I'd take a meaningless endearment from Lowry over a sincere one from just about anyone else, so it'll do.

"I'm more embarrassed than anything else. Really, I'm fine."

Everything is buzzy, and my head is filled with a rush. My fall must have looked really bad, but I feel surprisingly not terrible. Almost like I could go back to dancing, though this time away from stairs. Or ice. Yeah, not bad at all.

Lowry looks at me like he doesn't believe a single word that's come out of my mouth which he's always been good about *not* doing. "I don't think you are fine. I can call an ambulance. Or grab a cab and we can go to MGH. At least let me look you over before you get up. That was really bad. Did you hit your head?"

Ugh. I have been fussed over and poked and prodded enough for a dozen lifetimes. I know he means well, but I can't with this right now.

"I'm fine, really. If it will make you feel better, you can do your doctor thing, but after we get back to my apartment. Please, this is already mortifying."

Spending a lot of your life being "sick" means you always have a lot of people staring at you, examining you, speculating about you. I put up with it because, frankly, it helps keep me alive, but for anything beyond that, my tolerance for being regarded as damaged is bottom-of-the-sea low.

Lowry looks as though he might argue, and I am not having that. I'm a grown woman and I just humiliated myself in front of hundreds of people, not to mention the man I've been in love with for as long as I've known him. So I push up off the stairs, finding my feet and making damn sure there's no ice underfoot to send me flying again.

My bones feel out of whack, as though I had my own personal earthquake, which I suppose I did, but otherwise I'm fine. I'll be sore tomorrow and probably sport some super-attractive bruises for a few weeks, none of which requires medical attention.

I brush myself off with my gloved hands, wincing when I graze the spot I fell hardest on.

Lowry's still scanning me as though he could actually tell anything of use with his eyes—although how freaking horrifying would it be if he actually had x-ray vision—and he looks so serious, so very intense. To have that attention focused on me is heady, though I'd rather have it focused on me in some other context—not because I'm a foolish girl who didn't listen to someone I would fucking love to be my daddy, and as a result, I've fallen on the ice. Honestly, who does that?

"Lowry, I am fine. Let's go, please."

He clearly doesn't believe me, so I spread my arms and strike a pose. "See? Fine. Humiliated but fine."

"If you're sure."

God, he's handsome when he's skeptical. I mean, he's always handsome, but there's something about the way the crease between his brows gets deeper, the way he looks as though he's this close to scolding me and putting me over his knee for misbehaving and making him worry… Heaven knows why, but that totally does it for me. Stern, caring, would give me a lecture at the drop of a hat for my own good. Yep, would totally be on board for that. If I weren't so floaty, pretty sure I'd be getting turned on right now, so probably better that I'm feeling exhilarated instead of aroused.

He holds a hand out to me and I tip my head in thanks. Both for the hand, but also for not arguing with me further. Who knows, maybe once we're back at my apartment, it won't be so terrible to have him insisting that he wants to look me over. His hands running over my limbs looking for breaks, palms brushing over my ribs to seek out sore spots, his fingers sculpting around my skull to check for head wounds. Clearly I need to get laid if I'm looking forward to this for the sake of some human contact.

Once I have hold of his hand, I take a step, and...

My knees buckle, the world spins, and instead of holding Lowry's hand, which was sweetly mortifying enough, I'm now clutching at him while I faint. Fuck my life.

LOWRY

I've seen Starla unconscious many times. It was part of my job. But that was in a carefully controlled setting, induced by impeccably measured anesthetic, with dozens of medical professionals within shouting distance in case there was ever an emergency, and there never was. This is entirely different and smashes every panic button I have. She went from being insistently saucy to clinging to me as her legs gave out from under her, and now she's...

She's breathing, she's just passed out. Probably as a result of the adrenaline flooding her body draining away. But Jesus, what if she hit her head harder than I thought? It could be a million things.

Once I've managed to get us safely on the ground, I tell one of the gawkers to call 911. I know Starla said she didn't want an ambulance, but it's not her choice anymore because this is about safety. You don't fuck around with loss of consciousness, especially not after a fall like that.

Her breathing and her pulse are regular, but I'm still fucking terrified. There are very few times in my life when I have been as alarmed as I am right now. People think doctors are all sorts of stoic, that we're great under pressure. In fact, I have been. Gave a man on a plane CPR and didn't think twice. Simply had to be done. All of my calm, professional competence has fled, though, because it's her. I'd like to say it was different when she was my patient, but it hadn't been, really. For a while, yes, and then…

I knew I'd lost professional objectivity the night she tried to kill herself.

She'd been a junior in high school, still a minor, which I was at once painfully aware of but could also forget all too easily.

By the time I got to Harbinson after getting the call from Lacey I dreaded most in the world, Starla was sedated—pale with her wrists bandaged in the hospital bed, her father and Lacey talking while they stood in a corner.

When I arrived, her father turned on me, shoved a finger in my face. He'd been a slim man, compact and shorter than I am but rather threatening nonetheless.

"You were supposed to help her. You were supposed to be some fucking wunderkind. Look at what you've done."

He flung an arm to where Starla slept, and my heart squeezed with guilt. I was responsible for her, this had happened on my watch, but at the same time, he was being wildly unfair.

"I'm not the one who put that razor to her wrist. People's depression changes, it evolves, sometimes for the better and sometimes for the worse. Starla—"

"Get my daughter's name out of your mouth, you piece of shit. If she dies, I'm suing this entire place for malpractice. You'll lose everything, you'll never see another patient again. Your name is going to be mud."

I hadn't been afraid, though I'm sure Jameson Patrick could've done any and all of those things. He wasn't shy about using his power. The only thing I'd been afraid of was losing Starla, and that made me bold.

"Your daughter has been doing her very best to fight this thing that I don't think either you or I can fully appreciate. For her to think this was her best option…"

I'd wanted to vomit. Wanted to yell. Wanted to kick Jameson and Lacey out of the room so I could put my head in my hands and offer Starla choked apologies because I'd allowed this to happen. But to some extent, my hands had been tied. Despite my recommendations, despite his daughter's pleas, despite Lacey's support, he'd steadfastly refused ECT, and it made me fucking furious that he wouldn't put his daughter's needs over his own fears. I felt a little bad about taking advantage of his vulnerability, but not guilty enough to not press my current advantage, to use his desperation against him to do what I'd been urging for months.

"Perhaps now you'll consider a course of ECT."

"You and your fucking—"

And then Lacey was there, resting a restraining hand on Jameson's forearm. "You need to listen, Jameson. Doctor Campbell has no vested interest in trying ECT. It's simply that it's a good option for treatment-resistant depression, which is clearly what we're dealing with here. I know it seems scary. It does. And I can't offer any guarantees that it will be effective in Starla's case. What I can guarantee is that Doctor Campbell and I are on the same team as you. We're all on Team Starla. We all want what's best for her. She's said she's willing to try it, so perhaps you should be as well."

The anger seemed to drain from him then, and all I could see was an older man who felt hopeless and defeated. Who was having to face the idea that yes, this time Starla's attempt at suicide hadn't been successful, but next time it could be.

He scrubbed his hands over his face. "What if it doesn't work?"

I'd kept my mouth shut while Lacey nudged him, knowing he liked her far better than he liked me. But I couldn't keep it shut anymore because my—no, not my patient. I mean, obviously, yes, but more importantly, *Starla* was suffering, and he wasn't doing anything and everything in his power to make it stop. That was unacceptable. "But what if it does?"

He stared at me, fire back in his glare and I wouldn't have been at all surprised if he punched me. He hadn't. He punched the wall instead, stunning Lacey into stepping back and me into moving between them. Jameson had no intention of hurting Lacey or anyone, though. Just couldn't seem to find another outlet for his devastation and despair than putting a fist through some drywall. I suspect, though, it was mostly the fear of losing the daughter he doted on to the same thing to which he'd lost his beloved wife.

I thought he might break down again, but instead, he puffed up, looked nothing short of furious, and started bellowing.

"Anything," he said. "Do anything! Even...even...Jesus Christ, yes, do it. Just fucking do it."

These are the things I think about as I hold her against me, keep her off the ground with my body, and try to wake her. Say her name while I cup her cheek, stroke my thumb across her skin. Please let it be nothing. Let it be overwhelm from the adrenaline drain. Please let her eyes flutter open and have her righteously indignant, slap me in the chest because she said she didn't want a fucking ambulance and how goddamn dare I.

God, please, let this foolish, reckless, joyful act not take her from me.

I don't often pray; my relationship with the church is fraught. But I do now, dredging up memories of Catholic school for any saint I can invoke because I'm only human and I need all the help I can get. It's when I get to John Licci that her brows draw together and she turns toward my chest as though someone's shining a too-bright light at her, and then she's searching my face with those big hazel eyes.

I can breathe again.

CHAPTER 10

 tarla

AFTER A TRIP to the ER where I took full advantage of having a wing of the place named after my father, and Lowry took advantage of having privileges to get me in and out as soon as humanly possible, we're back at my apartment.

I'm exhausted and sore and the burn of humiliation hasn't completely faded. All I want to do is try to find a comfortable position to lie down in, curl up, and cry. Not exactly how I pictured the first time I lured Lowry back to my place.

In truth, I had no plans to lure him here because he'll think it's odd. Everyone thinks it's odd. I am one of the richest women—if not the richest woman—in Boston and I live in a studio. A well-appointed luxury studio with a beautiful view and a prime location, sure, but a studio nonetheless. I didn't particularly want to have this conversation ever, and I'm not up for it now.

But since he's here and under less-than-ideal circumstances, I keep up a brave face so he doesn't realize exactly how taxing all of this has been. I don't want him to pity me and treat me like a sad, broken thing he needs to fix because he's got perfection leaking out of his pores that he uses like glue to mend other people's cracks.

I take off my hat, unwind my scarf, and start to take off my coat. When I suck air through my teeth because my arm fucking hurts, there are hands at my shoulders, helping me with it.

Goddammit. I love his kindness and at the same time it makes me feel shitty. Are there people who can accept small kindnesses without feeling like a failure? How can I be one of those people?

When I've stripped down to my jeans and sweater, I shrug. With my good shoulder.

"Well, you can go now."

Clearly those etiquette classes my father forced me to endure didn't really take. That was rude. And though I don't think Lowry gives a goddamn about etiquette, he also doesn't look like I've convinced him to leave.

"I'm not going anywhere, at least not until you're settled in bed. What if you need help with something? You heard Doctor Kwon. You're supposed to take it easy. Why don't you get ready for bed and I'll make you some tea."

There is a long list of things I want so very badly, and having Lowry put me to bed has always been rather high on the list. There is a significant subset of that list of things I can never have for various reasons, and Lowry tucking me in is *definitely* on that list.

"Really, I'm fine. You don't need to stay. I'm going to have to manage on my own tomorrow, aren't I?"

Lowry's face gets that stern set, the one that makes my stomach flip. "The last time you told me you were fine, you passed out ten seconds later. And while I can't do anything about you being alone tomorrow, I can do something about you being alone tonight. Your stubbornness has served you well, but it's not doing you any favors right now. So, for the love of God, Starla, let me look after you for a bit."

Look after me? My eyelids sink closed, and I hope he mistakes it for trying to summon patience instead of what it really is, which is me trying not to die of happiness and break down in tears because my feelings are rioting and I can't manage them all at once.

"Fine."

I turn on my heel and head over to my armoire, pulling out some pajamas, and then walk into the bathroom. Peeling off my jeans to use the toilet is an exercise in how many swear words I know, and I feel sick at how much it hurts when my knuckles graze over where I landed on my hip. Taking my sweater and bra off isn't much better. And while I manage to pull on my softest pajama pants with a minimum of wanting to die, the top is far more complicated.

Everything hurts and I can't bend my elbow correctly, and it's so frustrating that I want to throw shit. If I were here by myself, I'd shove one arm into my bathrobe—both if I could swing it— and collapse. I'm not alone, however, which is both a boon and a curse. A curse because I can't half put on my bathrobe and then have a tantrum in my bed. A boon because…perhaps I could actually ask for help and not be stuck in an uncomfortable bathrobe all night. Imagine that.

Swallowing every ounce of pride I possess, I crack the door.

"Lowry?"

"Yeah?"

His footsteps sound on the wood and the rug, carrying him closer until I'm guessing he's right outside the door.

"I…I need help."

"Of course. What do you need? Can I grab you something?"

If only. My cheeks heat and I want to shrivel up, but on top of being wrung out and in pain, I'm cold now too.

"No. I…I can't put my shirt on. The sleeves, and the… Putting it over my head, I can't…"

Rage and embarrassment thicken my throat, and Jesus Christ. Is there not someone else who could use a lesson in humility more than me?

It might be my imagination, but I'm pretty sure there's a swallow on the other side of the door.

"Sure. I've got your tea ready when you're dressed."

Perfect.

I stand there, hand on the doorknob, eyes shut, head leaning against the door, and it would be great if I could stay here forever. That would also be a perfectly good solution. Use a bath towel as a cloak so my goose bumps would go away. I'm so tired I could probably fall asleep like this, and everything would be perfectly fine.

"Starla?"

Shit.

"Yeah?"

"Are you going to come out? Or would you like me to come in?"

Right. No matter how much I'd like to, I can't *actually* stand here until Lowry leaves. I may be stubborn as hell, but I have proof he can be just as bullheaded. There was more than one session during which we sat in silence the whole time. Because he's an asshole. An asshole who I'm keeping from his own bed and a good night's sleep by being ridiculous.

So I grab a bath towel, wrap it around myself as well as I can, and push open the door with my shirt in my hand.

He takes it wordlessly and has an entirely blank expression. Do they teach that in med school? How not to be fazed by anything? Whether they do or not, he's got it down pat, and he looks completely neutral as he shakes out my shirt and finds the neck.

"Ready?"

As if I need to give him permission to dress me for bed when it is a thing I want more than almost anything else in this world. But I nod because he's trying to be kind and I did, after all, ask for this.

He stretches out the neck of my shirt and eases it over my head, careful to not graze the part of my skull where a lump is forming and it's tender to the touch. I offer up my good arm, but he shakes his head.

"Probably easier to do the other one first. More wiggle room, aye?"

I swallow and nod again, because he is close. So very close. And he's being so very careful with me, it makes me ache. He always has been, but not in a way that made me feel weak, like some people.

This is an actual, physical hurt, one that it should be much easier to accept help for. Would I not get a cast if I had a broken leg? Would I not get glasses if my vision weren't perfect?

Wordlessly, I switch my grip on the towel, and together we maneuver my arm into my shirt with only one sharp pain that makes me suck air through my teeth. I'd like to tell him I can take it from here, but the truth is, it'd be a bit of a challenge to get even my good arm into its sleeve since I can't much use my other arm to help.

I switch my grip again, and finally my damn shirt is on. Quite the production.

Before I can, Lowry scoops up the towel from the floor and goes into the bathroom, and I wander over to my kitchen area and there's a mug, still steaming, on the counter. Picking it up with my good hand, I feel its heat. It hurts my cold hand like when you're chilled and trying to run yourself a hot bath and put your fingers under the stream to check the water.

I take a sip, and holy shit, that is not just tea.

"What the hell did you put in this?"

Lowry comes back, a sheepish, one-sided smile making his

dimple appear. "Ah, yeah, should've mentioned. It's more like a hot toddy than tea. So, whisky. And lemon and honey. But—"

"Mostly whisky."

"Aye, well, my gran said it would fix just about anything. Figured it couldn't hurt."

It doesn't. Hot enough to singe my tongue and my throat, but I'm not entirely sure that's all the steaming tea. Could also be the more lingering burn of the liquor. I think I'd like Lowry's gran, though I doubt she's alive anymore. If she were, I'd send her a case of the world's finest whisky.

~

LOWRY

Starla's standing there, taking slow, deep sips from the mug in her hand. She looks like hell, which is understandable, given what she's been through, and knowing how she feels about going to the hospital for anything other than her ECT. That's a necessary evil, and everything else feels like pile-on.

"Why don't you sit, love?"

When I moved here, I had to practice beating "love" out of my casual conversations since Americans don't use it in the same way as everyone back home. But with Starla, it comes out. While I did my utmost to never utter it when she was my patient, my tongue has loosened and I have more important things to spend my efforts on than not calling her love. Like forcing the stubborn hen to take a rest, for the love of God.

She wrinkles her nose and scrunches her mouth. "I can't actually figure out how I'm going to do it comfortably."

That'd do it.

"Well, come on then, let's figure it out. You're not going to be able to stand forever, especially since you look like a stiff breeze could knock you over."

She's clearly exhausted because she doesn't even snap back at me, or insist that she's a tank. Which she is, just…a tired one. One who's already been through a lifetime of combat, not to mention a particularly nasty battle today.

Shuffling over to the couch, she looks like she might collapse. I don't think I could handle that again. The first time it was as though my heart had gone through a shredder. Then she stands there, looking at the couch like it's a damn Rubik's Cube. Finally, she sets her tea down and lowers herself onto the plush cushions, wincing and sucking air through her teeth when she lands.

Frowning and looking miserable, she blinks up at me. "The entire right side of my body hurts."

I can imagine. And I can imagine the ugly black and blues she's going to have tomorrow, and how sore she's going to be. What I'd like to do is wrap her up in a blanket and take her onto my lap, rocking her to sleep while I convince myself she's okay because I can feel her steady heartbeat and the rise and fall of her breath. But there's no way she would stand for that, even when she's beat. Since that's not allowed, I'll try something else. There are several throw pillows on hand that I pile onto one end of the couch.

"What if you lean up against this with your left side? That should take some pressure off your right side."

She tries it, arranging the pillows, but still looks like she might burst into tears from pain and frustration.

"Not working?"

She shakes her head and tries to burrow into the pile. It's adorably pathetic, like a bunny trying to make a nest in leaves. She would hate that I felt that way, though, so I toss that idea, along with the pillows, and take their places at the far side of the couch, resting my arm along the top and patting the seat beside me.

"Come here. You can lean on me. Come on, before you lose consciousness."

She regards me for a blink, clearly trying to determine if she has enough energy to fight me on this, but then decides no and scoots closer, snuggling into my side to rest her head on my shoulder. At first she keeps her arm curled into her chest like a bird's broken wing, but eventually thinks better of it and snakes it around my waist, sighing when she lets the tension go.

"Better?" My voice is half a croak and I hope she doesn't notice.

She nods into my chest and makes a small "mmm" noise, and then next thing I know, her hand is curled into my shirt and she's breathing the perfectly regular and soft beats of sleep. Me? I will not be sleeping anytime soon. Even if I didn't want to stay awake so I wouldn't inadvertently move and hurt her, be ready should she need anything, I'd want to savor this. How could I possibly sleep when there's something so precious and fleeting to be enjoyed?

CHAPTER 11

tarla

I WAS HAVING the very best dream about cuddling with Lowry, and now I'm awake. While I do appear to be curled into his side and resting my head on his chest, I also hurt. All over. Worth it, maybe, if the result of my injuries means I get to be this close to him. *On* him.

He's as solid as I'd ever hoped, and it's heavenly to get to inhale him with every breath. But it's the middle of the night, and I'm not going to do either of us any favors by sleeping through the night like this. As much as I might like to stay here, like this, forever and ever, I should get up. I try to be sneaky and sort of slither my way away from him, but there's a rumble in his chest as I try.

"I'm not asleep, Star. You don't have to be sneaking about."

Of course he wouldn't be asleep. I've been sprawled on him and probably snoring and drooling, and he's endured every moment of it because he's a nice person. That's fan-fucking-tastic.

I do my best to sit up in a graceful manner, but I feel like the Tin Man left out in the rain overnight: rusty and stiff. Though I definitely have a heart and it's beating quick from Lowry calling me Star. Lots of people have, it's an incredibly obvious nickname, but he's never done that. I've always been Starla, always. Does this mean—

No, I shouldn't read anything into this. It's late and he's tired, and the extra syllable was too much effort. I get it.

Once I'm upright-ish, it's becomes obvious why I was leaning over like that—it fucking hurts to put any weight at all on my right side. To relieve the pressure, I try to stand but that was, like, whoa, too fast. Dizziness swirls my brain and I sway. And then, again, Lowry is coming to my rescue, standing in front of me and resting his big hands on my waist.

"Not so fast. You're going to take another tumble and you'll be sorry for that."

I'm sorry already. The dizziness dissipates, but I'm still feeling lightheaded and queasy. I use a hand on Lowry's arm to steady myself and focus on his face. His tone had been easy, but his expression is one of genuine concern. My god, am I a disaster human. And I have once again asked too much of him. Though I'd like to curl my fingers around his biceps for hours, test and measure his strength, that is a thing I absolutely cannot do. So I yank my hand away as though he's a hot stove. He could, in fact, burn me.

"You should go home. You have patients tomorrow and I'm fine. I mean, maybe I'll have some more whisky, but otherwise, yeah. Fine. And if you're worried about me being alone, I'll call Holden."

Holden mostly manages my bills and the finances of the business, but he also takes me to and from ECT. He's my employee, but sometimes being my PA constitutes some kind of weird shit.

Coming to sleep on my couch because I fell down some steps won't be the worst thing I've ever asked him to do, not by a long shot.

"I'll tell you what. How about I'll stay until you figure out a way to lie down that's comfortable enough for you to actually fall asleep and then I'll go. But I can't in good conscience leave you standing here knowing it took you several tries to find a good way to sit on the couch."

Maybe I should ask him to sleep in my bed since that seemed to do the trick for being reasonably not in pain on the couch, but I don't relish the idea of the horrified look I'd get in response. Yep, really don't need that.

"Fine. Whatever."

I move carefully away from the couch, completely mortified that Lowry is following close behind, probably with his arms out in case I fall over again. Could I be any more of a mess? Really wish poise were something I could buy.

Looking at my bed is a bit daunting, though. Lowry must sense my hesitation because he walks past me and pulls the covers back. I've always liked the way a million pillows look on people's beds, but when I tried that they all ended up on the floor and stayed there, so now the only decorative one I keep is a BB-8 pillow.

Lowry's a nice person though, so he doesn't comment on my childish decor, just moves the adorable white and orange droid to the side.

"How do you usually sleep? On your back? Side?"

"Stomach." Unless there's someone to spoon me, which I will not bring up.

"Right, then." His brow does that sexy furrow thing and he looks like he's trying to work out some kind of complex equation. "Do you have a side of the bed? Or do you sleep in the middle?"

"Do *you* have a side of the bed?"

Dammit. Exhaustion is making me ask questions I have no business asking.

"I do. Only because Maeve liked to be on the right. I still sleep on the left, even though we haven't shared a bed for years. Funny, the things that become habits." He shrugs as though that's not a weird thing for me to have asked.

"It, um, probably makes more sense for me to sleep on the right side. Since I'll have to sleep on my left side, and I like facing the edge."

"Okay. In you get, then."

He folds the covers down farther and I slip in, careful to lie on my left side. I'm going to flop over though, I know it, and wake myself up with a start. I'm about to tell him so when he holds up a finger. "Not done yet."

He grabs the pillow I'm not resting my head on, fluffs it, and then places it in front of my legs before holding out BB-8. I take the little droid and hug him to my chest, leaning over onto him and hiking a bent leg onto the pillow. Not bad, which is better than I have any right to expect given how much my body hurts.

"Does that feel all right? I know it doesn't feel good, but hopefully less bad?"

I nod as much as I'm able and…I don't know. I should be mortified by this and I am, but it also feels weirdly good. To have someone care for me, fuss over me, arrange my goddamn pillows so I'll be as comfortable as possible. Makes me feel small and squishy and needy and full of wanting. Wanting to ask him to stay the night. Not because I have any reason to worry, but because I just fucking want someone here, okay?

Someone to get me some Tylenol, someone to bring me water, someone to brush the hair off my forehead and ask how I'm feeling. I want these things and I want them from Lowry, but I can't bear to ask for them so all I do is roll my lips between my teeth.

LOWRY

Christ, her eyes. And the way she's clutching that fucking pillow. If only I could replace that pillow with my head. Give her something to focus on other than the pain. Perhaps by gathering up that pajama top until her breasts were exposed and then spending rather a lot of time with them. Licking, kneading, squeezing, suckling—figuring out what she likes.

Wouldn't go any further than that because I wouldn't want to hurt her. Could she come from that? I'd enjoy trying to make her. And if not, perhaps she's got a vibrator in one of those bedside table drawers. I wouldn't be able to fuck her to orgasm without causing the bad kind of pain, but I bet I could use one of her top-drawer friends to do the trick.

What does she look like when she comes?

That isn't what I should be thinking about when I'm supposed to be getting her settled into bed after she's been through a traumatic event. But the way she's looking at me... I have got to get out of here. Because if I don't leave now, I'll try to talk my way into staying, and that's not okay. Not tonight of all nights. She's hurt, she's vulnerable, it wouldn't be right. Way more than it's already not right, which is not an inconsiderable amount.

"I...I should be going. But can I get you anything before I leave? Something to eat? Glass of water?"

"My enemies encased in carbonite?"

The smile on her face is killer. Sweet and mischievous, it makes me not want to leave, but stay. Get on my knees beside her bed, take her face in my hands and kiss her silly. Thread my fingers through her hair close to her scalp and twist enough that she feels the pull. In my mind, she'd gasp but then melt, surrender to me, make little pleading noises, and Christ...

"If you like, though I'm sure in a couple of days you'll be able to acquire those yourself."

She rolls her eyes but I really do have that much faith in her.

"There is one thing."

Please, God, let it be me. She needs me. Wants me to stay, wants me to be here for her today and always, trusts me to maybe not take all the pain away but make things as easy for her as they can be. I'm choked by all the things I wish she would say, and barely get out, "And what's that?"

She wrenches her mouth to the side and her cheeks pink. "I can't reach… Could you… The covers?"

Sweet mother Mary, the woman is being asked to be tucked in. Why this should send a flood of arousal through me… I don't want to think too closely about that, because I suspect I know why but I don't want to admit it. It dances too closely to something that makes me nauseated. Fuck.

My voice is probably overly gruff as I tell her, "Aye. Course." I don't mean for it to be, but my head is buzzing and I'm fighting off the urge to do far more than tuck her in. Not tonight, of course, because she's hurt and I would never want to cause her pain. The bad kind of pain at any rate, because perhaps she'd like to be spanked. The way her leg is draped over the pillow makes the curve of her bottom so… What would it be like to take her over my knee? To have her glance over her shoulder, pleading look in her eyes, and promise to be a good girl. Why can I not get these ideas, these images out of my head when I'm around her?

Before my head explodes, I need to get out of here. Before I do, though, I finish pulling the covers over her, all the way up to her chin and she smiles when I do.

"Thank you."

And then my hand, my goddamn hand, which seems to have a mind of its own or is perhaps more closely wired to the animal part of my brain that only thinks about what it wants and not about what's wise, reaches out and runs through her hair. Her mouth opens, forms a near-perfect O, same as her wide eyes, and for a split second before I'm horrified at what I've done, it makes the desire so much worse. It's as though it's all I'm made of, all I have.

"Please do call Holden to be around if you need something. And if he's not able…even if he is…I am, I am always here for you, and I expect you to call if you need me. I will be here, no questions asked. For anything. That's not an offhand promise, and you know that, so please do take advantage, if you need."

Shut up, you lovesick puppy masquerading as a responsible man.

"Good night, Starla."

"Good night, Lowry."

Somehow I make it out of her studio, down the hall, to the ground floor where I stumble out into the freezing night air, but even that doesn't cut my lust. I don't know that anything is capable of doing that.

But as I tell my patients over and over, it's not about your feelings. Feelings are always valid. You're permitted to feel however you do. What matters, though, is what you *do* with those feelings. How you apply logic and empathy and the general rules that govern a so-called civilized society. *That* is what matters.

It is not my feelings for Starla, the impulses I have toward her, that are the problem. I'm just a man; I can't help the things that spring from my imagination any more than any other human can. What I can do is protect her from those, keep them buried like unexploded munitions. Though as anyone who's ever lived near a war zone can tell you, that ordnance is far from harmless and can detonate at any time.

The subway is stifling with the overworked heating of the HVAC. Perhaps it would have been better for me to walk home, even if it had taken hours. At least that way I would have exhausted myself, given myself something to focus on other than images of Starla from tonight. But no, they're still vivid in my mind. And continue to be as I walk from my T stop to my building and until I walk through my door.

All I can see is her. Eyes and soft curves, teeth sinking into a plump bottom lip, expanses of skin even though I did my damnedest not to look at her when she needed help with her top. At least I kept from audibly groaning. Thank God for small favors. Though a bigger favor would have been her sleeping through the night, resting on me. That was more than I could ever ask for, yet still not nearly enough.

Inside my own home, still a relatively bland and sparse bachelor apartment, I can't escape her. There's nothing here that interests me more than her, and restlessness prowls in my chest. I wish there were a way to get rid of this feeling, to be less obsessive. I could try meditating, but in this state, it would only result in meditating on her, which wouldn't be any better.

But…

Would it truly be the worst thing to get myself off to thoughts of her? Would it make being around her easier or harder? I know how she feels now, the weight of her in my lap. Too, I know the maddening worry and hands-raking-through-hair torment of waiting for a verdict on whether or not she's all right. Perhaps selfishly, I'd rather focus on the former. She hadn't gotten up when she'd come to earlier. Wisely, I'd say. But she could have demanded I put her down. She didn't.

Can I think of her willingly cradled on my lap and looking up at me as though she trusts me to keep her safe? May I pretend she'd allow me to see her vulnerable and understand I don't resent her soft spots but treasure them?

It's not that I want her weak. She's not. Anyone who thinks so is completely daft. But everyone needs help sometimes, everyone needs a shoulder to cry on, a hand to help them up when they get knocked down, a safe haven when the world is a fucking awful place. I want to be those things for her, be worthy of her most tender thoughts and feelings.

I'm not the physically strongest man; I'd fight for her without question if it came to it, but that's not where my strengths lie. I do like to think I'm responsible, measured, can shoulder a considerable psychic burden, would let her be carefree to the extent that she wishes it because I could handle everything she didn't want to, or couldn't bear. Wouldn't my head and my heart swell if I could have those things from her?

To what extent are those desires intertwined with the thoughts I've had about her before—the ones where she calls me *daddy*, the ones where she bites the pad of a finger and gazes at me from under her lashes with those doe eyes, the ones where it's not a single item of her outfit that's darling but all of it?

It's a lot. More than I can parse, more than I can handle. How can I want these things, how can I want her like this, but also be so terrified of my own desires? It's not the same as if she were still my patient, still a girl instead of a woman, and yet it's hard for me to logic my way out of this as it's all part of my relationship with her, part and parcel of what makes her both my basest and most precious desire.

Because the truth is I did want these things from her back then. I did. And doesn't that make me the kind of man who's always turned my stomach? Don't those desires make me the worst kind of vile?

Or do they?

I left, didn't I? Didn't take the things I wanted though she may have been willing to hand them to me. I had convinced myself that all of those feelings were bad and wrong but perhaps they weren't. Oh, acting on them would have been. I'd've wanted to slit my own throat for that had I taken action other than leaving.

But she's not eighteen anymore. She's thirty-three, and that hasn't slaked my thirst for her, hasn't changed the feelings I have toward her. If anything, the craving has grown. Sharpened in a way I wasn't expecting, and every time there's a hint of it, it's another pass over the whetstone.

There's more, too, always more. I'd like to discipline her, whether for real or as a game. Whatever she'd agreed to. Not only have her sit in my lap, but turn her over my knee and scold her. Or perhaps she wouldn't need scolding, just a reminder that she's mine, and if I'd like to spank her bottom, then I will. For my pleasure and hers as well.

I make quick work of getting ready for bed, scrubbing my face, brushing my teeth, stripping off my clothes that smell like the hospital in favor of some loose cotton pajama pants and a tee, one for the Cubs because no one in their right mind is a White Sox fan.

Once in bed, I still can't shake Starla from my thoughts. Indeed, my brain is playing the worst parts of tonight over and over on loop, making my pulse race and my stomach twist. If I ever want to get to sleep, I'm going to have to replace those thoughts with something else. Surely the universe will forgive me if I rub one out to thoughts of her so I can sleep and be my best for patients tomorrow? I'd ask God, but I don't think much of the one I grew up with anymore.

So, I close my eyes and let my thoughts jog to the place I so rarely let them go. To Starla, sweet in a dress the hem of which swishes around her legs at mid-thigh. If she twirled—and she would, for me—I'd catch a glimpse of toothsome panties. A golden yellow honeycomb with bees buzzing about. A hint of the playful and darling the small black sundress wouldn't entirely bely. Those are the things that make my brain hum, the secrets she keeps from others that she'd give to me.

In a meadow, because sure, why the hell not, she'd be picking wildflowers while I lounged on a picnic blanket and watched her. And when she was done, a handful of riotous color clutched in her fingers, she'd come back to me, show me her bounty and smile because I'd tell her they were lovely, just like her.

"Do you want a treat?"

Her eyes bright and wide, she'd say of course, because there's little she likes better from me.

From the basket we'd carried our picnic in, I'd take out a pouch, cold to the touch because it would be full of freeze packs, and from their midst, I'd extract a Popsicle. Honey lemon with edible flowers frozen in it, it would have to be pretty enough to be seen with her. She'd grab for it, forgetting her manners because she would covet it so badly. I'd know what she likes, how to make her happy and desperate.

"Ah, what do you say?"

"Please, Daddy?"

"Aye, that's a good girl."

But I wouldn't hand it to her, no. I'd hold it in front of me and she'd crawl on her hands and knees toward me, dress loose enough at the top that I'd catch a glimpse of lush, bountiful cleavage, and my mouth would water.

In the present, I've shoved my pants down, taken my cock in hand and begun to stroke, because this fantasy is too good. Almost never do I let myself indulge in these thoughts, but this fantasy's run wild and for once, I'm not going to rein it in. I'm going to let it run.

She'd lean over, use that sweet kitten tongue to take a few licks of the Popsicle, and my head would about explode. It's not fair, the power this woman holds over me. I would've been turned on before, but how she slowly, sensuously, purposefully uses her mouth to tease… She'd know exactly what she's doing and bat her lashes at me because she's a saucy little minx.

"Ah," I'd say, tugging her treat out of reach. "You'll have the rest in my lap."

She wouldn't be sorry for that, but climb eagerly into a straddle, be able to feel precisely how her show's made me feel. She'd rock up against me on purpose to make me groan and shut my eyes. Probably not entirely so she could snag the Popsicle from my hand.

Her giggle would make me open my eyes and then narrow them.

"Brat."

She wouldn't bother to argue, and her nod as she sucked the tip of the frozen treat would make me half laugh, half die inside because I'd want her so badly. Until she was done, I'd have to settle for wrapping my arms around her and holding her close, or perhaps clutching her delicious bottom in my hands and kneading, squeezing. Not spanking, because I wouldn't want to jar her while she's eating.

The picture is making me grip myself harder, to the point of pain, because I want to make this last. See where this story will end, because while her eating a Popsicle is sexier than it has any right to be, I'm certain my mind can come up with something even better.

Indeed, it does. Her rocking against me as she licks and sucks, and offering me some. I'd take a lick to please her though it'd be a bit sweet for me, but she'd reward me with a kiss, her lips and tongue cold but quickly warming as I explored her mouth, moved my lips against hers and licked the sweetness from her flesh. She'd squeak when the juice had started to melt down her fingers and rush to finish her dessert before any more of it was wasted.

When she'd finished, she'd lick her fingers too. One by one, savoring them, taking them deep into her mouth and making me fairly growl.

In my bed, I'm gritting my teeth because this is good, too good. But I can control myself, hold off, wait, because I can be patient. Especially when it comes to Starla, I will wait as long as it takes. Though in my daydreams, I'm guaranteed it will arrive, unlike in real life where I might wait forever for something that never comes. Also fine. Better than fine because I can't ask for this, ever, never mind *have* it. But that makes me relish this all the more.

Done, finally, she would kiss me again, and this time I wouldn't hold back, clasping her flush against me with one arm snaked around her waist while I'd bring my other hand down on her bottom, a solid *thwack* that would make her jump and mewl, but then melt into my grip. Yes, she'd enjoy that.

"What do you say, little girl?"

"Thank you, Daddy."

It'd be music to my ears, that, and a feast for my senses when combined with the shy way she'd smile at me. Despite my raw pleasure, I'd tsk at her and her chin would dip, her gaze questioning.

"Your manners could use some work, little miss. I shouldn't have to remind you, now should I?"

She'd shake her head, clued in to the game we'd be playing.

"You know what the rules are. Bad manners means?"

"Daddy spanks me."

"That's right."

Without me having to tell her, she'd drape herself over my lap, skirt barely covering her cheeks. Very few views can compete with that, but I'm a greedy bastard and I'd want more.

"Pull up your skirt."

She'd do it, but with a whimper, because being forced to bare herself mortifies her. The sweet bite of embarrassment would add to the intensity, the wrongness of it all, which in turn would arouse her more. She'd shift, and I'd be able to smell her. I'd lay a hand at the small of her back and then begin, palm meeting the flesh of her behind which would give under the impact.

I'd take my sweet time warming her up because in the fantasy realm, I have all the time in the world to lavish attention on her bottom, to turn what flesh I can see a lovely shade of pink. And when it became too frustrating, I'd pull the darling fabric up, wedging her panties between her cheeks and exposing the rest of the flushed skin. She'd squeak when I do, and grind her pelvis against my thigh.

"Not yet, naughty girl, or I'll make this a real punishment."

The threat would do as I intend; the rocking would stop, but the squirming would not, and she'd makes a helpless, pleading noise.

"Hands behind your back," I'd instruct, and she'd obey so I could gather her wrists in one hand and begin to lay into her properly. Not to hurt…not much, anyhow, but to remind her with the ghosts of bruises on her pale skin, of what we've done here. Leave her something to admire over her shoulder in the bathroom mirror, to graze with fingertips, or press into her bed at night to make the soreness come alive again, and send an erotic thrill through her with the memories.

The way my slightly cupped palm meets her bottom would be exquisite. I'd hit her over and over again until my hand would be tingling and her sounds would be a symphony of whines and gasps and all the things that'd send blood coursing straight to my cock. She wouldn't be hurting in a bad way, she wouldn't actually want me to stop—we'd have words for that, and she would have used them when we were first getting used to each other. Sometimes she still would, though not as often because I pride myself on the attention I pay to her reactions.

Finally, I'd stop the barrage, and delve between her parted legs with two fingers where I'd find her hot, swollen, and slick. Perfect.

I'd ease her onto her back, draw her panties down her legs and then spread them wide for me, followed by pulling the low neckline of her dress until it rested beneath her breasts. She'd flush and fist her hands in the blanket but she wouldn't cover up or try to close her legs because she's my darling good girl, and she'd know it no matter what I might say when we play our games.

"Time for my dessert since you didn't leave me much of that Popsicle."

She'd open her mouth to protest and I'd take the opportunity to push her panties between her teeth. I'd want her to taste what I'm tasting, how delectable the flavor of her own honey is, to experience what I'd be lapping up with my tongue. Wouldn't hurt that I'd like the way her pleading sounds are muffled when she's gagged, and she'd know how to stop if it got to be too much. Pinch my earlobe and it'd stop.

And then I'd be between her legs, spreading her pussy lips wide so I could lick and suck and nip at her, teasing round and round until I'd slick my tongue over her clit and then suckle, making her writhe beneath me, pressing her thighs to my ears so I could barely hear a thing, and my other senses would have to suffice.

My cock in my hand is aching, full to bursting, imagining what Starla would taste like, how she'd buck her hips into my face to ask for more, and though I'd wait in real life if I ever have the chance, I'm going to let myself come when she does in my dream. My eyes are closed and my grip is rough—I want this to be a bit punishing, the way I think about her, because she'd likely be mortified. Would wish I wouldn't think about her like this. So, she'll never know, I'll never tell her, I'll simply have her in my dreams while I take myself in hand, and then I can be a gentleman when I need to.

In my mind, her muffled cries are getting louder, she's rocking her hips to get the contact she needs to go off, and goddammit, I would give it to her. Push fingers into her pussy to give her something to fuck up against and suck hard on the tiny bundle of nerves until I felt her cunt start to grasp and pull at my fingers, until her back arched and didn't go down again for seconds, until her cries had grown near deafening even behind the gag.

That's when I spend on my stomach, a hot mess of release, the aftermath of pent-up desire, a sticky viscous reminder of everything I want from Starla Patrick but can never have.

tarla

"Would it be the worst idea in the world to text Lowry, or the worst, worst?"

"You are not drunk enough to be asking questions that ridiculous."

I knock back another mouthful of prosecco and scowl at Holden over the Star Wars Monopoly board. "Shut up! It's not the very worst idea I've ever had."

"No, that would've been when you stayed with Tad a year longer than you should have because you wanted to make your father happy."

"Would you kindly fuck all the way off?"

Holden lands on one of his very few property holdings which is annoying because I'd at least like to charge him money for being obnoxiously right. I've always had the impulse to make my father happy wherever I could since it was so rare that I could make him happy.

"No, you pay me not to."

He's right again, because I do indeed pay him to argue with me, and to not always give in when I demand something. Yes, we have a code if he does actually need to fuck off, but sometimes I just want to push up against something and it not actually move.

"But…"

Now it's Holden's turn to glare.

"No, hear me out, okay?"

He rolls his eyes and makes a go-on motion with his finger in the air.

"But what if this was a good idea?"

"How on Endor would this be a good idea?"

"Because if I drunk text him, I'll be so mortified I'd never be able to look him in the face again, and then I wouldn't have to worry about this anymore."

"Why don't you stop seeing him and avoid the whole being mortified thing?"

"You've met me, you think I have the willpower for that?"

Holden takes a drink of his own prosecco and looks at me, his gaze penetrating. I don't like it at all. "If this were anything or anyone else at all? Yes, because you're one of the strongest, most determined, self-aware people I know. But this guy…"

Yeah, I know. Lowry gets under my skin. Or rather got there almost twenty years ago and has never gotten out.

"I worry about you. I know you think Lowry Campbell is some kind of saint, but I'm not so sure about that. Don't you think it's weird that he spends so much time with you? He's what, like twenty years older than you?"

"Eighteen," I mutter. "What's your point? Are you saying couples with age gaps can't be happy? You've dated a few cougars and silver foxes in your time."

"Yeah, but none of them have been my ex-psychiatrist."

Point, Holden.

"And you're not dating. It's some bizarre, maybe-want-to-date-but-guilt-complex thing with some other weird shit thrown in there for good measure. Maybe you should get drunk and go to a bar and pick up some random dude. Should be easy enough to find a daddy type who would take you home."

"Sure, but A) they might have been friends with my father, and B) I don't want a daddy type. I want a *daddy*. Those things are not the same."

"They sure aren't."

Holden doesn't totally grok my daddy kink, but he gets it well enough to know what I mean. Some random older guy isn't going to cut it. Silver foxes are all well and good, but just because a man's got grey hair doesn't mean he's going to do it for me. No, my tastes are very particular.

My phone rings and it's Tad. Again. He's upped his campaign from once every three days to once every two, to now he's calling me every goddamn day and I can't with this on top of all the other shit I'm now handling on the regular. His number flashing on my screen makes me want to cry. But I also know if I completely lose my shit with him or stop responding altogether, he'll use that as evidence I can't be trusted to hold a controlling interest in Patrick Enterprises and I won't let that piece of shit be the reason I lose my father's company. He won't, absolutely will not, be the reason I throw in the towel and say fuck it all and become the ultimate disappointment, the apex of failure in my father's eyes.

"It's Tad."

"Ugh. That guy is the worst. Want me to stay?"

"No, this is probably going to take a while and no one wants in on that action, least of all me, but I have a fiduciary responsibility to the shareholders, blah blah blah."

Holden points and laughs because he's an asshole, and then grabs his coat from by the door, slinging it over his shoulders and then opening the door.

"Remember," he says, pointing an accusatory finger in my direction. "Worst, worst. Don't do it."

LOWRY

My buzzer rarely goes off unless one of my neighbors has forgotten their keys. It's on the late side for that but, yes, they might buzz my unit because they know the Scottish doctor doesn't have any children to wake up.

"Hello?"

"Lowry?"

Starla's voice is near the last one I expected to hear, not least because it's raining cats and dogs out.

I don't bother responding before I'm pressing the button to let her up, and thoughts are racing through my mind in the couple of minutes it takes her to make her way to my door. She doesn't make it all the way down the hall when I can see she's not her usual put-together self, but looks more like a scraggly drowned rat, and her shoes are…squelching with every step.

"What are ye doing here? It's pouring rain outside, and you're soaked through. What on god's green earth are ye—"

"Did you know your accent gets thicker when you're upset? It's rather remarkable," she says, rolling her Rs in a mocking way and putting her hands on her hips, still standing in the hallway. Yes, I'm aware my accent makes a roaring comeback when I'm getting worked up over something or other, or when I've been hitting the bottle too hard, but I haven't been imbibing and even if I had been, that's not the important thing here. What is with this woman and not being able to remember to bring an umbrella to save her life?

"Get in here, and take off those clothes straight away before you catch your death."

Her eyes get very wide, and she blinks up at me with a certain kind of gleam in her eye before she ducks into my apartment.

"You're a medical professional. You can't honestly believe that I'm going to 'catch a chill.'"

"I can't, can I? You have no idea how strong my gran's superstitions were if you think she didn't drill all these old wives' tales into my thick skull when I was a wean. So, yes, you're never going to convince the me with a medical degree that my gran was wrong."

It does occur to me that it's not perhaps the best idea to demand a woman come into your apartment and take her clothes off, but Starla doesn't seem to mind, just looks around at my living space. It's not as nice as her apartment or anywhere near as well-furnished or decorated, though more spacious because I've got two bedrooms.

Why, anyway, does Starla live in a studio? I would've asked her last week when we had dinner at her place, delivered from the very swank restaurant on the first floor of her building. Nice perk, that. But I'd been happy she'd agreed to not go out since she was still hurting from her fall the week before so I hadn't pressed.

She's here at my flat now, though, which is odd. She's had my address for a while but she's never made use of it. And it's surprising it's without warning since she plans everything. But perhaps...

"Really, you're making me nervous. I'll get you some clothes and show you to the bath, you're going to take a hot shower before you get dressed."

I'll have to find some clothes that won't fall straight off her —*Christ*—but I've got to have some clean sweats that will do the trick...

"Not a bubble bath?"

That nearly knocks me on my arse—the image of Starla in a tub full of iridescent bubbles, soaking and splashing and giggling like she hasn't got a care in the world. I can't even see her naughty bits in the picture and yet it still gets me short of breath and there's heat creeping up my neck. I've showed her down the hall to the bathroom and she's followed me inside.

When I turn round to face her, I notice something I hadn't before because I'd been so zeroed in on her being soaked to the skin. She's a bit flushed and she's got that slightly blurry look to her that says she's probably been at a pub. Ah, fuck's sake.

"I don't have any bubbles for ye, lass."

She laughs as I let my speech take on an even heavier burr. I like to please her, make her laugh, and she won't feel as guilty about enjoying it if she's buzzed.

"That's too bad. Although I didn't really come here for a bath."

"No?" I've got to dig out a spare towel from the linen closet so I turn my back on her. Coming up with one that's not exactly fit for guests but it will have to do, I face her again as she's stripping off her soggy sweater, dragging it over her head, and leaving an expanse of her midsection uncovered.

She's... I... Yes, I've seen her naked before. In a towel, recently. And I've certainly seen other naked women in the not-so-distant past—what counts as distant, anyhow?—but that plane of smooth skin, and the way her breasts are displayed in the bra she's still got on, I...

How can a man be expected to think under these conditions? It's not right. So I thrust the towel in her general direction and turn on my heel to head out the door, muttering something about dry clothes.

~

STARLA

Perhaps this was, as Holden said it would be, the worst, worst idea. Yes, I'm naked and wet in Lowry's apartment, but this isn't how I saw this going. At all. I suppose I could have foreseen he'd think of me showing up soaking wet on his doorstep as a problem to be solved and not a romantic gesture—why does it always seem romantic in the movies?—but then... He never did ask what I was doing here if it wasn't for a bath. Isn't he curious? I'd be curious if our positions were reversed, that's for damn sure.

If nothing else, I'm in Lowry's home, which is so bland compared to the man himself. He's renting though, and hit the ground running when he moved back by getting back to work straightaway. Probably hanging up some pictures or buying a vase or whatever wouldn't have been high on his list of things to do.

I'm also in his shower. Like a lot of men, his toiletry selection is rather sparse. But I didn't come here for a spa visit. I didn't come here for a shower either, but here we are. His shampoo and his soap smell like him, and I possibly take longer than absolutely necessary soaping myself up and inhaling the concentrated scent of Lowry.

It would be weird—like real weird—to stay in here for too much longer, so I rinse everything off and step outside, feet sinking into his soft, fuzzy bathmat. It's not pretty or sophisticated, but it's comfortable and I like it. The towel he shoved at me before running away is—

Oh my god, what if he has someone here? What if she's in his bedroom and they were...canoodling or something? This is why Holden said it would be worst, worst. Except, Lowry would've said, right? He wouldn't want me to be embarrassed if there were someone else here. He still would have scolded me and made me get out of my soaking wet clothes, but he would have told me. I'm certain of it.

Past that jolt of panic, I towel off, eyeing my bruises in the mirror. They're still there and ugly as ever since they've passed the deep purple pretty stage and are yellowing now. Nothing says sexy like mottled swamp skin. At least they don't hurt so badly anymore.

And then I'm in a towel with stringy wet hair and no blow-dryer in sight, nor any clothes. There's not a robe hanging on the back of the door either, which means when Lowry showers, he's wandering about his apartment in a towel. Except I suppose he's mostly showering at the gym at work thanks to my brilliant idea, which he mentions every time he sees me. How well it's working. How much his life has improved, and his performance as a clinician. It's maybe overkill for him to mention it every single time, but I like it when he says nice things.

It should go without saying—that whole "you catch more flies with honey than vinegar" thing is a saying for a reason—but people get better outcomes from me when they're nice than when they're not.

Tad stopped being nice to me some time ago, but he's recently gotten outright nasty. Tonight's phone call was a fine example.

"Your father would be so disappointed in you."

My eyes had burned and my sinuses tingled, and I'm angry they're doing it again now, a couple of hours later.

"You're driving this corporation into the ground."

Which isn't even true. Yes, the stock had tanked upon my father's death, and dipped lower still when it was announced that I was inheriting all of his shares and would hod a controlling interest. That's not exactly a vote of confidence. But since then, it's been steadily climbing. Not back up to where it was prior to my father's death, but people's confidence that I'm not going to set the place on fire or anything has gone up. I may be making extremely conservative decisions, but they aren't bad.

"Everyone on the board was concerned when you started and I tried to allay their fears, but you've been worse than they'd imagined. How am I supposed to pull your ass out of the fire now, huh?"

I'd wanted to punch him, wanted to yell and argue, but...what if he's right?

What if heaven is real and my father is looking down on me and thinking: "What the ever-loving fuck have I done?"

I made my father's life hard enough, now I'm making his afterlife a misery too? I know, I *know*, that Tad was doing it on purpose, poking at a spot he knows is vulnerable, but that's because it fucking works. I can tell myself all I like that there's no such thing as heaven or that I'm not doing a terrible job, or that Tad is so fucking toxic not even a rancor would eat his corpse, but jeez.

It's possible I downed another one of those tiny prosecco bottles Holden had brought over after I hung up with Tad because I've developed coping mechanisms for a lot of things, but someone using my recently deceased father's approval or lack thereof against me is a new one, and I haven't had time to develop a scab over the wound yet. Not even a temporary bandage. Nope, just a gaping wound that Tad can pour salt and citrus juice in like my psychic trauma is a goddamn margarita.

A knock on the door pulls me out of my ruminating.

"Starla? Are you finished? I've got you some dry clothes."

I swipe at my eyes because I don't want Lowry to ask what's with the tears. Because he will. I don't want to talk about that. I want to talk about my feelings for him because… What else do I have to lose? I don't want to keep playing friends if I'm some sort of extracurricular pity case for him. I can fucking well pay for my mental healthcare, thankyouverymuch.

And for fuck's sake, what would I do if he meets someone and wants us all to be friends? That would be too much to bear. I don't even like thinking all that much about Maeve and she's his *ex*-wife. Which isn't fair and I should be a grown-up. She does seem cool. Does a lot of charity work in Chicago, including for immigrant kids. I should like her, and I probably would, if I wasn't jealous that she got to share Lowry's bed, his life, and I haven't.

"Star?"

Shit.

I plaster a smile on my face when I open the door. Lowry's standing there, a pile of navy blue, grey, and crimson in his hands.

"I didn't know what you'd like best, so…"

He holds them toward me without totally looking at me. Right, I am wearing a towel. And that's probably awkward for him. But the question is, why is it awkward? Is it awkward because he *does* want me or because he *doesn't*? If it's the former, we're in business because I want him and we're both consenting adults and yes, I get that for quite some time he was in a position of power and significant influence over me, but he's not anymore. I'm the one with a shit ton of money, I'm the one who said I didn't want to see him, and he respected that. I've got a pretty good bullshit meter and Lowry doesn't register. The man is earnest to a fault.

Also, it's been fifteen goddamn years. Yes, he's got some street cred with me because of our time together before, but… I am a grown-ass, adult woman. Give me some fucking credit. Trying to take that away from me by saying I can't possibly make a real decision is some paternalistic trash that can jump in a dumpster fire. It's…possible I have some feelings about this.

If this is awkward because he doesn't want me, then this is all going to go according to plan. I'll come on to him, he'll be mortified and explain nicely that I am an attractive woman, just not one he personally finds attractive and then I can go back to my apartment and medicate my mortification with some more prosecco. And a bubble bath. And calling Holden to make him come eat tuna salad out of a bowl with Doritos. It tastes better than you might think. But only the Nacho Cheese ones. Not that Cool Ranch nonsense.

I take the pile from him, but not fully receiving them until he looks me in the eye. Like he'd be able to tell if he let go, they would fall. *Look at me, Lowry.*

"Thank you."

And then I step back and shut the door in his face. There. Enough for now. I need a minute to, I don't know... I need one of those boxing coaches who would rub my shoulders and get me all psyched up and shoot me up with painkillers because let me tell you, this prosecco is some weak-ass sauce. I can barely tell I drank any at all. But that's for the best. If I were obviously sloshed, Lowry would pat me on the head and probably try to distract me with an animated movie, and let's be real, that would probably work, especially if he let me sit next to him on the couch. And like doubly work for me to pass out if he cuddled me or petted my head. I'm so fucking easy.

CHAPTER 13

$\mathcal{L}$owry

W<small>HEN</small> S<small>TARLA</small> <small>EMERGES</small> from the bathroom, she looks more bonnie than any woman wearing mismatched, oversized sweats has a right to.

"Thanks for these, they're, um, warm." She shrugs and looks even more darling, if that's humanly possible.

"You're not going to win any fashion contests, but, uh, aye. I'm glad you're warm."

I swear to God I have a decent vocabulary that I often make good use of.

"Not going to catch my death now."

I shake my head because I'm too far gone to say anything. No, she's safe from that mysterious chill my gran was always so worried about, but my heart might stop. It feels painfully right to have Starla in my home, freshly showered and wearing my clothes. Perhaps not the pants because they look somewhat ridiculous, but maybe if she wore some of those leggings women all seem to wear now, and the grey Hopkins sweatshirt I've had for…well, a long enough time, that she's currently swimming in.

No, I can't think about that at all. What I ought to do though is ask her why she's here. I never did find out because I was too busy getting her undressed. *Way to be a professional, Campbell.*

"No, you aren't. And now that that's taken care of, did you want to tell me what you came here for?"

I have to stop myself from saying more like, "Don't get me wrong, I'm glad to see you, but…" Because I am all but encouraging her to drop by whenever, so we can… I don't even know, but it's not a good idea.

Her face is flushed which is a good reminder that she's been drinking and whatever she says needs to be taken with a grain—nay, a boulder—of salt.

"I came here…"

She takes a few steps forward and I take a few back, landing myself against a wall because apparently all of my spatial abilities desert me in the face of a woman I'm very likely in love with. At least I don't have any knickknacks to knock over.

I'm not afraid of her, not at all. I am afraid of myself, afraid of what I might do, afraid I won't be able to marshal my control and keep my hands to myself, because this isn't right. People say things like "The heart wants what it wants," which of course it does. But that doesn't mean the body and the brain have to go out and get it.

Self-control, decency. These are things I've prided myself on my entire life. Doing the right goddamn thing—hence the title Saint Lowry—and for fuck's sake, I took a vow to do no harm. I should've switched seats on that plane. I should have never called to refer Lois to her, could've had Lois do it herself. I should have listened when Starla told me she never wanted to see or speak to me again. Christ, I'm a sorry excuse for a human.

The way Starla is looking at me now though says she doesn't think so. A few more steps and then she's standing directly in front of me. When we've both got bare feet, she's small enough that I could tuck her under my chin if I held her to me, and the idea makes me want to weep. I am a weak man and she deserves a strong one. One who is not so fundamentally flawed and haunted. But because I'm weak, I don't stop her. Don't tell her to go.

I allow her to take another step forward and Lord in heaven above, I stop breathing when she lays her palms flat against my chest and looks up at me.

"I came here to tell you that I like you, Lowry. Not as a friend. Not as my former doctor. But as a man. You're thoughtful and intelligent and handsome and funny, and I…I like you very much. It's, um, really hard for me to say this out loud and to be so earnest, because you know that's not really a thing I do, but I'm saying it now because I wanted you to know, and I'm hoping you like me back. Not as a friend. Not as your former patient. But…as a woman. Who you might like to kiss. I'm, like, right here, so if you did…want to, that is, now would be a good time. Just saying."

Goddammit. Goddammit all to hell. I've done a lot of difficult things in my life. My career requires me to do difficult things nearly every day and usually far more often than that. Everything I've ever wanted for over fifteen years is standing in front of me, hand literally over my heart and telling me she wants me too, her eyes round and bright as she offers herself to me. God-fucking-dammit.

Having to peel Starla Patrick's small hands off my chest when I would like nothing better than to heft her up, instruct her to wrap her legs around my waist while I rutted into her with her back against the opposite wall, is among the most personally difficult things I've ever had to do. Nevertheless, I do, slipping thumbs under her fingers and breaking what seems to be a seal between her hands and the thin fabric of my shirt. So thin I could feel the warmth of her hands pressing against me, and Christ—I feel as though I am stripping away a level of my soul as I pry her hands from my body and guide them back toward her.

Hell, asking Maeve for a divorce was easier than this. Likely because Starla looks a thousand times more devastated than Maeve did. Chin wrinkled on the verge of trembling, a crease formed between her brows, tears brimming on her lower lashes. It crushes my soul to think I've hurt her that much. But I can't —*cannot*—ever have an atom of doubt in my mind that any feelings Starla might have for me are fake. That they were fueled by alcohol. It needs to be her choice. Her stone-cold sober choice.

"I'm flattered. Very, very flattered. But...you've had a drink or maybe more. I can't—"

"I'm not drunk. That's not why I'm here. It's not liquid courage. I know how I feel."

She's angry now, so mad she might stomp a foot. While I might deserve her heel coming down on my toes, the grinding of bone against hardwood, perhaps the snap of one of those devilishly small bones you can't really do much for, it would likely also ping that delighted part of my brain that likes to see her let go of how she thinks she ought to act and give in to her feelings, her impulses, reckless as they may be.

"Be that as it may, I would never forgive myself if you woke up in the morning and felt like you'd done something you'd regret. So, for my sake, please. We can't do this right now."

Her face has gotten that dusky coral color that passes for blush on her olive-toned skin and instead of about to cry, she looks like she might physically assault me. Wouldn't blame her for that a bit. Her eyes flash dangerously and fury twists her sweet features.

"Can't or won't?"

"Either one."

And just as fast, she looks as though she might cry again, and it breaks my heart. It would be so simple to take her in my arms, kiss her hard, explore her flesh with my hands, carry her to bed and have my way with her there. Simple, but not easy, and I can't do it, no matter how much I'd like to.

Hands on her hips now, she cocks her head. "Are you going to send me home?"

Och, am I? I hate the idea of her being alone in a car or on public transit having had something to drink. It'd make her a target, and I'd never forgive myself if something happened to her.

"No. But you're going to bed. I'll sleep on the couch."

That scowl is masterful. "That's ridiculous. I'm not kicking you out of your own bed."

"You're not. It's my choice."

"And what if I say I'll sleep on the floor if you sleep on the couch?"

Her arms are crossed, stubborn as can be, and it makes me feel as though my cerebrospinal fluid is sloshing about in my skull. What an infuriating woman. I'd like to threaten to pick her up and deposit her in said bed, but if I do that…if I do that, then all my protests are for naught because there is no way I'd be able to stop at tossing her on the bed. I'd surely follow.

"Fine. We'll both sleep in the bed. Now, march."

There's a glint of satisfaction in her eyes as she turns to flounce toward the bedroom, but she'll learn I'm as clever as she is. Well, probably not, but in this one instance I can outwit her.

I pull back the covers and point to the expanse of sheet.

"In you get."

There's a smile on her face as she hops up, tucks her feet under the blankets and lies down, head on the pillow and arms by her sides. It kills me to cover her up, pull the linens up to her chin and tuck them under the mattress. I've often wished I could keep Starla with me, look after her, put her to bed when she's tired, make sure she eats when she's hungry and drinks water before she gets thirsty, give her constant reminders of how loved she is. Having her here, the opportunity to do just that within my grasp and refusing it all, is fucking with my head.

Saint Lowry. Fuck me.

STARLA

It's six in the morning, and the late-winter sun is trying its best to force its way through Lowry's curtains. I know this because I am in Lowry's bed. So is he. But not holding me in his arms, not even with his head on a pillow beside mine. Oh, no.

I can still hear the deep, even breath of sleep coming from the foot of the bed where he is sleeping crosswise. I cannot believe he is for real doing this. That he honest-to-god slept like that. All night. When he first lay down, I made to join him and he made one of those distinctly Scottish noises. I don't know how they do that, make a single sound that contains so much meaning. This had a distinctly warning note.

And then he'd said it: "*Star. Don't.*"

I should have been insulted. I should have gotten up, called a car, and left. I should have told him to make up his goddamn mind, to either be with me or not, but this was bullshit. To want me here, to want me to be well and safe and *in his goddamn bed* but not have anything beyond a polite concern for me. It doesn't make any sense.

But… While I had felt chastised and frustrated, I'd also felt a twinge of arousal. *Star. Don't.* His tone had contained all the best things about being scolded. Restrained power, confidence. Brevity because he believed I would obey. The way he said my name… Could be making this up because I want it so badly, but it sounded almost as though he wanted me but was holding himself back, a verbal bite of his fist. Giving himself a warning as much as he was warning me.

I'd had half a mind to get myself off imagining what might have followed if this were my perfect life instead of the one I'm actually living. I'm not a brat, though. Never have been, beyond a little sass. No, I desperately want to please, be a good girl, and I don't think that masturbating in his bed with him right there would qualify, especially since he hadn't even been willing to grant me the intimacy of sleeping side by side. After some pouting, I'd fallen asleep because apparently I was exhausted and the comfort of his bed overtook me. So now I'm frustrated in more ways than one.

I should get up and go home, start my day. Read over some more of those reports my advisors have compiled about the state of Patrick Enterprises and what different scenarios would look like. Not what I want to do, but apparently very little of my life is about what I want. Which seems wrong somehow. I can buy any goddamn thing I want in triplicate, but the things I want most desperately, I can't buy.

There's movement from the end of the bed, and I hold my breath. Lowry slips off the mattress, and even in the gloom of the early morning I can see that at some point last night he took his shirt off so he's only in cotton pajama pants. Doctor Lowry Campbell, shirtless, is a sight to behold.

Not because he's built; he's not, really. He's that middle-age thickened torso that's sturdy as hell but with none of the definition other women seem to drool over. I don't want chiseled, hard muscle. I want thick, solid, warm flesh with strength underneath. And yeah, some chest hair isn't going to hurt.

Before I can start drooling, he snags a T-shirt from the floor and pulls it over his head. Does he always sleep this way?

"Starla?"

Caught.

"Yeah?"

"It's six thirty, do you need to get home?"

"Soon, yeah."

He reaches for the curtain and pushes it aside, letting more sunlight in, and I squint against it. Maybe I was a mushroom in another life. Or one of those cave-dwelling fish or some shit.

"Your clothes are dry and on the bureau," he says, gesturing with an arm. He must have been busy last night, I don't remember him getting up at all. "I'll make you breakfast before you go."

"You don't have to do that. Don't you have to get ready for work?"

"My first patient canceled so I've got a bit of wiggle room. And I know I don't have to but I'm going to. Pancakes or eggs and toast? Or all three?"

Bossy man. But a bossy man who's going to make me breakfast, so I guess I can't be too mad. "Pancakes. Please. But only if you have real maple syrup."

Because I'm spoiled like that. Lowry doesn't react with anything other than a nod, though.

"Why don't you get dressed? I'll meet you in the kitchen."

By the time I do, I'm mortified anew by what I did last night. And also his response. Reminds me that we're scheduled to have our regular dinner tonight, and I don't think I can sit across a table from him again.

He must feel the same way because by the time I settle myself at the breakfast bar in the kitchen, there's a stack of pancakes on a plate set out with a mug of coffee, a cup of orange juice, butter, and the requested—nay, demanded—real maple syrup, and he's wiping his hands on a dish towel.

"Help yourself to anything else you'd like. More coffee's in the pot, there's fruit and yogurt in the fridge if you're still hungry."

I won't be, since I rarely eat this much in the mornings, but god, it's sweet of him. "Okay."

"I'm, uh, getting in the shower now."

Yep, awkward. So I dig into my hot breakfast, the pancakes fluffy and perfectly cooked, and break out my phone to text Holden.

You know the only thing that would've been worse than texting Lowry last night?

Oh my god, you didn't.

I send him a pic of my half-devoured breakfast with the text "Pancakes at Cafe Campbell" splashed across it because I sure as fuck did.

Oh, honey, no.

Don't I know it. Can we drink tomorrow night? Please?

Sure can. I've got a date with Ben tonight and I think I'm going to tell him I don't want to see him anymore so that'll be fun.

Wait, I thought you were dating Anna?

What's your point?

Fair. Holden for realsies goes out on dates, and with multiple people at a time. I could never, but he seems to enjoy it.

I finish my breakfast, the only noise accompanying my meal the muffled sounds of Lowry getting ready for the day. I start to think about heading out before he returns, leaving a note, because honestly, I don't think I can deal with seeing his face for a week at least, maybe ever. Except that I can't even manage that because what do you say to a man who you confessed your love to and he tucked you into bed like a small child and slept at the foot of his bed instead of next to you? Those vaguely warm feelings I'd had about the experience have drained away, leaving me only with shame and mortification. And not a little anger with a glaze of indignation.

Mission accomplished, I suppose. That's what I wanted, right? To be so humiliated that I wouldn't be able to speak to him again? It's worse than I expected though, far worse. Should've listened to Holden. I hope he'll at least refrain from I-Told-You-So-ing the shit out of me.

I gather my things, check twice before I bail that I haven't left anything else of mine that Lowry will have to clean up. He's cleaned up after enough of my messes already.

tarla

"THIS ONE HAS a vertical layout and this one has a horizontal. Does either of those play nicer with your brain?"

Lois wrenches her mouth to the side and studies the planners I've laid in front of her.

"I don't know that my brain has a preference about that."

"Cool. Sometimes people feel really strongly one way or the other. Like for me? I cannot even with a vertical layout. Makes my head hurt. How about Sunday versus Monday start? Because this one has a Sunday start, and this is a Monday."

Helping people pick out planners is definitely one of my favorite parts of my job. Especially when they super nerd out over them and develop elaborate systems of stickers and color codes and washi tape and whatever else. I can't do it myself, so I stick to a super basic system. Only because I invariably let it slide toward the end of my ECT cycles when I start dragging and then

I feel bad for failing. But I love looking at other people's pretties, they're works of art. I get the feeling Lois might be one of those.

"Oh, I hadn't even noticed that. But now that you mention it, I definitely prefer the Monday start so the weekends stay together. Is that weird?"

"No, not at all. That's why I asked."

I smile at her and she smiles back. She's doing a lot better with her short-term, day-to-day getting shit done using a white board that has the everyday things labeled with washi tape so she doesn't have to write those over and over, and blocks of time left to let her brain do whatever it wants. It's good mix of keeping up with the basics but also letting her brain run wild sometimes so she doesn't feel frustrated and restless and always eyeing the new shinies. Now we're tackling the best way to keep track of longer-term plans so she doesn't double-book herself, which has been a real problem.

"So why don't we go with the Monday start for now? You'll use it for a couple of weeks and we can check in on it during our next meeting. Make sure you write down what you like and what you don't, so if it's not working, we can tweak it. If there's not a perfect planner for you on the market already, I can help you customize one. There's nothing wrong with being picky as hell. I don't go for that right away because they tend to be pricey and it sucks when what you think you want and what actually plays nice with your brain aren't the same thing. Hopefully this way saves you some money and some headache."

A lot of my meetings I do by phone or video chat, but Lois works close to my apartment and it turns out we both like sushi and boba tea, so we've started doing our meetings over lunch. It's nice.

"This is awesome," she says, flipping through the pages. I can practically see the stickers and washi and pens and clips dancing through her brain already, and I can't wait. "I've always liked the idea of a planner, but I never had the patience to go through a whole bunch of them and figure out which one would actually work best, so I always ended up using them for like a day and going back to my Post-its."

"Hey, Post-its are awesome, right? But for one-off reminders that you can stick on your fridge or the edge of your monitor. Somewhat less than ideal for organizing your entire life."

"Ugh, exactly. You're so freaking smart."

I have to laugh. "Smarter than a box of rocks, anyway. But it's more about paying attention and translating people's strengths and weaknesses into systems that emphasize the former and minimize the latter. I've been doing this for a while, so I've usually got a good baseline of where to start depending on what people struggle with the most."

Gives me a warm fuzzy feeling that I've been able to help her, and will hopefully be able to help her more. Super satisfying. As is this almond milk tea with tapioca pearls. Cold, creamy, and sweet, I suck some more through my straw and get the ideal number of bubbles with it, which is obviously three. Fight me.

"Well, I think you're brilliant. Between you and Doctor Campbell..." She trails off and looks up at me, pursing her lips conspiratorially. "He's real cute, isn't he?"

I almost inhale my boba. That'd be mortifying. I can see it now: *Billionaire Heiress to the Patrick Enterprises Fortune Chokes to Death on Tapioca Pearls.* Not today, motherfuckers. I pound against my chest with a fist and swallow.

"He is an objectively good-looking man, yes."

"But not your type? Not even with that accent? God, I think it's killer."

Can she not see the flames emanating from my face?

"I've known Doctor Campbell for a very long time," I say carefully because I can't admit my real feelings for Lowry, but I'm not going to outright lie. Especially when she's sharing. I think we could be friends.

"Oh yeah? How do you know him anyway? He never said."

Of course he wouldn't have. Because privacy.

"I was his patient back in the day. He saved my life."

"Oh, wow." She really does look impressed as she dips a piece of cucumber maki into the soy sauce/ginger/wasabi concoction she's mixed together with her chopsticks. "That doesn't surprise me. He's good at his job, like you. But still, that's cool."

"Yep. Very cool."

And isn't that enough for you, Starla? Jesus, what else do you want from the man? You ask too much. Far, far too much. I need to stop. Stop wanting him or at least stop tormenting myself with this fraction of what I want. Knowing he's probably with a patient because it's just past the hour, I text him.

I have to cancel for tonight. Sick.

And shove the phone into my pocket until lunch ends and I part ways with Lois, only to pull it out when it buzzes as I'm walking into my apartment.

Ugh, of course.

"Why are you calling, Lowry?"

"You left without a word this morning so I was going to check in with you anyhow. But now you've said you're sick. I'll bring you something and we can have dinner at your place if you're not feeling well. I've met you, Starla. I'm not going to let you eat a bowl of cold cereal or Doritos dipped in tuna when you're feeling poorly."

I am "feeling poorly" because I'm mortified. I want to crawl in my bed and never get out again because I am so completely humiliated. My stomach aches with embarrassment, and chicken soup or whatever the hell he would bring me isn't going to help with that. What I want is to flop on my couch and cover my face with a hand.

"Stomach flu. You don't want a piece of this so you definitely shouldn't come here. I've been puking and..." I can't quite bring myself to lie about having diarrhea. "You get the picture. So you definitely don't want to come here and be doing the same thing.

You have patients to see. Can't do that when you're glued to the toilet."

Why can I not stop talking about toilets? For fuck's sake.

"Okay," he says slowly, because no one wants the stomach flu. Even the most hardened anti-germaphobes will keep away from that ish. "But I doubt you have Gatorade and saltines and ginger ale hanging about. I'll drop by and leave them on your doormat."

He's far too goddamn decent. "Please don't. Don't come. I don't want you here. Why won't you take no for an answer? Weren't you the one who taught me that 'no' is a complete sentence? Why are you pushing this?"

There's silence on the other end, and I regret snapping. It's not his fault. He's trying to be kind because that's what he does, and I shouldn't discourage him from being that way because it's one of the best things about him. Besides, I'm the one who showed up on his doorstep last night with no invitation, no notice, and he welcomed me. Gave me clean, dry clothes, a comfortable bed to sleep in, and made me breakfast when he could've turned me away. Would probably have been more comfortable if he had.

"That's fair and I apologize. You're right. Did you know my brothers used to call me Saint Lowry? Always trying to help even if people didn't want help. It's a bad habit of mine, and I'm sorry I'm inflicting it upon you. You deserve your privacy. I won't come by if it will really bother you."

Goddammit, there he goes again. Being a good, respectful person. Which is of course why I concede. But only an inch.

"Fine. I like the purple Gatorade. And the white. Orange is the worst. You bring that shit here and I'll puke on you."

"Brilliant. I'll be by round seven thirty. Take it easy for the rest of the day, aye?"

Sure, sure, I'll coddle myself so I recover from my fake illness. I do my best to imitate one of his Scottish grunts and fail, likely sounding as though I'm about to have another round of vomiting because I'm sexy like that, and then I hang up.

LOWRY

Armed with a bag full of Gatorade and crackers, I make my way down the hallway toward Starla's apartment. The odds of her actually being ill are near zero, but props never hurt. Particularly when I've bought my way into seeing her or at least being near her with the promise of the sort of food you only resort to when sick. Except maybe not Starla. She probably eats this for lunch regularly because for a rich girl, she's got some dime-store taste when it comes to cuisine.

I knock on her door and am utterly unsurprised when she responds with a shouted, "Just leave it. I told you that you don't want a piece of this. I have the plague."

The woman is... If she weren't so infuriating, she'd be adorable. I mean, she is that too, which is part of the reason she's infuriating. If only she were sick, she might let me take care of her. But since I suspect it's more her emotions than her body that feel like utter shite—and because of me—it's no wonder she's yelling at me through the door.

I'd called Maeve in between patients and told her about Starla showing up last night and her text claiming illness since.

"You know, for such an intelligent man, you're awfully dense sometimes."

"I'm offended, how—"

"You're no such thing. You're calling precisely because you want someone to tell you that you're thickheaded and I'm only too happy to do it."

I'd made a noise to let her know she was right, but I wasn't happy about it.

"Here's the deal: you want her, she wants you. I know you've got some sort of complex about it because you're Saint fucking Lowry, but you need to get over that. And you're going to have to go after her and fall on your sword real hard. You need to tell her you fucked up. Give her all the explanations you want, but the bottom line is that you hurt and embarrassed her even though you want the same things. So go apologize before I have to fly halfway across the country to drag you over to her apartment by the ear so I can smash your faces together already. Honestly."

I did not want Maeve doing anything of the sort, so here I am with a sacrifice of only the best colors of Gatorade and some actual saltines. Which are frankly, getting heavy, so I set them down, and lean my forehead against the door. I don't have a sword handy, so this will have to do. I take a deep breath before I fall. Or rather, throw myself.

"I know why you canceled dinner. And it wasn't stomach flu. I'm sorry if I embarrassed you last night. That wasn't my intention at all. But for my own peace of mind…"

I shove my hands into my pockets because there is no peace of mind in this situation. I suspect I will always feel uneasy on some level and wonder if I'm taking advantage of her, speculate about whether we would've ever gotten together if Starla had never been my patient. I'd like to think so, but how would I ever know for sure?

Starla's got this theory about why Padme married Anakin, even though he's, and I quote, "a whiny-ass, insecure, volatile, abusive man-child." It's because Anakin is inadvertently exerting mind control on her. I'm no *Star Wars* expert like she is, so I can't say whether this theory holds water, but what I do know is if something similar is going on here—if I'm using my knowledge of Starla's psyche to manipulate her—I would feel like the lowest creature that ever walked the earth.

Much as I want her, much as I want to believe I could make her happy and take good care of her, I can't take just any opportunity to have her. If there's anything I can do to reassure myself that she is reasonably, rationally, choosing me of her own free will and not because I'm performing some kind of Jedi-psychiatrist mind trick nonsense on her, then I'm going to do it.

Part of that means I can't have her under the influence of anything when she says...

My heart constricts, squeezes tight, and I lose my breath when I remember her palms on my chest, her nails scratching at my pecs as she looked up at me and confessed that she likes me, as a man, and that she'd like to be kissed. By me.

I shake my head to clear it, but there's no getting Starla out of my head. It was unfair for me to send her off and put the burden of vulnerability on her again. *Be a man, Lowry. You want this woman, and the least you can do is tell her the feeling is mutual. If she wants you back, all she has to do is call and you'll come running. Hell, she can tell you to go away and you'd still come running, because you're a bloody fool.*

"I...I'm here to tell you that I like you. Very much. Not just as someone to have dinner with, not only as someone to fetch hot cocoa for after I've forced you to muddle about on ice skates. I like you, Starla Patrick. As a woman. A woman I would like to date because you are intelligent and beautiful. You are captivating, funny, sexy, and stubborn. I'd like to believe that you feel anywhere near the same way about me, but given how our relationship started, I want to be very careful. Make sure you don't— that we're actually—that I'm not..."

Her door swings open, and I nearly take a header into her but catch myself on the doorframe. She might not be sick, but she's no longer dressed for work or wearing the pretty clothes she usually sports for our dinners. No, she's got on some socks that go above her knees and tie with ribbons—pink goddamn ribbons, in the name of everything holy—some black ruffled shorts, a Hello Kitty sweatshirt that's falling off one shoulder, and her hair's up in what my admins would call a messy bun.

With her pink cheeks and wide eyes, the most hopeful expression on her face, she's never looked lovelier to me.

"Anakin to my Padme?"

"Aye, that's the right of it. I'd even been thinking that. Should've put it that way in the first place, but sometimes I talk too much, and how could I do that if I used an apt allusion you'd latch onto straight away?"

She nods, her mouth pinched in a way that makes me feel as though she's trying not to laugh at me. I ought to say something else, but for the life of me, I can't think of what else to say. So I stand there, like some sort of numpty.

"Lowry?"

Thank God she's not speechless. "Yes?"

Instead of saying anything else, she takes a couple of steps toward me, closes the gap between us. I try to suck in a breath as she crosses the threshold. She's knocked the wind out of me, and my whole body is straining, alight, primed, and ready. *Touch me please, Starla. I wasn't prepared last night but I am now and I swear I won't let you down again.*

Her hands come up, and she hesitates oh-so-slightly before she gingerly lays them on my chest again, same as she had before.

Something crackles between us, and I nearly swallow my tongue as she slowly slides her palms up to my shoulders, curls her fingers around my neck, and finally slips them into my hair. It's enough to make a man short-circuit, and every part of me seems to be on the fritz. Breath coming quick and shallow, heart beating wildly against my ribs, muscles in my stomach and my hands contracting, and hell, I'm blinking too much. I need a damn reset button, perhaps a rewind that would let me try this over again because I must look rather daft.

But Starla seems to either be oblivious or not mind. She comes up on her tiptoes, using her hold on me for balance, and tips her head, studying my face as though she's never seen me before. Perhaps she never has, not like this. With the confirmation that my interest in her is not platonic, nor is it in the least professional, but is in fact, deep, romantic, sexual, and more abiding than I hope she'll ever know.

Her lashes flutter as she leans closer and I have to swallow. Speech is out of the question but I could at least breathe well enough to not pass out. When she's so close our lips nearly brush together, so close that I can feel her breath on my mouth, she says, "I've dreamed of this."

And then she kisses me.

CHAPTER 15

 tarla

AT FIRST I think I've made a terrible mistake. His mouth said one thing, and now his…yeah, still his mouth, is saying something else. Yes and then no.

In all the times I imagined kissing Lowry and how it might be, never did I imagine he'd be so…stiff. Except in the appropriate area, of course. That, I had pictured being long and thick and so hard it was nearly bursting with his desire for me. But the marble-statue thing hadn't ever appeared in my fantasies, not even during my *Twilight* phase. Lowry was always warm and passionate, and he'd always touch me. He's not touching me, nor is he moving at all.

He regrets this already, his attachment to being righteous and honorable and professional overtaking the confession he just made, and the thought has me pulling away from him, parting my lips from his. Yeah, no, this was not how I'd pictured things at all and mortification is starting to twine around me.

His hair is softer than I thought it would be, and the stubble on his face scratchier, but the feel of his shoulders and traps as I skimmed my hands over them were precisely as I thought they'd be. Now I know that for sure. And if I can ever bring myself to rub one out while I think of him after this—the hurt and humiliation will take a while to burn off—then I'll know how it feels.

I start to stagger back, holding up my hands and shaking my head, issuing apologies for I'm not quite sure what, but this has gone very badly and somehow it's my fault, probably. But as I'm wiping our kiss off my mouth with the back of my wrist and about to shut the door to my apartment, he's there.

Covering the distance my dozen stumbling steps put between us with two of his own quick strides, Lowry takes my face in his hands with a sound that can only be called a growl.

"Not on your life. I've fucked up enough things with you, and not on your life am I going to be that big of an arse again."

And then, then—

Yes, this is much more like how I'd pictured it. Lowry's lips against mine, not at all shy or still now but slanting over my mouth with a pressure that makes me want to give in, yield to him. Which I do with a sound I'd be ashamed of except that I'm too busy being kissed.

It's not just his mouth, either. One of his big hands slides up and his fingers spear into my hair until he makes a fist around the strands, holding me fast in a way that makes my knees weak. Lucky for me, his other arm has come around my waist and he nearly hauls me against him. Draws me in until we're pressed together from chest to thighs.

This is more like it, oh yes, far more like it. His tongue coaxing my lips to part and then licking inside as though he wants to taste every inch of me. As though he's been thirsting for years and I'm the only source of water that could possibly satisfy.

There's a slam and I open my eyes for a blink to see Lowry's kicked the door closed. That's good because some of my neighbors have children, and I don't think this is going to stay G-rated for very long. Hell, with the way Lowry's hand is coming down to take a firm hold of my ass cheek, I think we're into maybe PG-13 territory already? And the way he squeezes, kneads, pulls me closer even though we're already touching—it's heady. As is the feeling of...

Oh yes. His erection is hard against my stomach and I want to be closer, feel it at the apex of my thighs, so I wrap a leg around him. Which doesn't quite work because he's too goddamn tall. He withdraws from my mouth and I chase after him, but he's not going far. Just letting out a soft, strained laugh before bending his knees slightly and then hefting me up. I wrap my legs around him and hook my ankles at the small of his back to take some of my weight off his arms and, oh god.

"Is that what you were looking for?" he asks, rocking my hips against his length, and all I can do is whimper. And kiss him again. Hard. Greedily, like I'll never get enough because I don't think I ever will.

It's a funny thing, to have one of your dreams come true. There are things I want that I'll never be able to have, but the universe has seen fit to give me a chance with this man and you'd better believe I'm going to hold onto him with everything I have. And a bit unbelievingly, because I'd thought even if he did in fact want me, he'd never dare to have me because of what it would say about him as a doctor. As a person people put their deepest trust in. It's an overwhelming feeling to think he wants me so badly that his desire would overcome his sense of honor, his commitment to being the consummate professional, his precious ethics. It's enough to make my head spin. Or perhaps I'm not getting enough oxygen because of how fervently I'm kissing him.

It's been a while, and I'd like to believe that's why I start grinding against him shamelessly. I suspect, though, that this would've been my reaction to Lowry-in-the-flesh whenever I would've gotten this chance.

It's perhaps a strange thought to have, since I do in fact regularly have electricity shot through my skull, though I've never been awake for that. No, I'm always very carefully anesthetized so my body doesn't actually bear the physical effects of the seizures they induce. But that's the only way I can explain how this feels—like there's electricity coursing through my entire body and I'm buzzing with it. Giddy, but not drunk—everything is razor sharp and in hyperfocus. The way Lowry tastes as his tongue plunders my mouth, the way he smells at this distance, and Jesus, yes, the way he feels between my thighs.

He carries me over to my bed and lowers me onto it, careful not to fall with all his weight on me as he follows. I laugh, because oh my. This is impossible. It is impossible that Lowry Campbell is hovering over me, looking down at me like I am some kind of miracle and he can't believe this is happening. Impossible.

"What's so funny?"

He's looking down at me with a gentle smile, twirling a lock of my hair around his finger.

"Nothing's funny, it's… I'm…"

"It's a lot, yes?"

I nod. "Yeah. I'm kind of overwhelmed. I never thought this would happen and now that it is, I don't even know what to do with myself? Because when I try to figure it out, all I can think is that I want everything."

He releases the curl he'd wound around his finger and threads his hand into my hair, kissing me at the corner of my eye. It's so swoony I might die.

"I know how you feel. It's the same way for me, when I look at you. I don't even know where to start."

Indeed, his gaze is roving all over me and I can feel it almost as keenly as where he's actually touching me. Though if I had to choose, I'd pick his real touch every time.

"And I feel as though I might have gone about this a bit wrong already. I got carried away and I didn't think to ask. Is this okay? Me, like this, on you? Or is it too much? I can—"

"Don't you dare."

To make my point, I fist my hands in his hair and pull him down to kiss again, possibly squirming and pressing a bit against him, because how can I not? This is marvelous, he's marvelous. And a damn good kisser, which surprises me not at all.

"Mmm, Star…"

It's hard to find the space to answer him, but I do, between kisses.

"Yeah?"

"I am enjoying this. So much, but I…"

"Yeah?"

Apparently my vocabulary has shrunk to one word but who can blame me?

He leans up, seeming a bit short of breath, and samesies. I can barely breathe and not because he's lying on top of me. I let go of his hair reluctantly and knit my hands behind his neck instead. I'm unwilling to let him go entirely.

"It's very important to me to be careful with you. Not because I think you're fragile. I know better than almost anyone that you're no such thing. But it's also…" He swallows, his Adam's apple bobbing in his throat. "I feel very protective of you, and I'd never want to hurt you if it can be avoided. I'm saying this, and yet I've already manhandled you and hauled you to your bed like some kind of brute."

"I, um, like it. The manhandling that is. And the hauling."

His lips part and he seems to stop breathing.

"And see, that's good for me to know. I'm not going to treat you like some kind of porcelain figurine if you'd rather be…"

"Manhandled."

"Aye, that."

"But?"

"But I need to know. So, perhaps before this goes any further, we could talk? About the things you like and the things you don't? If you want to take this slow—"

"I don't."

It's his turn to laugh, his entire torso vibrating with it, and I'm pretty proud of myself. I like making him laugh.

"Noted. I'm not particularly inclined to take things slow myself given how long I've waited for this, but whatever you want, I'll be respectful of your wishes."

How long he's waited? How long has he waited? What, like a few months? I've been waiting for almost twenty years, but sure, several months is the absolute same. I won't be petty about that now, though. Maybe later.

"And what about your wishes? Don't those count at all?"

"Aye, course they do, but..."

"I swear to god if you pull some weaker sex bullshit, I'm going to headbutt you."

"I would never. But I suspect my appetite for you is basically insatiable, so I'm going to have to rely on your better sense to reel me in."

"The assumption that I have better sense is, well, questionable at best."

"Be that as it may, I think we should talk. Because of consent and all that good stuff. And probably not in your bed because the odds of me getting distracted by you if we stay here are approximately one hundred percent."

I roll my eyes, faking exasperation. "Fine. Under one condition."

"What's that?"

He kisses just below my ear and it makes me shiver. Perhaps I should have insisted upon multiple conditions. But hopefully we'll get this done blip-bloppity-bloop and then the making out can start again. And then beyond making out.

"You manhandle me over to the couch."

He answers me with a bite to my earlobe and now I *really* regret not making more demands.

"Deal."

Then he's scooping me up, and I have to cling to him. Gee, darn. Super hate having to wrap my limbs around him and hold on for dear life while he's carrying me across my apartment. I'm only too happy when he sits, with me landing in his lap. I was worried he was going to make me sit on the opposite side from him so we could do this properly, whatever that means. This is better, way better. A straddle is not my favorite way to be in a man's lap, but I will take this for sure. Particularly when his hands land on my waist and it's only seconds before they drift down to my hips and his fingers skim over the curve of my butt to rest on my thighs, right between my stockings and my shorts.

"Will you be insulted if I say you look very cute?"

I roll my lips between my teeth and shake my head. "No. I like looking cute. I would only be insulted if you said it in a condescending way while patting my head. Don't get me wrong, I like to be petted but that's different from patting."

He cocks his head.

"What? There's a goddamn *distinction*."

He laughs again and the resulting smile lingers. "What's that exactly?"

"Why don't you try it and see? I'll tell you which one you're doing. Here…"

I pull the elastic from my hair because while perfectly sufficient patting can be achieved with a messy bun, any petting that results would be subpar.

"Okay, go ahead."

I'm kinda mad he has to remove a hand from my thigh, but I suppose I'll live. He reaches out, and sort of taps the top of my head.

"Yep, see, that was patting for sure. Not as good."

"Not as good as…"

"Petting. Try it."

"Bossy britches," he mutters, but I forgive him almost immediately because his fingers delve into my hair as he smooths a hand over my head, making me a puddle.

I tilt my head, close my eyes, and enjoy the calming motion, how safe and loved it makes me feel. Cherished, if you want to be sappy about it, and when I'm being petted, I do.

LOWRY

I've seen Starla happy before, many times. Except for when things were at their very worst, she could still smile. But I don't think I've ever seen her look as peaceful as she does right now. Straddling me in the most adorable outfit imaginable, with her hair down to make it easier for me to pet her. Yes, *pet* her. She's practically purring.

"You really do like this, don't you?"

"Mmm." There's a nod, but she doesn't bother to open her eyes.

"You're like a wee cat. If I do this for long enough, are you going to roll over and show me your vulnerable underbelly?"

That does make her crack an eye open.

"I think we both know you've seen plenty of my vulnerable underbelly."

True enough.

"Do you only like having your hair stroked or do you like this other places as well?"

"You think I'm going to give you all the answers? I think you'll have to conduct an experiment. For science."

"Ah yes, science. Very important."

On the next pass of my hand over her head, I keep going, gently rubbing her neck, her shoulder that's bared by her sweatshirt, and then her arms. The dreamy look hasn't left her face; more than her head, then. Good to know.

"Shall we do this for the rest of the evening, then?"

Truth be told, I probably could. Not that this would top the list of things I'd like to do to Starla, but making her feel this way is something I enjoy very much. Fills me with pride, pleasure, and some other things I can't identify. Good, I suppose, is the bottom line. Making her feel good, happy, makes me feel good. That's not magic. What it is, is good fortune.

"No, I guess not. Don't get me wrong, this is really nice and I like it a lot, but pet play isn't really my kink."

My stomach flips, hearing her talk about kink. She's said it lightly, perhaps as a joke, but I have to swallow to keep my voice from coming out all strangled. "No? What is your kink, then?"

For the first time since I've started petting her, Starla's muscles tense. It's not as though she jerks or does anything so obvious, but there's tension in her body where there wasn't any before. Her throat works, that delicate jaw of hers tightens. I don't think this is a joke to her.

I don't want to prod or pry—that's never worked well for me with her in the past and I doubt very much it would go any better now—but I do want to encourage her, make her feel that it's okay to tell me. I want to know.

So I continue to pet her, go back to her hair because she did—according to my extremely rigorous research—seem to like that best. After a minute of silence during which her eyes stay closed —not, I think, because she's relaxed but because she doesn't want to or can't look at me right now—I speak.

"It's okay, Star. You can tell me. I promise I won't judge you harshly. I want to know because I want to make you happy. At the worst I'll simply say it's not exactly to my taste, and we'll figure out something we both like. That's the absolute worst. I promise you."

She does that thing where she rolls her lips between her teeth and God, she looks scared. Hurts my heart. What have other people said or done to her to make her so afraid? Course it doesn't have to be a personal thing. Society at large can be pretty crap about kink.

After minutes during which my thoughts run away with me in all sorts of directions, she finally blinks her eyes open and her gaze is pleading.

"I promise," I say again. "And you know I don't make promises lightly."

I've only made her a promise once before and it's in that moment that I realize she may feel that I broke that vow and that my promise isn't worth jack shit to her. That possibly, I couldn't have said anything worse.

"I'm not going anywhere, if that's what you're worried about."

"I really want to believe that."

Oof. That is a punch to the gut I might never recover from, and worse, I don't know how to reassure her it's not going to happen again. Not without explaining why I left in the first place, which carries its own risks. For me. Because what if she thinks the very thing I've always been the most afraid of? Though I suppose I don't need to disclose the entire story. Just the bit that has to do with her, which is bad enough. Seems only fair, though, that I should take a risk when she will also.

"Shall we make a bargain, then?"

"A bargain?"

"Yes. Seems as though we've both got some things we're not keen to talk about, so we'll trade."

"The old 'I'll show you mine if you show me yours'?"

"Aye, well, I thought we might be able to play that later."

That got her to crack a smile at least, and I chafe her shoulders. "I can go first if you like."

Her mouth—Christ, her mouth, now that I know what it's like to kiss that mouth, I'm not sure I'll be able to look at her ever again without thinking about that—wrenches to the side.

"No. It's okay. I can go first. You just have to...you have to promise not to make me sorry about it later."

I could make a joke about some outlandish thing to try to make her laugh again, but there's something I've learned from talking to hundreds of patients rather intimately over my career: if you shit on something they can draw parallels to their own experience from, they're never going to trust you. So, though I love to make her laugh, I value her trust far more, and I'm not going to risk something so precious on a throwaway line.

"I promise."

CHAPTER 16

S tarla

JUST AS THERE is a distinction between patting and petting, so too is there a difference between being *ashamed* of being kinky and being *shamed* for being kinky. Hell, there is even kink-shaming in the kink community which is...table-flip-worthy. Sometimes I think about what it would be like if kink were discussed in sex ed like just another thing. Which has its own issues because kink isn't always sexual, but I'll take what I can get.

I would also take not feeling all tied up and twisted on the inside thinking about telling Lowry what I'm into, what I want from him. If only it could be as simple as he's said: if my kinks are not his, we'll keep talking and find something we both like. Anyone who thinks it's that simple is willfully ignorant or their brain simply isn't wired for self-consciousness.

To be fair, it's not usually this brain-melting to tell partners what I want. If they don't like it, they can shove off—it's that simple. This thing with Lowry, though, is anything but simple. It will shred me in ways I can barely imagine if this goes sideways. But the potential for this to go well makes it worth the risk. Doesn't stop my stomach from churning but it will get me to step off the cliff.

His hands are resting at my hips again and I lay my hands on his biceps, trying not to dig my fingertips into his muscles. Holding on for dear life isn't going to help.

"Do…do you know anything about…" Oh god. I need to spit it out, otherwise my heart is going to beat out of my chest and it'll fall on Lowry, and I really like the shirt he's wearing. It's blue and white plaid and the shade where the checks overlap is almost precisely the color of his eyes. Wouldn't want to ruin it. "Daddy kink? DDLG stuff? That's—"

"I know what that is."

His voice is soft, encouraging, and he squeezes my hips lightly. Not dumping me off his lap and running for the hills yet, so there's that.

I shrug. "So, I'm a little. Sometimes. Not all the time, obviously. I like to wear cute things."

I look down at my Hello Kitty sweatshirt, and back up at him. Lowry has the barest smile on his face and it's…it's not a big blown-out reaction, like drunk girls shrieking in a bar bathroom: "Oh my god, you like that too? Besties!" I don't need that. His slightly warmer than neutral affect is encouraging.

"I like to color, especially when I'm feeling overwhelmed. I like spankings. Usually more for fun than discipline, but I've done those too, and if I'm in the right space, I can be into more pain. I like being coaxed into things, and when I'm feeling stubborn, I like to be sort of forced. It's tricky, though. Like I want my top to prove they're smarter or stronger or have more endurance than I do. I need to be convinced that I can rely on them even if it means making me fail. When I'm little, I get very cuddly, need a lot of affection. I want to feel safe, you know?"

He nods and I try to think of the other most salient details to share before my bravery runs out.

"When I'm little, I can get disoriented easily. Almost like my brain knows someone else is looking out for me, so it can take a break from some of its regular functions. But that also means my anxiety kicks up more easily. I like to be called *little girl*, other pet names like that, and I…" Here comes one that could be difficult for Lowry to swallow. It's so typical, and this isn't usually something I hesitate to share because even a lot of people who aren't really into daddy kink can enjoy it. But for him? Eh… "I don't have to, but I like calling my partner *daddy*."

I can feel the way he sucks in a breath, and something in me starts to crumble. I've been holding it together pretty damn well, have also tried to steel myself, prepare for disappointment, but now that he might actually be not cool about this, it's hitting me hard. Like my chest is a gong and he banged my heart with a big-ass mallet. Great. He won't be mean, he won't be, but I'd held out hope that he would want this too. My catastrophizing horse is out of the gate and galloping toward the finish line of *way to fuck this up, you foolish girl*, when he loosens his hold on my hips and sets his hands on my shoulders.

"Starla. Hey, where'd you go? What's going on?"

Trying to breathe and formulate thoughts at the same time seems suddenly overwhelming, and things are kind of greying out. I'd climb off him, stand up, and get away from him if I didn't feel dizzy.

"It's fine if you don't want to. It is. I mean, I have a partner I play with sometimes. Not recently, but that's because…" I definitely don't feel like spilling any more of my guts to Lowry right now, and that includes the painful and awkward matter of me having control of my father's company and not really wanting it, but not knowing how to get rid of it without disappointing him. Yeah, without disappointing my *dead father*, okay? But I haven't dared go to see Jade because if Tad found out, I'm sure he'd find some way to use that against me in his battle to control my father's empire. "But I totally can. I could call her. So, it's fine. Just, you know, say it. That it's not to your taste. Because people's most personal and private kinks are totally like not really enjoying olives. It's fine. I'm totally fine."

Clearly, from the word vomit exploding out of my mouth.

"Who said anything about it not being to my taste?"

Sometimes when I was his patient, we would talk about something someone had said to me. Could have been my father, someone at school, hell, sometimes it was Lowry himself. And he would want me to repeat very carefully what the person had said —*The literal words that came out of her mouth. Tell me what they were.*

Because like some shitty, useless hardwired translator, my brain can take what people say and turn it into something awful. Seriously, someone could ask me to pass them the salt and because of my goddamn depression, I would hear it as, "You worthless piece of shit. How the hell did you not realize I needed the salt? I've been waiting for like twenty minutes because you've got no sense in your head and you're basically a waste of oxygen. Fuck off."

I've gotten better about that, partly through doing ECT so depression doesn't hit me so hard, but also through therapy and having these conversations over and over and over. Turns out I can be taught. Sometimes. So, yeah, a lot of times I can replay the videotape all by myself and realize that no, she asked for the salt and that's it. But sometimes? Especially when I'm stressed? It's like I'm being dragged behind a runaway horse, and it's crapping on my face as I'm tumbling through the dirt at great speed.

The point here, though, is that...

"No one?"

He nods slowly, seriously but encouragingly. "That's right. No one said that. Can you take a guess why not?"

"Because you're trying to figure out a nicer way to say it or maybe planning your escape route? I can tell you the sole means of egress is right there."

Like a flight attendant, I two-finger point with both hands toward the door to the hallway. He squeezes my shoulders and then runs his hands up my neck to cup my face, forcing me to look him in the eyes.

I don't want to. Makes me feel vulnerable in a way I'd really rather not, like offering him all of my fears and insecurities and deepest, darkest desires on a platter for him to do with what he likes. I feel my own frailty—which I fucking hate—down to my bones. But I do it anyway because he's given me so much, allowed me the luxury of trusting someone with my most disturbing thoughts and urges without being judged, so I can at least give him the simple courtesy of listening while looking him in the eye.

"It's actually because what you've said sounds absolutely brilliant. I mean that. Having that kind of relationship with you wouldn't be something I would tolerate, it wouldn't be something I'd gloss over and make you fulfill your needs with other people."

His face is open, brows lifted—though not so far as to be surprised, he's too sincere for that. Staid and impassioned at once, if a man can be such things at the same time. If anyone can, it's Lowry.

"It's... I..." He actually blushes, his pale skin turning ruddy and coloring all the way down to the collar of his shirt. Then he half smiles, shakes his head, not quite shrugs. "I don't have any experience with it in real life, but I'd like very much if you were to be my little girl. I might not be very good at it at first since I haven't done it before, but I'd like to think I could learn to be a very good daddy to you."

I am clearly deceased because the only way this is happening is that I've died and was a good enough person in life that I've been escorted straight to my personal version of heaven.

Lowry blinks and draws in a deep breath. It's possible I should offer up a response but I don't have one yet. So, I let him exhale and stroke his thumbs over my cheeks while he looks at me gravely from under his heavy brows.

"Do you think you could be a bit patient with me?"

I'm finding it difficult to locate words, any words, which is probably why I come up with "how patient?" and he laughs.

LOWRY

"I don't mean that we'll have to put this whole thing on pause while I study up and get some kind of daddy doctorate or anything, if such a thing even exists. I am, in fact, rather impatient to do these things with you, but I'm not going to be perfect. I won't be perfect—ever—but especially not right out the gate. That's all."

How is this real, how is this possible, how is this happening? When she said she enjoyed being manhandled, I thought it might be my lucky day.

But to have her say she wants these things, that she is basically everything I could ever wish for and some things I wouldn't have thought, wouldn't have dreamed, to ask for? And the poor girl panicked because she thought I might not want those things too. I could see that simply talking about being little has had an effect on her. It's as though saying the words had the effect of scraping away some of the enamel of adulthood and leaving her an exposed and painfully sensitive nerve.

And hell, do I understand that. I'm feeling raw myself. It's one thing to have your mind conjure these things and give in to the sweet temptation in the privacy of your own thoughts, your own bed, your own home with no one else there as witness. It's another to say them out loud. *I'd like to think I could learn how to be a very good daddy to you.* It's dizzying in more ways than one.

"Okay," she whispers, unbelieving, her gaze darting about my face, searching for signs. Signs of what I couldn't say—perhaps signs that I can be trusted or that I'm indeed the worst sort of person and am fucking with her head. I wouldn't.

It's fair, though, that uncertainty. I'm not insulted. I feel the same kind of bewildered disbelief because what are the odds? I want to rush ahead, take a cannonball into this lake I never thought I'd even get to dip a toe into, but it also seems important to be cautious, careful. Because that's something a good daddy would do. Makes me warm with pleasure to think of that, the possibility of being that for Starla. Also chokes me a bit, but I'm trying to focus on the positive, the good here.

"Can I ask…is being little, is that a sexual thing for you? Or do you enjoy it purely for the affection and the respite it gives you?"

Dammit, Campbell, why do you always leave it up to her to take the leap? On the whole, especially in my professional life, the ability to open doors and stand around pretending I have no stake in which ones people choose to walk through is a great skill to have. It's served me well with many of my patients, and indeed, with people in general. Most often people don't want advice, they just need someone to talk to until they figure it out on their own.

But with Starla, regarding this in particular, it's unfair to make her volunteer all of these things, especially knowing how difficult it was for her to say them out loud in the first place. It might be nice if I instead showed her the door I wanted to walk through and asked her if she wanted to come with me.

She's had more experience than I have, to be certain, but if I'd like to take on this role, and I think I would like that, very much, then I have to take some responsibility for her. She said herself she gets disoriented, and I can feel it, the way she wavers a bit when she's feeling little whereas I've always thought of her being clear as an undisturbed lake. So I'll put it out there, for her, and hope my words belie the confidence and comfort I don't yet feel.

"Because for me, the idea of being your daddy is a turn-on. More than anything else my pea brain can come up with, anyhow, though I am open to suggestions. Is that…is that how you feel as well?"

She bites her lip and, still looking a bit dubious, nods.

"Did you maybe get turned on just now, talking about it, or were you too nervous?"

Her mouth doesn't exactly purse, it more forms a precursor to a laugh. "Oh, no, I definitely got turned on. Thinking about it. Doing those things with you. Not as much as usual, but, yeah."

Not as much as usual? Thinking about doing daddy kink things with me is *usual*? Christ almighty…

"Look, I know I said I wanted to talk, and I still think that's a good idea, but I'm also just a man and I am dying here. I got to kiss you and hold you, and now you've been sitting on my lap for some time, and if it would not make me a terribly irresponsible individual, I would like to do more of that."

"I would not object to that. But there's something else I'd also like to do."

"What's that, sweetheart?"

Her smile dazzles me. Sweet like that Popsicle she enjoyed in my fantasy the other night.

"I want to fuck."

Jesus, Mary, and Joseph. It's a good thing I wasn't drinking when she said that because I would be spitting it all over what I'm sure is a very expensive rug.

"Ye do?"

She nods, more enthusiastically, still wide-eyed and looking… I don't know. There's something softer about her, something more innocent even though she was anything but just now. I need to get some clarity for myself, though, before I jump in headfirst.

"I know you don't want to take it slow, but…"

"If you don't want to fuck, we can do other things. But I want to. We're both adults, we've both had sex before, and it's not like we just met. And I have condoms."

"Of course you do."

Starla's eyes narrow. "This isn't some slut-shamey kind of thing, is it? Because I've got to tell you, I have no time for that. Less than zero. I like sex, I've had a bunch of it, and I'm not going to be coy about asking for it. I mean, I might be for a role-play, but not like in real life."

"Ah, no, not at all. I was surprised. Delighted, yes, that too. So, if you're sure, I'd be happy to oblige."

"As my daddy?"

If she keeps saying that, I'm going to spend in my pants before we get there. Good thing I'm not a green lad anymore because I probably would have already. "If you like. I'll do my best, though I might be a bit awkward."

"I don't care. Back to the bed, please."

"Is that how it is?"

She nods again and I can picture her doing the same with pigtails dancing on either side of her head. Maybe a little sassy, which doesn't come as a surprise. And I may need to start lifting more at the gym if carrying her about is going to become a habit. I'm in no danger of dropping her, but I'd like to do this more easily, make her feel safer, and—as it's clearly something she enjoys—I'd like to do it more often.

Once I've carried her back to the bed, I lie down beside her, kiss and stroke her, savor everything about her. She's somewhat lacking in patience, though, and grabs at my shirt, untucks it from my pants and unbuttons the thing, wrestles it over my shoulders and then heads straight for my belt. I'll have to return the favor shortly, but for now I can't help but be flattered by how ravenous she is for me. I like to think of myself as confident but not arrogant, but how much she wants me is going straight to my head.

Indeed, she's single-minded in her pursuit of stripping me out of my clothes, and it doesn't take long until I'm naked as the day I was born. And though I'd feared she wouldn't be impressed since

I'm not exactly the fittest specimen on the planet—though I hope not bad for fifty-one—she seems anything but disappointed. Runs her hands along my arm, my chest, along my side, and down to my arse.

I would have never pictured her to be so forward, but I'm glad she is. Makes the scales tip a bit back into balance. Speaking of balance, I'd like to even the score on how many clothes we're sporting. But when I reach for her, she reaches right back and circles my cock with her hand, which ends any coherent thoughts I've ever had.

It's been a while, yes, but that's not the entirety of what's making my head blank like a freshly erased blackboard. I don't want to disappoint her already, so I circle her wrist with my hand.

"Ah, not yet, you greedy little thing. I want to see you."

"Okay."

Her voice isn't exactly a mumble, but it's not anywhere near the assertive Starla I'm used to. Really drives home precisely how delicate she is when in this state and how careful I'll have to be to balance treating her as the capable and brilliant woman I know she is, but also the fragile and intensely vulnerable girl she also is.

I roll her onto her back and elect to start with her stockings, though someday I'd like to have her in those and nothing else because, Christ.

The pink ribbons must be satin, smooth and soft between my fingers as I fondle them.

"I like your stockings very much. So pretty and soft, just like you."

To emphasize my point, I run my hands down to her ankles and then back up over the thin knitted material. Once back up over her knees, I tug at the ribbons to undo them and the ties fall apart in my fingers. Will she be as easily undone?

Loosened, it's easy enough to push her stockings down her legs and peel them off her feet. Her toes are a shimmery pink today whereas the last time I saw them they were a thistle color, but if she's anything like Maeve—both women who are rich and who grew up that way—she likely gets them done regularly.

Her black ruffled shorts are next, and I hook my index fingers into the waistband before kissing her stomach. It makes her giggle and reach for my hair. I like that, her fingers running over my scalp—I'll bet it would be an absolute delight to have her tugging on it while I licked between her thighs. God, I can't wait to taste her. But though sex can mean a lot of different things, I'm pretty sure of what Starla meant when she requested to fuck.

So, before I get too distracted, off they go and then she's in a pair of these darling panties with Hello Kitty printed all over them. They match her goddamn sweatshirt and it's not even fair.

I must make some sort of noise or be gawking because she brings her knees together as if to hide herself, shy away from me. Perhaps I ought to be more careful, but I grip her knees and pull them apart so I can look my fill.

"What are you hiding for, love? I wanted to admire your pretty panties, how well they match your sweatshirt."

"You like them?"

Suspicious again.

"Oh yes, I like them very much indeed. Do you have many of these matching sets?"

She nods, her big eyes holding my gaze, still not sure I'm earnest in my appreciation.

"I'll think about you wearing them every time I see you, then. Wonder precisely what print you've got on that day. Or all they all Hello Kitty but in different colors?"

"No. Hello Kitty, Wonder Woman, Star Wars, She-Ra, lady-bugs, butterflies, unicorns, um…more than that."

It's possible my voice is hoarse when I say, "I'd like to see them all."

"Now?"

"No, silly girl. I have things of greater import to see to at the moment. You said you wanted to fuck, and that's what I intend to do. But I wanted to be clear that I adore your darling little outfits, and I'll enjoy it very much when you wear them in front of me."

"'Kay."

I'll give her time to get used to the idea that though the men who have come before me—no, sorry, she said before she has a partner who's a woman—the *people* who have come before me might have been tolerant of her inclinations, but I will be downright enthusiastic. I don't know as I'd go so far as to say I *need* it, but it's so enticing I'm near drunk on it.

"Can you sit up a bit for me?"

She does and I take her sweatshirt off, revealing, Jesus... I thought I'd be seeing a bra or one of those camisoles or anything but the expanse of her skin that I've revealed. Her torso, her breasts. It makes sense given that her shirt was falling off one shoulder and I didn't see any straps. She's lovely. Maeve had been more angular, the sharper thinness she felt pressed into. Starla, on the other hand, is all lush curves and full breasts. They look like they'll be weighty as they spill out of my palms; round and tipped with dusky pink nipples that have gathered into hard points.

I could spend all day marveling over her tits, and I will someday, but not today. Today, I'll strip off the rest of her clothes so I can see all of her. Every last inch that I held myself away from for years upon years. There's some irony, of course, in having seen into the depths of her psyche without having seen her body, and now learning I may have had no idea about what lay beneath. Perhaps these sensual, curious, needy parts of her didn't exist then, but perhaps they did and I was simply locked out, which is only appropriate. If I wanted her as badly as I did and I didn't know those things, I can't imagine how I would have managed if I *did*.

I'd like to think I wouldn't have done anything because she wouldn't have been a real adult. It would have been wrong, it would have been... A cold frisson runs down my spine like the breath of a ghost and I don't want to think about it. So I press it back, push against it until it's given up and retreated into the ether...for now.

Which allows me to pull Starla's underwear over her hips and down her legs to be tossed onto the floor. I'd like to say I take my time, savor this as I've savored the rest of her, but I've used up all of my patience, all of my better instincts. No, instead of marveling at her and telling her how lovely she is and how much I've ached to see every inch of her skin, I simply prowl over her until I've notched my hips between her soft and willing thighs.

CHAPTER 17

 tarla

"How do you like it, Starla? Fast and hard and rough? Or sweet and sensual and slow? I'm happy with whatever you'll let me have."

He rubs his thick, hard length along the seam of my sex and I almost die. It feels good but like such a tease. I don't want a glancing tease of his erection. I want it—him—inside me. And for this time...

"Mostly I'm more of a thorough pounding kind of girl, but I..."

I look up into Lowry's eyes, suddenly so very self-conscious. I have dreamt about this moment a million times. Have fantasized about this very man taking my virginity over and over again. How he would be gentle and patient and kind and loving. That ship sailed long ago and I'm not a big fan of romanticizing the "loss" of one's virginity. Honestly, it's ridiculous. But in some ways, I'm back there again. With my serious crush and feeling like Lowry Campbell is the most perfect man to ever walk the earth. Or to ever grace the gap between my thighs. And I...

Would it really be so bad? To have this thing I wanted so very, very badly I would sometimes cry with all those unruly feelings adolescence can bring? If it were a different role-play, I'd be less shy, but since it's blending fantasy and reality in some fairly uncomfortable ways, for Lowry especially, I don't want to ask for it and ruin everything.

But on the other hand, wouldn't that be magnificent? If all of us could have the option of a do-over? And instead of the three junior prom night thrusts I had with Mike Baxter in the state-room of his family's yacht, I could've had an attentive, experienced lover who would've made me feel so, so good. Would've been concerned about me and not his parents' sheets when I bled.

The pass of a thumb over my cheek drags me back to the present where Lowry is hovering over me, the crease between his brows more prominent than when his face is in repose.

"Are you okay, love? Did you change your mind? We don't—"

"Oh, no, not at all. I did not change my mind. I want this, I want you, so badly, but I... Can I ask you for something? You can say no and it'll be fine, and I promise not to make it weird except I'm kind of making it weird right now, aren't I?"

The corner of his mouth turns up, and he cups my cheek before leaning in to kiss me softly, sweetly, and rub the tip of his nose alongside mine. "You can ask me for anything you'd like. On my honor, I'll do my best not to 'make it weird.'"

Why is it that Lowry's American accent is so very, very strange? But it is and it makes me laugh.

I run my hand down his ribcage, careful not to tickle, and focus on how good it feels to be here like this with him. Nothing has ever felt so right in my life.

"Would you... Could we..."

"Making it weird."

Snort-giggles are so sexy. As is smacking his shoulder. But

how can I help it with his ridiculous American accent? "You know, I don't think you'd be half as sexy if you were American."

"Aye, ye're probably right, lass."

More giggles, because now he's laying on the brogue very thick.

"Lucky for me, these cheeky American lasses seem to like my wee accent."

"You're ridiculous."

"And you're brilliant. You have the nicest laugh, did you know that? I used to…"

Ah, his turn to trail off. He turns his head, his expression somewhere between rueful and bashful.

"You used to what?"

He blinks back to me, eyes clear, gaze steady.

"I always tried to make you laugh because I loved the sound of it. But that wasn't my job, so I'd only let myself do it once. One single time when I saw you, and then I'd stop trying. Because it wasn't right, how much I liked it."

Meticulous, conscientious man with a ball of guilt the size of a boulder on his back. So I smile and tip my chin up, telling him I'd like to be kissed again, yes, I would. And he doesn't deny me because he almost never does.

"Would it be awful for you to pretend I'm a virgin? Not that I'm seventeen or that I'm still your patient or anything like that, but…that. That's what I want our first time to be like. Is that weird and gross? I don't have a virginity fetish, so I don't think this would be a regular thing, but for our first time…"

I shrug, which is awkward given that I'm lying on my back. "I thought it might be nice to pretend it's my first time, is all. Since…I mean, I totally wished it had been you. Not that I haven't had some good sex in the meantime, but…I don't know. I'm making a mess of this and you're probably like, 'What are ye on aboot, ye wee dafty?'"

Now it's his turn to snort-giggle, and that's fair because his

American accent is far superior to my Scottish one. When he's recovered some, he kisses my temple, which also means his chest meets mine and the hot hard length of him slides again against my labia. It makes me whimper, whine, because I want him.

"Will you think I'm a monster if that sounds like a very sexy idea to me? You said you want it, and I'm more than happy to oblige, but I'd rather not if you're going to think me a pervy old wanker afterward."

"I feel like I'd think that if you went around deflowering virgins or fucking ex-patients all the time. But it's different, you know?"

"I know. And that's what this is. Pretend. Hell, everyone likes to pretend sometimes. And if we're both on the same page, then it's okay. We're not hurting anyone, we're not coercing anyone. I feel like there's been pretty explicit consent here."

The words are coming out of his mouth, and I think he's trying to encourage me, but it feels a bit as if he's trying to convince himself that it's true too. I can't exactly blame him for that. It took me a while to tell someone what I wanted, and longer to be at peace with the idea that there's nothing pathological here, nothing that needs to be psychoanalyzed. We like what we like, and at the end of the day, if it's all consenting adults and no one is being harmed, then what the fuck is the problem?

"Mmm, yes."

"So we'll try it, aye? See how it goes. And if it gets…what's that word you like? Squidgy?"

"Squicky. Like, squicked out."

"That. If either one of us gets squicked out, then we'll stop. Go make some popcorn or something."

"Yeah, popcorn."

"But for now?"

"For now…"

I close my eyes and try to get that feeling back, that nervous excitement that used to surround sex. Not the jaded, wary boredom I mostly feel toward it now. It's not hard with Lowry's hips pressing my thighs wide—I summon the shyness I would've felt at being naked with a man for the first time, a touch of fear because it's supposed to hurt, and that soul-deep vulnerability that comes with being a sexual woman.

So many expectations, so much pressure. Don't be easy, but don't be a tease. Nice girls don't want to get fucked, but when you get it on, you better be a sex kitten. Maybe that's part of why I'd like to be coaxed, cajoled. He already has my permission; he already knows I want it. What's so terrible about putting on a facade of bashful reluctance?

I've got doe eyes, I know I do. It's one of the things I like about my appearance. So I open them wide and bat my lashes while sinking my teeth into my bottom lip.

"I...I'm nervous."

The click into his role is visible. And sexy as all hell.

"That's okay. You're allowed to be nervous, so long as you know I'd never hurt you. There's a big difference between nervous and scared, isn't there, sweetheart?"

Oh.

He scoops a hand behind my neck and bends down to kiss at the juncture of my ear and jaw.

"Yes."

"And are you one and not the other?"

His murmur is soft, as are the kisses he's planting down my neck, and he's reduced me to a quivering puddle of Starla jelly. I would give anything to this man.

"Nervous. Not scared. I'm never scared of you."

"That's good, sweetheart. I'd never want my—" There's the briefest pause and my stomach clutches. "I'd never want my little girl to be scared of me. I'm going to take good care of you, make you feel good. Do you trust me?"

Oh my. *Sweetheart. Little girl.* He's going to take care of me. I've never felt like such a mushy ball of pleasure and arousal in my whole life. It's confusing, this; I want him to fuck me hard, but also take me in his lap and tell me I'm pretty. We're making up the rules, though. Who says I can't have both of those things? Doesn't sound like it's going to be Lowry—he's moved down to my collarbone, kissing and nipping at me, outright licking when he gets to my suprasternal notch.

"Yes, I trust you."

"Hmm? Who do you trust? Tell me, sweetheart."

I'm so wet between my legs, I want to squirm until he's seated deep inside me, but my role is that of the shy ingenue and so far it's as good as I hoped it would be. Maybe I lied when I said we wouldn't do this often. It's really fucking hot, stoking a fire in my belly and making my nipples ache. It's all I can do to not buck my hips into his, grind myself against him.

"I trust you, Daddy."

He groans and sinks his teeth into my trap, forcing a squeak from my throat. Also, if I thought I was a quivering puddle before, it had nothing on now. There's something about saying those words. Out loud. To him. It sets me on fire, burning my own candle until I'm slippery, malleable hot wax. He releases my flesh, and licks where his teeth had sunk into me, loving away the sting. But fuck me, he could do anything other than take a bite out of me and I'd enjoy it. I hope, in fact, that he's left a mark. An outline of his teeth marking me or a half-moon of bruises that I can pull down my shirt and admire in the days to come.

"That's a good girl."

The man is trying to kill me for sure. He said he'd be an amateur, but he's proving himself willing and eager, and best of all, a quick study. I do want to be his good girl, more than anything.

He nuzzles at my shoulder, his beard tickling the sensitive skin, and I'm trying to breathe. Which is harder than it sounds. Lucky for my prospects of not passing out, he pauses and looks up at me.

"I want to touch your beautiful tits. Kiss them, maybe suck on them. Is that okay?"

Jesus. Is that *okay*? There is a very short list of things I would like better than that, and I suspect many of those are on his list of Things to Do to Drive Starla Mad.

"Yes."

"Yes, what?"

I don't know whether to hate him for this, or love him, but I think it's the latter. It's just difficult. Will it get easier or will there always be this delicious sense of taboo that has me squirming? I'm not totally sure what to hope for.

"Yes, Daddy."

"What a good girl you are, and how I'm going to enjoy eating you all up."

He puts his weight onto one elbow and leans to the side, cupping my breast in his hand and giving it a squeeze that takes my breath away. I wasn't expecting it to be so hard, but I'm not sorry at all. And then he's dipping his head and taking my nipple in his mouth, tonguing the stiff peak and then, holy Mary mother of god, suckling. Drawing on me as though he might actually get something out of me if he tries hard enough. It feels fucking phenomenal and sends a burst of want straight to my pussy. And I nearly orgasm when he closes his teeth around the taut little bud.

"Ah!"

He lets up the slightest bit and strokes my ribcage. He's waiting, I think for me to object if I want to, but I don't want to. I actually wish he had two heads or at least two mouths so he could do the same thing to the other breast simultaneously. But maybe it's best he's only got the one since my brain is practically melting out my ears as things are.

He squeezes my neck softly, rubbing his thumb below my ear, and it makes me purr. Also makes me feel pliable and supple, more so when his hand that's been cupping my breast circles my wrist and pins it to the bed.

I'm being held and cradled, but also controlled and turned on. It's about as perfect as I could ask for. He bites me once more and I gasp. As much as I'd like it, he doesn't switch immediately to the other breast, but studies my expression. Can he see how turned on I am? What he's done to me? Or do I merely feel as though "Daddy's Horny Little Slut" is written across my forehead?

"Do you like this, little girl? Does it feel good?"

"Yes."

He raises his brows expectantly, and I choke on a half laugh, half cry.

"Yes, Daddy. That feels good."

"What feels good?"

"When you suck on my tits and bite my nipples."

Oh god, my face is going to burn off. And then I won't have a face. That would be really unfortunate. Because I kinda like my face. Lowry also seems to like my face. He's smiling into it now, like I'm the best, prettiest, and most important thing he's ever seen. It's kind of embarrassing, but also an incredible feeling. Like maybe that could actually be true?

"You're the sweetest thing I've ever seen."

He kisses me then, pressing his lips to mine, first softly and then not as softly, but still gentle, seeking permission to lick into my mouth, and I open for him because what else could I possibly do? I want to give myself over to him. I want to be as good as he thinks I am, as special, as remarkable, as precious.

I take his kiss, receive it like an offering, and sacrifice myself to it. He can set me on fire, burn me all up, but I don't think he will. I'm not a candle, I'm a phoenix.

His fingers tighten on my wrist and I groan into his mouth, feeling almost delirious with it. Feeling out of sorts and like this is a fever dream, like it can't possibly be real because it's too perfect.

When he finally sees fit to draw away from me, he looks a bit dazed himself.

"Have you ever played with yourself, Star? Rubbed your clit, pushed a finger or two inside yourself? Made yourself come?"

"Yes, Daddy."

"That's good. A girl should know her own body, what makes her feel good. Would you like it if I touched you like that too?"

My response this time is more of a whine than a sentence, but he lets me get away with it, perhaps sensing that there's not much left in my head besides wanting and feeling.

"Then spread your legs, pretty girl. Let your daddy make you feel good."

I've never thought of myself as shy in bed. Hell, a guy I dated broke up with me because he said I was too "aggressive" sexually. I think what he actually meant was he didn't have a clue how to get a woman off and wasn't open to suggestions, but whatever.

My point is I'm not a nervous, wide-eyed, inexperienced, or prudish woman. But playing this way feels so good, and even better when Lowry slips a hand over my knee, because I haven't moved fast enough for his liking, and pulls, drawing my leg out and exposing my very core.

"There now, that's not so bad, is it?"

I roll my lips between my teeth and shake my head, even though I've never felt so naked in my life, like I'm naked in front of a room full of people.

He slips his hand down the inside of my thigh and something inside me pulls tight. My interior muscles are almost fluttering with need, craving something to hold onto, something to clamp down on. I feel empty and I want to be full. Which is what I say to Lowry, who is taking his sweet time tracing blue veins toward the apex of my thighs.

"Daddy, please. I need you. Please touch me, I want you to—"

In a single smooth movement, Lowry parts my labia and runs a finger over my clit before delving farther back and gathering moisture from where it's pooled at my entrance, only to slick his fingers back up to my clit and start making leisurely circles, barely touching that wildly sensitive bundle of nerves. Oh, I'm dead, dead, dead, dead. I am going to die here in my apartment from sexual frustration and that will be difficult for him to explain, indeed.

"Like that, love?"

"Oh, no. Daddy, please."

"Tell me how. I'll think about you tucked in your bed at night and spreading your legs while you think about me, touching yourself. Tell me how you'd do it, Star."

"Smaller circles, tighter. Don't even lift your finger. Just rub it around, make my... Oh yes. Like that."

Wanton, that's how I feel as he touches me the way I told him I do when I think of him at night. I won't tell him I've done this for years. Like, a person old enough to vote's worth of years. Maybe he knows anyway?

As I'm panting and heaving and trying to hold off, he leans down to whisper in my ear, and I think he's going to tell me to go on, come for him, and I likely could. Instead, he says, "I want to fuck your sweet little pussy with my finger. Maybe two or three. Would you like that, sweetheart? My fingers pumping in and out of your cunt until you come all over my hand?"

What a dirty talker. I had no idea he was capable of such things. Which is probably a good thing because I would've left a wet spot every time I saw him in his office if I'd known.

"Yes, Daddy. Fuck me, please. I want your fingers in me."

He doesn't hesitate, doesn't wait for any more begging, but slides his fingers back until he can press one into my entrance. Almost immediately, I know it's not enough. Better than nothing, yes, because god, I love penetration, but there's not nearly enough. I get the urge to dispense with this game altogether so we could go straight to the fucking part, but I won't do that. Especially since he's curled his finger just right and is rubbing the tip against my inner wall, searching for my G-spot, and heaven above, finding it.

"Oh."

One corner of his mouth kicks up and he looks very pleased with himself.

"Do you want more, sweetheart? We've got all night and I'm in no rush. I want to make sure you're good and ready for me. I'm going to use my fingers to stretch out your pretty pink pussy before you take my cock. And you're going come for me before I fuck you because I want you all slick and ready. So, tell me, can you take another finger? Is there room for it in your sweet, hot cunt?"

"Yes, Daddy, please. More, I want more."

"What a greedy little thing. Don't worry, Daddy's going to take care of you. I'm going to make you feel so full."

"Yes, please. Fill me up, please."

He drops a kiss on the tip of my nose, which ought to be at odds with the filthy way he's plunging a finger in and out of me, but it feels right, the mingling of sweet and filthy, of tender and dirty. And then there's a second finger sliding into me alongside the first and it feels so good, so very very good. He's still stroking my G-spot but moving a little faster, more aggressively now, and I want to beg him to get this over with and fuck me.

Lowry fucks me for a few minutes like this, my hips bucking up to meet each thrust of his fingers, and if I angle my pelvis just right, I can rub my clit on the heel of his hand. I'm close, so close. My orgasm is gathering like a storm in my belly and my body tenses all over. At which point he slips a third finger inside me and pumps into me, harder now.

"That's right, little girl. Take it all. I love finger-fucking you, your sweet honey getting all over my fingers. After you get off, I'm going to push these fingers into your mouth so you can see what you taste like. Come on. Rock your hips, take me all the way inside like the greedy little thing you are. Get your pussy ready to take my cock."

Apparently that's what it takes to get me off: some enthusiastic finger-banging and a bunch of wicked daddy kink dirty talk.

I clench around his fingers and he keeps thrusting through the rhythmic pulses of my climax until they slow and then he does as well. Plus, he's holding me like I need to be eased through this incredible orgasm. Like it's too much for me to take. I'd be okay if he weren't sheltering me in this way, but I like that he is, and I take the opportunity to burrow into his shoulder and let my fingers scramble for purchase they won't find because there's no place for them to dig in without hurting him and I don't want to hurt him. What I do want is to taste him, have his faintly sweat-salty tang on my tongue, so I lick and suck at his skin. It's nice, settling after I have been so thoroughly unsettled.

My heart is still beating hard and fast and Lowry's fingers are still buried inside me. I like them there, but I'm also curious. He said he was going to put his fingers in my mouth and I've never done that before. I have an idea of what my arousal smells like, but not tastes. Will it be as consistent as onions which smell and taste so much the same it's almost difficult to determine how you're experiencing it? Or will it be like vanilla with one sort of scent and a dissonant taste that rattles your brain?

I think I'm about to find out, because Lowry is finally easing his fingers out of me, after I've milked every last pulse out of coming.

He nudges the top of my head with his nose. "You're so gorgeous when you come, Star. I loved watching you and knowing I'd had a part in it. And you're so wet for me now. I'll give you a minute, but now that I've had my fingers stuffed inside you, I can't wait to slip my cock into your perfect little pussy. Before I do, though, I told you you're going to taste yourself. Don't hide your face, little girl. Let me see you, and open wide."

I do as I'm told and it's so viscerally carnal and filthy. Not that

Lowry treats me this way and not that I'd want him to, but the occasional insinuation that I'm only good for my holes and that he's going to use every one of them as he sees fit... Well, it might feel threatening and demeaning in a not-fun way in real life, but in this situation, with him, in my head, it keeps my arousal at a simmer.

Yes, I'm Daddy's good little girl, and I'm going to do as I'm told—and he's told me to open my mouth wide. It's nearly as dirty, and in some ways more so, than being told to spread my legs.

And then his fingers are in my mouth, and I automatically lick them and then suck. That's a knee-jerk reaction to something pushed into your mouth, right? I find that I actually prefer the taste of my slick fluid to the smell. It tastes less musky, less earthy than the scent and a touch sweeter than I expected.

I'm so absorbed in trying to discern the small details of my flavor that it takes me a second to realize Lowry is staring at me. More specifically my mouth, and to be precise the way I'm laving the fingers that were inside me moments ago.

"Did you know you're the sexiest thing I've ever seen? You take my breath away."

I try to smile at his compliment but my blush will have to do the talking because he's still got his fingers pushed inside my mouth, and is now fucking my mouth with them, slow and filthy, an echo of what he'd been doing to my sex mere moments ago.

I'd been a little skeptical that he would be able to make me come again when he fucks me, but I can feel it gathering again— that slow burn of a line of gun powder straight to my core, and Lowry is the match that will set me alight.

Lowry pulls his fingers from my mouth and I chase them. It was nice to have something in my mouth and I didn't mind that they were covered in my essence. But he replaces them with his mouth, so I'm not too distraught.

He fucks my mouth with his tongue, an echo of how he was

using his fingers, and it makes me feel empty. Not in a depressed, desolate kind of way, but in a "fill me up, Daddy," kind of way. I want that motion, that plundering, between my legs again. And I wouldn't be sorry if he could keep kissing me like this when he settles his hips between my thighs and presses his cock where his fingers used to be.

Fill me up, Daddy.

CHAPTER 18

owry

THERE ARE APPROXIMATELY ten hours until I need to be back at work tomorrow morning, and frankly, that is not enough time. I need more. It seems cruel that I'm only now getting to have my wicked way with Starla, and I'll have to stop before I really get to know her body. I'd like to call in sick tomorrow and keep her in bed through the weekend, but Lacey's been looking at me as though she knows what's going on, so I won't be taking any chances.

I hadn't been prepared for Starla despite my fantasies. All the dirty talking I've done to Starla in my dreams is certainly coming in handy and I've been trying not to hesitate before I say the words aloud though they make my skin burn hot. Yes, I'd sometimes say dirty things to Maeve, but not like this. No, never like this. Aside from the filthy things falling out of my mouth like I've rehearsed them, I hadn't been prepared for her body, all her sweet flesh that's now mine to feast upon. For planes of smooth skin, for how soft she is, for the stark delicacy of the scars across her pale skin which I haven't remarked upon. Won't. But that doesn't mean I didn't look. I have, many times.

I'll treat her as fragile not because she is, but because life has already tried to shatter her on the floor one too many times, and wouldn't it be nice if someone cradled her for once? Plus, I fucking love having my hands on her, in her. I could touch her all day and not be satisfied. And hearing the way she calls me *daddy* is like shooting up with heroin. Or so I've heard, wouldn't know for sure; that shit scares me to death. So I'll indulge in another vice: Starla Patrick.

So sweet she ought to be able to give me a toothache by looking at her, this Starla before me is so different from the snarky, snappy, aggressive woman I encountered on the plane a handful of months ago. She's pliant and shy, *vulnerable*, and while I wouldn't trade the other Starla for anything, I like her very much like this as well.

She's let down her walls for me, literally let me inside her body, and it's enough to make a man get a swelled head. She trusts me enough to see her like this, to share her fantasies, and my God, what a fantasy it is. There's a sharp edge to it given our history, but that's part of what makes this fun—the risk, the taboo, the wrongness. It's like gliding a razor along your skin— one false step and it's not fun anymore. But this is a heart-pounding thrill and probably the most turned on I've ever been.

Kissing Starla and tasting her wetness in her mouth makes it so tempting to go down on her, drink directly from the source, have my face covered in her arousal, but I think not this time. Some other time when I have the patience to toy with her more and my cock isn't going to burst.

I run my hands over her body while we kiss, kneading a breast, pinching a nipple, grabbing her buttocks, and making a fist in her hair that has her whimpering into my mouth and pressing—no, more like rocking, undulating against me. I'd thought she'd need more time given how spent she'd seemed when she came, but I'm delighted to be wrong.

Unfortunately I have to stop kissing her, but fortunately, she pouts when I do and makes a tiny mewl when she realizes she can't chase after me because I'm pinning her to the bed with the hand I have in her hair.

"How are you feeling, little girl?"

Calling her that makes my cock throb. I thought it would be harder, but it's not. It's easy. Calling her *little girl* and saying filthy things to her comes so naturally to me it's almost terrifying. All of it awakens a primitive part of me I wish it didn't because I like to think of myself as a progressive feminist. Can I still if I want to infantilize the woman I love? What if she enjoys it? What if she wants it? And can I keep myself from adopting that attitude elsewhere? I think so, but I want to care for her all the time. And because I like the shy, blushing smile that steals over her face when I call her my little girl. God, she's precious.

"Good, Daddy."

"Not too sore, I hope? After Daddy stuffed three fingers in that pretty little pussy of yours?"

She makes a tiny peep and flushes a darker shade of pink as she shakes her head.

"Do you need a little while or are you ready for more?"

"More?"

Her eyes and mouth widen into perfect circles, and the doe eyes and the lash-batting almost do me in.

"Yes, more."

"I don't know if it will fit. It's too big."

She looks up at me, biting her lip and looking genuinely nervous. She's very good at this, the role-playing. Makes me want to tease her, fire up the blush and stoke the heat in her cheeks. Is it turning her on even as it's embarrassing her? I can play this game too, want to play with her.

"What's too big?"

Her hips and shoulders shift, a sweet squirm that makes me want to groan and sink my teeth into her flesh again, suck at her skin until I leave marks on her.

"Your…your…"

"Go on. My what?"

"Your cock, Daddy."

Fuck me. Her choked near whisper and the way there's white all round her irises make me want to dispense with this and rut into her.

"You're worried it's too big, eh?"

I lean up and wrap my hand around the aforementioned cock, letting the head stick out from my fist as I stroke myself a few times. Too hard of a grip to make me come, but her gaze is pinned to the tip as though she's expecting me to spurt come all over her at any second. Someday I will.

Someday, I'll cover her tits and her torso in sticky white semen and then rub it into her skin, marking her. Not today. Today I want to bury myself in her to the hilt and imagine filling her cunt so full of come it spills out of her. I'm a medical professional, I ought to know better, and yet there's something about the image that makes me burn for her, has me going up in flames and not wanting them to be put out. *Set me aflame, Star, until I'm mere ashes. I'd be grateful and proud to be the conflagration you warmed your body upon.*

She sinks her teeth further into her plump, pink lip and nods.

"I'd never hurt you, Star. Not really. I might spank your bottom if you're naughty and make you whimper and cry, but I'd never give you something you can't handle. You believe that, right? That I know what's best for you?"

"Ooh."

I give my dick a few more pumps while I look in her eyes, and she looks dazed, perhaps a bit stoned. Her dark eyes are glossed over and wide, pupils blown with desire, and whether she means to or not, she's squirming underneath me, pressing her hips up as though she wants what I'm offering her; is, in fact, begging for it.

"Tell me, little girl. Say it out loud. I want to hear you. I...I need to hear you."

Yes, I am absolutely getting off on the illusion of being in charge of her, holding her in the palms of my hands, being in control of what she gets and how much she can take, but I need my own assurances.

She's perhaps a little too convincing at this wide-eyed innocent routine. Perhaps when I've gotten more used to this, used to her being this sweet, vulnerable thing I hold like a ripe peach, waiting to sink my teeth into, I won't need her to anymore and maybe she'll prefer that, but today I need to check.

"I know you'd never hurt me. Daddy knows best."

Fireworks. In my brain. Colored explosions go off against a background that's gone black, and if I'm not careful, everything will end in a smoky haze. She deserves better than that from me, so I'll take a breath and provide it for her. Fulfill her fantasies that she's been brave enough to ask for, and perhaps someday be worthy of everything she's ever trusted me with.

"You'll be good for me, then. Take everything I give you."

"Yes, Daddy, yes."

"You seem like you want this, actually. Like your sweet little pussy is dripping wet for me and you want me to fuck you with my big, fat cock. Look at you, your hips bucking, your eyes bright, your pert little nipples rock hard, begging to be sucked."

Her eyes close and she moans, almost as if she's in pain from waiting. I know how she feels. I'm going to die if I have to wait any longer.

"Ye don't have to wait anymore. I'll go slow at first, work my thick hard cock inside that tight cunt of yours, and when you're ready, I'm going to fuck you, Star. Drive into you until you cry out my name. Until your legs are splayed wide open and you're getting hammered. I'm going to absolutely pound you until you're wrecked. That's what I'm going to do and you're going to love it, aren't you, my horny little girl?"

"Yes, Daddy, please. Please. Give it to me, please, I want it."

Yes. With that resounding and enthusiastic consent, that I can do.

"Condoms, love?"

"Oh, fuck, right."

She wrenches open a drawer and tosses a strip at me. I tear one off and rip it open so I can get suited up as quickly as possible because I can't stand not being inside her for another second.

And then I'm in between her thighs, her pussy swollen, pink, and glistening in front of me like the Promised Land. Leaning forward and settling myself, I notch the head of my cock into her so all I have to do is push to be inside.

I can't believe it. If anyone would've told me sixteen years ago I'd be doing this, I would've punched them in the face, kneed them in the groin, and wrung their goddamn neck. And yet here we are and there's no place I'd rather be, nothing I've ever wanted more.

Leaning over her, I slip a hand behind her neck, cradle her head, and study her face. I want to remember this forever. The light in her eyes, the way her lips are parted, how she feels as she breathes beneath me. Though I can't imagine I could ever forget —this moment is going to be seared into my brain.

"Relax for me, sweetheart. Let me inside."

She closes her eyes, lets out a breath, and sets her hands on my biceps, her lashes fluttering as she finally gazes up at me. "Please."

That's the final invitation I need to press forward, by an inch, to get a taste of what it will feel like to be surrounded by her slick, wet heat, and in doing so, I make her gasp.

"Shh, shh. You're all right, Star. Aren't you? Feels good to have the head of my cock stretching your pussy, doesn't it?" My coaxing is met by a tiny nod. "Good girl. I'm going to put more of it inside you. Real slow until you're stuffed full. You're going to take all of Daddy's big fat cock like a good little girl."

Christ. Jesus fucking Christ this is filthy as hell, but also achingly sweet, and the combination is going to do me in.

She clings to me as I press farther into her tight passage and I take my sweet time. Draw out a bit to ease my way with her moisture when I rock forward again, the whole time telling her she's such a good girl and that she feels incredible. That I love her is on the tip of my tongue, but I can't say that to her. Not now. When I say it, I want it to be under circumstances where she'll never doubt it's true, that I mean it down to the marrow of my bones—and not just with my boner. So I tell her in other ways, nuzzling her throat, kissing the junction of her jaw and her ear, murmuring sweet things, and passing the pad of my thumb across her cheek.

"Gorgeous girl, you feel like home to me. I love being inside of you."

STARLA

Home. That's how I feel with Lowry surrounding me, penetrating me, his weight pushing me into the mattress, the thick length of his erection filling me up. Full. That's how I feel. Not just physically either. For all that I've craved love, belonging, and understanding my whole life, and lusted after Lowry thinking he might be the one to give it to me, perhaps teenage Starla wasn't so foolish.

He was 100 percent right not to have taken advantage of that and I doubt we'd be here now if he had. But we are, and having him above me, between my spread thighs, pressing into my very core with this intoxicating mix of bossy dominance, poking gently at the parts of me this has laid so very bare, and also being the sweetest, most attentive lover I've ever had is... Well, it's everything I ever dreamed it would be. Right down to feeling as though he could split me in two if he weren't so very cautious and conscientious.

"Daddy..."

God, my voice is breathy and small, almost a soft squeak.

"Yeah, sweetheart?"

"I...I'm full, Daddy. I can't take any more."

He pauses, levers up on his elbow and searches my face. I could say stop and he would. I could claw my way out of little Starla and be grown-goddamn-woman Starla for long enough to tell him it was too much for real. If it were. It's not. But I want more of that cajoling, more of that easing, more of that dirty talk that came so easily to him.

I want him to...*make* me isn't right. I'm not bratty. But the sweet coaxing and the assurances that Daddy knows best is enough to render me molten lava. Enough, perhaps, to make me come if he made that promise before driving his cock home with a brutal thrust.

It's probably a good idea to have a safeword before we do this again. Will we get to do this scenario in particular again? I know I said it was a one-time thing, but god, it's fun to play a virgin who needs to be taught the ways of sex. Hopefully Lowry will think so too.

If only I could beam my thoughts into his brain. It sometimes seemed like I could—or that, in fact, he could draw them out—when he was my doctor. And as convenient as that might be in some situations, I'm glad it's not actually true. But that means I have to find another way to let him know I'm fine, that he doesn't need to stop—*please don't stop* —that I need more, *want* more of that delicious taboo persuasion. So I work the small muscles surrounding my mouth, forcing up the corner of my lips into the smallest quirk, willing him to understand so we don't have to break the spell further.

Relief breaks over his rough features like a wave dashed against rocky cliffs—abrupt and startling. And then it's gone, replaced by sternness.

"What did I say, Star?"

"That I'm to take everything you give me."

"And what else?"

He tightens his grip on the back of my neck and it renders me into a quivering dollop of girl, as though he's pressed a button that makes me limp and pliable, so very very soft and willing to hand myself over to him. To believe in him wholeheartedly.

"That Daddy knows best."

"I do. I know you, little girl. I know what you're capable of, I know what you can take. You are one tough cookie, and even if it makes you nervous, I think you want to take the last couple of inches of my cock. You want to feel so full you might burst, like you might get torn in half. I'm not going to be rough with you until you take it all, until you're stuffed full, and then I'm going to fuck you so hard your tits bounce. And you're going to love every stroke, every thrust. You're going to make helpless little noises while I ram my cock into your tight cunt over and over and over until you come on my throbbing dick."

I whimper because I can.

"Say it, Star. Say it while I'm fucking into you. Say it until you can't anymore because you're coming all over my cock and saying my name."

He grabs my wrist that's not pinned to my side and drags it over my head, holding it down against the mattress, and that resistance I'd put up, the one I ached for him to crumble, falls to pieces in the face of him handing me exactly what I need.

"Daddy knows best."

"That's it. Come on, again."

"Daddy knows best."

He pulls out slightly, only to press back in, farther than he'd been before, and I let out an "ooh."

"That's right, little girl. You can take it. Make all the noise you want, but you're going to take every inch of Daddy's cock."

He draws out again, then takes one of my nipples in his mouth and sucks hard. Tightens his grip on my neck and my wrist until it almost hurts and then bites my nipple hard enough to make me cry out and buck against him. And then he presses in harder and the friction is incredible. Add in his dirty words and the feeling of being pried open and so very vulnerable, and it's almost blinding.

"Daddy knows best."

And there it is. The entire fat length of him is seated inside me and I'm pinned like a butterfly to a specimen board, all spread out and vulnerable. Lowry stops suckling me to lift his head and meet my gaze, the intensity of his expression pinning me even more.

"There you go. I knew you could do it, knew you could fit Daddy's cock into that tight little pussy of yours. And now I'm going to fuck you until I spill my come inside you."

Oh, fuck. I've never been particularly turned on by a man shooting his load inside me in erotica or in person. But coming from Lowry today, in this moment? It's now the only thing I can think of, everything else has been crowded out of my brain, and the only thing I can think to beg for is, "Fill me up, Daddy. Please, fill me. Put your come in me, please."

A groan that sounds as though it's been ripped from his lungs escapes his lips and he dips his head, resting his forehead against mine.

"Perfect, Star, You're perfect."

And before I can tell him that he's perfect right back, he lifts his head and drives into me so hard I make a sound. Ngh, maybe? Unh? Whatever it is, it's not pretty and it's not calculated, and I want him to make me do it again. Fuck me so hard I can't *not* make a sound. And that's what he does.

Starts driving into me over and over and over, the rhythm and the force brutal and so, so satisfying. Makes me feel helpless and used, but also respected? He believes I can take this because I'm strong. Not only that, but even though he's rutting into me with abandon, I know he wouldn't leave me.

Though I accused him of it and it still smarts if I think about when I felt he had abandoned me, Lowry would never do that. He's attuned to me; my sounds, the movements of my body, my very breath. Despite seeming as though he's lost in his own desires, his own pleasures, I have no doubt that I am first in his mind. Which is made all the clearer when he grits out, "Come on, little girl. Come for Daddy. I know you're close. Come for me now while I've got my cock buried in you. I want to feel your cunt tighten around me, and then I'll give you what you want."

Oh. Yes. He's deep inside me, grazing my G-spot with every thrust, and as he's promised, he's fucking me so hard my breasts are bouncing on my chest and it's just the right side of degrading. I tip my hips to take him a fraction of an inch deeper and that's when it hits me.

"Lowry, yes. God, yes. I'm coming. Lowry, god."

It's like one of those massive explosions where the shockwave hits you before the sound, before you see the target shatter and spread into a billion tiny little pieces. And no matter what, no matter how hard you try, no matter how long you spend, no matter what kind of space-age adhesive you might have at your disposal, it's never going to be the same again. Rocked. Shattered. Wrecked. That's how I feel as this climax rips through me, and I know I am forever changed.

CHAPTER 19

L owry

STARLA'S MUSCLES pulse around me like a tightly squeezed fist, and I come so hard I think I might pass out. Seriously. Is it possible to shoot one's load with such force that it breaks a condom? It's a ridiculous thought, though I really feel I ought to check, because God. My God.

My vision's gone spotty, there's a low tone in my ears, and the universe seems to be spinning around me. Wouldn't surprise me if that sex changed the gravitational pull of the earth. Hell. I thought I'd had good sex. With Maeve, the sex had been good. Yes, it had been, and I shouldn't take away from that, shouldn't downgrade that experience because it had been pleasurable, satisfying. It's just that sex with Starla is something I hadn't even conceived of as being possible.

Gasping like I've run a marathon, I try to catch my breath. I ought to open my eyes which I've screwed tight shut because they probably would've burst out of my head otherwise. Take stock of Starla and see if she's okay. Yes, I'm pretty sure she had a wicked orgasm, but that's one thing. A great thing, but only one. That was phenomenal, but also a kind of intense I wasn't entirely expecting, and it wouldn't surprise me if it hit her hard. How is she feeling about the things we said? The way we fucked? Did I leave bruises on her from grasping her so tightly? How is she going to feel if I did?

When I finally manage to open my eyes, a lazy grin stretching my mouth because I'm too wrecked to do anything else, it's to Starla's lovely, flushed face, yes, but she's wide-eyed with over-whelm and her chin trembles.

"Starla, darling? Are you—"

And then she starts to cry.

I've heard the expression "bursting into tears" many times, but I don't know I've seen it myself until now. It's a violent spilling of tears that must have been welling for minutes judging by the sheer volume of them. Christ, what have I done?

"Oh, sweetheart, hush."

Her sobs are convulsive and I want to make them stop. It's an impulse I've had to fight against for as long as I can remember. The urge to fix things. Patch them up, make them better. Which is why I went to medical school, yes, but it's all the more satis-fying and frustrating to dig around in people's heads and help them sort themselves out than it is to patch up a bullet wound. Not everyone feels that way, I know.

There's a rush my colleagues in the ER get that never did much for me. Too quick, over too soon. Not enough buildup. It's perhaps a bit sick of me, but there's not enough intimacy. Not enough time to get entwined with another person and their fate. Yes, losing a patient is difficult no matter what, but there's a difference between having dedicated yourself to a stranger for a few hours and having coaxed someone to trust you with their innermost thoughts and secrets, the very clockwork of their minds, familiarized yourself with their emotions and basest and most generous impulses for a period of years. I'm enough of a masochist to have a strong preference for the latter even though it takes a toll.

The point is I shouldn't be shushing Starla. I should be holding her. I can rock her, tell her I'm here, that she's safe, but stop her? No. I want her tears to stop because the way my brain receives that message is that she's in pain, but what if she's not? I need to give her the space to do what she needs to do. Have emotions without making her feel as though I'm allergic to them, as though they scare me and she needs to keep them hidden because I can't handle them or they disturb me. I only want her to stop hurting, and I need to let her tell me what hurts before I make another move.

In the meantime, I will disentangle us as quickly as possible so I can cradle her, wrap my limbs around her and lend her the warmth and shelter of my body, and try to be a port in the storm, something solid to cling to as her emotions swirl around her.

It's maybe unfair of me, and definitely not something I would say to her, but it's a relief in some ways to feel her quaking in my arms, the maelstrom of feelings overwhelming her. The scariest times with Starla, the times I was most terrified I was going to lose her, were when she would come sit in my office, her beautiful face blank, staring off into nothing because it was as worthwhile to look at as anything else. She's most certainly not numb now, and even as most of me is fretting over her and fighting the urge to ask how I can fix this, I allow myself a small drip of pleasure that she *feels*. Deeply.

Eventually her tears and her breathing slow, and while she's still clinging to me, her nails aren't digging into my skin. Her keening's died down to an occasional hiccup and humming whines. It's not out of the realm of possibility that she'll fall asleep and we'll talk about this when she wakes. I'll hold her until morning if I have to, but I'm human and, though I've learned well to hide it, impatient.

When she pulls away, there's a beat of panic until she offers me a tear-streaked smile. "Need tissues. I'm so gross. Like the definition of ugly cry."

I suppose it's true her eyes are swollen and red, and her skin is splotchy, but... "I'm not worried about that. I'm worried about you."

It takes her a few minutes to wipe her eyes, her cheeks, her chin. Blow her nose and push the hair that's gotten stuck to her forehead out of the way. And then she looks sheepish. Like she wants to hide. She's not going to hide from me.

"Starla."

"Mmm?"

She blinks at me, and I want to laugh. Is she really going to pretend she didn't bawl her eyes out for the past twenty minutes? Not on my watch, absolutely not.

"Can you talk to me? Tell me what that was about?"

I'm not trying to play shrink, but there are some things that can't be helped.

She studies the tissue crumpled between her fingers and I let her have the silence, hopefully give her the space to say what she wants to say.

"That...that was incredible. Really. And I'm not upset with you, at all."

A good start. Maybe?

"But it was really..." Her brows crunch together and she frowns at the tissue as though it's offended her. "It was really intense. Like, I've done daddy stuff before with partners. Being little isn't...it's not new to me. I didn't get thrown into the deep end of the pool without water wings, you know?"

I nod to acknowledge her but not interrupt.

"But I kind of felt like I was drowning anyway."

Oof, punch to the gut, and it must show on my face because she backpedals. "No, no. Not in a bad way. I think it was terri-fying because it was so good and it felt so right and it was the sexiest thing I've ever done in my life and…it was with you. It's edgy to be with you like that, more than it is with other people."

Drowning, terrifying, edgy. Those aren't words a man usually likes to hear associated with his sexual performance. Although I'm sure there are people out there for whom that would be a point of pride. But those aren't the only words she said. Incredible, intense, so good, so right, sexiest thing she's ever done in her life. That helps to balance the scales a bit, and if this is what's going on in her head, no wonder she cried. That's a damn lot.

"It's… Can I tell you something and you won't regret this?"

I don't like making promises, but there are very few things—I can think of less than a handful—that could ever make me regret what we've done.

"You can tell me anything you like. I hope you will."

She closes her eyes and punctuates her discomfort with a breath blown hard out of her nose before looking up at me.

"This is so embarrassing. And I don't want to gross you out."

I shrug because there's not much that can shock or appall me. "I doubt very much that it will bother me at all. And as for you being embarrassed, I hope I've never made you feel that way. I've certainly never meant to."

It has been my mission since the day I met her to always leave her feeling better when she's left me than when she arrived. Or at the very least, no worse. It wasn't always easy because she was dealing with some heavy stuff and sometimes therapy means feeling worse before you can feel better, but whether I succeeded or not, I did always try. No matter what her confession is, I won't make her feel abandoned. If nothing else, I will always show up.

⁓

STARLA

Will there ever be a time when I don't feel like I am one step away from losing everything? Probably not. I'm wired to feel insecure. To feel as though whatever I have, I don't deserve, so it wouldn't be surprising if someone yanked it all away. I wouldn't even be able to argue. Except when I do the math, it makes sense why I can feel this as more of a real possibility. I'm a little over a week away from my next ECT and this is when the depression starts creeping up for real, the whispers grow louder in my ears. It never gets nearly as bad as it was at its worst, but I can feel it. It's not real. My brain likes to lie, isn't that great?

What is truly great, though, is that I am snuggled against Lowry and he's holding me as close as I ever dreamed he would. He never did embarrass me. Which is not to say that I was never embarrassed in front of him, because I was—frequently, wildly— but it wasn't because of anything he'd done. I can at least try to explain why I had a major fucking meltdown just now.

"I, um…"

I can't look at him while I say this. Instead, I tuck myself under his chin and curl my fingers against his chest. And heaven love the man, he holds me tighter.

"When I was your patient…" Oh, so much vomit, so much. "I…I had the biggest crush on you."

He kisses the top of my head and cradles the back of my neck in his hand, stroking my hair.

"That's not unusual, Star. It happens to a lot of people. Adults too. It's almost hard not to when there's someone you feel is so invested in your well-being, who genuinely cares for you."

"Yeah, well, I never felt that way about Doctor Gendron. Still don't."

He snorts and it makes me feel a little better, makes it a bit easier to continue.

"It felt different to me, though. Like, I had minor crushes on boys I went to school with, even dated some of them." His frame goes rigid, probably remembering Milo, but this isn't about him. I don't even know where he is now. I could probably find out but I don't think I want to know. "But you were the one consistent thing. It didn't feel shallow to me, it wasn't passing. I knew it wasn't okay and I didn't want you or anyone else to know, partly because I was afraid Doctor Gendron or my father would've taken you away from me if they did. But I…"

When I think back on those years—the ones where I was walking closest to the edge, the ones where I wasn't certain if I was going to make it to college and wasn't sure I wanted to because what did it matter anyway and why did I deserve to take up any space at all, especially so goddamn much of it—there are very few things I remember fondly, and Lowry is one of them.

"I think even then I loved you. I don't say that lightly. Whether you knew it or not, I thought about you all the time. Thinking about disappointing you was one of the things that kept me from, well…"

I thought about killing myself far more frequently than I actually tried, which he knows, but I don't think he realizes exactly how powerful he was as a motivation for me to not. "It sounds over the top, I know, and maybe I'm being melodramatic, but you of all people know emotion isn't always logical and—"

"Starla. Can you look at me? Or is it not safe yet?"

It doesn't feel safe, not at all, because I've basically vomited my soul all over him and I'm not sure how he feels about that, but at the same time it seems like such a small, simple thing in exchange for everything I've forced him to bear.

I peel myself far enough away from him that I can look at him as he asked. Kinda feels like I'm peeling my own skin off to do it, but it's also kinda nice because he's so goddamn handsome and he looks at me so kindly.

"It's not gross and I don't think you should be embarrassed. I knew you had feelings for me, before. It didn't offend me, and you never behaved inappropriately, never made me uncomfortable. It's nothing you need to feel badly about, for any reason. You did absolutely nothing wrong and you needn't worry on my account."

It's a relief to hear him say that. And while it *would* be wrong and it *would* be inappropriate, a part of me aches for him to confess that he'd felt the same for me. Such a selfish wish, and one that I don't dare voice because I've asked him for far too much already. I remember the last time I asked for too much—he left. I won't let that happen again. I'll take what I've been given and be grateful for it, because it's 98 percent of everything I've ever wanted.

"Okay."

"And hearing that makes me understand why—"

"Why I'd have a complete and utter meltdown?"

"That's not what I was going to say and I don't want you to think of it that way either. What I was going to say is that I could understand how this could be overwhelming and you'd need an outlet. I can't tell you how to feel, but I wish you would believe me when I say I'm not afraid of any of your feelings and you don't need to hide them from me. Course you don't have to share everything with me either, you have a right to privacy, but I hope that's why you'd not share something, because that's your prerogative and not because you're afraid of how I might feel about it."

God, he's so earnest it kills me. And I try so hard not to wonder why I deserve a man like this and instead enjoy the fact that he seems to think I do.

"Okay."

"I do think, though, that it's late and you ought to get some sleep. You have clients tomorrow morning, aye?"

"Yes, I do. But—"

"No buts. We'll have plenty of time to talk more later. Do you have plans for tomorrow night already? If you don't, I'll pick up some takeout and be over at seven thirty."

"I don't."

Holden had texted earlier because his breakup didn't go quite as planned with Ben, and apparently he and Ben and Anna are all meeting up tomorrow night? Kids these days, I don't even know. But let's be real, even if Holden hadn't ditched me for a potential threesome, I would cancel with him because there's pretty much nothing I'd rather do than eat some lo mein with my daddy.

"It's settled, then. And it's entirely up to you, I don't want to be a bother or disturb, but if it's not too much, I'd like to spend the night with you. I'll have to get up early to head back to my place, but…"

Is he worried? Does he seriously believe there is any possibility of me being like *Nah, check you later*? It seems from the way he's regarding me with a smidge of tightness around his eyes, around his full mouth that yes, he is, and yes, he does.

"I'd like it very much if you stayed."

And to prove my point, I cuddle in closer and lock my arm around him. I like the gentle way he huffs a laugh, and the way he uses his arm to gather me still closer, and most of all the way he murmurs into my hair.

"I'm glad. The night's a better place with my Star."

CHAPTER 20

Lowry

IT WAS MORE than difficult to climb out of Starla's bed this morning and head home, and she was all I could think of on my way into work. All I could think of from my car to my office. I may not have an overflow of emotions like Starla did last night, but it sure does feel like a dream to me.

Now I'm on my way up in the elevator in her building, this time with a sack full of Chinese food instead of yesterday's props of saltines and Gatorade. My God, does that feel like forever ago.

When I rap on her door, my heart stops because I hope I haven't hallucinated this whole thing. Haven't dreamed that Starla is mine now, that I've finally had her—and if I'm a very lucky man, will continue to have her—in all the ways I've always fantasized about.

But when she opens the door, it's with a great big gorgeous smile which renders anything else invisible except for her clothes. A bright pink tutu with a ribbon hem and bow at the waist, and a black and white T-shirt that proclaims "Don't Mess With the Princess" below a picture of Princess Leia. Jesus Christ.

Will she find me presumptuous if I step over her threshold, drop our food to the ground, and take her in my arms to kiss? My God, I hope not because I can't possibly do anything else.

My sweet girl goes on tiptoes and throws her arms round my neck, returning my kiss full force, and I could get swept up in her again, much the way I did last night. Except I'm not going to make her not eating dinner a habit. I am, after all, supposed to look after her. But I'm not going to turn her away, not now, not yet, especially given that I know how she frets. I hope she hasn't been fretting about me.

When we come up for air, she looks at me, suddenly shy, though she doesn't let me go.

"Hi."

Though I'd desperately like for her to say "Hi, Daddy," I understand why she might not. Perhaps she has the same concern that yesterday was all a fantasy. Or even parts of it. Why would she risk that? But I will. For her, though my stomach still clenches as I say the words.

"Hello, little girl. I'm awfully glad to see you."

And in that instant she's transformed. Her cheeks flush, she blinks bashfully, and dips her head. Absolutely darling.

Her "me too, Daddy," is practically a whisper, but she may as well have shouted it for how my body reacts, primed all day and now raring to go for her. Christ, this is what makes me want to set upon her, forget to feed her, strip her bare, and make her come over and over and over. So I kiss her more, grab her bottom and knead her flesh, groan into her hot, wet, willing mouth when she hitches her leg around me because God almighty, this woman.

When at last I can breathe again, I unhook her leg from around me and withstand her mighty pout.

"You, little miss, need to eat dinner. And I'm not going to be the irresponsible daddy who keeps you from it. So we'll behave for a bit, you'll tell me about your day, and then I have intentions where you're concerned."

"I hope you intend to fuck me into next week."

Such filthy words coming out of such a sweet mouth, I nearly perish.

"What a naughty little thing," I say, circling a hand around her wrist and leading her over to the couch where we sat and ate off the coffee table when she'd been injured. She's better now, though I noticed last night some of the bruises linger in the form of yellowed skin. "Now sit and eat your dinner or you'll get nothing at all."

I don't mind the scowl she delivers from her seat kitty-corner to mine. I know I can't sit next to her and control myself, so for now, I'll be over here. From the takeout bag, I dig out our food and hand her some beef lo mein, which I happen to know is her favorite because she's mentioned it before, and a pair of chopsticks because I've seen her devour immense amounts of sushi with them—the woman's got skills.

Starla doesn't wait for me to crack my honey walnut shrimp and rice open before she's digging in, and I have to roll my eyes—fondly. The woman was clearly ravenous but would have starved herself to keep kissing me. I'm not going to lie, that feels good, although also proves that she does in fact need someone to remind her to eat. Though if I weren't here, she wouldn't be distracted.

"How was your day?"

She slurps a noodle into her mouth, and then chews thoughtfully, her legs crisscrossed on the couch.

"Mmm, fine. I signed a new client today."

"That's great, congratulations."

She smiles and pauses with a few inches of noodles hanging from her chopsticks. "Thanks."

"You know, I'm really proud of you—this business you've built is filling a very important niche, and you're clearly excellent at your job. I'm not sure if you hear that enough."

Starla looks at me, noodles dangling from in between her lips, and it's rather comical.

"I don't mean to embarrass you or to be condescending, but you need to know that, and perhaps I'm making an arse of myself because people are constantly telling you how phenomenal you are, but on the off chance that no one else does tell you how incredible you are, well, that's my job now."

Her only reaction is to blink, so I urge her, "Don't forget to eat your noodles, don't want to drip on your shirt. Which is very cute by the way."

She eats, looking at me the whole time she chews.

"What?"

Did I say something wrong? Have I overstepped already? Am I mistaken and she actually has numerous people falling all over themselves to tell her how brilliant she is? In which case, she ought to dump her lo mein on my head and tell me to get the fuck out, but I don't think I'm mistaken.

"You said you didn't know anything about how to be a daddy because you've never done it before, but you're good at it already. So, um, thank you. I don't hear that a lot."

I don't press, but tell her as much about my day as I'm able, given that I can't talk much about my patients, but she understands that and presumably is glad for it, knowing I've always given her the same privacy.

"Can I ask you something?"

She looks at me over the takeout container, chopsticks poised to dig into the lo mein again. "Have you ever not asked me something?"

Many times. If she took a minute to think about it, she'd realize that. But that's not something that needs to be discussed, at least not right now. I don't respond because Starla's sass doesn't always require a response. Indeed, she huffs and rolls her eyes.

"Yes, what did you want to know?"

"Why do you live here? I mean, in this studio."

I know why she lives in Boston. It's her home and she's not great with change. Sure, if her job had necessitated a move, I have no doubt she would've found the wherewithal to do it, but if there's one thing that has been made exceedingly clear over the last several months, it's that Starla has a talent for shaping the world around her to fit her particular strengths and needs.

Not that I didn't know that about her before—she's had a talent for sculpting her environment, unapologetically, since the day I met her—but her capability is sharper now, honed like a knife she wields not just on her own behalf but also to advocate and plow paths for others. In this, as in so many things, she is remarkable.

She shrugs and stuffs a clump of noodles in her mouth. If I didn't know her so well, I might leave off there. She likes it here, what's the big deal? Except I know some things that make this a more invasive and particular question. Since Starla seems content to nosh on her beef and onions and snap peas until I drown in my curiosity, I nudge.

"I know you didn't sell the house in Chestnut Hill."

Which doesn't surprise me. Starla isn't one to throw away something perfectly good, and I know how attached she was to her father. No, it doesn't surprise me at all that she still owns the sprawling estate. What does surprise me, particularly given her distaste for change, is that she doesn't still live there.

"It's a good investment."

Likely true given the real estate climate in greater Boston.

"Sure. But it would still be a good investment if you lived there. Better, even, perhaps?" Then she wouldn't also be shelling out rent on this place which, while small, is in a prime location and must run her a few thousand dollars a month.

"It's too big for one person."

I can understand Starla not wanting to wander around an enormous house with no one to talk to. It would highlight exactly how alone she's been since her father died. Remind her every day of how much she misses him.

"Okay, but why don't you rent it out?"

Up until now, she's answered my questions rather docilely, especially for her, but now she's getting annoyed, stabbing her chopsticks so hard into the container it's a wonder they don't come out the bottom.

"I don't think my father would care for having other people living in his house."

It would be a dick move to point out her father is deceased and that, given her lack of religious convictions, it's not as though she believes in the afterlife. It's not as though she actually thinks Jameson Patrick is floating around the estate, measuring the grass with a ghost ruler or swiping a gloved apparitional finger over a thin layer of dust on a mantelpiece.

She must sense my continued skepticism, though, because with another huff, she drops the lo mein, chopsticks and all, onto the table, crosses her arms across her chest and leans back into the corner of the couch. I have perhaps poked too hard.

"That much space makes me nervous. And while I'm capable of keeping this neat and organized, there's no way I'd be able to stay on top of things in that house even with a housekeeper. I'd end up living out of a single room and that would be far stranger than having this place to myself. So I can't live there, and the guilt of letting someone else live there wouldn't do me any favors. I know my father would want that for me, but I can't right now. Someday. Maybe. I'd like to. But today? Not going to happen. So, yes, it's expensive and ridiculous, and every time I go over these things with my accountant, she shakes her head, but I've had about enough of it. It's well within my means to maintain both properties even if it seems wasteful. Because honestly, how much is my mental health worth to you?"

I'm such an arse. Yes, I wanted to know, and yes, I'm allowed to ask, but perhaps I could've done so more delicately. One thing I know for sure, though, is what Starla is worth to me, and tied irrevocably to that is her mental health.

"It's priceless. You're priceless."

I reach for her hand that's resting on the couch and she doesn't snatch it away but allows me to take it up, bring it to my mouth where I kiss her knuckles, the top of her hand, before turning it over to reveal her palm.

So many lines and I know my gran would say Starla's life is an unpredictable, riotous, beautiful disaster. I'm not sure she'd be wrong, but Starla's done her very best to keep it from falling into disrepair and I shouldn't do anything about that except allow her to run her ship as she sees fit. She's a fine captain, and if she'll let me, I'd like very much to stick around and be her first mate.

I kiss the inside of Starla's wrist before biting the meaty padded section of her palm that joins her thumb and then each fingertip in turn. She lets me. And when I'm done, I press one more kiss to the palm of her hand before taking it and sliding it into the open neck of my shirt until it rests against my heart. Her hand is cold, as ever, so I'll warm it with my body and let her feel that the muscle pumping my very lifeblood through my body beats for her, and always has.

～

STARLA

Lowry's warm. And charming. And brought me my favorite

Chinese food. Which makes it easy to let the fit of pique dissipate. I know it's foolish to live here while holding onto my father's house, but I do. Oh well. I could do a lot worse things with the ridiculous amounts of money I'm currently sitting on.

Tad had called earlier today, as had a couple of the advisors I've been talking to, and it's clear they're all frustrated with me. The whole my-father-just-died thing is apparently wearing thin in the face of the grinding wheels of commerce. Part of me would like to hand it all over to Tad because what the fuck do I care? But the truth is that I do care and I don't trust Tad to handle the business as my father would like. Although to be fair, I don't trust myself to do that either. Which is a whole different smack in the face.

I need to shake myself loose of these thoughts. There's nothing to be done about any of this tonight. What could be done, though...

Why does Lowry always smell good? And he looks so... I don't even know. Precisely how a daddy should look, I suppose, with his heather-green collared shirt open a few buttons even as it's tucked neatly into some dark grey slacks. His cuffs have ridden up enough as he sits that I can see his goddamn argyle socks. See, what I'd really like to do is crawl into his lap and straddle him, but I suspect he won't allow those sorts of hijinks until I've eaten dinner to his satisfaction.

And right on cue, he's drawing my hand out of his shirt and pressing another kiss to the inside of my wrist, which makes me all kinds of swoony for him.

"If you've forgiven me for needling you, I think you ought to eat some more."

Yes, I suppose I should.

"Fine, but you're going to let me have your fortune cookie as penance."

"You drive a hard bargain, Ms. Patrick, but I accept your terms."

He gives my wrist a little nip before letting me go and settles back with his takeout carton. I take a couple of bites from my own and then look over the white peaks of my open takeout box. He looks pensive, which you'd think I'd be used to, but I'm not. He's usually so easy and present that him thinking about something other than what's in front of him is noticeable.

"Penny for your thoughts. Or even your fortune cookie back."

He blinks up at me with a sheepish smile. "Sorry, love."

"Seriously, where'd your head go? Something going on with one of your patients? I know you can't talk about them much and I'm not sure what to offer other than listening, but if you tell me what would be most helpful, I'll do my best to do it."

"It's not that."

He shakes his head and takes another bite of his shrimp. It looks really good and I wonder if he would share. Probably, if I asked nicely. If I were a brat, I'd reach over and snag one, but that's not really my jam. I get that for some people that "in trouble" feeling is a rush. For me, it feels like nausea. I get enough of that when I've done my ECT, thanks.

"Then what is it? And can I have one of your shrimp while you oh-so-carefully formulate how to say this?"

The corners of his eyes crinkle when he laughs and holds out his food. The shrimp is sticky, so when I snatch one, it comes away with clumps of rice stuck to it. It's far from ladylike, but I stuff the whole thing in my mouth and chew. It's really fucking good—the crispy fried coating gives way to the specific tenderness of the shrimp and the whole thing is covered with honey sauce and tiny bits of crunchy walnuts, and I don't know, it's like a symphony in my mouth. I'm totally getting this next time. Or just eating more of Lowry's. Whatever.

Indeed, he doesn't seem to be composing his thoughts into sentences but watching me eat. It's possible I made a noise.

"You seem to be enjoying that immensely. Would you like to trade?"

If I were a grown-up, I'd rebuff his offer. But I'm not, so I shove my half-eaten lo mein at him and he looks at me from under his ginger brows like I've pleased him somehow as he hands over the rest of his food. Yep, it's so good.

"Well, now that I've buttered you up with my dinner, what I was going to say is that I have more questions for you, but I feel as though I've poked you enough for one evening."

It's clearly been a while since Lowry was a thirteen-year-old boy, because I make the obvious joke through a mouthful of shrimp and rice. "I think you've poked me not at all and that's nowhere near sufficient."

"I meant mentally."

"Yeah, that's different." And now I'm wary. The shrimp is still incredible, though, so I'll focus on that. "But is that a thing people do? Not ask questions because they feel like they've asked enough questions already? Or is this a you-thinking-I'm-fragile kind of thing?"

"You're fragile like a tank, little girl. I prefer to think of it as being respectful because it's emotionally taxing to talk about difficult things."

"And this is going to be difficult?"

He shrugs and spears his chopsticks into the box of lo mein. "Might be. Or maybe it's fine. I don't know. But I could imagine how it would be a sensitive topic."

"Will you go ahead? I'll tell you to shush your face if I don't want to talk about it."

"All right, then. Have you always thought of yourself as kinky?"

Sure, let's dive into the deep end of the pool. Although now that he knows about the daddy kink thing, the rest of this is more academic, not nearly as stomach-churning.

"I guess so. For as long as I've known that was a thing, anyway. I knew I always felt like the love I saw in movies and on TV and stuff wasn't quite right, that it was…missing something isn't it exactly, but it was like everyone around me was satisfied by it but it didn't taste right to me? And when I learned what kink was it was like, 'Oh, yes, that!' I know labels aren't always great, but sometimes they're helpful."

"The World Health Organization and the American Psychiatric Association agree with you. Although I'd argue they're a bit overzealous."

He's such a nerd.

"Was that it? Or do you have more questions?"

"I have so many questions. And I'd get a beer, but I've heard playing after drinking is frowned upon."

I shrug. "It's like driving. You can have a single drink and then play, but yeah, being any kind of intoxicated is bad news. That whole consent thing kind of goes out the window, and if you're doing impact play, you want to have your reflexes and hand-eye coordination at their best, you know? If you want one, there's a mixed six-pack of Brew Dog in the fridge."

It starts out as a nod but turns into a cock of his head. "You got me Scottish beer?"

"I did. You said your brothers liked this brewery and you wanted to try it but it was hard to find around here. If it can be had, I can have it. So, I have it for you."

That's one of the other things I like about Lowry. He's never tried to take advantage of my wealth. We take turns paying for dinner and otherwise don't talk about money much. Which is wild amounts of privilege, I know, but when you have that privilege, it's nice to feel wanted for other things.

He goes and fetches a beer from the fridge and cracks the can, taking a first sip before dropping back into his chair.

"Ah, I can see why Alex likes this one. It's not subtle, just like him."

I've heard a little about Lowry's brothers, know he's the oldest, have seen a couple of pictures of the four of them lined up with their ginger hair. I'm perhaps biased, but I think Lowry is the best-looking. His brothers, however curious I am to meet them, aren't the point.

"Now that you're fortified, did you have other questions?"

"This daddy kink of yours..."

I'd like to point out that I'm not the only one sitting here with my daddy kink. Lowry's obviously got a daddy kink as well, just from the other side of things. But I'll let it slide because as he's said, he's new to this. He might not identify that way yet and that's fine.

"Do you feel like it comes from somewhere or you're hard-wired that way?"

"I've thought about this a lot, actually, and I've come to the pretty firm conclusion that it doesn't matter."

He opens his mouth, no doubt an apology on the tip of his tongue, but I don't need an apology. It's a reasonable question, if not a particularly useful one.

"I mean, do I have daddy issues? Probably. But it's not like I can tell how much of my kinks are from where. I'm pretty sure I would've been kinky no matter what. I feel like most people who are into kink would be, no matter how or where they grew up. For some people it's nurture, sure. But I'd bet mostly it's nature. I do think, though, that nurture can have something to do with how people's kinks and fetishes manifest. I feel like there's some shit people can't touch because of how they were raised and there are also things they like because of it."

He's listening as intently as he ever has to me, and I've got to wonder if he's itching to make notes. If he is, he covers it with another sip of his beer, so I continue.

"I mean, I suspect I'd probably enjoy a lot of the physical things that I do, like the impact play. And being a bottom. But as for the daddy stuff, kinda hard to say. Maybe things would've been different if I hadn't desperately craved my father's approval and attention, but I did." Still do, which is kind of fucked up and not something we need to discuss at the moment, if ever, so I press on. "And maybe that has something to do with how I like to play or maybe not. I can tell you there are people who enjoy role-playing incest scenarios as if they were fucking their actual parent and that's not what I like. If anything, I crave what I didn't have, not what I did. I mean, can you imagine me calling my father *daddy?*"

CHAPTER 21

Lowry

THE SHALLOW CURVE of her mouth and the way her eyes are large and luminous say no. And honestly, when I think back to Mr. Patrick...

"No. No, I doubt that you did. Was he always 'Father' to you?"

She nods and laughs a little. "Always. Can you picture it?"

I can. Of course, I didn't meet Starla and her father until she was in high school, but I've seen pictures of her as a small child. Her eyes were even bigger then, as children's are, but I doubt she'd ever acted all that much like a child. *Father.* And he was the person she was most comfortable with in the world. My God.

"Was it...was it very difficult for you, when he died?"

That is a ridiculous and insensitive question, and I'd like to suck it back between my teeth because of course it was difficult for her. It was difficult for her to make friends by the time I knew her—even if her classmates hadn't known and gossiped about why she wasn't in school—which they absolutely did—the fact is she was only ever there part-time. She didn't have many friends, and while I think she enjoys spending time with some of her clients and Holden and has had some relationships, she still doesn't seem to be a sociable, outgoing person. So, whereas it would be difficult for anyone when their father died, I doubt Starla was left with much of a support system. Probably why I couldn't stop myself from getting on a plane and coming out here.

Thankfully, I have a stockpile of goodwill with Starla, and I seem to have only cashed some of it in by being thickskulled.

"Yes," she says, not looking at me. She rolls her lips between her teeth and looks into the middle distance, and I hate myself more for bringing this up. I could have been pulling her over my lap, rucking her skirt up, tugging up the back of her panties until they separated her nice, plump, oh-so-spankable cheeks, and then laying my hand on her over and over until she was squirming across my thighs. I hope, anyway, though I don't really have any experience with that. Doesn't matter because, instead, we are talking about her dead father. *Way to go, Lowry. You always did know how to muck things up.*

But I'll take it as a sign of how deeply she's come to trust me again that she answers. The truth is I can't imagine how devastated she must have been. My mum and dad and all three of my brothers are alive and well back in Scotland, and I never relied on them the way Starla had leaned on her father.

"Yes," she repeats.

How bad was it? Was it so bad that she won't say? Won't risk me thinking less of her—I wouldn't—or is she worried that I would end things here and now because I believe she's literally trying to replace her father with me? I don't.

"I'd had my depression managed really well for a long time. Was keeping up with my ECT, and though it wasn't perfect, it was fine. I was fine. I know it's never going to go away. The best I can hope for is to manage it and I was. And then he was gone, and I..."

She sighs. And I can see it. How disappointed in herself she was, how embarrassed she is even still. Which is ridiculous.

"It wasn't managed anymore. There's a difference between depression and grief, but for me, they got all mixed up. The grief made the depression worse, and the depression made it impossible for me to climb out of the grief, and I was... I should've been scared, but I was so far gone that mostly I couldn't locate fear. Just despair. Disappointment. Pain. And it was so dark, so deep, I couldn't even imagine the possibility that it wouldn't last forever. I did manage to tell Doctor Gendron that, though, so I checked myself into Harbinson for a while until I felt like I had a reasonable grasp on reality again. Took a while. Longer than I want to admit, but at least I got there after I thought I might not be able to."

It hurts me to think of her adrift in that sea of loneliness, of not knowing if she'd be okay again. Ever. Of having fought so many battles and won, but to be faced with one that made her want to lie down and give in because what was even the point?

I'm also fucking furious with myself for not being here for her when she could have used me the most. That's nonsense though because I wouldn't have been any good to her if I showed up then and only then. Like a fellow soldier who abandoned you in battle riding up on a shiny silver horse while you've been dragged through the mud and almost died half a dozen times. Pretty sure "Fuck all the way off" is the only reasonable response in that situation.

"I'm sorry I wasn't here for you."

She lifts a shoulder. "Why would you have been? You lived in Chicago. I hadn't seen you in fifteen years. Why on earth would I have any expectation that you'd show up?"

Except that's the thing, isn't it? Awkwardness makes my throat thick and I've got to wonder if telling her that I was in fact here will make this better or worse. I'm almost certain the answer is worse. And yet, I feel as though with all of the things she's told me and with everything I'm still holding back from her, this is a time and place where I should tell her. That I owe her the truth.

"I…" My throat works around a swallow and I send up a prayer that this won't spell the end of things for us. Though Starla's never been one to throw things away. She might be angry at me or disturbed, but *over* is probably a reach. "I was here, actually. In Boston. After your father passed."

Her hazel eyes narrow and her chin presses into wrinkles. "You were here? Like for a conference or something? Interviewing for your job? Or apartment hunting? It wasn't that long before you moved back."

I scrub a hand over the back of my neck because I've started to feel a bit sweat-prickled and cold-veined all at the same time. I'm not used to this and I'd like it to stop, but the only way to the other side of this is through.

"No. No, I decided to move back after I was here."

"Why? I mean, why were you here, and what about your visit made you decide to move back? It's not like you came at a nice time of year. I love Boston, but August isn't when the city's at its best."

I should've had more to drink, made my tongue looser, so this would be easier to say even if the outcome is hard to take. "I saw that your father had died and I…I'm a foolish, arrogant man. I thought…I thought you might need me."

"Need you?"

Her question is almost an echo, as if she's bouncing my words back at me in the hope that when I return them again, they'll make more sense. They won't, because this all sounds rather daft.

"Yes. Like I said, foolish. But I couldn't shake the feeling that you'd be in a bad way and if so, that you'd need all the support you could get. And I…" This isn't about me, we're talking about her and her father's death. But I can't explain this without telling her. "You remember yesterday when we agreed to a trade? We'd both tell our secrets, the things we weren't all that keen to talk about?"

"Yeah."

That slight tug up of her lip, an echo of a snarl, perhaps, makes me fear the worst. She's going to be horrified, disgusted, and as soon as this began, it's going to be over again. And worse, I will have left her with a sick feeling that no one can be trusted.

"Aye, well, mine is… There was a reason I left all those years ago. And it was you."

STARLA

This is what it must feel like to get slapped in the face with a freshly caught fish. Mortified, hurt, shocked, and slimy all over. That's what I'm experiencing in the instant Lowry makes one of my worst nightmares a reality.

I'd always feared I was the reason he left, always believed it was my fault. I've used all of the skills I've picked up in twenty or so years of therapy to be rational about it, but it's stuck around like cigarette smoke or cat pee in carpets: no matter how much you try to scrub it away or cover it up, it's always fucking *there*.

Now he's confirmed it—my fault. I was the reason. He didn't beat around the bush or try to couch it in kinder terms. Oh, no, for once, his psychobabble bullshit has abandoned him, and at the worst possible time. *Really could've used some coddling right about now, but thanks. This heart-shredding shame will work too.* God, I want to crawl under my coffee table and curl up there until… forever. For-fucking-ever because life is getting too big for me and I can't handle it.

My brain and my body are having a hard time processing this

shock to my system, and all I can do is laugh and look at my hands. "You know, I'd kinda hoped that wasn't true?"

Turns out, it was. I asked for too much, practically begged for things I couldn't have, and it's no wonder Lowry ran away. Who wants that kind of responsibility? Who can handle those kinds of soul-sucking demands? Who wants to be a party to this big of a disaster? Not even the most patient, well-intentioned, and steadiest man alive.

I wish I'd known this before. I wish I'd made him show me his first. Because there's no way I would've given all of myself to him like that if I'd known he couldn't handle far less than that. Why did he even come back? Why did he even start this? Why, why, why? The little inside me is throwing a fit, stomping and throwing shit because this all seems so wildly unfair. But I'm not going to let him see that part of me again because apparently he can't take it when I'm desperately needy. Fine, that's fine.

"Starla, I—"

"No. I don't want to hear anything else. I do wish you'd go. Because if you couldn't handle what I needed then, you sure as hell won't be able to handle what I need now."

I haven't even told him about Tad and my father's company and these looming decisions I'm supposed to be making, this business I'm supposed to be running but instead am finding myself paralyzed—because who wants to be a failure? Who wants to ruin lives because they made a bad decision? Not this girl, but I'm also not capable of managing a multibillion-dollar corporation because as much as I'd like to deny it, on any given day, my mental health is like a house of cards. Could be blown over by a stiff breeze at any moment. Goddammit. God-fucking-dammit.

I won't, will not, let Lowry see me cry again. I will swallow down all the tears, bite them back until my lip is bloody if I have to, but I will not cry in front of this man again. Now I'm mad about everything. I'm mad that he brought me my favorite Chinese takeout. I'm mad that he traded me when it became apparent I preferred his food. I'm angry that he tucked me into bed, and I'm absolutely furious he let me call him *daddy* and play a skittish virgin when we fucked.

"Sure, let me bare my soul and all of my secrets, intimate yourself into the core of my body, and then tell me it's my own fucking fault you abandoned me."

Okay, so I'm not going to cry, but apparently I'm going to yell.

He's a blur of green and grey and ginger hair because the tears in my eyes have rendered him out of focus, so I scrub my fists over them, and apparently I'm standing now.

"How dare you. How fucking dare you. You were supposed to protect me and care for me and you left without a goddamn word and now you're going to tell me it was my fault? No, thank you."

"I don't think you understand."

Wow, does he look miserable. But I'm too angry to care. What did he think was going to happen when he told me? That I'd laugh, we'd clink champagne glasses on a yacht or some shit and then we'd fuck? Does he not know me better than that?

"You're right. I don't understand. Aren't you supposed to be Saint Lowry or some shit? You're the worst. The absolute worst and I hate you. I hate you."

There she is. Little Starla is so mad she can't even access her grown-up vocabulary anymore. She is—I am—hurt. All the way down. I wish I had a door to slam, but I live in a studio and my bathroom has a pocket door and my closet doors slide. It's enough to make my frustration and fury boil over, and I want to hit something, but there's nothing to hit and I'm fuming and mortified and tired, and I can't anymore.

He'll leave when he leaves, and short of calling the police or my doorman, there's not much to do about it. I don't feel like causing more of a scene than I already have, and Lowry doesn't actually make me fear for my physical safety, so I'll sit on my couch and tuck my knees up to rest my head on, wrap my arms around my shins, and make it clear that we're done here. I'll be a little Starla egg until he leaves. Again.

Except he doesn't leave. He sits next to me. Doesn't touch me, perhaps sensing I might punch him if he did, but still quite close.

"Starla. I am so sorry. I didn't mean for you to understand it that way. Because that's not what I meant, at all. I left because of you, but it wasn't your fault. There's a distinction, and I should've made it. I apologize for making you feel like…"

He makes a frustrated noise.

"You might hate me as much for this, maybe more, and I'd deserve it. I do deserve it, because it was never okay and it still isn't, and I oughtn't have started something with you under false pretenses but… For fuck's sake, Star."

Anguish, that is what's coloring his voice, and I maybe turn my head a tiny bit so I can sneak a glance at him from over my knee. He looks desolate, racked with suffering, raking his hands through his hair. I'm not ready to offer him anything yet—no succor, no acceptance—but I am curious. And the way he can't even spit it out… I've never seen him such a mess.

"So, why don't you tell me why you really left, if it wasn't my fault? I thought I broke you. Asked too much of you and you couldn't stand it, so you left for Chicago. Stopped even working with kids and adolescents altogether. Why'd you do that? If it wasn't my fault, what did you do it for?"

LOWRY

"The job I took in Chicago was for working with adults."

It's my knee-jerk response, the one I give to anyone who asks. It seems obvious, yeah, that's the job that was available so that's the one I took. I had to do some studying up to get the latest on treating adults, but I think that shift is far easier than going from treating adults to adolescents.

Starla, though, knows oh-so-much better. And from where she sits, head still resting on her knees but fully turned toward me, her eyes narrow. There is no way in hell I'm getting off that easily. Nor should I. Yet I can't seem to continue my explanation. Perhaps she'll take pity on me. Play the therapist and ask leading questions that will compel me to answer. It's not fair to put her in that position, not at all, but when you're bogged down in self-loathing and hypocrisy and throat-closing disgust…

"Okay, but you could've gone anywhere. You were an incredibly well-regarded children's psychiatrist with a specialty in treating difficult and persistent cases of depression and anxiety. Any practice or hospital would thank their lucky stars to have you. So, nice try, doc, but I'm not buying it. Next?"

It's strange how the very things you can love about a person can also be the ones that drive you most mad. Starla is persistent, intuitive, and intelligent, all of which mean she's perfectly reasonable to demand these answers. Doesn't mean I want to give them to her any more, though. If anything, I want to hand them over less. Should've kept my mouth shut, took this secret to my grave, and perhaps gotten to live happily ever after. Though I wouldn't have deserved it and probably would've wizened under the weight of getting a fairy tale ending I didn't at all deserve.

"It's…it's not a nice reason."

I can't even meet her gaze anymore. There's a nonzero chance she's going to be horrified and demand I get out of her apartment, and I'll go, no argument, no cajoling, just walk out and maybe throw myself into the Charles because all I could say to that is, "Aye, ye've got the right of it, lass."

Also, I don't want her to feel guilty. There's no reason for her to, but she might anyway. She always takes too much on herself, makes things her fault when they aren't. When the people around her should've been better than they were and they failed her. Like her father did. Like I did. But I'm not going to fail her now, keep this secret from her when she ought to know and then decide if she really wants to be with a man like me. If I even still have a chance after she's said she hates me.

I force myself to look up at her and she's regarding me, calmly, kindly, chin now perched on her knees. She probably thinks I'm exaggerating. I'm not.

"Did you know I grew up Catholic? Not like church on Easter and Christmas Catholic, but church every Sunday, Catholic schools, went to confession every week, was an altar boy. That kind of Catholic."

"I bet you were an adorable ginger altar boy."

I force the corners of my mouth up to acknowledge her gentle teasing. How do I deserve this kindness from a woman like her?

"I don't know about adorable, but I took my duties very seriously. Unlike my brothers, of course. But that's neither here nor there. My mother thought about becoming a nun, but she met my da and changed her mind. Had a gaggle of kids she swore to raise up as good Catholics to make up for it. Her brother, though, he became a priest."

I have very clear memories of Uncle Sean. He had red hair like me, and was always ready with a joke or a little magic trick. I thought that man had hung the moon. I haven't talked about Sean in years, though I think of him often.

"We'd go to his church and see him give mass sometimes, and he was the kind of priest every parish wants. He was engaging, funny, warm, flirted with the old ladies, and..."

My throat closes, which is fine since it keeps the bile in my throat, not spilling out of my mouth and onto Starla's expensive carpet. Best get this part over with, though, rip off the Band-Aid as it were, because the story's not going to change no matter how long I wait. So I clear my throat, trying to breathe through the roiling in my gut.

"Turned out he was molesting little boys. He's one of the few who went to prison for it, so at least there's that. He's out now, though I haven't spoken to him. Can't bring myself to. But when I was a boy, I was jealous of those lads. The ones he spent extra time with, who he seemed to take a special interest in."

Makes me sick even now to think of it all these years later. I imagine it will for the rest of my life.

"Maybe if I hadn't been so self-centered, I would have noticed the boys themselves weren't so thrilled about it. Avoided him, more like. But I was a kid and it never occurred to me. It just seemed wildly unfair that Sean was my uncle and though we got to see him most Sunday evenings for dinner, he wasn't around more than that."

Starla's uncurled herself from her protective snail shell, and I hate that I'm sullying her with this. Not that she's naive and doesn't know these things happen because the world is an eminently fucked-up place, but there's a difference between knowing these things happen in an amorphous kind of way and having the vile show up in your own backyard. She doesn't look horrified, though, more like angry. More like she might fly over to Scotland, hunt down Sean, and throttle him herself. I've thought to do it myself to be honest, and though I dissemble when my family asks, I know he's one of the reasons I so rarely go home.

"So your uncle was a sick fuck who got what he deserved. I'm not sure what that has to do with you."

Oh, my sweet Starla. She should know better than I do that men who seem good aren't always.

～

STARLA

"I think maybe I knew about it?"

The icy sensation that's been lapping at my feet hits me full-on in the face.

"You knew?"

He shrugs and his cheeks have gone ruddy. A deep, searing burn of embarrassment and probably worse. Humiliation? Guilt? Remorse?

"It was during a time when it was in all the American papers. People whispered about it, made it sound like it was a problem over here, but not in our own backyard. But that didn't make any sense to me. I should've put it together. Should've figured it out. Should've said something to someone even if I wasn't sure."

"Lowry…" Though a few minutes ago I was so angry at him and so hurt I could have thrown a full-on tantrum, I have the urge to touch him, comfort him. I'm not sure what this has to do with why he left, but he's a human being, one I care for very much, and I don't like seeing him in pain. So, I put a hand on his shoulder, and he stiffens but doesn't shrug me off. "You were a child. That's what you would tell any of your clients, and I'm sure what your therapist has told you."

I've come to understand that most mental health professionals see a counselor themselves, in part to process all the care-taking of other people they do and the difficult topics they've had to help patients through. Lowry mentioned his therapist to me a few times when I was his patient, perhaps in an effort to build rapport or whatever. It helped, a little. Knowing this person I held in such high esteem also saw a therapist. Helped to reinforce what he was always telling me that, yeah, I needed help, but that didn't make me broken or a failure.

His knuckles knock together between his spread knees as he looks at the floor and mumbles something.

"What?"

He blinks up at me, that perma-crease deepening between his brows.

"I didn't tell her. Couldn't have without explaining why it was such a problem. Why I was racked with guilt."

"Whyever not? You were suffering. She could've helped you. You always told me that was your job. That I could tell you anything. Is it not some kind of...breach of professional courtesy or respect or something *not* to tell her? At the very least it was a waste of your time and money."

Lowry's brows go up as though he's suffering through my lecture. "I don't think you understand. It wasn't simply guilt over not having done anything for those boys, though that was bad enough. It was—I thought—I was scared—I..."

I've never seen him so at a loss for words. And he has heard some deep, dark shit from me, and I can only assume many of his other clients. He was always compassionate and composed, made me feel like even though the terrible thoughts in my head weren't okay, that I, personally, wasn't wrong. That I wasn't irreparably broken. That I hadn't done anything to deserve them and I shouldn't be embarrassed that I was unlucky enough to have these ghosts whereas most other people escaped that fate.

He meets my gaze, blue eyes imploring me, but for what, I don't know. My anger at him is lurking in the background, but I have a sense that it's about to be sorted out. So, whatever he needs, I'll give it to him. He literally saved my life. I owe him everything I have.

"Before I left..."

The thought of that time is still a gut punch for me. But I don't let it show because for once, this isn't about me.

"You'd barely turned eighteen, and I'd never been as fascinated by a woman as I was by you."

He shakes his head, looking like he wants to melt into a puddle and seep into my rug. What he's said works its way through my brain. He...what? It's so at odds with why I thought he'd left that I have a hard time reconciling those thoughts. Although it's like those movies where there's a plot twist and there's a montage with all the pivotal moments and you can see how every assumption you'd made was wrong and how those moments actually add up to what's being revealed in this moment. I have to make sure, though, because really?

"You…you liked me? Like that? Then? Is that why you…"

"That's why I left. That's why I couldn't tell you why. It wouldn't have been good for you. It was incredibly inappropriate. I hated myself. I had started to resent you. I would've lost my license, my calling, and then what would I have done?"

I…don't even know how to begin to answer that. I can't imagine Lowry not being a doctor, not being able to use everything he's learned, everything he's taught himself, to help people, heal people.

"I wrote you letters I never sent because I couldn't tell you why I'd left and I couldn't bring myself to lie to you. The whole thing made me sick. Not you, but the idea that I could have anything in common with my uncle. That I had the potential to take advantage of someone who trusted me. Someone who was recently a minor and I was responsible for. That's why I didn't tell my therapist. She was a mandated reporter—"

"You never touched me."

I'm angry on his behalf, but also bewildered and sort of furious at him. Emotions are rioting all over the place and I'm not great with them on a good day. This is beyond anything I ever thought I'd have to process.

"I know that. God, do I ever. But she would've been right. I could hear her answers in my head, d'ye understand? I knew what she'd say—to remove myself from the situation as soon as possible. So I did, but in a way that didn't involve you in some traumatic scandal or me losing my job or my license. I didn't like it, but it was the only thing to do. I'm not proud of it and maybe I should've taken my lumps but—I'm not like him, Star. At least, I hope to God I'm not."

"You're not." There aren't a whole lot of things I'm dead certain of, but that is one of them.

He dips a nod in thanks, but I'm not sure he feels that even as he acknowledges it.

"But if they'd said I was—my peers, my colleagues, my bosses, people I respected, then I would've been as good as, and my career would've been over.

"So, do you see now, why I left and in the way I did? It wasn't okay, and I've felt terrible about it since I decided that was the thing to do, but I didn't see another way out. I knew it would be hard on you, though not exactly how hard. And it's no consolation, I know, but it was god-awful for me too. But mostly I'm sorry for leaving you in a way that made you think any less of yourself instead of just being furious with me. So I apologize, again, and I should have told you sooner. Before you were so brave and shared with me, I should have laid everything on the table for you. I should've given you all the information because you were sold a bill of goods, but you didn't actually know what you were getting. I'll understand if you want me to leave and never come back."

"You think I'm going to be angry at you for what your uncle did? It's sickening, I absolutely agree with you, but I don't see what that has to do with me. Even if you both had the same feelings, he acted on them and you didn't. You removed yourself from the situation, and even though it hurt me more deeply than I can fully explain, I understand why you did it. So, unless you're going to tell me that you had these feelings for some of your other patients and didn't show that same self-restraint…"

"No, of course not. I've never felt that way about anyone before, never mind one of my patients."

"Then you're not the same. At all. And maybe it makes me a terrible person, but I'm mostly flattered. Probably because you did leave. Things would've gone a lot differently if you hadn't— namely, my father would've had you killed—but I don't think you're a monster, not of any sort. I mean, who can blame you for being fascinated with me? I am a spellbinding individual."

It's perhaps not kind to make light, but I'll do whatever I can to make him believe he shouldn't be crushed by his guilt over this. It's not even a matter of that math people sometimes try to get away with when horrible people are geniuses or great artists or whatever so we should forgive them their heinous sins. Lowry's presence in this world has been a nearly unmitigated good as far as I can tell. Yes, I still have trauma scars from how he left, but I do get it now. I don't like it, and it doesn't erase those old feelings that are carved into my psyche with a jackhammer, but at least I can empathize with the choice he made.

I don't think he'd welcome advances from me right now, not when he's mired in guilt and shame and remorse and whatever else he's got floating in there, but I can sit with him. Hold space. Hold his hand. So that's what I do.

CHAPTER 22

$\mathcal{L}$owry

IT'S GENERALLY a cause for celebration when one of my patients seems to be doing better. Perhaps they've had some sort of breakthrough in therapy, maybe the medication or drug cocktail they've been taking is working well, or they tried a new treatment like TMS or ECT and it's precisely the right tool.

I love that feeling. It's why I do this job. Helping people live better, fuller lives is why I spend hours poring over medical journals, going to continuing ed classes and conferences, why I mine my colleagues' knowledge and experience. That's all I've ever wanted to do: help people. There is nothing so satisfying as watching the expertise you've accumulated over most of your lifetime be used in the service of giving someone their life back. Or giving a family their loved one back.

There was one case I had when I first got to Chicago where an elderly woman who'd dealt with chronic low-level depression for as long as she could remember was thrown into a nearcatatonic state after her husband passed away. I was one of her team at the hospital and we tried everything. Elderly patients can be challenging in very different ways from kids and I felt out of my depth. Felt terrible every time I saw her children and grandchildren come to visit her because I knew they were looking at me and wondering why I couldn't do more. And why couldn't I?

I spent hours upon hours in the library making lists of medications and therapies and drug cocktails and everything I could think of to try because there was something about her—she still had so much life in her, so much love to give, and I felt as though if I could only find the right combination, I could crack her out of the locked safe of her grief.

Eventually we got her sign-off—and her daughter's approval—to try ECT, and it was... It's not always a miracle. But for this woman it was. After her first course of treatments, I went to check on her and she was with her daughter and some of her grandkids. Looking at photo albums, smiling, laughing after she'd barely looked at her loved ones for months. Warmed my heart. I'd been about to leave when there was a tug at my lab coat and I looked down to see a little girl. Five, maybe six. I'd squatted down because she clearly had something to say.

"Are you my grandma's doctor?"

"Aye, one of them."

"You made her better?"

"I like to think I helped. There's a lot of people here who've been trying to take the best care of her we can and help her feel better."

"I felt like she went away even though she was still here."

"That's a good way of putting it. She probably felt that way inside too."

"She's back now, though. You found her."

And then she hugged me, her small arms around my neck, nearly making me fall on my arse with the strength of her embrace. My throat had gotten thick and my sinuses burned as I patted her back.

That's one of the memories I dredge up when I'm having a shite day, when nothing seems to be going right or I'm dealing with new computer systems or red tape and paperwork, which aren't the reason I got into psychiatry at all. Or when I'm dealing with a difficult patient and I can't seem to find the combination to their safe, can't figure out how to help them.

Some of my colleagues have become hardened to it, are convinced there are some people who simply can't be saved. Perhaps that's smarter or at least easier, but I've never been able to feel that in my bones. And I don't feel it now while sitting across the coffee table from Tony.

He's...calm today. Not angry, not frustrated, not desolate. Which could be good, but I'm almost certain it's not. There's a thing that happens sometimes with severely depressed patients who are suicidal. You'd expect them to keep tumbling down the hill of their disease until they reach the pit of despair and appear to be at rock bottom before they end it all. That's how it was with Starla.

Things got worse and worse and worse, and the last appointment we had before she slit her wrists in the bathtub, it had seemed like it was painful for her to be alive. Everything hurt. Sitting hurt, standing hurt, walking hurt, breathing hurt, talking hurt; anything and everything was a misery.

But sometimes they seem at peace. They've made a decision, they've made—or are making—a plan. All the misery they're feeling, all the hurt they believe they're causing other people, all the wasted space they're taking up, it's going to be over soon. They give things away, they make arrangements, they write letters, they donate money. One of the benefits, I suppose, of orchestrating your own death.

Tony's not wearing one of his Bruins shirts today, and I have to wonder if it's because he's already passed it on for someone to enjoy when he's gone. He may be at peace, but I am very much not. And I'm irrationally angry at the Bruins for losing the Stanley Cup and at the NHL for being in the off-season right now so I can't talk to him about hockey, perhaps remind him in a sneaky way that there's something he'd like to live for, even if it's seeing the next face-off. I don't care what gets the job done, so long as it's done.

"Tony, I'm very concerned about you."

"What for? I'm feeling pretty good."

"If that's true, I'm glad for it, but I'm having trouble under-standing what's changed over the past few weeks. We haven't tinkered with your meds, you haven't tried anything new in terms of therapy. Maybe you took up yoga and you forgot to mention it? Or…"

I don't want to say it out loud. Perhaps if I keep my suspicions to myself, they won't manifest. That is the worst kind of supersti-tion and I won't allow it to overtake my professional acumen. Also if I don't do everything in my power to stop him from taking his own life, I'll regret it. No matter what, I'm sure I'll come up with something I could've done differently, better, because why couldn't I have done more?

"Or maybe your suicidal ideation has become rather active and you've been making plans. Suicide is never the answer. We still have things we can try, and you have a family. Emily and Portia and Clara. You're a good man, and I know you wouldn't abandon them."

His brows gather for a split second before he smiles at me. It's creepy as hell. "Don't worry, doc. Everything's going to be fine."

"You're not giving me reason to believe that's true."

Tony looks up at the clock and pushes out of the chair. "Time's up, I gotta go."

I want to block the door, prevent him from leaving, call up inpatient care and get the process started on committing him, but

I can't. He's given me no concrete reason to believe he's going to take his own life, and my hands are tied without it.

In desperation, I stand in front of the door. Not so close he can't leave, but close enough that it's going to be uncomfortable for him to get by. I don't like it, but my panic has reached stomach-twisting levels.

"You don't have to do anything yourself. Just say you're thinking about harming yourself or others and then it's out of your hands. Then I can do something. Please, let me help you."

"You have."

And then he shoulders by me. Not roughly, only the same jostle you'd experience on a crowded subway. No way could I call it an assault. Unfortunately. It's only when I sit down at my desk that I realize he didn't say it. Same thing he always says on his way out. There was no "See ya, doc," and I hope to God I'm wrong, all wrong about this, and I will in fact see him again.

~

STARLA

When I do my accounting, I like to listen to music. Loud music. I always deal with numbers during the day because my brain is sharper for them then, and it didn't occur to me that many people would be around my building during the day since, you know, working. I was promptly disabused of this notion when my neighbor dropped by one evening and asked if I was planning to audition for *Wicked*.

I've never gotten over my embarrassment sufficiently to sing at all anymore, and while I still like to blast something in my earholes while I take on my finances, I do it with headphones. Today I'm listening to all the things Rick Astley is never going to do to me on repeat because I don't know, I am. Does Lowry know what rickrolling is? Maybe I should teach him...

I pick up my cell to text him when a hand lands on my shoulder.

I'm very on top of who is supposed to be in my apartment at any given moment. Holden, my housekeeper Sofia, any maintenance people. Lowry doesn't have a key yet, though I don't know why not, he should, but he wouldn't just…show up. No, only women who've had the precisely wrong amount of prosecco do that. All of this probably explains why I throw an elbow and, after standing up, a punch.

My headphones have been ripped off my head and the cord out of my laptop, so now my entire building is being serenaded by the baby-faced British rocker. Great. Also, my knuckles hurt and Tad is sprawled on my floor with a hand to his cheek.

Oopsies.

"What the hell, Starla?"

"What do you mean, 'What the hell, Starla?' I think I've got more of a right to ask, 'What the fuck, Tad?' What are you doing here? Don't you know how to use a buzzer or knock or pick up a fucking phone? Jesus Christ, you scared me half to death."

"Well, you've probably given me a black eye."

"I don't feel bad about that at all. You're lucky I didn't do worse. How did you get in here anyway?"

He shrugs. "I still have my key."

Note to self: get Holden to change the fucking locks.

"And you thought it was okay to use it? We haven't been together for years. What the fuck is wrong with you?"

Tad is clearly expecting me to offer him a hand up, but he is clearly mistaken. I shut my laptop instead, so we can stop shouting over Rick.

When I turn back, he's on his feet, brushing his hands over his thighs. "Aren't you going to offer me an ice pack?"

"No. I'm going to offer you a nice tall glass of get the fuck out of my house, though."

"Such language. Doesn't your daddy wash your mouth out with soap for having a potty mouth like that?"

The wave of emotion that crashes over me is complex. I hate this fucking fucker for a thousand different reasons, and I have no idea why he'd know about Lowry. I've certainly never mentioned him in a board meeting. I wish I had some witty comeback, but I'm overwhelmed and then ticked off at myself because he clearly takes my silence for confirmation that I do in fact have a daddy.

"Huh. I knew you were seeing someone."

Now I'm even angrier at myself. That dickhead was bluffing and I've as good as confirmed it for him. I wish I'd have punched him harder, shoved a knee into his junk. He's not going to fall for a denial, but I can at least play it cool. "And why would you think that?"

"Because you weren't here when I stopped by this morning."

"This isn't the first time you've showed up uninvited and unannounced at my apartment? You are such a trash heap of a human being."

And thank god I brought my laptop to Lowry's last night. Would Tad have tried to break into it? What the hell? I'll have to be more careful. But what can I do about it if Tad wants to follow me or have someone follow me on his behalf? There's not really a damn thing I can do and fuck if I'm going to stop seeing Lowry while this shakes out. Not only do I not want do, I don't think I *could*.

"You should know he'll be here soon and I would advise you against being here when he arrives. He won't take kindly to you violating my home and my privacy."

I feel like there are bugs crawling all over my skin. So gross, so fucking gross. And while my use of *soon* might be overstating things a bit because Lowry won't be here for hours yet, he will be here and he will want to murder Tad. Well, he will if I tell him about this, but...I don't want to. If I have to, I will, but I don't have to yet. I can handle my own business. Like a grown-ass woman.

Tad spreads his hands like he's being the reasonable one here and I'm the overreacting shrew. "Starla, I came here to offer you my help."

I believe that not at all. "You've been badgering me for months and now you want to help me? Pardon me if I don't buy that story for a second."

"You can believe whatever you like, but it's true. I heard that Jerome Garrett has been sniffing around shares of Patrick Enterprises."

Jerome Garrett has been my father's biggest rival for years. Had been? They were often competing in the same industries, with one of them always one step ahead of the other. My father mostly despised the man because they'd been so fiercely competitive. Not in the way that you have drinks at the club after one of you wins either. More like I wouldn't have been surprised if one of them clubbed the other one to death if they'd found themselves on the same golf course.

"Why would he do that? He's got his own empire to run."

"Probably because he smells blood in the water. Knows you're weak. Let's face it, if I'm an investor in Patrick Enterprises, who would I rather have steering the ship? Jerome Garrett, who has successfully run a multinational, multibillion-dollar corporation for over thirty years or little Starla Patrick, who can barely run a tiny boutique consulting firm for other nutjobs like herself?"

Rage and embarrassment burn my sinuses, but I'm not going to cry in front of this dickhead. Even when we were together, he never knew what to do with me when I was upset. He sure did pick up on my sore spots, though.

"You are an investor in Patrick Enterprises and I don't think it would be in your best interest to have Garrett take over. You're one of my father's people, and I can't imagine that one of his first orders of business wouldn't be to get rid of you."

"Maybe so, but I'd be leaving with a pretty sweet golden parachute—not to mention if I sell out sooner rather than later, I'll get a nice chunk of change."

Five years ago, I would've said Tad wasn't capable of such a dick move, but now I'm not so sure. Or is he bluffing? How do I know? Although I'd never admit it to him, I'm not cut out for these corporate games of cat and mouse and double-crossing and whatever else these mostly old white guys do while they fuck around with other people's money. It's not an exhilarating rush like it was for my father—it scares the shit out of me that I am playing with people's futures. I don't want that. But I also don't want Tad doing it, because at least I'd try to be responsible. Whereas this fucking guy...

"What do you mean 'sooner rather than later'?"

"You really are just a pretty face, aren't you?"

He's lucky I only punched him in the face. Now I'm wishing I would have kneed him in the balls or stabbed him with my scissors or otherwise done more significant violence to his person.

Tad revels in my ignorance for a few more beats, smirking.

"This could get ugly. Very ugly. You think my little taunts hurt your feelings? In this kind of corporate warfare, there are no holds barred and Jerome Garrett is one of the most vicious people I know. He's going to go after your mental health, he's going to go after your sex life, he's going to after anything about you that could be used to embarrass or discredit you. When he does, the stock of Patrick Enterprises will tank, and he'll be able to snap up a controlling share on the cheap."

"It would be almost impossible for him to—"

"Didn't you listen to your father at all?"

I close my eyes against the image of my father sitting at his desk in the evening while I was still small, before my traitorous brain had ruined everything. "We're in the business of the impossible, Starla. Someone says you can't do something? That means you're going to."

It had taken me a while to realize that he stopped saying that to me when I was about fourteen. Probably around the time he realized I wouldn't "snap out of" my depression. Around the time I started to feel like he'd given up on me. He'd started saying it again in the past few years and my relief was palpable. He possibly thought I was worthy. That I hadn't entirely failed. I only felt the desolation of how much I'd let him down, shamed him, when it stopped. So, fucking yes, I listened to my father, but Tad won't let me get a word in edgewise.

"Even if you didn't, Jerome Garrett sure as fuck did. 'We're in the business of the impossible'? It won't be easy, but he could make this happen."

Fuck. I'll have to run some numbers and look in some of those piles of reports and figure out exactly how difficult it would be for Garrett to get a controlling share of Patrick Industries. I hold 49 percent of the stock, he'd have to basically form a coalition of every other stockholder to override me. One would assume that would be nigh on impossible, but shit. Shit. I need to study up and then I had best make a decision.

Before anything else, though, I need Tad out of my apartment because I sure as fuck can't think clearly with this douche canoe messing with my head.

"Perfect. Thanks for the heads-up. Do you need anything else? Didn't think so. Get the fuck out before I call building security and have you escorted out of here."

Again with the "whoa, crazy lady, take it easy," hands, and he's backing toward the door. He steps into the hallway but doesn't close the door until he sends a parting shot: "Tick tock, Starla. Better make a decision quick otherwise your father's legacy could end up trashed and you'll have no one to blame but yourself."

It's so tempting to throw something at the door, but he'd probably enjoy that and I don't want to give him the satisfaction. What I do want is to talk to Lowry. My watch says it's three forty-five, so he should be on his way back to his office from the gym. First, I'll compose myself because even though I want the comfort of his voice, I can't take him digging. I'll surely spill all my troubles, and then he'll back away slowly because that isn't the kind of disaster he signed up for. I take a few breaths and then make the call, having to wait only a couple of beats before he picks up.

"Well, this is a nice surprise."

Yes, that's what I needed. My shoulders sink down from my ears at hearing his gentle burr, the way he sounds genuinely delighted that I'm calling him unexpectedly.

"Maybe I'll have an even better one for you later. Are you still coming over?"

It's not flattering to sound insecure, but that will raise fewer red flags than having a meltdown, which at this point is my other option. Maybe he'll think I'm being flirty. Sure, let's go with that.

"Wouldn't miss it."

"And hey, I was thinking if you don't have plans next weekend, maybe we could go see Jade, and you could get a little, um, demo. If you want. Maybe even a lesson?"

There's a jostling sound I can't quite discern and then I hear Lowry offering someone an apology.

"Warn a man before you say something like that, will you? Nearly knocked a person into a bush."

That's not funny, but... Okay, yeah, it's kind of funny. Only because no one got hurt.

"Sorry, I didn't know asking if you wanted to watch one of my kink partners spank me and maybe get in on the act yourself would be so...discombobulating."

"Now you're doing it on purpose. Lucky for you, I was expecting it that time."

And I am expecting a very good time tonight and perhaps an even better one next weekend. Tad Harding can go jump in a sarlacc.

CHAPTER 23

L owry

THE HOUSE we drive to doesn't stand out in this part of Jamaica Plain. One of the grand Victorian homes that's been split into condos and apartments, it's well-maintained and painted a dark grey with aubergine shutters and doors. Does it matter? No, because this is where Starla's brought me and this is where we'll go.

Starla's been quiet on the way here, fingers knotted together in her lap, and I'm not sure what she's nervous about. Is she always an anticipatory bundle of nerves when she comes to see Jade? Or is it because I'm here? Is she worried I'll be turned off by this? Is she worried I'm going to embarrass her? I might do the latter entirely by accident, but I'm almost positive I won't be the former. I've had to keep my mind firmly on running through diagnosis codes to keep from being uncomfortably aroused the entire way here.

Once I've found a parking spot less than a block from the

house, I go round to open Starla's door and offer her a hand out. She'd said when we were discussing the details of this meet-up that, for her, going to see Jade isn't a thing that happens solely within the few hours that she sees her. It's a headspace she enters before the play even starts, and I can see it.

It was in the way she asked me to drive—she almost always takes the wheel if we'll be in the city. She's more confident in the crowded streets, and the road rage doesn't seem to seep into her in the same way it works its tendrils into me.

It's in the way she's dressed as well. The weather hasn't warmed up yet, but instead of the black nylon and down coat that goes down to her knees, she has on this very pretty blush-pink, not-exactly-peacoat. It's not boxy enough to be a true peacoat, and it looks—I don't know, is *twirly* a description you can use for coats? With big buttons and a bow at the belt and slightly puffy sleeves, it's nothing short of darling. Of course the black beret and houndstooth gloves don't do anything to take away from that impression either.

She clutches my hand as we walk up the sidewalk, and I'm at a loss for words. Squeezing her hand is almost always a good idea, though, so I do and she looks up at me, shy. It pokes at something in my chest. No, not *something*, I know damn well what it is. It's my heart.

I've seen Starla vulnerable before. It was something I prided myself on; her trusting me enough to tell me how she was really feeling even if it was unpleasant, even if it was downright scary or embarrassing. I hope that all holds true, because Christ. Her eyes are almost impossibly wide and the way she tips her chin and a smile flits across her face is... Ach, may as well be stabbed in my chest and die right now because I'll never see a more perfect look in all the rest of my days.

"I..." I clear my throat is what I do, because there's something trapped in my gullet. As soon as her face falls, though, I press on, choking be damned. I can choke later. "I'm looking forward to this. Bit nervous, though."

She laughs in a skittish way, short and edgy, like how a crystal chandelier sounds when someone slams a door. Lovely but fragile.

"Mmm, yeah, samesies."

Despite our nerves, I feel as though there's also a warmth flowing through us. Good intentions and a genuine...affection isn't strong enough. I knew a long time I ago I loved Starla. From each strand of dark hair on her head all the way down to the polished nails of her sweet, small toes. That has to count for something, right?

One of the stairs creaks as we head up to the porch and the front door. It's funny the things Americans consider very old. And sure, this house isn't new, but it's not exactly Elgin Cathedral or Spynie Palace, both of which you can find not so far from where I grew up.

Starla presses the bell with no hesitation, and there's not a long delay before a figure comes down the stairs. The infamous Jade. Is she infamous, though? When Starla talks about this woman, she gets this dreamy, peaceful look on her face. Which inspires some envy on my part, I won't lie. Does she look like that when she talks about me as well? A man can dream.

The door swings open and a woman who is nearing my height stands there, looking rather stylish in some wool trousers, a dark red sweater that clings to her, and a paisley silk scarf tied round her neck. She and my ex-wife might get their clothes at the same shops.

Except that Maeve would never look so soft. Not the way that Jade looks at Starla, like it's a delightful surprise that she's turned up as opposed to this being a very carefully orchestrated meeting.

"Come in, come in. It's cold out. And you with your bare legs, what a silly girl."

Starla blushes and I wonder if she'll argue with Jade. Her legs aren't bare, not technically. She's got on tights. But Starla doesn't say a word, just flushes, her cheeks getting pinker than her coat.

Once Jade's herded us inside the foyer, she rests her hands on Starla's biceps and leans down a bit so she can look her in the eye.

"Starla, darling, so good to see you. Come here."

Obediently, Starla drops my hand with a fleeting squeeze and steps into the embrace Jade has on offer.

I am definitely not jealous, not at all, of the way Starla presses into Jade, wraps her arms around the taller woman's waist and snuggles her head against what I can only think of as Jade's bosom.

Jade circles her arms around Starla and holds her for long seconds, rendering me utterly superfluous. Perhaps I shouldn't have come. What am I here for, anyhow? Starla doesn't need a chaperone, and these two are obviously capable of taking care of themselves. Each other. But that's not the point. The point is for me to learn, to see what it might be like to do all of these things with Starla without so much fumbling first. I should be grateful I've been invited at all, and I am.

When their embrace has finally ended, Starla steps back and takes my hand again.

"Jade, this is Lowry. Lowry, this is Jade."

Jade holds out an elegant hand; slender fingers meant to play the piano or harp, though large enough to span more than an octave. I give her a firm, but not hard, shake. I am in no way trying to compete with this woman. I have no right to. After all, she's been here for Starla after I abandoned her. Which, if Jade chose to play that card, it's one I can't beat. I do my best to look at pleasant and open as possible as I dip my chin in greeting.

"Pleasure. Starla's told me a lot about you."

Jade eyes me in an assessing way, and I suspect she's well-practiced at taking the measure of people with naught but a glance. I can't tell from her expression whether she finds me wanting.

"And I've heard quite a bit about you, Doctor Campbell."

Oof. Not Lowry, not even Mr. Campbell. If she's trying to remind me that she knows exactly who I am and precisely how I met Starla, she's done a bang-up job. Yes, I know very well and my conscience reminds me of it frequently. She needn't worry about me forgetting.

"Be nice, please."

Starla's soft request turns both our heads, and Jade releases my hand. "I did promise, didn't I?"

Starla nods and Jade responds with a huff and a pouty roll of her eyes. "Fine, then. But only for you."

I help Starla with her coat and nearly choke when I see what she's had on under it. Not overalls, because it's got a skirt on the bottom. A jumper? Is that what Americans call it? It's got the suspender type things that frame her breasts and a skirt I didn't notice was so short because it was under her coat. And the little ankle boots she's got on make her legs look long, like way too much of them is showing between the hem of the skirt and her ankles. It's nearly obscene, even though she's completely dressed. Her shirt has a rounded collar and buttons shaped like…are those paws? Christ.

When I can breathe again, I notice both the women are watching me. Starla with a wide-eyed, slightly terrified, hope-in-the-throat type expression, and Jade with a look that tells me if I'm an arsehole about this, I should prepare to have my throat slit. Probably with one of the spiked heels she's wearing.

But I'm not going to be an arse. At least, not in the way Starla's likely concerned about, why she's waiting with bated breath for me to say something, do something, react in any way whatsoever. No, the issue is that I like it.

Too much.

Way too goddamn much.

When I saw Starla as my patient, she was mostly in jeans and a sweater or a T-shirt. Sometimes a dress if it was summer. On occasion, she'd be in my office straight after school and she wouldn't have had time to change and I would see her in the uniform that posh institution insisted upon. No matter what she wore, she never looked as…childish, innocent as she does right now. And fuck me, because it's got my engines revving so very hard, and while my cock is sure this is the best thing to have ever happened in the history of things happening, my heart is equally enthusiastic.

My brain is somewhat more conflicted. The professional part of me that's studied kink and fetishes insists this is a completely normal and healthy part of human sexuality and experience. Be that as it may, there is also a part of my brain that is bellowing at me. Not just unkind things, but downright vile things. That I'm a pervert, a pedophile. Abuser. Someone who would take advantage of vulnerable people. People I have power over. Children. That I have more in common than the shade of my hair with my Uncle Sean.

But Starla is not a child. She is a grown, intelligent, independent woman. There is nothing I can do about our history aside from stay away from her, and I've seen how that turns out. Selfish though it may be, I'm not willing to do it again unless she tells me to go. This was not a thing I asked her for. This wasn't even something I knew about, not really, nor ever would expect.

There's a jab in my ribcage that makes the breath I've been holding come out in a flood. I'll be lucky if I haven't been staring, slack-jawed, drooling all over the floor.

Jade is glaring at me in a way that makes it clear she doesn't think I'm all that bright, and I had best say something before she tosses me out on my arse and goes about her evening with Starla just the pair of them.

"Ye…ye look brilliant, lass. Truly."

I've seen a lot of beautiful women in my life. Hell, I was

married to a beautiful woman. But never in my time on earth have I been so enchanted by a creature as I am by Starla at this very second. Makes my bollocks ache.

Starla smiles, shy, and turns a knee in, her foot pivoting on the toe of her boot. There is something different about her, as she said there would be, but I didn't think it would be so striking. It is, that—striking. It's as though I'm being struck in the chest, and not an elbow to the ribs like I got from Jade.

"Manners, kitten."

The admonishment from Jade comes as a shock to me, but not to Starla who merely turns a slightly deeper shade of pink—verging on red—and says to me, "Thank you."

"Right, then. Would you two like to stand here all day making eyes at each other or shall we get started?"

It's meant to be a rhetorical question, I'm sure, but to be perfectly honest, standing here and letting my gaze roam hot over every inch of Starla's body doesn't seem like a terrible use of my time. But I suspect if I can stop my gawping, I might get to touch her, and that would probably be better than looking at her. Maybe too much better and my head will explode. Probably worth a shot to find out, though.

Jade makes a gesture to Starla who then follows her, grasping Jade's hand, and I'm left to trail behind them. Which is fine. Gives me a chance to look at Starla's short skirt swinging a few inches below her deliciously round arse. And Jesus, are those…

Yes, she's wearing stockings. Not tights. Stockings, and it's one of those bizarre man things. Really, what is it about stockings that renders a man's brain scrambled eggs? They do, and never more so for me than when part of an outfit that can't decide whether it's sexy or innocent, apparently. I nearly trip over my own two feet when I start to wonder what her panties might look like.

Jade opens the door to her apartment and I follow the women inside. It's a nice place, homey but sophisticated. Dark wood on the floors and fancy wallpaper surround solid, graceful furniture. Jade fits in this place like she came out of central casting and I've a bit of a pang that my home isn't as well-suited to my tastes. That's what you get when you rent a generic apartment, unsure of how long it will take for you to settle, or if you'll settle at all.

"Let's do your hair, lovey."

Starla's lips part and she looks over her shoulder at me, that nervous pallor stealing over her cheeks.

"Ah." Jade catches Starla by the point of her chin and turns Starla's head so their gazes meet. "Don't worry. We'll get to him soon, but this part is for us. We'll do as we've always done and he can watch if he likes. Do you understand?"

Starla rolls her lips between her teeth before she answers, but it's a yes, as I knew it would be.

This isn't how I pictured a session with a domme. Whips and chains and leather and crawling and her insisting on being called Mistress would be more like it. But I suppose the trappings don't matter as much as the feelings do, and it's clear Jade is in charge here and that we'll do as she says. Me because I'm not in a hurry to make enemies with this woman, and Starla because... Well, I think A) she likes it, but also, B) it's perhaps a relief for her.

Jade tugs Starla down the hallway and I trail after them into a room that's decorated much like the rest of the house, though this one has a bed, an armchair, and a bureau. And there's a dressing table where Starla sits. I park myself in the armchair and try to be invisible. A fly on the wall.

Jade removes the tie from Starla's pert ponytail and runs her fingers through the long, dark locks she loosed before picking up a hairbrush from the vanity.

When Jade starts brushing her hair, I swear to God Starla purrs. As when I petted her—not patted—her eyelids fall closed, lashes fanning over her cheeks, and she tips her head to the side. Jade takes her time and it makes my fingers itch. I've never had a strong desire to brush a woman's hair, and for the life of me I can't imagine why not. Starla looks so dreamy and pleased, like a kitten in the sun. I want to be her sun, something that gives her light and warmth and happiness.

After a few minutes, Jade murmurs something in her ear and a slow smile curls up the corner of Starla's mouth. Is this what angels look like? I think it must be. And then Jade is taking up a comb, moving more purposefully than her relaxed and soothing strokes of the brush that she was making before. When she's done, Starla has a straight part down the center of her scalp, her waves of hair separated into pigtails, and when she notices my reflection in the mirror, she gets that apprehensive look again.

My hand's been resting on my chin, fingers in front of my mouth, and I'm surprised she can't feel the weight of my regard. I've been staring, shamelessly, but there's no way for her to know that I like what I see. Very much. I've become so practiced at having a blank expression sometimes I have to remind myself a flat affect isn't always appropriate. Starla doesn't need equanimity from me right now. She doesn't need neutrality, a blank canvas to project her own feelings onto. She knows her feelings about this, rather well, and she needs to know mine.

Holding her gaze, I let my fingers slip to beneath my mouth, and stroke the growth of beard at my chin. Give her a smile. One I hope conveys just how okay this is with me, precisely how lovely I think she is, and exactly how badly I'd like to wrap one of those pigtails around my fist and pull her toward me to kiss.

STARLA

I've heard the expression *eye-fucking* before, but I didn't know what it meant until now. Because that's what Lowry is doing. His gaze hot on mine, his knuckles skimming the scruff below his lip, as though he'd like to be touching something else, but that not being available, an absentminded stroke of his coarse facial hair will do for now. He wants me. And I want him.

It's such a relief to have brought him here, to have seen so far how he feels about the things I enjoy. Yes, we've done some daddy play and he seemed to enjoy it a lot, but this isn't a passing thing for me, and he needs to understand that.

His initial positive response doesn't mean the rest will go smoothly, of course, but at least he's—I don't know, granted the premise? At a baseline level, he can see how these things I like to do could be sexy, fun. Not simply an indulgence. I've done that before, and I don't want to do it again. If he can't give me these things, it's not a deal-breaker. That's what I have Jade for. She understands my needs and she meets them. Without shaming and without judgment. With pleasure and I might even go so far as to say joy.

Speaking of Jade, there's a tug to one of my pigtails, a sensation that runs straight to my core, which she knows.

"Shall we get started, kitten? A spanking to begin, hmm?"

Oh. The synapses in my brain misfire. Not in the way that becomes increasingly obvious when I'm too far out from a treatment and my depression starts to drag me down again, but in a way that's caused by an overload of arousal and nerves. How many times have I told myself the story of Lowry taking me over his knee? For a punishment because I've been naughty and Daddy knows best what his little girl needs? Or because it turns us both on to have him warm my bottom with the palm of his large hand? Or perhaps because sometimes a person needs a good cry and I'm incapable of allowing myself to have one?

If it's because of feelings, it's not okay. If I cried because of feelings, it would mean I was weak, a failure, unworthy, and a mess. A disaster of a human being who can't regulate herself. But if he spanked me? Spanked me hard? For a very long time? Maybe with a hairbrush or a paddle or some other kind of implement or perhaps with those wide hands of his... That would be hard enough to hurt, now, wouldn't it? Physical pain is a completely acceptable reason to cry. Rational people do that all the time. And if we fucked afterward because I'd been writhing on his lap and I was soaked between my legs, then we would. Pleasurable side effect. Who couldn't use some of those?

So, yes, the idea of Lowry spanking me has held a central place in my fantasies, but that doesn't mean Lowry in the flesh will have this in common with Dream Lowry.

Regardless of how he feels about it, he's not going to be a dick. But I don't want that blank psychiatrist slate of a face, the one that is as unreadable as a chalkboard wiped clean. I want a human reaction. I don't want Doctor Campbell, I want Lowry the man, and it's terrifying to tell him so. To know the next couple of hours could change the way he feels about me forever. The thrill and the anxiety and the desire are almost overwhelming, but I swallow and shut my eyes, the image of Lowry still burned into my eyelids.

"Yes."

I'm not sure how I've gotten from the dressing table over to the chaise where Jade is sitting already, looking stern with the hairbrush in her hand. It's a special kind of twisted delight to be spanked with an implement that gave me such sweet pleasure a few minutes earlier. This too will be pleasure, but of a darker, more degenerate variety. Though who's to say? Floating off into subspace and becoming wet between my legs because Jade is brushing my damn hair could probably be considered degenerate. I'm not going to concern myself with that overmuch right now. Instead, the tension in my belly ratchets up and squeezes my lungs when Jade beckons to Lowry and pats the chaise toward the end where the back rises in an elegant curve.

He's been so very docile with her, which I like. He places a great deal of faith in expertise, and it would be the height of entitled male douchery for him to come in here, beating on his chest and insisting he be in charge because he has a dick. Jade is far more experienced than he is, and beyond that, this is our party—mine and Jade's. He's but a guest here. And if he's rude, he'll be asked to leave.

Like I knew he would, he goes over to the chaise and sits where Jade's indicated. And then they're both looking at me, and I think I might melt into a puddle on the floor.

Could this one day be a special treat? If I've been a very good girl, could this be something I ask for and receive? Two of my favorites, two of the people I hold in the highest regard, have the highest esteem for, topping me? Oh my. But that's not what this is. More of an informational session, and also, for Lowry, a job interview of sorts. Jade has been very skeptical that he could possibly be good enough for me, so I'm curious to see if he'll win her stamp of approval.

Jade curls a finger and I walk toward her until the rounded toes of my shoes nearly touch the pointed toes of her stilettos. Which is when she pats her lap.

This is always a fraught moment for me. Mmm, maybe fraught isn't the right word. It's a tipping point. The fulcrum of a seesaw, and which way am I going to tip? It's a familiar place, though not without tension for that, and I'm nearly trembling when I climb onto the chaise.

The low simmer of embarrassment when I prostrate myself over Jade's lap is usually part of the fun. It's not an absence of mortification but a tiny, manageable dose of it that somehow sends blood pulsing toward the apex of my thighs, making me swollen and sensitive. This, though, with Lowry here, is different. The humiliation cuts deeper. Which is the point, right? It cuts, doesn't scrape along the surface. It's that tip of the razor blade that digs into my skin where it's painful instead of being a shiver-inducing drag of excitement.

"Go on. Head in his lap, kitten." When I still don't move, her eyebrow kicks up in a dangerous curve. "I wasn't going to punish you, but I can."

Oh, definitely not. That is pushing this way too far. For the moment. I can imagine a day where Lowry might punish me himself—god, I want that—but that day is not today. For today I kneel on the chaise and close my eyes tight as I walk my hands over Jade's lap and then lower myself until my butt is in prime position for Jade and her hairbrush to have their way with it, my torso rests on the chaise between Jade and Lowry's thighs, and I…

I rest my head in Lowry's lap, my head turned toward his knees, and my hands resting on his thigh. Barely breathing, I want to squirm so badly. But I also want to be good. For them. So I try to locate my peace. I find it, yes, but it's more like I'm in the neighborhood than actually able to occupy it. Why did I think this was a good idea, again?

Oh, right. I wanted Lowry to get a better, more complete idea of what I like, to see if he likes it too, and thought it would be easier to have Jade here while he did. In the event that Lowry was not a fan, her presence would cushion the blow. And in the event he was, she'd be able to show him the ropes. And the paddles. And other things that might come in handy.

A touch on my thigh reminds me I haven't successfully paused time to dive into this morass of introspection. No, Lowry and Jade are both getting an eyeful of my dorsal side while my head spins. Overthinking and perseverating are specialties of mine and I'm making good use of them now.

Jade turns up my skirt, exposing my backside, and I suck in a breath, squeeze my eyes shut, my fingers tightening. This is for real, it's really happening. There's a sharp inhale above me a split second after my own, and I don't know if Lowry's gasping because the sight of my ass tipped into the air has taken his breath away or because I'm digging my fingers into his thigh. Could be either.

And then Jade is stroking my bottom. She makes a pleased low noise in her throat while tracing the embroidered straps that

271

make up most of this underwear. It's definitely more pretty than functional, but her approval makes me glow.

"Very pretty panties, kitten. I like these very much. They'll let me see that nice shade of red your bottom turns even before I peel them over your hips so I can see all of your cheeks."

My level of embarrassment has officially reached DEFCON two. I might die before this is over.

"Thank you," I mumble, wondering if Lowry can feel the heat of my breath through his wool pants. Always the professorial wool, it kills me.

"You can touch her if you like," Jade offers and then there's another touch in addition to the increasingly rough handling of my butt cheeks. Lowry's gently rubbing my shoulders with one hand while Jade has started kneading at the flesh of my buttocks. So many hands, and the contrasting touches are killing me. As Jade gets rougher, Lowry's hand moves to my neck and he rests it so that his thumb can stroke behind my ear, which makes me want to sigh and purr except that Jade's started pinching, grabbing, and...jiggling. That's the worst. So mortifying. But she likes it, and I don't dislike it enough to tell her to stop, to make it one of my limits that she's not permitted to cross. It's that goddamn embarrassment fetish of mine.

It's longer than it usually takes her to start laying into me when Jade says, "Look at him, kitten. Turn your head. I want him to see your pretty face while I spank your bottom."

Yes, I think Jade is quite enjoying this opportunity for additional embarrassment. I, on the other hand, am not. Am I not? Or am I? Perhaps it's the not being able to tell that has me buzzing like some heat-maddened fly. Regardless, I have to steel myself before I lift my head to turn my face.

Something I've always liked about being over Jade's knee is being taken from me—even as she's flipped up skirts or pulled down pants and underwear, spanked me, pushed her fingers inside me and brought me to orgasm, I've always had a measure of privacy in being able to hide my face from her. Now, though, I'm not afforded the luxury, and am instead being exposed, my innermost feelings flayed open for Lowry to feast on. And my god, would Freud have a field day with this scenario.

I force myself to open my eyes, to see the expression on Lowry's face, and when I do, what I see there stuns me. There's a mix of arousal and tenderness that goes straight to my heart, and zings quickly to between my legs. Yes, this is what I want. What I've always wanted from him. Benevolence and nurturing but also wanting to fuck me into next week. My lips part to say I don't know what, but as I hold his intense gaze, Jade's hand lands on my butt.

Open hand on the fleshiest part of my bottom, it's a stinging slap designed to get attention. Yes, we're getting started now.

$\mathcal{L}$owry

I HAD KNOWN there was something missing. Knew it in a restless, poked-at way. As though there were a mosquito buzzing about and I couldn't see it, only hear it, and couldn't slap the damn thing to kill it. The sound of Jade's hand hitting Starla's bottom and the way my Star's mouth forms a perfect O in surprise when it does... What I wouldn't give to have that be my hand.

Caressing Starla's shoulders and neck, cupping her cheek and toying with her pigtail are delightful, wonderful, don't get me wrong. I would take her head in my lap any day of the week over just about any other activity I can think of. But my God...I would like to make those expressions flit over her face, feel my hand bounce off the flesh of her bottom, force those noises from her throat. It's a symphony of gasps, grunts, squeaks, squeals, cries, and giggles as Jade lays into her. The way Starla squirms and writhes while trying to keep her movements in check is delightful. As is the press of her breasts against my thigh and the way she buries her face in my legs before Jade scolds her and forces her to turn her head toward me again so I can see her. Yes, I want to see her.

My beautiful girl.

And yes, I know very well she's a grown woman. An intelligent, industrious, indomitable woman. But in this moment, she's also a girl who's turned over Jade's knee and receiving a spanking for no discernible reason other than they both like it.

I had wondered if this was going to be a role-playing thing, but it's not really. It's a different side of Starla than I'm used to seeing, but it's still very much her. The her I've caught glimpses of. The one who desperately wants to be small and guided and taken care of. Not that a person needs a reason to want those things, but I can imagine why this would feel good to her. Being told for so long that there was a limit to the love she was allowed. That she could only take up so much of someone's time and energy. I get it, sort of. People are not bottomless wells of compassion and sympathy and nurturing. We all get tired at some point. Overwhelmed, overtaxed. But we all have different tolerances for being needed as well, and I suspect her father's was rather low. No shame in that, and I know he did his best by her, but...she needed more than that and I wasn't able to give it to her then. I can now.

Jade is striking her rather hard now, and Starla's arse has gone from a pale cream to a nicely warmed allover pink and is starting to turn red in places. The giggles have disappeared, and the noises now consist of mewls, whimpers, cries, and yelps.

Here's yet another surprise: I've always fancied myself a gentle man, but those sounds have my dick straining at the front of my pants and it doesn't help that Starla's pain-twisted face is within licking distance of my cock. Christ.

The thing is, I've seen her in true pain before, anguish. Not that this isn't hurting her, because I think it really fucking is and I can understand why—she's being hit awfully hard. But it's by *choice.* She could make this stop at any moment, and she's choosing not to. I'm not entirely sure why and maybe she doesn't know herself, although I'll ask her about it later because I'm curious, but she's getting something out of this.

"Hold her wrists, would you? It's time for the hairbrush and it's not meant for rapping knuckles. She's gotten a bit out of control as you can tell."

Tell? She looks incredibly composed while she's catching her breath. Yes, she'd been moving a lot, but who can blame her? I sure as hell wouldn't be able to lay there, draped over anyone's lap, being *hit.* Yes, I understand it's fundamentally different for her than it would be for me, and yet, it hurts, and she's allowing it. And she's going to tolerate a hairbrush? For fuck's sake.

Jade is eyeing me, likely speculating on whether I have the stomach for this. To hold Starla down while Jade beats her arse with a hairbrush. I absolutely do, because my cock is pulsing with want and arousal thinking about my hands circling Starla's slim wrists and holding her fast, and the idea of paddling her bottom isn't unappealing—at all—I just…need a minute. There's a difference between feeling that an act is fundamentally okay in a global way and actually performing it oneself.

Starla's caught her breath by now, though, her inhales and exhales coming slow and even, and she's looking up at me from where her head is cradled in my lap, scratching gently at my thigh through the fabric of my pants. Is she taunting me, daring me? Her sass is perhaps a front for fearing I won't do it. Either way, there's only one thing to do.

I catch up her wrists, one in each hand, and place them at the small of her back, gathering them into one hand. Aside from this being hot as all hell, I don't want her to get hurt. Not for real, anyhow, and reaching her hands into the path of the hairbrush is a sure way to do that.

After she's secured to my satisfaction, I look back to her face to see if she's still okay. Her expression reads to me like gratitude and it tugs at something inside me. Am I reading her right? When she mouths, "Thank you," I know for sure I am. Clutches my heart in a harder, more thorough way.

I don't want to say you're welcome, because I owe her as much thanks as she owes me. Not that she owes me anything. It seems the right thing to do is to brush some hair back from her face and stroke her cheek with the pad of my thumb. Tell her in more than words that I'm grateful for her. More than she could ever know. So, with one hand I restrain her, and with the other I pet and stroke her. If that doesn't encapsulate what Starla enjoys, I don't know what does.

$\approx$

STARLA

I could die happy like this. Not that I want to die—I've spent an awful lot of my life trying not to die—but if I had to, this wouldn't be a terrible way to go. Lowry's stroking my hair and dragging his thumb across my cheek and the only thing I could want more than this is to take his thumb in my mouth. Suck on him while his other hand is pressing my wrists into the small of my back. Hell, I wouldn't say no if he unzipped his pants and stuffed his cock down my throat. But that would be unwise given that I'm about to take a beating. I wouldn't put anything...delicate in between my teeth during that—it seems risky. God knows I wouldn't want to hurt Lowry at all, but especially not damage his beautiful cock.

Sometimes Jade gags me during this part, but she won't this time. Won't want to set a bad example for Lowry since she wouldn't gag me if we were brand-new to playing with each other. Nor will she want to spare him from what this is like, for better or for worse. She wants him to hear me, see my face contort, I know it.

And then there's the smooth plane of wood rubbing over my cheeks. They're sensitized, tenderized already from the hand-spanking I've had, and the sensation is far more intense than had Jade done this when we first began. A hand brushing over my skin would set me to tingling, and this is nearly electrifying. I shift my hips in anticipation and I get a short, sharp tut of the brush for my trouble that makes me gasp. Oh, yeah, this is going to be a lot. She was very thorough with her hand and that's going to make this a more intense experience for me.

Like that. *Shit.*

A more serious crack of the brush across the fleshiest part of my bottom has me gasping for breath and my shoulders rising, as though I could escape that way. Of course I can't. I know better than that. Even when it's only me and Jade, I can't, and now I've got Lowry ceasing his petting to press down between my shoulder blades in a way that makes me groan. There's no escape, I have to take this. And if I do, I will make them both happy and will have earned whatever kind of affection and care they see fit to bestow upon me afterward.

Which is maybe kinda messed up? Do most people assume they're worthy, deserving of affection? Kindness? Spoiling? Care? Cosseting? Or am I not as alone as I think in needing to prove myself worthy, of earning that, of repaying the person, or rather, putting a down payment on any sweetness they might have for me? Regardless, this is how I've chosen to receive this and it lets me have affection without embarrassment, without questioning why I'm receiving it. It's obvious.

Which is why, despite it hurting like fuck, I relish the way the paddle strikes my ass, builds up heat, and is surely painting the pale skin a mottled red. Perhaps, if I'm lucky, with some bruises that will remind me of everything we've done here for days to come. Trophies, yes, of being strong enough to handle what Jade dished out, but also souvenirs from a time very much enjoyed.

My mouth works in ways I can't control, parting on a yelp,

tightening on a squeal and squeak, flying wide open with a cry as Jade takes a crack at a spot she's been hitting over and over and over. My god, that's painful. And when Lowry swipes at a spot of saliva at the corner of my mouth, I can't help it.

I lick the pad of his thumb and then suck it inside, groaning with satisfaction when I can surround it with my mouth and suck it deep and hard. Makes it easier to take the stinging pain on my backside, how there's pain on impact, yes, but how it also radiates and stays long after the hairbrush has moved on to other parts of my bottom, the backs of my goddamn thighs. It's when Jade hits me there that I'm most tempted to swear, but I'm also acquainted with the consequences of spitting curses at her. So I'll keep sucking at Lowry's thumb and trying to breathe because I've been scolded often for forgetting.

You wouldn't think it would be possible to forget to breathe, but when you're being smacked and hit and swatted, it's easy to hold your breath. Trying to manage pain is a tricky thing, and all sorts of normal, everyday things get left by the wayside. Which is one of the wonderful things about this: when you're trying to figure out how you're going to accept the next blow, when you're trying as hard as you can not to break down into tears, it's easy to forget about pretty much everything else. That deadline you missed, that email you need to write, the nagging decisions you haven't made, how you've disappointed your father—yeah, everything.

I can feel it now, sneaking up on me, that feeling of being near the edge, of being so close to tipping over from *I can do this* into *I cannot fucking take this anymore*. Sometimes Jade will make me tell her—how many more swats I can take and I know she'll make them hard and that I'll have to count. It's a kind of game I play with myself. How many can I take for her, how many will it take before I break down? I don't want to guess too many because then I won't be able to make it and I'll feel shitty about disappointing her, but I also don't want to make it too few because I want to be strong for her and also prove myself. *I am tough, I am strong, look at everything I can take.*

I don't think she's going to force me to do that today, which is fine since I have too much swirling around in my head already, though at the moment it's static: a background thing, muddled together and happening somewhere in the distance. I've hit that deeper level of subspace now. Not the slightly disconnected pleasant feeling of letting things happen and not acting over-much to try to prevent them, but that push under the water that makes me feel surrounded.

Nothing matters now except feeling, and I am feeling. Every inch of my body is alive and I feel *more.* Hypersensitive as though my nerves are straining toward any stimulus and intensely aware of what is happening now. The only things from the past that matter are the ways in which Jade prepared my body for what she's visiting upon it now. Pain on top of more pain. Sting on top of ache, heavy thwack on top of an already stoked fire.

Which is when it happens. Really fucking hard on top of a spot she's been paying special attention to since she bared my bottom, and that was the hardest she's hit me all night, no joke. Most of the time, I have a hard time distinguishing between how hard she's hit me. A softer swat can feel ouchier after she's hit me there before. But this—*this*—I can guarantee that this is hard. So hard I almost choke myself around Lowry's thumb instead of laving it. Fuck, *fuck.*

All of a sudden, I am there, very fast. That point at which the pain stops being manageable and becomes way too fucking much. The reflex of fight or flight I've been able to control breaks free of the tethers that held it. All of a sudden, this stops being a fun game and becomes terrifying. My body no longer gives a shit that if I say stop this stops. Fear overtakes me and everything human about me flees.

I have enough presence of mind to look up at Lowry as the next strike falls, and as our gaze connects, I think he can sense it or can read the expression on my face. He must, because unlike before when he's silently studied me, even seemed painfully pleased with my predicament, he says, "I see you," a split second before Jade whales on me again. Those three simple words buoy me, but I still freak the fuck out when the strike lands. Because it hurts enough to force me to tears and pained gasps, to render me into a mass of panic.

I'm not fighting because I can, I'm now fighting because I can't not.

Lowry releases my wrists and I hear him say, "Stop," but not to me, even though he's looking in my eyes.

At this point, I'd usually curl up in Jade's lap, cry on her shoulder while she caresses and soothes me, tells me what a good job I've done, how strong and brave I've been, how pleased with me she is, and how I'm okay. I'm okay because it's over.

What she won't say is that I can lose my shit because I'm allowed to now. That I have earned the right to cry and fall apart because I've withstood pain and punishment and humiliation and anyone under those fucking circumstances would be within their rights to hardcore lose it.

But I hear it nonetheless when we're together because she knows. She knows why I do this, what I get out of it, even as my butt is bruised and sore for days, even during the times when I've yelled at her that I hate her and that this hurts like a mother-fucker and she's an asshole for doing this. Sure, I get mocked and punished for that too, but I'm allowed to say those things, allowed to be angry and hurt, which I haven't been permitted to for most of my life. Except with Lowry. He always let me have my feelings. He's letting me have them now.

I am a mess, a wreck. The tears are flowing uncontrollably and I'm scrambling at, scratching at, anything I can get ahold of because I need something. Someone. I need to be held, reas-sured. I've done my time and now I want my reward. I want to be cuddled and consoled. And now my mind is faced with a question when usually I don't have to deal with any: Jade or Lowry?

They're both here. I'm...on both of them. While my inclination is to climb into Lowry's lap, I don't want to betray Jade. She's been here for years. Met my needs whereas Lowry abandoned me, even if I understand why now. Will she feel badly if I choose him? I don't want her to. But isn't that what he's here for? To see what this is like? To make an informed decision? To see the full burden of what it's like to be with me, what I want? Because no one has had to take this on before. They've all gotten off easily. Or not, as the case may be.

Irritation pricks the back of my neck and frustration rises to the surface of my desperation because it's not fair that I should have to think about such things when this hasn't been part of the toll I've been expected to pay before. It's too much and tears of frustrated rage are about to join those of fear, pain, and release.

Could I be a little less of a disaster at some point? Pretty please? Although Jade can't be surprised by how overwrought I am, this is par for the course. And Lowry... Well, he likely remembers this kind of tantrum from the ones I would throw on occasion because it wasn't fucking fair. It's still not.

But I've come a long way since then, found people who can service my needs, including Jade who is as good as a mind reader sometimes. That's what really good dominants seem like sometimes. Even though they don't really read minds. They pay attention and observe to an extent that's mind-boggling to most people, myself included.

Jade's voice, soft but clear, thankfully cuts through my confusion. "Go to him, it's fine. You're not going to hurt my feelings."

Permission given, I crawl into Lowry's lap in a wildly undignified way and fling my arms around his neck, burying my face in the crook between his neck and shoulder. A space that feels like it was made for me, and that allows me to inhale him.

There's the scent of sweat and I can't tell if it's from now or if it's soaked into his shirt collar from past wears. It doesn't matter. It makes him more human. He smells like warmth and the faint tang of arousal and also the aftershave or cologne that used to make me go weak in the knees. It still does. And whether that's from memories or the present, does it really matter? I'm going to go ahead and say no. Because the fact is that at this very moment, I've never felt safer, more contained. My feelings aren't too big for Lowry, they don't scare him. The only time I've ever scared him was when I told him I was thinking about hurting myself, taking my own life, and frankly that seems fair. And still he kept it from me so I wouldn't hide it from him in the future.

In the present, his solid arms are wrapped tight around me, as though I'm the life raft he's clinging to instead of the other way around. But no—there's a quality to his embrace that there isn't in mine. Mine is desperate, wild, clutching. His is confident, strong, comforting.

Especially when he begins to croon in my ear.

The very sound of it makes me pause. Pause is maybe too strong of a word because I'm still sobbing uncontrollably. But control seems like a possibility now. Perhaps out of my reach at the moment, but a thing I have a chance in hell of attaining.

"Starla, love. Shh. You're going to be okay."

"It hurt."

"Oh, I know. You're a marvel, being able to take that. Really, flat-out incredible. I couldn't believe it. Still can't. You're so strong."

The wonder in his voice can't be faked, and even as I relive that panicked moment between the penultimate and ultimate strikes, pride laps at me, soothing the sting of the pain and the panic.

"Still?"

Has seeing me like this changed his mind? Does he think now that he's overestimated my capabilities? Was he impressed before and now that I'm bawling in his lap like a child who's skinned their knee, will he reevaluate and determine I've actually been exaggerating every damn thing I've come crying to him about?

"More than ever. You're my Star. You light the place up. You're so brave and I could never... Can you breathe for me, darling? Please? Nice and slow. You're not going to fall if you pass out because I've got you and I'm not letting you go for anything, but I know you can do it. If you can take a beating like that, a few inhales and exhales ought to be cake."

It's not the same, but I try to do as he's asked and it's made easier by homing in on his own respiration. Which he's maybe exaggerating for me to follow as his hand circles my back, but I don't care if he's pandering to me. That's what I do this for: to earn the spoiling and the coddling. I'll take it as I concentrate on the way the air moves in and out of my lungs. Slower, slower until we're nearly synched.

And because I can, I lick at the skin of his neck above his collar, lick and nibble and suck because it's a comfort and I like the taste of him on my tongue. He might have a bruise where I'm working my mouth over his flesh, but he doesn't complain, doesn't try to stop me. Just lets me comfort myself by soaking in the shelter of his body.

LOWRY

Starla's mouth is still open on my neck, her tongue occasionally stroking the light stubble there in a way that's making my pants incredibly uncomfortable. She makes these small noises as she nuzzles at me and her fingers are tangled in the cotton of my shirt. Sweet little Starla, who can take a beating that would make men twice her size cry.

I've been talking to her, telling her how incredible she is, how impressed with her I am, but she doesn't seem to be listening anymore. If anything, she seems as though she's on the verge of consciousness, slipping down to sleep.

Jade gets up from the chaise and brings over a fluffy blanket, a pastel pink and purple thing that looks starkly out of place amongst the dark elegance of our surroundings. She shrugs at my questioning look. "It's her favorite."

I'm glad Starla is sharing this with me, and I try to tamp down the envy I have for Jade—that she has been able to gather up these pieces of Starla, learn her innermost secret cravings, desires, and preferences. I want to know those things. I want to be able to hand them to Starla without her having to ask. I'd love it if she would and I wouldn't refuse her, but it's also hard to ask.

"You might want to scoot back," Jade offers with a lift of her chin. "She gets heavy."

Yes, that's a good idea since Starla is already weighing on me, and I don't think she's hit that deadweight stage of sleep yet. Her noises have drifted off into nothingness and her head has slipped down to be cradled in my shoulder instead of having her mouth at my neck. Probably a good thing because I might've died of one of those three-hour erections those ED ads are always on about.

Trying not to wake her, I shift so my back's against the high side of the chaise and my arm that's behind her is supported. I don't mind a bit of strain but I also don't want to have to wake her up because my arm's gone dead. When I'm settled, Jade drapes the blanket over Starla and tucks it in around her. She's obviously very fond of Starla, and I can't blame her at all.

"How long are you going to hold her for?" Jade asks as she sits at the opposite end of the chaise and slips off her shoes, revealing perfectly polished burgundy toenails.

I shrug as well as I can with the shoulder that's not occupied by a snoozing Starla. "As long as it takes, I suppose, unless you have plans and need us out."

Jade studies me and I try to maintain my composure under

her scrutiny but it's not easy because I feel as though her gaze is penetrating me, reaching into my brain to extract information.

"She's not as tough as she seems, you know. I mean, the woman can take a hell of a spanking and other kinds of torments besides, but she's..." Jade purses her lips and her gaze flickers to Starla, loyalty and fondness there. "But I suppose you think you know that already."

I have been on my best behavior here. I'm not on my own turf, Jade and Starla have a history and relationship of their own that I've been respectful of. But for this woman to tell me I don't understand the ways in which Starla is delicate? That's a load of rubbish and she ought to know it.

"Ah." Jade holds up a hand like she knows I was about to unleash a torrent of "I've known Starla Elizabeth Patrick since she was fourteen years old" and is not here for it. "She's told me about you. I know you were the savior doctor who she credits with being alive. Which, fine. My understanding is that she has her depression really well under control and a bunch of the best doctors in the world to help her keep it there. That's not your job anymore.

"What I'm talking about is that there's a very delicate balance you have to strike in the way you treat her. She's smarter than I am, tougher than I am, and god knows she could buy my entire life a million times over with all the money she has. I've never had to worry about all of that because it is literally my job to make her feel small, vulnerable, a little embarrassed. You know why she lets me do that?"

Yes, I would like to be let in on any secrets Jade can share with me. "Why?"

"Because I've never given her a reason not to. I have always stuck to our arrangements, I have always played our game. She can be like this here, with me, because I've never asked her to be anything else and at the end of a few hours, she takes out her pigtails and leaves. I don't ask her about the rest of her life, I don't inquire about her health aside from asking about new injuries that I need to know about. She thinks you could be everything to her, which I think is a risky proposition for anyone, but this isn't about me. My point is that if you tease her about this or make her feel bad about it in anyway, it will hurt her deeply. And then I will be forced to hurt you deeply."

"Are you…"

"Yes, I'm threatening you, and don't you think for a second that it's only a threat. I hurt people like Starla for pleasure, but I also hurt people for money, and if you make Starla feel bad or sick or wrong in any way for wanting this, for needing it, it will be my pleasure to hurt you for free."

I'd like to think I've led a fairly interesting life during my fifty-one years on the planet, but never have I ever been threatened by a dominatrix. I didn't know that she also does this professionally, Starla hadn't mentioned that. Only that Jade was a partner of hers.

"Understood, but I have no intention of hurting her. Ever. I have spent a great deal of time and energy protecting Starla Patrick and I will keep doing so until the day I die."

"Says the man who abandoned her fifteen years ago."

"You can't honestly tell me you'd have had me stay here and—"

"Don't you fucking even, doc. She was a child. You were an adult. You had a responsibility to her that you abdicated because you couldn't control your dick."

It's a shock to the system to hear it put so baldly though I've berated myself for the same reason for years upon years. I open my mouth but Jade shakes her head.

"Yes, Starla told me about your conversation but honestly it wasn't news to me. Just a confirmation of my suspicions of why you left. So you want to know what I would've had you do if it had been up to me? I would've had you do anything you needed to remain professional and care for her like you were obligated to. She literally could've died. Did you think about that? Because you couldn't keep it in your pants, you self-centered, oversexed, woe-is-me asshole with a fucking Lolita complex. Fuck you."

Starla stirs in my arms and the feel of her anchors me. I'd like Jade's approval because Starla clearly respects the woman a great deal. But I don't know that there's anything I could say to convince her I'm not a terrible person. She's right, and I need to live with that.

"I worried about her every day. I thought about her all the time. And you're right. If I were a better man, a stronger man, then I would have been able to shut down every inappropriate feeling I had for her. I like to think that if I'd stayed, nothing would've happened. But the only way I felt certain I could guarantee that was to leave. It's not an excuse. It's entirely my fault. If there were some way I could make it up to her, I would. The best I can do now is to love her and try to figure out how we can make this work now that we're both adults and we still have these feelings for each other. It won't be easy, but I'm not going anywhere. Not unless she tells me to. I swear on my life."

Jade stares at me, looking as though she wants to cut off my bollocks, stuff them in my mouth, and then cut off my head. She doesn't trust me and, if our positions were reversed, I can't say I'd trust her either. But the only way to earn those stripes is to do your time. Put in the work. Show up every day and prove that you're not a leaf in the wind, but a tree with roots grown deep. That I will shelter Starla as well as I can while trying not to stifle or suffocate her.

In response to my promise, Jade shrugs.

"Look, Starla's a big girl and she makes her own choices. She's choosing you. And I hope for her sake that she's choosing well. And if she hasn't, I'll be here to clean up the mess you doubtless will have made on your way out. Again."

CHAPTER 25

 tarla

LAST WEEKEND with Jade went well. Like, *really* well. And when we went back to Lowry's apartment, we had some of the best sex I've ever had, oh yes, we did. Tonight, Lowry's coming to pick me up and take me out for a late dinner. Late not because either of us had a late meeting or anything, but because we're going to play before we go out.

Yes, sometimes it's fun to squirm with anticipation through a meal, but sometimes it's equally as fun to have to sit on your freshly spanked ass at a really nice restaurant and have your daddy offer you bites of food from his plate. To anyone else, it would probably look like a well-off couple—with, yeah, a bit of an age gap—having a romantic dinner, but nothing scandalous. Nothing kinky. Certainly not anything that's making you wet under the freshly pressed table cloth because you're wearing frilly panties that not only make you feel little but also create added friction against the tender flesh of your bottom where your daddy left bruises and welts. Yeah, we'll probably fuck when we get home too.

Home.

I love my tiny apartment. Have always loved it. And Lowry has never said a word against it—I think after we talked about it he understands why I live here in addition to respecting that decision. It's not his to make, it's mine, so that's how it should be.

But I can't help but feel when he's been here for a while that perhaps I should move. Maybe to a bigger unit in the same building, even? My studio feels small when he's here. And not because he's one of those dickhead manspreaders who take up three seats on the T. It's felt more that way recently than when he first used to come. Perhaps because he stays for longer these days. Perhaps because in the back of my head, I can picture him staying for longer still. Like maybe even forever?

That's a dangerous thought and it's not as though we've talked about it, but I also have a hard time imagining what my future would be like without him. That path is cloudy now, fogged with uncertainty and improbability, whereas when I think of being with Lowry, that version of the future is clear. Sharp, even. So sharp it threatens to cut the vulnerable and paranoid part of me that is still so very certain he is going to abandon me again because although the reason for him leaving in the first place is no longer relevant, my brain can be a total asshole.

But if—*if*—he were to be a permanent fixture...I don't think we could live here. Part of me wonders if I'd finally be able to face living at my father's house, but that wouldn't be fair to Lowry. If I can't manage that, why should he? He has a busy and important job he won't want to give up, and I don't know that he'd want to spend his leftover energy dealing with an estate. God knows I choose not to allocate my spoons that way.

No use dwelling on that at the moment—or ever, but let's be

real, it's going to happen. But it doesn't have to happen right when I'm expecting Lowry to show up at any moment. I had a full day and maybe pushed myself a bit further than normal dealing with business shit, winding myself up into a coil of tension knowing I would have Lowry to unwind me...or flat-out shatter me because he's good at both of those things. He'll be here soon—oh, so soon—and I am freshly ready for him.

I'm wearing one of the dresses I ordered recently, finally brave enough to do it. My heart is racing some, though not a full-out sprint of panic. The picked-up cadence is a jog of anxiety plus a skip of embarrassment. I hope Lowry thinks I look darling with my long sleeves and short skirt that puffs out and makes a really nice twirl when I spin around. Will he be enchanted when I show him or will he think he's made a mistake? That he wasn't expecting this to be a thing. Not for-realsies, as a pillar of what makes us *us,* and not simply a once-in-a-while element to spice things up. I don't know, and I have to sit on the couch and reach down to fiddle with the buckles on my black patent leather Mary Janes, make sure the lace tops of my socks are folded down just so.

This dress is perfectly sized, but it feels too small. It's purposefully short, but I don't mean like that. More like it feels tight around my chest and forces my breath to be shallow. My whole body is already alive with arousal and Lowry's not even here yet. Can't imagine what I'll feel like when he stands on the threshold and gets that worshipful look in his eye like I'm the most beautiful thing he's ever seen, like he can't wait to get his hands on me.

Finally, there's a knock at the door and I'm on my feet before it's even finished. This is it. I suppose I could tear all this off, run my hands through my hair to mess up the perfect spirals I spent an hour taming it into. Unlock the door and beat a hasty retreat to the bathroom and tell him I've changed my mind.

I don't want to, but it's still difficult to force my feet one in front of the other to move to the door.

Please, Lowry, please. Please like playing this game with me. Please still think it's fun instead of icky. Please let it turn you on as much as it does me and not make you feel like a pervy old man—not in a bad way, anyhow.

A big breath in and then I open the door, trying to put a sweet smile on my face even as tension is making me feel anything but sweet—prickly and stressed, more like. But he can help relieve me, and for that I can be sweet for him.

~

LOWRY

I shouldn't have come. That's my first thought when Starla opens the door and she's standing there, hair in darling ringlets, mouth in a sugar-sweet smile, and her dress... God in heaven is going to smite me because of how I feel about her dress. Not to mention those shoes and socks sent from the devil himself to tempt a man like me. The combination of these things pricks my interest and desire like a short, sharp jab of a needle, but then it fades. Gets swallowed up in the other feelings that have been swamping me since this afternoon.

And my Star, love that she is, is trying so hard to be calm and lovely when she is, in fact, about to vibrate out of that smooth skin of hers. I can feel it, the waves of emotion coming off her. To some people—perhaps most—she can appear to be a sphinx, mysterious and inscrutable, but I know better, am tuned to her wavelength.

I should've called her, no, texted, and said I couldn't make it. She would've understood, or said she did, and I would've felt guilty but would've done my best to make it up to her. I didn't, though, because I have Jade firmly in my head, threatening me with a good chance of death should I abandon Starla again, and so here I am, regretting my life choices.

It's not fair to Starla for me to have shown up here like this, but it's not as though I can walk away at the moment either. No, I have made my choices and now I'm responsible for getting the both of us through them.

Starla's smile falters because her senses are like mine—she feels me. Though I've learned to mask my responses as a professional responsibility, she's never had to and she startles like a deer in the forest who's heard a shot. I'm sorry.

"Lowry, what's wrong?"

I look away from her, and the effort of coming up with how I'm going to tell her crunches my brows together. "I…"

Before I can finish, she's taking my hand in both of hers and tugging me over the threshold of her apartment, and yes, that would be better. Not doing this standing in the damn hallway.

"Come on, let's go inside."

She tows me over to the couch and I let her, feeling dazed. I got here on autopilot for sure, couldn't tell you anything about anything I saw. Good thing I wasn't going through South Station today, I'd hate to miss an opportunity to see Keytar Bear. Not that the busker's usually charming antics would have broken through this haze.

Starla sits on the couch, leaving a space for me at the corner, and… I don't sit. Can't, not with her looking up at me with those big eyes and concern etched on her pretty porcelain features. No, this isn't what she signed up for, and I should give her what she needs. Provide. That's what I do.

So I try to gather up some of my scattered thoughts, only the ones to do with her, and sweep the rest away to be dealt with later, after she's snoozing in my arms or later still when she's deep asleep and I've snuck out here to deal with my own emotions.

I drop my messenger bag to the side of the couch and paste a smile on my face, hoping it doesn't look too grim, and clap my hands together.

"Well, look at you, little girl. You look darling. I can't wait—"

"You stop that this instant."

Shock reverberates through me, scattering all my thoughts again. Is she scolding me? This is a turn of the tables I didn't see coming, at least not tonight. But she's looking rather serious, arms across her chest and glaring at me from under her brows. It ought to be a bit ridiculous, this little doll of a woman in her ruffly socks and ringlets taking me to task, but it hits me like a punch.

"Stop what?" I try, willing in some ways for her to let me have this, let me do it, allow me to wrest back the control I've lost. Give her what she needs so I can not fail at something today. But she's not to be deterred.

"You're pale, like, more than usual and that's pretty pasty, you ginger bastard. And you're scruffy, not like scruffy hot but kind of haggard. You know I think you're the handsomest man alive, but you look like shit, Low."

The way she says it rhymes with bao—I'm hardly a dumpling, and it ought to make me smile, but nothing is working the way it should. Pressing on because I'm so obviously and embarrassingly struggling, she stands, taking a few steps until she's pressed against me but not so firmly that she can't tip her head up to look me in the face.

"Seriously. You're not fooling me. And stop trying, because it's insulting. I'm not one of your patients, I haven't paid for you to attend to me. You're upset and I want to know why. Help you if I can."

The way she sort of mumbles the last bit—as if her efforts would be only that and she doesn't have much to offer—sends an arrow straight into my heart. I don't think she will be able to make me feel all that much better, but if anyone on this earth has a shot in hell of lending me some comfort, it's her. And she's right. It's not okay to treat her as though receiving care from me is the only thing she bargained for. It's hard, though, to give up that role I'm so comfortable in, and wade into one where I'm so very not. Which is why I give it one last try, slipping an arm around her waist and pulling her more firmly to me.

"But you got all dressed up and you look so pretty for me, and I want—"

Serves me right that she bangs her little fists against my chest.

"Would you stop it already? I know Scotsmen are supposed to be stubborn, but this is ridiculous. You can talk about your feelings or you can get out of here, Lowry Harrison Campbell. Up to you."

When faced with an ultimatum like that—I can't deny there's a shred of me that's tempted to walk out so I don't have to do this. But I'd so much rather be anywhere doing anything with Starla than be anywhere doing anything without her that it's only a momentary folly.

"You drive a hard bargain, lass, but okay."

She tips her head and nods in decisive satisfaction of getting her way. Someday when things aren't so fraught, I'd like to get her to stomp her wee foot in frustration. Not today.

"Sit," she commands as she shoves me toward the couch.

Weary and resigned, I do. She's still on her feet, hands on her hips.

"Where would you like me to sit? We're not fooling around but…"

Her gaze flicks to my lap, and yes. That is something I want too. Not for sex at the moment, but for comfort. I pat my thigh and her shoulders drop before she climbs on to me, settling herself in the cradle of my body. The feel of her weight, the scent of her skin and her hair, the way she leans against me and strokes the stubble that's grown overmuch at my jaw. Went to the gym and worked out, hoping to sweat out some of the angst, and went through the motion of showering, but didn't clean up my facial hair.

It's a comfort to have her in my lap, to be able to wind my arms around her body—the warm and very much alive flesh of her, which is the thought that tightens my throat. If I had lost her, if she hadn't survived me leaving, what would I have done? I never would've been able to forgive myself.

Thinking about it makes my chest hurt and my arms tighten reflexively around her. As though holding her is going to make her immune to the disease that whispers awful things to her, as though my will is strong enough to overpower the demons that haunt her, who might be strong enough to drag her away from me and into the darkness she's only ever given me glimpses of, but that I know is constantly nipping at her heels, beating at the firmly shut door of her sanity.

My breath is ragged when I inhale and I fairly crush her to me because I've allowed myself to think the unthinkable. It haunted me for months after I moved to Chicago. It was years before I stopped waking up in cold sweats having dreams about her and now it's all coming back. Grief, yes, for what's happened in the present, but also those years of crushing worry fall on me and tears press at my eyes as my sinuses burn. I cannot, absolutely cannot, put this on her.

But if I don't let it out, where's it all going to go? My hands are starting to shake already. I have the ridiculous notion that I might be able to get away with this if I splash some water on my face.

"Darling, if you'll excuse me for a moment..."

Starla looks at me in a considering way and then declares, "No. You said you would have feelings and I'm going to hold you to that."

"Yes, well." My jaw tightens and flexes because weeping in front of her is not precisely what I signed up for and my feelings are trending toward frustration and embarrassment. "It's not precisely a turn-on to see your daddy cry, now, is it? I don't know if I can stop it, and I'd really rather not in front of you, because…because…"

"Did you think any less of me all the times you've seen me cry?"

"No, of course not. But it's different for men."

"Which is foolish. You can take your toxic masculinity and shove it. I have no use for it."

She says it so kindly and in such a straightforward way. She may as well have said, "Lowry, don't be a numpty. Cry, for fuck's sake, if you need to."

It's been half a lifetime since I did. I've forgotten the sweet relief of letting the moisture that's been stinging and burning at the corners of my eyes spill over. The tears are hot and wet, cooling rapidly as they roll down my cheeks. It's such a foreign sensation and I…I don't know what to do with them. Not swipe at them with my sleeve. Starla solves my dilemma by kissing them away, her soft lips pressing against my cheeks and her kitten tongue darting out to sweep the salty moisture into her mouth.

"I'm so sorry you're hurting."

Clearing my throat so my voice doesn't crack, I say, "And I'm sorry I brought this to your doorstep. I didn't mean to, and it'll be over soon, I swear. I didn't mean for you to see me like this, so I apologize."

"Don't you dare. I'm not sorry. I want you to come to me when you're upset. It means you trust me. And that you think I'm strong enough to help you and not just the other way around. Don't get me wrong. I love when you take care of me, when I get to be your little girl. But I can give you more than that and it means a lot that you'll let me. Or at least let me try."

"You being right here helps." I give my heels a bounce and she lets out a surprised giggle, clings to me a smidge tighter and God, does that feel good.

"So, what is this about, really? Can you talk about it? I know if it's one of your patients, it's—"

"One of my patients died by suicide this morning."

No use beating around the bush. There's not a nice way to say it. Took his own life? Is that any better? Perhaps I should've tried harder to temper my language because Starla sucks in a breath.

"Oh, Lowry. I'm sorry. I'm so sorry."

I close my eyes and think of Tony. Of the pictures I've seen of his wife and his daughters. Beautiful family and now he's torn it all to shreds. Or blown it up, same way he blew his brains out with a revolver at the desk in his home office. His wife found him. At least it wasn't one of the girls.

"I couldn't stop him. I couldn't help him. He didn't trust me enough or believe in me enough to call me when he was thinking about it. How did I not see this coming? I thought we had a plan. I thought we'd made an agreement. I thought..."

It's been a while since I've lost a patient. Always a risk in my line of work, with the populations I'm drawn to. And every time, it's a punch to the gut. Like someone's forced a balled-up hand into my midsection at speed, grabbed a fistful of entrails and dragged it out of my body, forcing me to look at it. *Here are your worst fears come true. And you are as powerless as you were then to stop it.*

It's selfish of me, I know, to be thinking so much about what this has done to *me*. I should be contacting his family and seeing if there's anything I can do, any help I can offer. I will. I may have failed Tony in allowing this to happen, but I won't fail him in this. It's the least I could do to offer anything I have to his grieving widow and the children he left behind.

The anger I feel toward him isn't fair either. It's there anyhow, yelling and stomping and wanting to shake him because *How could you? How could you do this to the people you loved and who loved you?* But that's the shitty thing about depression, isn't it? He probably believed they'd be better off. That perhaps they didn't love him. And I didn't think so the last time I saw him, but perhaps he was so far gone down the path that he didn't think he loved them either. Perhaps he looked at them and felt nothing but icy numbness. I'll never know. Even if I did, would it satisfy? No, nothing will. Because nothing could.

"I know what you're thinking," she says softly, her breath warm on my neck. "But this isn't your fault. There's nothing you could've done. If he was determined and sure and his depression was screaming so loud he couldn't hear anything else, no one could do anything. You know that, right?"

She rests a hand on my chest, over my heart, and it's not anatomically possible, but I swear it lets in more blood so it can swell toward her touch, beats hard to let her know she was heard. Heard, yes, but believed?

In my head, I know that's true. Intellectually, I can repeat her words, and I would say the same to any of my colleagues who were in this situation. Have, in fact, done precisely that. But in my chest? In this muscle where the ache of loss seems to be centered?

"I know. But—"

"No buts." She sits up, not taking her hand off my chest. "Who's the expert in depression here, me or you? Not like the DSM and *Psychiatrist Weekly* and peer-reviewed journals and shit like that—you can wear that crown, I don't want it. But of the two of us, who is viscerally familiar with what depression can do to a person?"

The words come to my lips, ready to give Starla her due, but what comes out is a choked sob. Jesus, Mary, and Joseph, I'm a mess. All I can do is close my hand around hers and bring it to my lips, kiss her knuckles and assure myself she's here, and I don't need to worry anymore about losing her to the darkness. I say a prayer over her fingertips that that's true.

"You are. And I've thought about that every time I've lost a patient since I left. Every single goddamn time. It would've been awful enough without that added ton of guilt, but every time... every time."

Which is not her burden to bear and I'm a right tosser for mentioning it to her. I have no right to ask her to absolve me of any of my sins, but particularly that one. I shouldn't have handed that weight to her, but I can't take it back now. She'll have to carry it too.

CHAPTER 26

tarla

IT'S DISCONCERTING, having Lowry hunched over my fingers and in such obvious pain. I had no idea… But of course, I wouldn't have. When he left, I convinced myself it was because he didn't care for me, that I'd worn him out, used up all the nurturing and watching over he was capable of giving. That horrible thought was only borne out by never hearing from him once he'd gone. I had no idea he'd fretted over me, that he worried I would take my life, and that if I had, he would've believed it was his fault.

I don't think words will do any good at this point; I know they couldn't reach me when I was at my lowest. It would've been like someone trying to talk to me through a blizzard. So, I do what I can and thread the hand he's not clutching through his hair, murmuring things to him like how I am still here. I am very much here. I am not going anywhere. And the fact that I'm here is due in large part to him.

I doubt he takes enough credit for the lives he's saved, and takes on far too much blame for the ones he's lost. And as I told him, those are not his fault. Nor is it the fault of the people who killed themselves. It's near impossible, I think, for people who've never experienced it to understand exactly what depression is like. Not the occasional period of being blue, but a hole so deep you have no expectation, and indeed not even any hope, of climbing out. But when the call is coming from inside the house —inside your own mind—it's exponentially worse.

If you can't trust your own mind, who can you trust? If your brain is trying to kill you, why shouldn't you listen? Is anything you can experience with your muted emotions going to be worth the agony of walking this earth one more day? These are the questions I asked myself. And I was so, so lucky to have someone like him there to give me a hand up and out of the abyss.

Yes, it took effort and struggle on my part, and sometimes I feel myself slipping back toward that deep, dark well where I could drown, but I also appreciate how he and my entire medical team were racing around at the top of the crevasse trying to figure out how to get me out, like baby Jessica in the well. I couldn't see it then, I was convinced I was very much alone. But when it worked—I could see them and everything they'd done for me, and I felt—still feel—tremendous gratitude. And some other stuff because I was a teenager and hormones and adolescence are confusing enough even without the threat of serious mental illness looming over you, but my enduring feeling is gratitude. I am so very grateful for still being here, and to everyone who helped make that a possibility.

I try to pour some of that gratitude over him, into him, make him feel and not just know that he has helped people, that he hasn't been a failure. I'd ask how many more people wouldn't be here without his help, but I don't think that would be helpful right now. That would likely bring on more despair.

I comfort and soothe him until his broad shoulders stop quaking and then I hold him. Willing him to know how deeply I love him without having to say the words.

"Have I talked about my feelings enough?" His voice is gravelly, his eyes rimmed with red, and he's looking at me with a ravenous hunger. I don't have much in the house, but I don't think he's craving food anyway.

"You could be done for now, if you want."

"I want. Christ, I knew how draining it can be for my patients to talk to me, but I feel hollowed out."

I remember that sensation, one that would last for weeks on end, sometimes months. Well, I'm not going to let that happen to Lowry. Not that it could in the same way since his brain doesn't have that unfortunate wiring that predisposes him to be depressed, but still. For as many times as he's given me something to hold onto, I'm going to fill him so he doesn't feel empty any longer.

"And do you have any thoughts on what you'd like to do now?" I check my watch as if I don't know the time. "Our reservation is soon. We could clean up and head over if you'd like."

He shakes his head. "I can't stomach the idea of being out in the world. I only want to be here with you. And if you're up for it…"

He looks me up and down, the intensity of his gaze singeing my skin as it travels the length of my body. "The only sustenance I want to consume right now is you."

Oh. Yes, I could do that. Let him devour me.

"I think that could be arranged."

"Yes? And I'll finally get to see what's under that skirt of yours."

I roll my lips between my teeth and nod, starting to cede control back to him. Which is frankly a relief. I'd been wired when he arrived, and being the one to provide support and succor didn't alleviate the burden. If anything, it's become heavier and I don't want to carry it anymore, not if he's recovered sufficiently to take on some of the load.

We kiss and I can feel his hunger, feel the way things around us have shifted, and as he plunders my mouth with that clever tongue of his, I feel too the way I've been keyed up turn into desire for him, desire to be his.

"Come on then, love."

Lowry sits down at the edge of the bed, grabs BB-8, and places it to his side. I wasn't sure if he'd want to do any of this what with the emotional roller coaster we've already endured this evening, but perhaps this will make him feel as though he has control over something, even if he couldn't save his patient. Or maybe he just likes to spank me and he could use a little pleasure right now. Does it matter? At the moment, I think not. Especially because I'm eager to surrender myself to him, let him do as he will with me. And if that's spanking my bottom? So much the better.

I crawl onto the bed and drape myself over his lap, clutching BB-8 to my head. Well, the side of him that's soft and doesn't look like the droid. I mean, BB-8 must've seen some things in Poe's service, but I don't want him being corrupted here.

It's that peculiar mix of comfort and slight humiliation being turned bottoms up over Lowry's thighs that has me starting to feel spaced out and dreamy. And when he slides a hand under my skirt and drags it over the frilly underwear I picked special for today, he groans and I let out a small moan of my own.

"What are you doing to me, Star? I swear I used to be a fine, upstanding citizen and now all I can think of is you in your little outfits and your darling shoes, and this..."

He fists a hand in my hair and I don't even care that he's crushing the ringlets that took me an hour to perfect—they've clearly served their purpose.

"And how I want to turn you over my knee and spank your bottom until it's bright red before I stuff my cock inside this"—there's a slight pause because he's shoved his hand full-on inside my panties, nudged my thighs apart and speared his fingers into my core, making me gasp—"tight little pussy of yours. You're so wet for me already, darling. I love how wet my little girl gets for me."

I rock back against his fingers, trying to get more of them inside me, fuck back against him while I rub my clit against his thigh and get myself off. There's no way he'll let me, but a girl's gotta try.

Of course he tsks at me, knowing what I'm trying to do, and withdraws his fingers with a spank to my cheek.

"What a naughty little thing you are, trying to rub one off on Daddy's thigh. You didn't think I'd let you get away with that, did you?"

I whimper and collapse, feeling the loss of his fingers keenly. "No, Daddy."

"That's right, I'm the one in charge here, not you. You'll take what I give you, no more, no less. Perhaps you need a spanking to remind you of how things work."

He doesn't wait for a response, but tugs down the ruffly underwear until it rests in the crease between ass and thigh, and it's that delicious kind of humiliation, knowing my butt is perfectly framed by my dress rucked up around my waist and the ruffles at the bottom. He must be thinking the same thing, because he grabs my cheeks in both hands and squeezes them.

"Like ripe peaches. That's what your bottom looks like, Star, all round and firm and begging to be squeezed."

He kneads at me for a bit, and it's all I can do to keep my hips still for him, to not rut against his leg. It helps that I am dying of embarrassment, my face flaming with how much I like this and also with thoughts of why. Why do I like this?

But when he plants a palm at the small of my back and then starts to spank me, it doesn't seem to matter so much anymore. The point is that I *do* like it. Like the way his hand lands against my flesh, the sting of it followed by a heat that builds with every passing blow.

Lowry works me over, his hand making contact with what feels like every exposed inch of my ass, and layering the hits on top of each other. That's how the heat builds, the warmth radiating out after each spank, but part of it remaining until the slaps raining down on me are hard. Not enough to feel punished, as though I've been bad and need to be corrected—I think he'd make it very clear if I was really being punished—but enough to make me feel as though none of this is under my control anymore, none of this is my responsibility.

Lowry is going to spank my bottom until he's felt I've had enough and that's how things are going to be. I shouldn't bother to fight, but just enjoy the repeated contact, and how he's so carefully attending to me.

Which is maybe strange? That it feels so good to me that he's spanking me so very thoroughly. Would I feel the same delight and peace if he were attentioning me in some other way? I wouldn't be averse to finding out, but there's something about being spanked that is a perfect storm of everything I want and love. I love, too, the way he drags a hand over my heated bottom when he's done.

"You were such a good girl, Star, taking that spanking. Your bottom is the nicest shade of pink now, and all warmed up. Can you feel that?"

Oh, I can, and when he switches to fingertips drifting whisper-soft over my abused flesh, I get chills. Serves to provide a contrast that bows my spine and makes me squirm as a shudder runs through me. "Yes, Daddy."

"Good girl," he murmurs as he continues to stroke my bottom.

I could fall asleep like this. Or maybe I'm too horny to fall asleep? Especially when I think about how he had his fingers inside me before. I'd like for him to do that again. I'd like for him to fuck me again, make me take his big cock inside me...

Just then, he strokes a finger into the top of the cleft of my ass and it makes me start.

"Shh, love. I know we haven't done this before, but I want to touch you. If you don't like it or don't want me to or need me to stop for any reason at all, say 'penguin,' okay? You can say 'no' and 'stop' and I'll check in with you the first couple of times, but I thought you might like to tell me no but still mean yes. I know you've used safewords with Jade before. Just like that. Tell me you understand."

"I understand, Daddy."

And I like the idea very much. It's nice that he's not making me say yes to this, as it's something I've struggled with in the past. I don't know why. Lots of people enjoy anal play and I don't honestly think there's anything to be ashamed of, but those taboos and shame are really hardwired, aren't they?

So he's going to do this and I have the safety of being able to make it stop, but also the freedom of not having to affirm that this is something I want. Hell, can even protest that I'm a good girl and of course don't want this, but have him "force" it on me anyway so I can take my pleasure.

"Tell me your word so I know you remember."

It makes me smile, and huff a little laugh. Of course he would pick a ridiculous word so I won't forget it and if I have to say it, some of the tension will automatically be broken. "Penguin."

"That's right. Do you have any lube? I don't want to hurt you."

I have to bury my face in BB-8 before I find the nerve to respond because, conveniently, once I'm in this headspace, I get embarrassed even more easily. "Top drawer of the nightstand."

"Up you get, then," he says, and I push up on my hands until

I'm kneeling back, red-faced with my heels digging into my sore bottom. I get a once-over with his assessing gaze.

"I love your outfit, darling, but I'd like you better naked at the moment. Strip off and then get back over my lap."

I don't need to be told twice. As he rummages in the drawer, I pull my dress over my head and shimmy out of my undies, leaving my clothes a heap on the floor. And then he's patting his thigh and I do as he's asked. The cloth of his pants is a stark contrast to my skin and it makes me feel even more naked, knowing he's not.

He doesn't use the lube right away but must set it down. There's something about the delay that builds anticipation, makes me clench my thighs together. And then his hands are on me again. Same heavy weight at the small of my back, and smooth easy circles over my cheeks with his other hand before he switches to the drag of his fingertips. Whereas he'd stopped close to the top before, he eases a finger further into my cleft and it makes me want to squirm. Beg for more or tell him to stop or, I don't know, anything besides tolerating this insinuating, teasing motion that makes me think of everything while he's giving me nothing. Is this his plan? To get me riled up and make me beg? I don't like it, but I'll do it.

But no, I think he's taking his time, exploring and enjoying me. Possibly relishing being allowed to do this. The level of intimacy I have permitted this man is far above any I've allowed anyone else, and I think he knows that. Not just is aware of it, but values the trust I place in him. Perhaps enjoys it in the same way I like to soak in his care and attention. Does it make his heart light up with the knowledge that I chose him? Because I have. And would like to know him as intimately as he knows me.

His fingertip skates over my asshole and I want to die a little. Because ohmygod, that is my asshole. Maybe it wouldn't be so weird if there was a nicer word for it, but all the euphemisms I've ever heard are cringe-worthy, so asshole it is.

And oh god. He's so gentle and thorough as he touches me, rubs around my hole and strokes my perineum in a way that renders me into a puddle. Such a secret, small place that can make a person feel so very good and, for me, intensely submissive and vulnerable. And to be handled with such care tells me I'm not mistaken in having put my trust in him. He's earned it back, with interest.

A good thing too, because his hands leave my body and I'm guessing I know why. A snick of a cap confirms my suspicions, and there are a few beats before he's touching me again. He warmed the lube between his fingers so I wouldn't get a shock of cold gel, and I appreciate it.

I also—jeez, what is it about lube that makes everything even filthier? Like, this was getting dirty before, but now with the slickness, it's more so. Maybe because the prospect of him fingering my ass has gotten that much closer?

"Star? You doing okay? You're being such a good girl for me, but you're so quiet I wanted to check."

"Yes, Daddy."

"You like how this feels? Me stroking your tight little arsehole?"

Christ on a cracker. "Yes," I choke, and he takes pity on me, not demanding more but instead applying a bit of pressure to the aforementioned tight little asshole. Which at once makes me spread my legs in the ache for penetration but also squirm because, oh god.

"That's a good girl, open up for me, Star. Someday I'm going to get my entire cock inside you here, but today I think I'm just going to finger-fuck your arsehole."

Filthy, filthy, and I want it.

He takes his time, adding more lube and stroking me, lulling me into comfort with the sensation. It starts to be less strange that he's touching me here, and almost becomes obvious. Indeed, why *wouldn't* he touch me here? It feels so freaking good. Every so often, he presses against my hole, murmuring to me, encouraging me, telling me what a good girl I am, and soon he's pressing with intent. Not a diffuse sort of pressure, but with a purpose to penetrate. To push a finger inside of me.

"Come on, love, let me in. I'm going to make you feel so good, but you have to relax and let me in. That's it. There's my good, obedient girl."

Obedient. If anyone else described me that way, I'd laugh in their face. I have been respectful, dutiful, even, but obedient? That, I shape myself into only for Lowry—and I suppose Jade— and only at discrete times like these.

It's an odd thing to focus on, to let myself be open in order for Lowry to violate me with a finger. But violate isn't right. Conquer, perhaps, or breach, but I don't feel violated. I feel loved.

I'm rewarded by the advance of his finger inside me, still with the same easing stroke, and then he draws back out to apply more lube and press forward inside of me again. Again and again until it's easy for him to sink his finger into my bottom, all the way to his knuckle, and the strangeness of it has melted away into more attention to how much I enjoy being penetrated by him, having him inside me, the rocking motion of being fucked gently by any part of him.

Which is perhaps why I've started to squirm in earnest. Press my hips back to meet his finger, create more of a thrust than a slow stroke. Because I want to get fucked like this, get off like this. I'm so turned on that any modesty I had is gone now.

"Don't be naughty, little girl. Don't you dare come yet, or there will be serious consequences."

The threat of which makes me whimper and clench around him. Part of me wants to be punished. To provoke gentle, loving Lowry into a man who would hurt me more. But I can't imagine he'd lose control even then. Especially not then. He's too careful with me. But he also likes to push me.

He applies more pressure to the small of my back, holding me down and making me feel so very at his mercy before his hand is gone and I hear the short clip of the lube bottle opening again.

"You're going to take two of my fingers and then you'll be allowed to rub off on my thigh until you come. That's what's going to happen: I'm going to stuff your tight little hole as full as it's ever been and then you're going to hump my leg until you come like the dirty little girl you are. Understand?"

What has been soothing is suddenly electrified and takes on a different cast.

"No!"

There's the briefest pause in the rhythm he'd established.

"You can say no all you want, little girl. You know the word if you really want this to be over. But until I hear it, I'm going to keep going. You're going to take everything I give you, because Daddy knows what's best for his little girl. I bet you're feeling pretty horny and frustrated right now, aren't you? And maybe you like how I'm stroking this finger in and out of your arse, but you're going to like it even more when your tight little hole is stretched around two of my fingers and I'm fucking you with them, nice and rough."

"Oh…" My moan is pathetic and needy, and I rock back, because I do want that. But I can't *take* it. I want…I want to be coaxed, to be told, to have these things done to me because he knows me so well and not because it's my idea. "Daddy, please don't. It's too small, you won't be able to fit them in."

"Yes, I will. You were worried Daddy's big fat cock wouldn't fit in your tight little pussy too, and did it?"

Oh god, did it ever.

With faux reluctance because it's fun and it gives me a thrill, I concede, "Yes, Daddy."

"That's right. So, trust me when I say you can take two of my fingers up your arse and that you're going to like it. You're going to come so hard that your pussy is going to convulse around nothing at all, and you'll beg me to fill that hole too. Think about that, Star. Think about me plugging your arse and fucking your cunt. For today we'll have to take turns, so let's get started. I'll be gentle and go slow first, but you're going to take two fingers in your bottom, stretching that hole."

Oh, fuck. Fuck fuck *fuck*. How does he know? But he does, so there's nothing left for me to say but "yes, Daddy."

I have to close my eyes to even breathe because I can't take any more stimulation than what's already being heaped upon me. This is one of the things that are both a blessing and curse about Lowry: he makes me feel so goddamn much. Even when I've been as physically intimate with other partners as I've been with him, even when they've reached this far inside my body, never have they reached this far inside of my soul.

So, I breathe and relax, try to be open for him, because he's right, I know he's right. He's going to make me feel so good and I won't regret this. And while being bottoms up over his knee is delightful in its own squirmy, mortified way, I can't wait for him to fuck me this way too. To feel his cock fill me up and reach so very deep inside me, his hips flush against my ass and the backs of my thighs as he pounds me. It will feel so dirty and so good and…I don't know, complete in some way? As though every part of me is his, as though he's mastered everything about me and knows how to, yes, manipulate me, but instead of using that information to hurt me, uses it to care for me and make me feel good.

He's working his second finger in much the way he did the first, with great patience and caution, and also by sliding in and out, adding more lube as he sees fit. It's a little bit agonizing, the way my body stretches around the intrusion, but it does in fact stretch, it doesn't tear. I can do this, I can take this, just as he said I could.

"God, you're beautiful, little girl. And so fucking sexy, letting me push my fingers into your arse, stretch out your hole and fuck you like this. Makes me feel so good that you trust me enough to let me do this. And wasn't I right? I knew you could do it and that it would make you feel good."

"Yes, Daddy. You were right."

"That's my good girl. And good girls get rewarded. Would you like your reward, Star?"

"Yes, Daddy, please."

I'm not proud of how my voice comes out as a whimpering plea, but it probably makes him happy. Altogether, I know he's quite pleased because I can feel the hard length of his erection against my hip. Which is at once deeply satisfying because he's being turned on by me, but also scary in its own way. Lowry is... not a small man. When he fucks my ass with his cock instead of his fingers, it's going to be intimidating. I know he'll make it enjoyable, but jeez. I won't be entirely acting when I tell him I'm not sure if it will fit.

He squeezes my ass cheek and then gives the same side a spank, making my flesh heat up in an instant, as if it had forgotten about the thorough spanking I'd been treated to earlier and just now remembered. I have never in my life been this aware of, this focused on, my ass. And why the hell not, because this is amazing.

"Then spread your legs. That's it."

Oh. With my thighs parted more, I get more contact on my mound and my clit, and Christ.

"Go on, princess. Rut against my thigh and show me what a filthy little girl you are. I want to hear you, I want your sounds, and I want you to come. I want to feel your muscles clamp down on my fingers when you climax."

His dirty directives make me want to hide under a table but also grind against his thigh, and when he senses I'm stuck between those two impulses, he urges me on. "Come on. You can do it. Make your daddy proud. I want you to come all over me and scream my name when you do."

I don't know about screaming, because hi, apartment building, but the other things? Yes. I do want to make him proud, I do want to please him, and fuck yes, I want to come. So, a little shyly at first, I press back against his fingers, forcing them farther inside me, and there's something about being active now instead of the passivity of having him be the one to make all the overtures that is at once humiliating but also empowering and it's all so much in my head. I'm about to get lost in it when Lowry calls my attention back to my body with another spank, hard this time, to my cheek.

"I see you, princess. Stop thinking so much. Let it go. Let it all go. The only thing you need to worry about right now is getting off. That's it. That's all you need to do to make me happy, and nothing else matters right now. I want you to come for me."

It wouldn't normally be so easy to focus me, but he's spent the last hour or so filling my senses, making himself the center of my universe even though I can't see his face, that his words hold an immense amount of sway and drown out everything else. So, I swallow his assurances down and let that base, pleasure-seeking part of me take over. The glutton, the hedonist, she wants more. So we'll have it.

The wool of his pants against my pelvis is a tad scratchy and the friction is a delight. So I rock and push, hips working against him, rutting as he said, and that's a good word for it. I feel like an animal, one who is intent on following its instincts for taking pleasure. Life is short and brutal, so take your joy and ecstasy where you can. Snatch it out of the sky and hang on for dear life to enjoy the ride, it will be over too soon.

I can feel my climax coming, bearing down on me like a gathering wave. I couldn't stop it even if I wanted to. I don't want to.

"Oh, Daddy, please. Please. I'm so close."

"Yes, Star, come on, fuck yourself against me. I want to see you come with your arse stretched around my fingers. Come on, little girl."

Between his words, the sensations being inflicted upon me,

and the motions of my body, I am so, so close. The penetration, the friction, the taboo, the utter naughtiness of what I'm doing right now, the sweat gathering along my spine and hairline, the slick thrusts of his fingers inside me, the way his knuckles bump up against my ass as I hump his leg and his fingers…

There it is. The wave crests and crashes, and I feel as though I'm being pulled under and tumbled in the undertow of sensation. Everything is so much. The light behind my eyes, the tone sounding in my ears, how every nerve in my body has come alive and is pulsing with feeling, with the experience of being consumed and swallowed and drowned in pleasure. "Fuck, oh fuck, Daddy, fuck me, oh god, yes. Yes."

I can hear him but I can't, because his voice is coming from above the waves that have swamped me, but luckily I can feel him. The forearm pressed over my low back keeping me flush against his thighs, his fingers planted firmly, god, so firmly, in my backside that keep me anchored so I don't have to worry about being swept out to sea.

The squeeze and release of my orgasm consumes me until I'm wrung out and limp, breathing heavily while draped over Lowry's lap with his fingers still inside me. He's lifted the bar of his forearm from my back and is stroking me, my back, my flank, my hip, and praising me softly. I want to hear him better, so I turn my head, angle it so my ear can catch his words better.

"What a good girl you are, so beautiful, such a good girl for Daddy."

I practically purr under his ministrations because I like being told I'm good. That I've pleased him. That he thinks I'm pretty.

"I'm going to take my fingers out now."

I'm grateful for the warning, and now that I've come, it has started to feel a little strange to have him buried so deep inside of me. Of course, it's a bit awkward to have them withdrawn as well and then to feel the absence of them so keenly. There's a spark of embarrassment, but it doesn't manage to catch my mood on fire.

No, I simply turn over and nestle my bottom into his lap where his cock is still hard, bury my head in his shoulder and slip my arms around him. He's warm and he smells like himself; his body is strong, his mouth soft as he plants a kiss on the top of my head. I'd snuggle here forever because it feels so very right. As though on Lowry's lap is where I belong.

CHAPTER 27

owry

STARLA IS A WARM, heavy weight on me, and it's the most divine feeling. She's not exactly a rag doll because there's a specific feeling when a body is deadweight, but she's not far off. Blissed out and dreamy, her eyes are closed and she's nuzzled so close to me, all curled up. She's the sweetest thing. I doubt she notices she's doing it, but one of her hands has come to rest on my chest and she's scratching gently through my shirt while her breathing evens out.

I am…turned on is not a strong enough word for how that made me feel. Turned up? So much of a build and then her plea-sure was explosive, incredible. Focusing on her and her alone meant everything else had been excluded from my mind, which was a relief.

It's coming back now and there's some guilt that I'm here doing this, and Tony will never see his loved ones or have any bodily experiences ever again, but mostly I'm still tuned into the curled-up ball of woman who is making the most adorable noises of contentment I've ever heard. Sleepy little sighs and muffled huffs make me dizzy—she intoxicates me. It would be easy to become addicted to Starla. I may very well be already. And would that really be so bad?

I have...feelings about what we do, but not so many that it would keep me from doing it. I'll have to sort it out on my own because it's not for Starla to concern herself with. She has enough to worry about. Between her business, her mental health, and making decisions about her father's business, that's enough for anyone to deal with. I won't add my own burdens to the pile. And while I may lay awake at night with the dirty things I said to her and the way she chokes a little when she calls me *daddy* circling my head, I won't regret loving her. She's honest-to-God so special, I don't know how anyone could.

I rock her a little and she seems to like that, making a little "mmm," that makes my heart swell. Aye, I feel badly about it because it wasn't fair to her, but I never felt this way about Maeve. Was it not possible because of how my brain is wired and the fact that she didn't need these particular things from me? Who's to say? I shouldn't torment myself over that too because we're both happier now.

I kiss the top of Starla's head again, the pale, delicate skin of her scalp showing through the strands of her hair. There are still notes of her shampoo left amongst the human smell of exertion and the mix of the two is sweet.

"Starla, love."

"Mmm?"

"I've got to get up and wash. I'm going to set you down and tuck you in and I'll be right back."

I don't bother to ask because if I did, she'd beg me not to and I don't want to refuse her. Not now. As it is, her chin is contracted into a pout when I pull back the covers from her bed then ease her onto the mattress and cover her quickly, up to her chin because she's naked and won't have my body heat to warm her while I'm gone.

I make quick work of washing up in the bathroom because there is a naked woman waiting for me and I can't wait to have my hands on her again. Not sure if she'll be up for anything else, which is fine, even though I'm aching. If she's not, I'll put her to bed and when she's asleep, head into the shower to at least buy myself some time and sanity by rubbing one out to what we've done. If she is, though...

She's not asleep when I'm heading back to bed. Curled up and clutching something under the blankets, yes, but her hazel eyes are open and she tracks me with her gaze. Her cheeks are pink and her mouth is curled into a sweet smile. My darling girl.

"What've you got under there?" I ask as I sit on the edge of the bed, gesturing with my chin toward her chest where she's clearly holding something against her.

Her lashes flutter and she looks to the side, perhaps embarrassed. But she doesn't refuse me, simply tugs down the blankets to reveal a brown furry doll sort of thing. "Is that a—"

"It's an Ewok. His name is Wicket."

I knew he looked familiar. Though I might've called him Chewbacca, and then where would we be?

"He looks very cozy in there. But also like a fine upstanding creature who won't destroy your virtue."

"Not like I have much left," she shoots back, a smile on her face.

Perhaps not, but she seems untroubled by that.

"Are you tired?"

She shakes her head, eyes wide, a combination of innocent and instigating. She'll be the death of me for sure.

"Hungry, perhaps?"

We haven't eaten dinner yet and it's getting late. I should've thought to get some food in her before, but I was distracted. She shakes her head again.

"No, not really. But there is something I want."

It takes a great deal of my self-control not to say, "Anything. Tell me what it is and it's yours." The woman could get most anything for herself, she doesn't need me to provide for her. Not materially, anyhow.

"And what might that be?"

"I haven't..." Her teeth sink into her bottom lip and something about that drives me wild. Perhaps the innocence bit again. But no matter what part of my brain it's pinging, it's still a potent gesture. Makes me want to rush her, shake her. *Haven't what?* But as in most things with Starla, patience is rewarded. "I haven't had you in my mouth yet. And I...I want to. May I?"

May she? For Christ's sake, *may she?*

"Och, ye may if you'd really like, but you don't have to, especially not right now. You've just—"

I can't finish my sentence because she's on her knees and curling her fingers into the waistband of my pants, grabbing ahold of my belt and tugging me forward until I'm at the edge of the bed, poor Wicket discarded in the tousle. Well, he probably shouldn't see this, anyhow.

As before, she's got no patience when removing my clothes. Pops a button off my shirt in her rush to get it off, even. That's fine. My gran taught me how to sew—I'll sew all the buttons Starla wants to tear off my clothes. She pushes the fabric over my shoulders and works the sleeves down my arms until they slide off at the wrists. Takes a hand and lays it on my chest, looks up at me through her lashes.

"I...I like how you look. You're the handsomest daddy in the whole world."

I take up her hand and kiss her knuckles, put it back where it was resting over my heart.

"And you're the prettiest little girl a daddy could ask for."

It's not an exaggeration, she's perfectly lovely. Especially when she wiggles up against me, her sweet round tits pressing up against my chest. I have to kiss her, can't even help it, work my hands into her hair and rub my fingers over her scalp before I let locks of her hair run through my fingers like chestnut silk.

She breaks our kiss, but it's only a second before she's kissing down my neck and over the slope of my shoulder, running her little kitten tongue over my collarbone. She plants more kisses on my pecs, licks gently over my flat nipples then works her way to the center of my ribs and follows the narrowing trail of hair down to my waistband.

Unlike my shirt, she takes more time here, running fingers along the top of my slacks, and toying with the leather of my belt. Sliding her tongue across the plane of my skin until my hands have curled into fists so I don't lose control in the face of her teasing. If this were the first of our fooling around, I'd likely be able to tolerate it better, but given that she rubbed off on me earlier as I finger-fucked her arse, well. I'm ready now. So very ready.

Starla stops her ministrations at my waist and scoots off the bed, tugging my belt until my back's to the bed, and then… God, dear God, she sinks to her knees and reaches for my slacks again, this time making quick work of the buckle before sliding the belt out of its loops. I've got my eyes tightly shut, but when there's a pause in her movements, I open them so I can check in on her.

She doesn't look disturbed in any way, though, simply sitting back on her heels with my belt doubled over in her hands which are resting on her thighs.

"Would you…not now, but sometime, would you spank me with your belt?"

My voice is hoarse when I locate the wherewithal to answer her. "I think that could be arranged. Probably if you've been a very naughty girl. I would imagine that would smart rather a lot."

She nods. "It does. But sometimes I like that. Or need it. Sometimes I need an excuse to cry, you know?"

"I think I understand."

Even though I don't have the same inclination, I think I do. Even if I didn't, I would try to give it to her simply because she asked. I reach out to pet her head again, rub a lock of her hair between my fingers. Her lids sink closed and she lets me stroke her for a bit, looking very much at peace. My mind is still a mess from this morning, but if I can't save everyone, at least I can bring her joy, pleasure, a few moments of serenity.

After a few minutes, she blinks open her eyes, lays the belt aside, and kneels up again to undo the button and zipper on my slacks and then she's slipping them down until they puddle on the floor and I kick them off from around my feet. And then, Christ, there's only a layer of cotton between her mouth and my cock and she leans forward, ghosting a breath over my erection, and I can feel the heat of her through the fabric.

Still being a tease, she runs her hand along my length, making me groan and drop my head back. My breath comes shallow as she strokes, and stops when she hooks her fingers over the band of my boxer briefs and tugs them down until my cock springs free. A relief, to be sure, but also—

"Ah…"

She runs her fingers over my flesh and it feels as though sparklers have been lit in my brain; all sizzle and light and senseless wonder. Gentle, she's so gentle and cautious as she touches me, it's going to drive me out of my skin.

Taking pity on me—or deciding that she would in fact like to render my brain into porridge—she circles her fingers around my cock and then lowers her head until her mouth surrounds my crown. And then I'm muttering all sorts of blasphemies as she uses her hand and her mouth to work at me, licking and sucking, bobbing her head until all my attention is focused on my cock.

I'm not proud of it, but how am I supposed to think of anything else? With the slick heat of her mouth, her dextrous tongue, and the way she works the rest of my shaft with her hand, I'm lucky I'm still on my feet.

"Star, I'm getting close. Do you want me to come in your mouth? Or—"

She pops off to answer, lips swollen, but doesn't let go with her hand. "In my mouth, Daddy, please. I don't want to waste a drop."

Not waiting for a response, she latches back on and works me over. The sparklers have turned into full-on fireworks now and I slide my hands into her hair, fisting them close to her scalp and showing her the speed that's going to take me there. She hums when I do, a little noise of craving and pleasure, and that more than anything else is what finally sets me off.

"Get ready, little girl. Daddy's coming."

And I do, Christ, do I ever, my hips bucking and my bollocks emptying into her hot, wet mouth. It seems to go on forever as she milks my cock with her tongue and draws every last bit out as she said she would.

At last she stops and withdraws, resting her head against my hipbone, and spent as I am, my cock still twitches at the feel of her warm breath.

"Come on, Star, up you get. I need to lie down before I fall over. You did a real number on me, you know that?"

I settle into Starla's bedclothes and she snuggles up next to me, chest to chest.

"You liked it?"

"Did I like it? I've nearly forgotten my own name, so yes, I'd say it was fecking brilliant."

She laughs and cuddles closer, and I have to drop a kiss on the top of her head as I hold her. How in Christ's name have I been blessed with this woman? I can't ask too many questions because I don't think the answers will ever satisfy, but for now, I'll hold her and keep her close and try to be the kind of man a woman like her deserves.

CHAPTER 28

 tarla

"Hello, this is Starla Patrick."

"Ms. Patrick."

The voice is low and rumbly, like it comes from inside a barrel.

"This is Jerome Garrett. We met once when you were small."

I've been tweaking my ADHD resource list for Nora to include things that might speak to her more, like ADHD Alien and How to ADHD. Now my brain has to screech to a halt, back up on the freeway to half a dozen exits ago and then go into drive.

"I don't remember that. I do remember you weren't a great favorite of my father's."

That's a nice way of putting it. My father loathed Jerome Garrett, talked about him as though he were the devil incarnate.

Garrett laughs, a huge hearty thing, and I try to picture him in my mind. Unlike my father who was a smaller, wiry man,

Garrett's always looked big in the press, larger than life: tall, broad, with a big gut.

I should probably feel threatened by him, but I don't. Wary, sure, but not threatened.

"Oh, but your father was a great favorite of mine. I never would've accomplished half of what I have without him to compete with. Used to drive me up a fucking wall, but he was a savvy, ambitious man. 'Like' may be too strong a sentiment, but I always respected your father and I'm sorry for your loss."

His candor is disarming and I have to remind myself that Garrett is the enemy. No one who wants to do a hostile takeover of my father's life's work is someone I should be charmed by.

"Thank you. Aside from belated condolences, is there a reason you're calling?"

"As a matter of fact, there is. I have a business proposition to discuss with you."

Which makes my blood run hot.

"Oh really? I thought you had other plans for taking over Patrick Enterprises whether I wanted you to or not. And now you want to talk about it? It's a bit odd, don't you think, to fill me in on your nefarious plot? I suppose you'd like to do it over whisky and cigars. Or perhaps a cask of amontillado."

He laughs again, and I don't know whether to be insulted or pleased.

"Feisty like your father, I like that. I suppose we could do that, although I was going to suggest dinner in the seaport. We could sic the lawyers on each other if that's what you'd prefer, but I thought we might enjoy this more."

His words could be construed as gross, but his tone isn't insinuating or sexual, doesn't make me feel like he's a creeper. I still don't trust him, but at least I don't think he's going to assault me or say heinous things that will make me want to toss a glass of perfectly good alcohol in his face.

He must sense my hesitation, because he presses. "I realize

your father didn't like me, didn't trust me. But I think my proposal might interest you."

It feels like a betrayal of my father to say yes, to even be considering this. I suppose it's possible, too, Garrett could outwit me, but I have a team of lawyers—he's got to know I'm not agreeing to jack shit before I check with them. It's perhaps juvenile, but I wish Lowry could come with me. If I were a man and I brought my wife or girlfriend or just a pretty face, I don't think it would be construed as odd or weak. But I'm not a man. If I say my boyfriend—is he my boyfriend?—slash ex-psychiatrist will be accompanying me… No can do because that would be as good as tossing a bucket of chum into shark-infested waters, and I'm smart enough not to make my position seem any weaker than it already is.

Also, what's the worst that could happen? I'll have some other dickhead man make an offer I can totally refuse? What if this is legit? What if this is the answer? It's probably worth a couple of hours to find out.

"Fine. But I don't take kindly to people fucking with me, so if this is an effort to take advantage, I'd advise you to reconsider. I guarantee I have faced down bigger demons than you and won. As you found my phone number, I'm sure you can locate my email. I'll be free Friday evening after seven thirty next week, let me know where you'd like to meet."

Then I hang up, because that's what I do to men who make me nervous.

~

LOWRY

We've had our team meeting where we have an opportunity to discuss difficult cases and anything else we'd like to talk about.

Obviously Tony came up, and while it was difficult, it could have been a great deal worse. I've been in touch with Emily, attended the funeral—alone, though I would've liked Starla to be by my side; it didn't seem fair to ask her to come, given her mother, given her own complicated relationship with suicide. It's still a loss, I still wonder if there isn't more I could've done, but the guilt isn't crushing. I'm not sure if it's because I've grown as a professional and I'm learning how to handle these terrible but inevitable parts of my job better, or if it's something else. Something like having Starla there to comfort and hold me.

I've headed back to my office and sat down at my desk to review the patients I'll be seeing for the rest of the day. It's not an overly stressful slate, but I want to do well by them. Especially after Starla's helped me with my schedule. I can't believe the difference. I'm a far better clinician because the woman knows what she's talking about.

There's a knock on my doorframe and looking up, Lacey's there.

"Thought I'd check in with you. See how you're doing. I know what a blow losing Tony has been."

I nod, thankful for the empathetic but not pitying or disgusted way she's looking at me. She knows what this is like, she's lost patients as well, this is professional courtesy and sympathy, not that she thinks I've cocked this up.

"I keep expecting him to walk in the door, as though he's not gone. I knew things weren't good. I had a feeling things were that bad, but there wasn't a damn thing I could do. I wish I could've done something else, but even talking to Emily... It's god-awful is what it is, and about one percent for me what it is for her and those girls. Always hard to lose a patient, but I don't need to tell you that."

"No, you don't. It's hard to watch anyone spiraling and feeling as though they're out of your reach. You can't be flinging yourself over the edge to try to save them either, not if you want to be there for all the other patients who need you."

That's true enough. Put on your own oxygen mask and all that. It'll take time and it will never really leave, but we move forward, we have to, otherwise…what's the point? That doesn't seem to be the only reason Lacey is here, though. Indeed, her brows crease.

"I wanted to speak with you too…"

Something pricks the back of my neck because this is something she clearly didn't want to discuss in front of the team. Privacy is apparently called for because she steps fully into my office and closes the door behind her but doesn't take a seat.

"What about?"

"This is extraordinarily awkward, I suspect for all involved, but I have to ask. Are you seeing Starla Patrick?"

I knew this would come up sometime. Knew it, and yet am still wildly unprepared, have no response ready to give. Haven't talked to Starla about it even, which I should have done, but we always have other things to do. Things to talk about, sex to have, games to play, on and on. I'm consumed by her whenever she's nearby and honestly when she's not. I've even started thinking to myself when working with some of my patients, "What would Starla do?" because she's fecking brilliant.

I don't want to hoist this responsibility on Starla, but I also don't want to disclose anything to her psychiatrist that she wouldn't want disclosed. This is rather a spot to find myself in and I put my pen down, lean back in my chair. We haven't done anything wrong. At least Starla hasn't. Lacey may very well feel differently about me, knowing my history with Starla. But I'm hoping she also knows me and that will count for something.

"I don't know that this is my information to share. I'm not trying to be evasive, it's only, privacy is privacy. Obviously there's no doctor-patient privilege here—anymore—but Starla's wishes about what details of her life are shared and with whom are still paramount to me."

Lacey nods but folds her arms over her chest. "I appreciate that, but…"

A shake of her head and a sigh.

"I think you're a good man and an excellent clinician, and it's not technically a violation of the ethics guidelines, but I'm not sure this is wise. You weren't here to deal with the aftermath of your departure, but it was ugly. Not as ugly as what had come before, but it wasn't good. Of course, this is all hypothetical. I have no proof, just the gut feeling that comes from how she smiles to herself in my office when she's seen you passing by in the hallway. Or the way you studiously avoid my gaze when I talk about Starla in a team meeting."

I can't say anything else without betraying Starla's trust, but I feel Lacey's words like a knife to the chest. It must've been terrible. I worried about it every goddamn day when I'd left, and it never really went away. So I get where she's at, I do, but as she said, it's an awkward position.

"Of course," I echo, not sure where to go from here and feeling as though I've disappointed my boss who I respect very much and also Starla, the woman who's the love of my life, by saying too much but not enough at the same time.

Lacey levels me with a glare like, "I can't fucking believe you're leaving me hanging like this, you right proper numpty," but I've got nothing else to give. Not to her, anyhow. Her suspicions are bad enough, I'm not going to give her proof.

"All right, then. I'm sure we'll talk later."

"Of course," I say again because I'm not sure what else to do. I'll talk to Starla later, but beyond that…who the fuck knows. Not this guy, that's for sure.

Lacey departs, but I can't refocus on my patients. I don't have time for a trip to the gym or a run to get my head in order, and I feel too scattered and edgy for anything else to do the trick. Perhaps, though, calling the other most important woman in my life will be something at least. So I ring up Maeve, knowing I'll get an earful because it's been overlong since we spoke.

"Lowry, you delinquent. It's nice to hear from you. I understand the flush of young love is distracting, but you could show me a little more deference. What with being your first wife and all."

There it is again. Maeve thinks of this as a foregone conclusion—she's my first wife, which implies Starla will be my second. But I'm still not sure that's something Starla wants from me.

"Lovely to hear your voice, Maeve. How are you?"

"I'm good. Very good, actually."

Maeve isn't a shy person but she sounds a bit bashful now. It's wildly unlike her, and I've got to wonder what that's about.

"Aye? And what's that about?"

"I'm, uh, maybe, seeing someone?"

"Are you, then? That's brilliant. Isn't it?"

"I think so. So far."

"And who's the lucky bastard?"

Not that I'll know him. Unless it's one of those fancy blokes I met at some function I went to with Maeve. Then I might have a shot in hell. But Maeve's never had much of a taste for those society gents, seems to prefer downtown men even though she's a decidedly uptown girl.

"This is actually a bit awkward. I don't want you to think there was anything going on when we were married, because there wasn't, but I... Denny. It's Denny. I'm fucking Denny, okay?"

Denny? As in her driver, Denny? It's a bit of a shock, but I never would've accused her of fooling around on me—neither of us are built for that, and there was no reason for her to stay with me if she'd wanted to be with him.

"You don't need to get your dander up, hen. I always liked Denny, was glad he'd still be around after I wasn't all the time. He clearly likes and respects you. I'm glad for you both if it makes you happy."

"You are?"

I forget sometimes that even though Maeve is mostly a machete, sometimes the woman's got a soft side to her as well. Shouldn't surprise me at all that she values my opinion as I value hers, but Christ, I wish she weren't worried.

"Course. Why wouldn't I want you to be happy? I always wanted that for you more than anything else, and I hope he's the man who can give you what I couldn't because I've got no sense in my head at all."

"Fine, then. How's Starla doing? I've heard talk about Jerome Garrett sniffing around Patrick Enterprises. Even though that would be difficult to pull off, if anyone can do it, it would be him. She must be frazzled."

Normally I'd poke a bit more and ask the obvious questions about Maeve and Denny: How long has this been going on, how did you get together? But I'm distracted by Maeve's mention of Starla. Star has hardly said anything to me about her father's business, and I haven't been much keeping track otherwise, figuring she'd tell me about something if it were noteworthy. But this sounds major.

"She hasn't mentioned it, actually."

Something that's not exactly embarrassment burns high up in my chest, nearly in my throat. Maeve knows something about Starla I don't? Why didn't Starla tell me? I pride myself on her being able to share anything with me, anything at all, but it seems as though the business and fortune elite insiders have got information I ought to have. No, that doesn't feel good at all, but I'm sure there's a reason for it. Must be.

"Oh. I'm sure she has it handled, then. She's got a team of sharks for lawyers so they've probably got it all under control.

I'm sure she doesn't want to worry you with all that since you never cared much for industry gossip or goings-on."

That's true, but I do care very much for Starla. I try to shake it off even as I plan how to ask her about it later. In the meantime, I'll interrogate Maeve about her love life.

"So, you and Denny, huh? How did that come about?"

CHAPTER 29

 tarla

LAST NIGHT and this morning I've had Lowry around to distract me from my upcoming meeting with Jerome Garrett. Eight p.m. Friday at a steakhouse in the seaport. Jesus, what does one wear to something like this? I'll have Holden pick something appropriate out. Something that makes me look professional but also dangerous. Something that says, "I know what I'm about, don't you dare fuck with me."

For now, though, I'm ravenous because I'm somewhat insatiable when it comes to Lowry. I want him all the time. I want him calling me his darling little girl all the time, I want him spanking my bottom all the time, I want him inside me all the time. I cannot get enough.

It's a good thing he's a responsible adult who reminds me—us —that we ought to eat something, if only to be able to keep up with our shenanigans.

I said this morning after he finally managed to pry me out of bed that I wanted French toast.

"Rhoda used to make me French toast every Sunday. When I got old enough, she showed me how but I haven't made it in, eh, ten years? Not sure I'd remember how."

"It's like riding a bike."

"Which is only helpful if you know how to ride a bike," I mutter and instantly regret because Lowry's head is cocked as though he can't believe what he just heard.

"Do you...do you not know how to ride a bike?"

Argh, fuck my life. This is one of my great embarrassments. I'm a grown goddamn woman. I'm obscenely wealthy. I can have essentially anything I want at any time. I've had the best education money can buy. I can speak at length about art history. I understand complex business arrangements, and I can help people figure out systems to help themselves succeed. What I cannot do is ride a goddamn bicycle.

"I do not."

My nose is in the air and my tone is prissy and dismissive as I fold my arms across my chest. This is not something I like to talk about. I had a rarified childhood which sometimes meant I was going skiing in the Swiss Alps or summering on a yacht in the Mediterranean when I ought to have been doing more normal kid stuff, like learning how to ride a freaking bike.

Which has always been one of Lowry's criticisms of my father. Not that he ever said as much out loud to me, but I could see the way his mouth tightened through his scruff that he thought I ought to be spending more time being a normal girl and less time being molded and shaped and hand-formed into what I was supposed to be like.

And when that all came crashing down because I could barely function enough to get through school, never mind be a jet-setting socialite or pull off attending a Swiss boarding school or some nonsense, that was an added layer of disappointment and inadequacy to the shit sandwich my father must've felt like he'd been forced to eat.

I mean, he loved me, but while I was growing up I never did feel as though he was happy with me or proud of me. Not for what I could actually do. Another layer to add to the pressure I felt weighing me down. When I felt anything at all, anyhow. It was better for a time. My father actually seemed pleased with me, like I wasn't an embarrassment or a thing he had to make excuses for but a daughter he could actually be proud of. My craving for that approval ran—runs, I suppose—deep and I would've done anything in my power to have more of it. But now he's gone.

The crease between Lowry's brows deepens, and I don't know whether I should ask what he's thinking or if I don't want to know.

"We've got the whole day today. It's a little cool, but funda-mentally nice weather. Would you like to learn?"

When people find out I can't ride a bike—it doesn't come up often, thankfully—they're always aghast, always want to know why not, always shake their heads in wonder that of all people, *I* don't know how to ride a bicycle. But never have any of them offered to teach me.

This has the potential to be completely mortifying. Falling, scraped knees, and screaming because you're flying down the pavement with only a couple of wheels and some metal sticks to support you seems perfectly reasonable when you're a child, less so when you're a thirty-three-year-old woman.

On the other hand…it's so sweet of him to offer. And in a way that's kind instead of horrified, making me feel as though he's giving this to me willingly and it's not a huge deal. It's something he has and I don't, so why shouldn't he help me get it? Generous. That's what Lowry is, and has always been, with me.

"Are you sure you don't mind? I'm not the easiest student."

"Perhaps I'm a very strict teacher."

He raises a ginger brow and all of a sudden, I am far more

interested in learning how to ride a bike than I've ever been. It's going to be that kind of lesson, is it? That I could be down for.

"There's only one obstacle I can think of. I'd imagine you don't want this to be a public exercise, and since we both live in the city, it's not as though we've got a winding private driveway for you to learn on. Even if we could find a parking lot to use, odds are there'd be a lot of passersby."

Yeah, no one wants that, especially not me. Double especially if Lowry's planning to go all strict schoolmaster on me. Which would be a delight, but also not a role-play I'd ever want to do in a public space. But...

"I may have an idea. Let me make a call."

LOWRY

The drive is in fact winding and private. Lined with trees, surrounded with lush grass that's been meticulously maintained. I can't help but feel it's a bit of a waste, given that Starla hasn't set foot on the property for months. At least as far as I know, and I'd think she'd tell me if she were coming here. Or that I'd be able to tell that she'd been. Unless I'm inflating the importance of her father's estate in my mind. Possible, but not terribly likely.

Indeed, she's sitting in the passenger seat with her fingers knitted together in her lap and looking uneasy. Of course, I wouldn't be feeling at ease if I were to head home either, but it's not the same.

I rest my hand on her bare thigh, and she starts before covering my hand with her own.

"You okay, Star? We don't have to do this if you've changed your mind. It's a beautiful day. There are a million things we could do. Take a walk, head down to Newport and drive around to see the cottages, pick up some food and have a picnic on the Common. Anything you'd like."

I give her a squeeze and she smiles, shakes her head. She looks absolutely darling, and I feel so fortunate that she's willing to trust me with this part of herself. She's got on a jumper with suspenders—it looks like a skirt, but I've been assured it's shorts. Right after she grinned and stuck her hands in between folds of fabric and announced, "It has pockets!"

Between that and her Peter Pan–collared sweater and knee socks, I am about to die. It's been torturous to have to sit out here and pay attention to the Boston traffic instead of taking her over my knee.

Probably for the best since it's not as though if I did drape her over my lap that I'd be able to flip up her skirt and give her a spanking. Damn skirt. Or rather, not skirt, which is the trouble. It does appear to have plenty of room for me to snake a hand under, though, and push aside the gusset of her panties to have access to her pussy, which I'm guessing is already slick… Jesus Christ, must stay on the goddamn drive. Don't want to run my car into one of these perfectly groomed trees.

Finally the house becomes visible, and…

I can feel Starla's gaze land on me, waiting for my reaction. She must've gotten a whole variety of them since the time she brought friends home from grade school, and I don't want to be one of the people she writes off because of how they react when they see this enormous place and realize exactly how rich she is. Not that they'd know, precisely, though I've got a pretty good idea.

"It's a nice pile of bricks you've got here, princess. I'm going to park over here so I don't sully the view."

She snort-giggles, and something in me loosens. This is as much an audition for me as it seems it is for her.

The drive curls round into a circle with a sizable fountain in the middle, and I park to the side you wouldn't be able to see coming down the drive. Not, at least, until it's too late. It's a rather impressive place: grey stone and cream trim round the many windows, some columns at the front door, and spindly iron fencing along the balcony on the second floor. Yes, it's lovely, and I can imagine Starla being scolded as she ran about this place. Because while I can't imagine her running now or when I first knew her, I have to remind myself she wasn't always depressed. It wasn't always threatening to take away her happiness or her life.

She takes a deep breath before opening the door and then lets herself out, the back of her skirt swishing after her. I'd like to follow, but I'd probably trip on my tongue with the way I'm drooling after her.

Instead, I get my bike off the rack on my trunk and fetch my helmet from the back seat and head to where Starla's inspecting a bike that's been parked in the drive near the house. I'm not a cycling expert, but it looks like a fine bike. Not a fancy racing bike, it doesn't seem built for speed. If she decides she'd like to do anything more than tool around on this driveway with its gentle hills, she'll need to get a real road bike, but this is the most darling cruiser I've ever seen.

Mint green with off-white tires and a wicker basket on the front, it's about the most Starla-like bicycle I could imagine. And there are some bags next to it that she extracts a few helmets from and tries them on. In some ways Starla's life is a constant struggle. I'm probably more aware of that than almost anyone save Starla and Lacey. But in some ways it's downright magical. She makes a single phone call and a bike with all the trimmings pops up in front of the estate that she owns but probably hasn't been to in months? It's something all right.

Having found a helmet she likes—cherry red and cream with a hole in the back for her ponytail—she fastens the clip under her chin and looks at me expectantly.

"Okay, now what do I do?"

$\mathcal{L}$owry

SHE'S GOT IT. It's taken a few hours, and a lot of effort, but Star-la's learned how to ride a bike. No longer will she have to confess, shame-faced, that she was excluded from this childhood rite of passage.

I'm a bit sweaty and red-faced myself, having chased after her with a hand on the back of the saddle to make her feel as though she wasn't going to fall. I think it's helped for her to feel little as we've been doing this. Easier to try and fail and try again because that's what you do when you're small. Of course, that's what we all do when we're big as well, but somehow the shame's not so intense when one is young.

We're taking a break on a back patio now where a round, older woman rolls out a cart of lemonade, iced tea, crackers and cheese, fruit, and cookies and then quickly excuses herself. It's amazing the things that can get done in the span of two hours when one has essentially limitless funds.

Starla's added some strawberry puree to her lemonade and it's a shade of pink that matches her cheeks, flushed with delight.

"Can you believe it?"

"Can I believe what? That you learned how to ride a bike? I absolutely can."

Her lips form a scrunched up rosebud as pleasure and embarrassment war on her features. I suspect she wants more praise but doesn't want to ask for it. Hell, no one likes to ask for things, it's hard, and after she's already worked so hard today, I won't make her.

"I believe it not only because I saw it with my own two eyes, but because you're a very talented girl and you work really hard. I know it wasn't easy for you, but I'm proud you were so persistent."

She's so lovely when she blushes. God knows she's lovely all the time, but there's something about the way her cheeks color and round like apples when that shy smile spreads across her face.

I don't want to ruin it, but something's been niggling at me and I can't seem to let it go.

"I wanted to ask you, actually, how things are going with Patrick Enterprises. You haven't mentioned it much, but it's got to be taking up a lot of your time. Everything okay on that front?"

The sweet smile vanishes immediately, and yes, this is why I didn't want to bring it up. It's not even any of my business insofar as I don't give a shit what she does with her father's company. I do care about the effect dealing with it may be having on her, though.

"It's kind of a shitshow, actually."

My Arnold Palmer nearly comes jetting out my nose. I wasn't sure what to expect when I asked her about it, but I wasn't expecting that.

Starla picks up a cookie and doesn't eat it but begins to break it into tiny pieces, dropping the crumbs on her plate.

"It's hard, and not the good kind of hard. You know, the kind of good where you're satisfied afterward?"

She's looking at me expectantly, verging on desperate, but I'm not going to interrupt her. I want her to tell me all about the shitshow.

"I hate it. I hate it and I don't want to do it anymore. But I also…"

She sets down what's left of her cookie, closes her eyes, and sighs. When she meets my eyes again, I can see the toll this has been taking on her, the toll she's been hiding from me. I bristle, but I'm also impressed. Strong as an ox, my little girl is.

"In the past few years my father had started talking like I might take over his empire when he retired. He'd started grooming me for it, asking me to come to cocktail parties where he'd introduce me to important people, asking me to sit in on calls, talking more business when I'd see him. I maybe should've nipped that in the bud because I have no interest in heading up Patrick Enterprises, but…"

For fuck's sake. I know how much her father's attention and approval mattered to her when she was a kid. Given how central he was in her life, it wouldn't be surprising if she'd never moved on from that. I mean, hell, most things being equal, I think most people would like their parents' approval.

Starla shrugs and her brows gather.

"It'd been kind of a long time since he seemed happy with me, proud of me. Really interested at all. And maybe it's silly, but I didn't want to let that go quite yet. Every time I saw him, I'd think, 'This time I'm going to tell him,' and every time, he'd seem excited at the prospect of me taking over and I…I just couldn't. So you can imagine I had really mixed feelings when he left me the whole thing."

She shakes her head, a rueful smile curling up the corners of her mouth.

"And maybe I should've already sold it off, but I keep dragging my feet. Not because I think I could actually pull off being in charge like he was, but I also don't want to make a royal hash of it, you know? It's not what he would've wanted, but I think it's as good as I can hope for. Which I also hate."

My stomach twists, because Christ almighty. It's nice that Jameson finally recognized how capable Starla is, but trying to force her into the mold he occupied after having watched her struggle for years is... I always thought the man was selfish, but this makes me want to wring his neck. How could he? She's found success on her own terms and in her own way, and how fucking dare he make her feel as though that wasn't enough?

"So, uh, basically my goal has been to not fuck this up too badly? I don't know that I'd be able to look at myself in the mirror if I destroyed everything he's worked for or if I just fucking lost it because it's 'too much' for me. I mean, I think I could live through that, not like..."

She waves a hand and the word may as well be spelled out in smoke. Suicide. She wouldn't kill herself. But what *would* she do? I wait a beat for her to tell me.

"But I would feel like a real piece of shit, you know?"

Her throat works as she swallows hard and nods. She can't meet my eyes, and I'm sorry for bringing it up. But only somewhat because at least I know now. And as I know from some of my pediatric patients before I left that line of work, knowing is half the battle. So I have more information now. That can only help. Me, anyhow. Starla, I'm not sure.

"So yeah, shitshow. I've got a meeting Friday that might help, might make it worse, but I can't tell yet. Maybe Rhoda's got some vodka in there, or something else to spike this?"

She picks up her glass of pink lemonade, tips it side to side.

"I might be able to offer something else to take your mind off it?"

This massive worry I've reminded her of, forced into her mind when she was just feeling satisfied and accomplished. Starla's not the piece of shit here. I could've gone for the professional, rational choice of talking it through, but perhaps we'll try that later as a longer-term approach to making her feel secure about her decisions. In the short term though, I'm going to go for something that will lift her burden quickly, clear her mind instead of burdening her further.

The way she perks up says she's far more interested in my less responsible but more immediate solution.

"Yeah? What's that?"

I push my chair out from the table and pat my lap. "Come here, princess."

Her eyes and mouth widen into circles and her color gets even higher. "Here? Now?"

"Not if it's not okay with you, obviously. We're on your turf and I know you must be having some complicated feelings about that, so this is entirely up to you. But if you're comfortable with it, or perhaps even if you're not, but you're curious and willing, I suspect I could make it worth your while."

Starla's shoulders make their way up toward her ears and she picks up her glass of lemonade with two hands and takes a sip. I'll wait and watch, because as I said, this is her call.

If this is too much—and I can absolutely see how it might be—it's truly fine. We'll go home and have our fun there. But there aren't many places where one can fool around outside in the city, and even fewer that offer the additional twist of danger or shame or that shock of taboo that comes along with being at the house she grew up in.

I'd like to take her inside, tie her down to her childhood bed, and ravage her, but that would definitely be a bridge too far, so I won't even raise the question. I'll simply think about it while I wait for her call.

While I wait, I take a sip of my Arnold Palmer, which has got to be one of the most delightful nonalcoholic drinks known to mankind. We're both learning lots today, Starla and I.

She's still clutching her lemonade between her fingers and looking at me over the rim of the glass, and I do my best to keep my expression neutral, because while I would very much like to have her in my lap—hell, over my knee—it's as I've said. I'm not the one who's in an awkward position here. Aside from interest because this is where my darling girl spent her formative years, this place means nothing to me.

After a few minutes of sipping our drinks while I squint up at the sunshine, Starla puts down her glass and takes up her phone, swiping a finger over the keys faster than I'll ever be able to—she's lucky I don't still have a flip phone. Probably would, if Maeve hadn't intervened.

Then there's a thunk as Starla tosses her phone onto the table and a screech as she pushes the chair back on the flag-stones. Apparently, someone's made a choice. But whether it's to come nestle her fine, round bottom into my crotch while she leans against my chest or to tell me it's time to go home, I'm not sure.

She closes the gap between us, her expression one of skittish determination, and proceeds to sit on my lap with more of a plop than was probably necessary, then perches there as though she's been instructed to demonstrate excellent posture. I have to keep from laughing because while I don't think that would be appreciated, this is rather entertaining.

"No one will bother us," she says primly, her hands folded in her lap, and all it takes to set my blood aflame are those quiet words. Of course she'd want to guarantee our privacy—probably hers more than mine since I get the sense the people who maintain this place have known her since she was a child—and I have

blood is gathering there because her labia are thick and hot. If I could see them, they'd be a lovely shade of dusky pink. It's probably best I can't see because then I'd want to heft her onto the table, yank her skirt-thing and panties down and force her legs wide open so I could feast on her sweet pussy. As it is, I can smell her arousal and, God. My God.

"Little wider, sweetheart. Have to make room for Daddy to push his fingers into your tight little pussy."

She chokes out another one of those tender moans and does as I ask.

It's something, really, to have her follow my instructions. I'm entrusted everyday with people's welfare, with their mental health, and I take that responsibility very seriously. Anyone who doesn't shouldn't be in the psychiatry business. But there is something incredibly special about a woman like Starla entrusting me with not just her body but her secrets. The ways in which I can light her up, send her into the stars via climax.

It can't be an easy thing, to tell someone that what gets you off is being cooed to like a small child and that what you'd really like is to have someone take away all the power you've earned though lifelong struggle and clawing your way back from the brink. To be permitted to do as you're told. Also she's so brave to allow herself to be so goddamn pretty like a doll when she's had to fight for her autonomy since before I've known her.

It seems almost a cruel joke: to force this woman to seek out things she's fought against in order to take her pleasure. There's nothing wrong with it, to be sure—people like what they like, and no one is being hurt by what we're doing—and I wouldn't want for her to be any other way, but Christ. Especially the first time, she must've been a nervous wreck even considering telling her partner that this is what she wanted.

And hell, she was the one who made the space for me to indulge in this with her. It's all thanks to her, really, this incredibly strong person who's tucked against me and still swinging her

Mary Janed feet with her shins encased in knee socks. I'm more than a little in awe of her bravery, and also so very grateful. For letting me have her like this, for letting me have this, period, and for letting us be here and do this. For being so goddamn resilient that she could let me back in after what I'd done.

I hold her tighter and bury my nose in her hair, breathe in the delicate scent of her scalp mixed with the shampoo she uses. I think I'd very much enjoy bathing her, working my fingers through her long, chestnut locks as she surrenders the weight of her skull to my hands; soaping and rinsing every inch of her until she's pink and warm and smooth and then I could dirty her all up again, rinse and repeat. Perhaps when we get home. For now, I'm going to make my little girl come all over my hand while she rides my fingers outside her childhood home.

STARLA

I should maybe be embarrassed by exactly how tightly I'm clinging to Lowry's shirt, but I can't be. If he weren't holding me so tight, I have no doubt that I would be breaking into pieces and tumbling all over the grass.

Exhilaration and exhaustion from learning to ride the bike earlier have made my skin thin. It didn't take much for me to slip into this headspace where I want nothing more than to be cuddled and coddled and yes, okay, given orgasms at his hand. This is my reward for all my hard work, and also for…I don't know, being me? That's never something I thought would ever be looked upon favorably. But here we are, his hand between my legs while I sit on his lap after having been taught to ride a bike. When the fuck did I get a genie who grants wishes?

Lowry's thick finger runs along the cleft at the apex of my thighs, and I want to beg him to push it into me already. I want to feel him inside me, but I can be patient, I can be a good girl. For a little while, anyway. I can still wriggle a bit and be considered well-behaved, right?

I rock my hips forward, trying to get firmer contact, begging with my body for him to stroke my clit or fuck me with his finger, or do something other than keep up this maddeningly slow, sensuous stroke.

"Don't be greedy," he murmurs into my hair, and it makes me all the more desperate.

"Daddy, I *am* greedy."

Which of course makes him laugh. It's not mean, and even in my fragile state I don't feel it that way, but it does dial my feelings and arousal up even higher, to the point I think I might burst. At least that's my excuse as to why my clinging has turned to clawing.

"Oh, oh. Easy, love. I've got you."

He strokes me and envelops me as I lose my goddamn mind, squirming in his lap, licking and biting at his neck where he tastes salty from his earlier exertions, and digging my nails into the soft cotton of his shirt.

"You're okay. Come on, settle down for Daddy. I want to fuck you with my fingers but I don't want to hurt you, so you've got to be still for a minute. Long enough to stuff my fingers into your tight, hot cunt."

And now I'm a sex-crazed lamprey, having latched onto his neck with my mouth. Good thing he can rock the Mr. Rogers look, because the man is going to need some high-necked cardigans or some shit to cover up the hickey I'm going to leave him with.

I do, however, manage to quiet my body enough for him to part my labia with his finger and skate over my clit before delving back to my entrance to gather up some of my copious wetness, and come back to slick it over my clit and start rubbing in small, tight circles.

I gasp and moan against his neck, the tension inside me building until I feel as though it's going to spill out of me and gush all over the flagstones. That would be embarrassing; don't need anyone on what I guess is now technically my staff cleaning that up.

"Please, Daddy, please, please."

Have I ever been this desperate? I don't think so. It's something about him that makes me able to hand over control, to entrust him with my pleasure that I've always held so tightly with both fists because I know he's not going to let me down. Lowry has the capacity, and perhaps more importantly, the desire to provide for me, to care for and nurture me, and yes—as he slides two fingers into my very core—fulfill me.

I cry out and press my heels to the edge of the seat we're in to get better leverage.

"Yes, Star, yes. Just like that. I want to you to ride my fingers till you come. Think about how when we get home, I'll peel you out of these clothes and fuck you. You're going to sit on my lap and ride my cock like this, aren't you, little girl? Hmm?"

"Yes, Daddy. Oh, god."

That's what finally launches me into the throes of orgasm, is thinking about straddling Lowry with his big cock stuffed inside me and rocking up against him, my hard nipples grazing his coarse chest hair, his hands gripping my freshly spanked bottom as he urges me up and down on his thick, hard shaft.

I come hard around his fingers, bite his shoulder, and get a stranglehold on the cotton between my fingers. He's lucky I haven't ripped the thing to shreds. No, that's just how I feel, clinging to him with my legs splayed, buzzing on the downslope of my climax while still clad in my darling outfit, complete with knee socks and Mary Janes: shredded.

He's torn me into a million pieces with his patience, understanding, acceptance, and dare I say, love. It's the making me come like the Fourth of July fireworks over the Charles, sure, but it's more than that. He's right in this with me, not doing it solely to please me and otherwise grimacing while we play these games.

And while it's kind of fucked up—okay, very fucked up and I would never admit it, not even to him because he'd be horrified—I like to think we could've always been like this. It would've been wrong no doubt, and it's better this way, but god, I could've saved myself so much torture and angst over the things I wanted if I'd known there was a man like Lowry who would want them with me.

CHAPTER 31

$\mathcal{L}$owry

ON THE RIDE HOME, I've been thinking about Starla riding my cock.

"You've been quiet," she says, glancing at me out of the corner of her eye.

Her hands are folded neatly in her lap and I'm gripped by regret because she must have been fretting. I need to be careful. Not that she isn't an incredibly strong and capable person—she is —but when she's allowed herself to sink into that little girl head-space, it renders her more vulnerable. And I've asked that of her, encouraged it, coaxed it out of her. If I want to be worthy of her trust in me, then I need to do better.

I put a hand over hers and give her a smile.

"Just thinking about what I'm going to do with you when we get inside, that's all."

Her answering blush is so lovely.

I guide the car into my spot in the parking garage under my

building and lean over the center console to kiss her cheek, take in the sweet smell of her. It might be my imagination, but I swear I can smell the slightly musky scent of her climax lingering on her skin.

"Come on you, I'm not finished with you yet."

"Yes, Daddy."

The ride up to my apartment feels as though it takes for-goddamn-ever. Wouldn't it have been wonderful to heft her over my shoulder and smack her on the bottom while I hauled her into her childhood home? To have climbed the stairs until I reached her bedroom and then tossed her onto the bed to have my way with her? *So, there was a car ride in between. Don't be a selfish git, Campbell.*

And now we're here. I close the door behind us and turn on her.

I thought before I'd wanted her. Indeed, left because I did and that was a far distance from okay. While I'd like to think that I did love her then, I had no idea I could be consumed by how I feel for her. I knew her struggles, I knew her fortitude and strength, I knew she was beautiful and intelligent, but I had no idea…

Can't even say for sure what it is about her. Yes, the sex is incredible, but it's not only that. She's funny and sly and stubborn and kind and I think I might like to spend the rest of my life figuring out what else she is. And yes, because I can't help myself, supporting her in the hard times so she can have more joy and freedom and energy to use on things other than simply being alive. She's taken care of herself and I wouldn't go so far as to say she needs me—probably would feel uneasy being here with her if I thought she did—but I like to think I make her life better and that my understanding means she doesn't have to work so damn hard to explain on top of everything else.

Aye, Maeve and I made a promise to be that for each other and then we broke it. Had promised to love and cherish each other until death, but I feel as though even when we were standing up at that altar making our vows to each other, it was more like we were swearing to enjoy each other's company to the fullest and hold each other in the highest esteem. A recipe for a respectful and fond relationship, certainly, but perhaps not what I would call being in love. I suppose I know better now and I hope she will someday as well. Perhaps Denny will be the one to give her that?

Would Starla want to marry me? I suppose I don't need the legal documents and the rings and all that—may be a bit much to ask of her anyhow. Especially yet. And if she did, would she want to live here? Or, no, someplace bigger than her studio but that we both could enjoy. I don't need to live in that grand old place we were at today—maybe would be better for Star if we didn't, actually—but perhaps somewhere with a bit more space. Whatever happens, I won't be an arse and ask her about that house again.

She's right; she can afford to be a bit eccentric—hell, she could be hundreds of millions of dollars' worth of eccentric and still be obscenely wealthy—and what does it matter that she's chosen to spend a minuscule bit of her fortune keeping a house she doesn't live in? Wasteful? Sure, but as she pointed out, if it lets her sleep at night then I can hardly call it a waste.

Perhaps keeping the house will ease the sting of divesting herself of her father's company. At least in that one thing she might let herself believe she'd succeeded. I'd never take that from her.

"I believe I said something about peeling you out of those clothes and you riding my cock, aye?"

She blinks at me. Perhaps she's changed her mind? That was more of an emotionally charged day than I had anticipated. Perhaps she doesn't want to fool around but could use a rest instead.

"Would you like that, Star?"

"Yes," she says, her chest collapsing. "Yes, Daddy, please."

Yes it is, then.

I make quick work of her clothes, not even letting her get to the bedroom before I've stripped her, and then I join her naked and in my bed. Mostly I like to take my time, but giving her that much space now seems like giving her too much time to think, too much time to torment herself. No, I won't have that, not right now. I aim to give her what peace I can.

Her skin is smooth and soft as I rub from her round bottom all the way up to her shoulder blades and back again. My sweet, sexy, squirmy girl who so enjoys these games we play. I do too, though that disturbed feeling about how we play lingers.

Sure, give my little girl peace, but God forbid I allow myself any.

Why? Why do I enjoy her this way? Is it poison in my blood? What does it say about me as a man, and as a doctor? But I won't let those dark thoughts take me away from the sunny little peach who's pressed the length of her body to my own, worked her leg between mine, and begun to wriggle on my thigh. Christ almighty, she's going to be the death of me for sure.

Leaning over her, I brush some hair off her neck so I can set my mouth to work at her sweet skin. Tongue and teeth, the taste of her is sweet and her flesh gives way to the pressure of my bite until she squeals and I ease the pinch with a lick. When I get to that sensitive part where jaw meets ear, I murmur to her. "And what did you think you'd be doing? Playing pat-a-cake?"

She giggles and it fills my head, makes it feel as though champagne has penetrated my brain.

"If you want, Daddy."

If it's wrong to think of a pig-tailed, poufy-dress-clad Starla straddling my lap while playing those silly games that delight children to make her laugh like that again...well, it's probably sending me straight to a well-deserved hell, but at the moment I can't be arsed to care.

"Not now. Can't bear to think of having you in my lap

without also having you ride my cock."

Perhaps someday I'll be coordinated enough to play cat's cradle with her while she's working toward an explosive orgasm on the aforementioned cock, but my brain's already scrambled, so rolling us both to seated and hefting her into my lap will have to do.

She gasps, her mouth turning into a perfect pink O, and that I definitely do have to kiss, take advantage of the shape to slip my tongue into her mouth and let it tangle with hers. Push against her and explore the shape of her, caress and tame her. My God, I love kissing this woman.

I enjoyed kissing Maeve; it was pleasurable. But that's what it was: a single dimension of pleasure, like skating on a frozen pond. Kissing Starla is more akin to being plunged into an icy lake. Icy in that it makes me feel vibrant and alive, but it sure as hell doesn't make my balls crawl up inside my body and my cock shrivel. Ah, no, not at all.

She wraps her arms around my neck and kisses me back, rubbing her already slick pussy against me and there is nothing I want more in this life than to be inside her and watch her come again. And fuck yes, come myself, because it's as though my body's remembered that earlier this afternoon I watched the sexiest woman in the world orgasm at my hands and is wondering when precisely I'll get to follow suit. Starla seems downright eager, so hopefully the answer is now.

Indeed, she's so enthusiastic I feel as though I need to tap the brakes.

"Darling. As much as I'd like to feel you, we can't..."

I gesture between us with my chin. Can't have her with no condom. Someday perhaps I'll be able to. But Starla's got enough on her plate without an unplanned pregnancy. And while I'd like to be a father, it scares me half to death. Mostly, though, I'd be concerned for Star. If she feels overwhelmed by the thought of managing a house, how would she feel about being responsible for a human being? Even if it weren't solely her responsibility? Not something we need to address or worry about because I wouldn't put her in that position. We'll be safe, every time.

It's clumsy, but I tilt so I can grab a condom out of the drawer. Rip it open as well as I can and then roll it over my cock. Can't hardly wait. Should've asked if she was ready first, but she doesn't seem to think I'm a selfish prig. No, she's coming up on her knees and grabbing my length to guide inside of her, and Christ. My brain might melt out of my head because she feels so good.

It sounds twee, but I feel as though we fit together, as though she's the piece I've been missing. She makes me feel whole, and loved for everything I am. And forgiven for the things I'm not. Or haven't been.

"Star..."

Her name on my lips is a prayer, and also a word of thanks so deep that "gratitude" doesn't cover it.

I hold her to me just as she is, her body encompassing me in a warm, welcoming embrace. This feels like love to me, and I hope it feels like love to her.

"Daddy?"

An anxious tone to her question makes me hold her tighter. While I could hold her like this for a good long time, I'm not sure that forever is what she intended to sign up for. I'm not sure if being with me is working out some of the abandonment issues I caused. If she'll leave *me* because she can now. One thing is for certain, I won't be leaving her unless I'm dragged away. She's simply too dear to me.

"Are you okay?"

"Oh, sweet girl. Yes, I'm fine indeed. I just like holding you. Is that so terrible?"

I give her shoulder a teasing nip and she laughs.

"No, not terrible at all."

"Are you perhaps getting impatient? Hmm?"

While I could soak in her body for a good long while and let how much I adore her flood my brain, I don't think that's what Starla was expecting, and it's perhaps not what she wants. Not now, maybe not ever. Couldn't say for sure. Don't know if I want to know.

How badly would I be crushed if this is sex for her and nothing more? It was never just sex for me and it's definitely not now. I promised her a good fuck though, and that I can deliver.

"Is having Daddy's fat cock stuffed in your pussy making you a horny little girl?"

She whimpers and sets my brain alight. Those sounds she makes hit very specific pleasure points in my brain.

"Yes, Daddy."

I lean her back enough that I can see her face with its pretty blush and her hair tumbling around her shoulders, and Christ, she's lovely and perfect.

"You know I haven't played with your tits yet today? And that's a damn shame. They're so pretty, and your nipples are begging to be pinched."

I do just that, tweaking both of them, and she sucks air through her teeth but doesn't tell me to stop. Sinks her teeth into her bottom lip, though.

"Are you a little sensitive today?"

She nods, widens her eyes as though she's embarrassed. "I'll get my period soon. They get sore."

"Mmm."

I weigh them in my hands, thumbing her nipples until she squirms.

"Just your nipples or all of your tits?"

To emphasize my point, I squeeze and she gasps. She doesn't need to confirm my suspicions, but she does anyway. "Everything, Daddy."

I hum thoughtfully again and continue to play with her, being a little rough, and it seems as though she might be sore, but that doesn't bother her. No, it might make breast play even more enjoyable for her. I can work with that. Yes, I'm getting a bit distracted by the way she's grinding on my lap—okay, a lot distracted—but I can still toy with her, push her, make her squeal and whimper and hopefully have another satiating climax.

I squeeze, knead, pinch, and yes, add the occasional slap. And when I've got her panting and rutting against me, mewling and begging, I sculpt my hands around her breasts and clamp my thumbs and forefingers around her nipples. And then tug.

She makes one of those sexy, muddled pleading sounds, and yes, she likes that. Which is nice, but I also want to prod at her embarrassment buttons. Not hard enough to verge into humiliation because I don't think she'd enjoy that, but a thin varnish of shame can add a dimension to these things and I want her to feel it all. To feel as deeply as I do.

"Now you do it," I say, not letting up on the grasp I have on her nipples. "Lean back and show me how hard you want your sore nipples pinched and tugged."

She looks at me with widened, unbelieving eyes. I want her to do *what*?

"Go on then. I'm not going to move an inch. If you want that feeling—and I think you do because you're a naughty, filthy little girl who likes Daddy to be rough with her perfect tits—then you're going to have to get it yourself."

Her chin wrinkles, and like the demoness she is, she squeezes my cock with her internal muscles. Oh, she wants to play this way? I don't think so.

"I felt that. You think you can outlast me? I could lift you off my cock, put you across my knee and give you a punishment spanking for not following my instructions, but I think you'd rather grind your way to an orgasm on my cock while we make your tits even sorer. I for one would rather come inside your tight, hot cunt than have a wank in the shower. Up to you, though."

Her frown deepens, and she's cute as a frustrated kitten when she pouts. Still restive as one too. But much as I suspected she would, she pulls back experimentally from where I still have her nipples pinched between my fingers and closes her eyes, a slight wince crossing her features. But, hands gripping my shoulders, she does it again, and again. Harder this time. Farther. And now she's determined.

Bucking on me like she can't get enough of my cock or the torment we're subjecting her breasts to, she whines and holds on to me harder.

"Are you going to come, little girl? Be my shooting Star?"

"Yes, Daddy."

"Soon?"

"Yes, Daddy."

Thank God, because I don't know how much longer I can hold out. Hoping to send her over the edge, I tilt my hips and she lets out this choked little gasp.

"Yes, Daddy. Please. More. Just like that, please."

And since it feels damn good to me too, I match her rhythm, thrusting up farther, gripping her tits even harder, and then I feel it. A split second before I hear it.

"Oh. Ooh. Daddy, yes. Yes, I'm coming. Fuck, fuck. Daddy, please. Oh."

Her nails dig into me as her pussy milks my cock and I spill. Spill my longing, desire, and pent-up sexual energy into her.

It's wildly satisfying, exhilarating to be shooting my load inside her. A lightening sensation as though I've been carrying this weighty craving for her. Which I suppose I have, but I never thought of it as a physical weight. But here she is: in my lap, in my arms, making the most intimate love to me, and even as the pressure of my own orgasm is relieved, there's a swelling in my chest.

I never want to let her go.

tarla

I'M GOING to have to talk to Doctor Gendron about my anxiety. Yes, I've dealt with it more or less throughout my life, but I've always thought of depression as my primary diagnosis. Maybe she can write me a temporary scrip while I'm dealing with this Patrick Enterprises shit? Because I've never had such physical, such visceral manifestations of it.

Even after this incredible weekend with Lowry, I don't feel any more relaxed, any less stressed. No, my agitation is off the charts and talking to him about my father didn't help any. If anything, it cranked up my guilt, my shame, made me feel like I have the most terrible secret. What kind of grown woman is desperate for her dead father's approval? Allows it to influence her decisions? Not that Lowry made me feel ridiculous, but ugh. Talking about my father and how much I still desperately want to please him sure as hell didn't help with the ratcheting up of my anxiety. Occasional pounding of the heart, blood running cold or whatever, I've dealt with before, but not nausea and that's what's been dogging me lately. Not to the point that I've actually thrown up, but that doesn't feel far off.

If there's one thing I've gotten better at, it's nipping things in the bud. Telling Doctor Gendron about them before I'm paralyzed or really sick. It doesn't make a ton of sense to waste time feeling like ass when I don't have to.

It makes me feel foolish that I avoided telling her about things that were bothering me for so long. But since time travel isn't a thing—even for me with all my money—I'll try to be gentle with myself even though that's never been a thing I'm super great at.

I take a last look in my mirror before heading out to meet Jerome Garrett. The outfit Holden picked out for me makes me feel powerful, but not like myself at the same time—I can't wait to take it off and put on some cutesy pajamas because aside from the peplum on my short jacket, I don't have any of those soft, adorable details Lowry likes so well because I can't afford for Jerome to see me as soft or weak.

My most expensive black heels, knee-length black pencil skirt with a slightly less than modest slit up the back, a dark turquoise silk shell, and my pretty peplum coat. Plus...

Diamonds. Yes, they're my best friend, not you, Jerome. No matter that I prefer kitschy and twee things. For tonight, I'm rocking my favorite grown-up bling and now I'm ready to go.

Holden's driving me, and he doesn't blink an eye at my lack of acknowledgment when I climb in. He knows I've got to focus. The ride there passes in a blink, though my stomach seems exponentially angrier by the time I reach the maître d'.

"Starla Patrick, I'm meeting Jerome Garrett."

"Yes, of course, welcome. Mr. Garrett's already seated, I'll show you to your table. Right this way, please."

He shows me through the restaurant to a banquette facing the harbor and there's my nemesis-I-didn't-choose slash possible-solution-to-my-problems.

Jerome stands, offers me a hand which I shake. My impressions from photos are borne out: the man is enormous. He's got to be six and a half feet tall and I'm feeling all five foot four of my very average height, plus like three more inches from my heels, I guess.

"Ms. Patrick, thank you so much for joining me."

"Don't thank me yet."

His grip is firm but not threatening, his hand warm and large enough to basically envelop mine. He's not trying to use his size to intimidate me, he's just really fucking big.

He's a handsome older Black man, and this is the sort of guy Holden would pick out as a daddy. Except the little in me doesn't get that instantaneous ping I sometimes do from a man who turns out to be not a daddy type, but an actual daddy. Not always, though, and definitely not what I need to be contemplating.

We slide into the cushy seats and Jerome looks across the overly extravagant table.

"I'm sorry again for your loss. Your father and I had our issues, but he was an exceptional businessman and I know he loved you very much."

How the fuck would Jerome Garrett know that when I was never certain? Doesn't matter. He's only making polite conversation before we get down to brass tacks. I'm certainly not going to let the childish words slip from my tongue into the air: *He did? How do you know? Did he say something about me?* A million times no.

"Thank you."

A waitress comes to take our drink order, and while I'd been dreaming of a full-bodied Douro red, the idea of it now makes my stomach turn. Goddammit, I was really counting on alcohol to ease the way of what will no doubt be an extraordinarily difficult conversation.

When she departs, Jerome's intense gaze settles on me.

"How's your health?"

"Excuse me?"

That's pretty fucking rude. And yeah, I expected this to be difficult, but not from this angle. How's my health, a.k.a., how far away am I from checking into Harbinson as an inpatient again? That's what he means and I'm not here for it. What the hell?

"I don't mean to be overly familiar—"

"You're failing spectacularly, then."

His mouth tightens, but I'm not even sorry.

"Look— May I call you Starla?"

"Sure."

He's already poked at my mental health, so what the hell difference does it make if he does it using my first name or my last?

"Starla. I'm fully aware of your depression diagnosis. I know you treat it very successfully with ECT. I would imagine the grief of losing your father compounded what you deal with every day. I have no illusions that your depression makes you helpless or anything less than formidable. It's—"

He seems to take a breath, collect himself, and I'm curious what he's going to say.

"I'm not sure you know my sister has bipolar disorder. So, I don't know what it's like to be you, but I probably have a better idea than most people."

"I didn't know that. I hope she's well."

I genuinely do. Depression can be really fucking rough, but I'm not dealing with the one-two punch of depression and mania.

Jerome shrugs. "We're lucky we have an effectively unlimited amount of funds to throw at it. She's been able to access the best treatment available, and I've done my best to let her be independent to the fullest extent possible, but there have definitely been some rough times. Right now she's doing well. She's an incredibly talented artist. Would you—" His face lights up, and then as quickly falls. "No, I'm sorry. That's wildly unprofessional."

"What were you going to say?"

He looks a bit sheepish and spreads his hands on the table, as though he's laying out all his cards for me to see, inspect.

"I suppose your father told you I'm a ruthless businessman. Which can be true. But I'm also a total softie when it comes to my family." He shrugs again, the considerable breadth of his shoulders rising and falling as he takes a sip of the wine he's ordered. "I was going to ask if you'd like to see some of her paintings, but this isn't show-and-tell nor is it a nursing home where it's fair to expect everyone to ooh and ahh over pictures of your grandchildren. I apologize."

He's embarrassed, and I get the feeling there's something about me that renders him vulnerable, soft. Which I could—should—use to my advantage. But I've never been inclined to be cutthroat. I've been one of the people who end up bleeding out from the knife wound across their windpipe for too long to find that appealing.

"I'd love to see them."

"Really?"

This whole thing could be a ruse, but I've fallen for it. I won't buy it hook, line, and sinker, though, nor would my advisors let me. But what's the harm in looking at Jerome's sister's paintings? What's the harm in either him thinking more kindly toward me or that he's fooled me?

"Yes. I'm not much of a collector, but I majored in art history. Over my seven years of college."

The corner of his mouth quirks, but probably trying not to laugh, he tames it. I used to be embarrassed it took me so freaking long, but now I'm mostly proud I did it at all. Jerome ultimately reaches into his coat pocket to pull out his phone, the enthusiasm blooming on his face again. He hits a few buttons and then hands me his phone.

"That's her website, you can scroll down and see more."

It's hard to tell from the images how large the paintings are, but they're vibrant and saturated with color. Mostly bright and lush with shades that make me think of the rain forest but sometimes the colors swing darker, moodier. This isn't overblown brotherly pride, though, she's really quite good. Bertryse Garrett. At the end, there's a photo of a woman who I assume is Bertryse standing next to one of her paintings. It's a huge canvas, and her smile is almost as wide. She's gorgeous, as are her paintings.

I hand him back his phone, saying, "She's lovely, and very talented. You must be very proud."

"I am. My little sister's been killing it for a long time. Sometimes I just feel like I'm along for the ride."

His expression tells me he's not just saying this, not trying to butter me up with saccharine platitudes. I can almost always pick up on when people resent the ever-loving hell out of their relatives or friends with mental illness but are trying to be martyrs. I don't get that from Jerome at all.

"I'm sure sometimes you are."

He laughs, a hearty thing, and offers me a toast. "Ain't that the truth."

BY THE TIME we're finishing our entrees, I have decided that despite my earlier reservations, Jerome Garrett might be the answer to some of my prayers. Not all of them, certainly, because my advisors will be wary, Tad will be ripshit, and I'm guessing my father's ghost will be so distraught he'll be pissed he was cremated so he can't roll over in his grave. But after talking to Jerome, I feel like perhaps my father took everything that happened between their businesses as a personal slight instead of the exhilarating game Jerome seemed to see it as.

If everything checks out, I will be selling a good portion of my shares in Patrick Enterprises to Garrett Industries. Which will mean I'll still maintain the largest stake in the company, and as a voting bloc, Jerome and I will have the final say on any decision that comes to the board.

I'm not giving him an answer until I can review everything, but after speaking with him and reviewing the portfolio he brought for me, I feel as though we have a lot of the same sensibilities. We both feel more responsible to our employees than to our shareholders, are committed to doing our best to be environmentally conscientious and innovative, and share a dedication to diversity at all levels of the company, but especially in the C-suite.

Yes, I'm going to have my people go through his proposal with a fine-tooth comb and tear it to shreds, but fundamentally... this might be okay? My heart doesn't shrivel at the idea of leaving my people in Jerome's care the way it does when I imagine doing the same with Tad. Will I always agree completely with him? No, of course not, but I do fundamentally think Jerome will do a good job of steering the Patrick Enterprises ship. Which is what I tell him.

"I'm going to have a lot of questions, and I'm sure the lawyers will have a lot to say about all of this, but I do feel, at my core, as though this is a real possibility. I wouldn't waste your time by telling you it was if I didn't mean it. I am cautiously optimistic about what we've discussed."

Jerome looks pleased as punch, and he should. This would significantly increase his presence in certain sectors and introduce his presence in others. It would make an already powerful man more powerful. But from his treatment of me, the way he talks about his sister, I feel as though I can trust him—within reason, of course. I don't mind having to check on the ship, make sure it's still headed in the right direction, but I sure as fuck don't want to have to be steering it myself all the time which is what the past several months have felt like.

I like the way he rises when I stand to leave, offers me his hand again.

"Thank you again for meeting with me. I hope this all works out, and even if not, it's been a pleasure."

"Likewise. I'll be in touch."

And then I head toward the exit.

It's still difficult. I hate the idea of disappointing my father, of handing his legacy over to someone who isn't me or someone he trusted, like Tad. But the thing is…I cannot do this. I cannot run this company without sacrificing my mental health. I'd like to be able to power through and do the difficult thing, but I can't. It is not within my capabilities. Admitting that blows. Makes me feel incompetent, less than worthy, all the worst things people have said to me for my whole life. Not to mention having to admit that my father was wrong about me and giving up on the approval I'd finally been able to win from him after feeling like a disappointment for so long. That…that will be the worst part of it, I'm sure.

But possibly, by making an informed and responsible decision, I'm actually not fucking this up as badly as I thought? God, I hope so because I cannot handle feeling nauseated like this forever. There is some shit that I have recognized as my depression being an asshole and I can ride through it, but I cannot chill on the feeling-like-I'm-going-to-hurl express. Not gonna happen. Indeed, I'm not chilling anymore—it's an effort to not be puking up my excellent dinner on this carpet on my way down to my car.

I want to go home. I want Lowry. He'll understand and let me lay my head in his lap while he pets my hair, and he won't complain while he holds my hair back as I puke. He'll get that my anxiety has grown beyond the bounds of what my mind can bear so it's visiting itself upon my body in an effort to be like, "Hey, Dickhead, pay attention to me. You should do something before I move on to other things like chest pains. Wouldn't that be fun?" Ugh. He'll encourage me to talk to Doctor Gendron about it and make me feel smart and responsible for doing it instead of like a failure.

Before I go home, though, I need to make a detour to the restroom because for fuck's sake, I can't not vomit.

I head straight to the last stall and barely lock it before I'm on my knees and hurling all the things into the toilet. Perfect, A-plus. At least it doesn't take long for my stomach to empty its contents. The bile burns my throat and tastes god-awful in my mouth. I don't think I can wait until next week to see Doctor Gendron, I'll leave her a message when I get home and she'll either call me back and put in a scrip or she'll fit me in tomorrow. She always does.

When I make my way out, there are a couple of other women washing their hands, checking their makeup, gossiping at the sinks. And they all totes heard me tossing a sidewalk pizza. Awesome.

In case I had any doubt, as I wash out the foul taste from my mouth, the woman next to me gives me a sympathetic smile.

"Morning sickness? God, I had it the worst with my first baby. Don't worry, the second one was so much easier."

Uh, what? I could protest, "No it's just a physical manifestation of my overwhelming anxiety. Obviously." The thought of being knocked up had never entered my mind. But now it does, even as I smile politely because there is no goddamn way I'm pregnant. We use condoms, every time. There is no fucking way. No. Fucking. Way.

I walk out feeling like I'm in a fog. Trail over to the car feeling the same and ride back to my apartment without saying a word to Holden, other than handing him the information Jerome Garrett gave me and telling him to sic my lawyers on it immediately. I walk into my building and wait until he drives away, but then—just for the hell of it—walk to the nearest drugstore a couple of blocks away. Just for shits and giggles, just so I can sleep tonight, just so I can prove to my sometimes worthless brain that no, I'm not pregnant, I must be throwing up because I'm so stressed. Because that would be oh-so-much better.

So I drift through picking up a pregnancy test and wander back to my apartment. Everything is surreal under the street-lamps. People are going about their business as if everything is fine, totally fine, and the earth is not flailing on its axis. So one woman said something in a bathroom. That doesn't mean anything. It doesn't. If wishes were fishes and all that. But this is not a wish I've ever had. Ever.

I've certainly worried about getting pregnant, but never had I thought beyond that. The outcome always seemed obvious: I would end it because I can't have children. I can maintain my own very small life—anything beyond that is too much. Plus, I hate the idea of knowingly passing on the kind of suffering I've endured to someone else who had absolutely no say in the matter. Yes, I'm okay now, but it wasn't easy to get here, and who knows if I'm going to stay this way? What happens if I have more in common with my mother than I think? There have been so many days when I wish I'd never been born and I don't want to put anyone else through that.

Except...

Things wouldn't be the same for a baby of Lowry's as they'd been for me. If he wanted to be a father, for us to be a family, and I could survive the pregnancy? I'd never let myself think about it, but now that I have—and wasn't that a terrible idea?—it's maybe something that I want. That I covet. There's no point in even dwelling on the possibility, though. I don't know if I'm pregnant. If I am, there's no saying that I'll be able to carry a baby to term. My depression could rear its ugly head violently and to save my own life, I'd have to end it. Jesus, I don't need to be considering how to terminate a pregnancy I don't even know is real yet. I need to clear my mind of all of it—because I've always been so good at letting shit go. For fuck's sake.

I've made it back to my apartment, into the bathroom and the thought of being like my mother... It sends a chill down my spine and I have to turn away from the mirror where all I'd see is reminders that I'm her daughter.

CHAPTER 33

owry

I WASN'T EXPECTING to see Star tonight, but I wasn't sad when she texted.

Are you still awake? Are you too tired to come over?

Sweet girl.

Yes, I'm awake. And I'm never too tired to come see you.

Which is true. The idea of seeing her buoys me, wakes me up. Even if I were exhausted, I would find the wherewithal to make the trip to her apartment. And here I am. I knock on her door and then there's a grand shuffle before she's standing before me.

In her sloth pajamas, hair disheveled, she's the one who looks exhausted. Eyes red, face drawn and pale, she looks as though she's been crying. I know she had some sort of meeting about Patrick Enterprises tonight but she hadn't said what exactly it was and I hadn't pried. I'd hoped whatever it was would make her feel better, more settled—instead I find her like this.

I barely open my arms before she's walking into my embrace, burrowing her head into my chest and hugging me tightly.

"Oh, Star, sweetheart..."

I'm hit with a wave of bewilderment, sympathy, and a good heap of inadequacy. Why is she so upset? What can I do? Why don't I have the answers already? I'm supposed to care for her and I've failed.

I wrap myself around her as well as I can, an arm at her waist, a hand cradling the back of her head, and I wish I had more limbs or other ways to hold her closer, shelter her. I've got the urge to demand who hurt her so I can go fight them, but that's not what she needs. She can fight people herself. I'm just the lucky bastard who gets to hold her after she does.

"Think we could go inside and do this? I don't mind standing on your threshold, but I thought you might like a bit more privacy."

She nods into my chest and it's adorably pathetic. She's not kick-ass, professional Starla right now, she's sweet, lost, overwhelmed Starla who really needs her daddy. Okay. I can do that. To prove it—to her as well as myself—I pick her up and get a startled laugh for my trouble, as well as a crackle in my knees.

I kick the door closed behind us and bring her over to the couch, get her settled on my lap, and she's still clinging to me. All I want is to pull it out of her, what's happened, how I can help, but I don't want to pry too hard and crack her open.

"Little girl, do you want to tell me what's happened, or do you just want hugs?"

"Just hugs right now. Please, Daddy."

She's not crying, but she doesn't sound too far off and it breaks my heart. But I can cuddle her, cradle her, give her comfort until she's ready to hand me more than that.

"Okay. You're okay."

After a few minutes, she sniffles and looks up at me.

"I had a meeting tonight."

"I know."

"About my father's company."

It's her company, but I suspect owning it in that way might overwhelm her, so sure, yes, her father's company.

"Mmm." I hum my agreement because I remember but I don't want to be obtrusive.

"With Jerome Garrett. Do you know who he is?"

"The name's familiar, but I can't say why."

Although now it's seared into my brain as someone who's made Starla unhappy.

"He's the head of Garrett Industries, which has been Patrick Enterprises' biggest competitor for as long as I can remember. My father hated Jerome Garrett. Like, a lot. Thought of him as his nemesis."

Interesting she met with him then. And what for?

"Anyway, I had dinner with him and I...I think I'm going to sell him enough of my shares of my father's company that Jerome will effectively be in charge. And I'll maintain enough that if we vote as a bloc, no one can override us."

She makes a sad little squeaky noise that sounds like she's trying so hard not to cry.

"I'm not sure why that's so upsetting? Can you explain it to me? Is he bullying you into this? Trying to take advantage? Black-mailing you? Whatever it is, you can tell me, and I'll do my best to help you work it out. Or just listen. Whatever you need."

Starla shakes her head, still looking miserable. I know she's not keen on selling the business, but if she's planning to, I'd think she'd make wise decisions about what to do with it because that's who she is. What about this Garrett fellow has her in such a state?

"No, he's not doing any of that. I...I actually like him. I don't agree with him on everything, but on the whole I think he'll be a good shepherd for Patrick Enterprises, and he'll treat our employees fairly and help the company flourish."

"Starla, love, you're going to have to help me out here because Scotsmen—skulls like boulders, ye see? I'm still not sure why this is a problem."

I get a smile out of her which I almost always do when I turn up my brogue, but then she's back to looking gutted.

"Because I feel like I'm betraying my father. I won't be able to stand it if I lose control or ruin this thing he worked so hard to build. I feel like I'm a failure for not being able to take the helm myself and I just want to do one thing—one fucking thing—right. The only time I can remember him being happy with me was after he'd started to think I could take over from him one day. I've been so anxious that I've been getting sick and I—"

Her chin trembles and I can see the tears brimming on her bottom lashes. One blink and they could overflow. I knew she'd been worried and overstressed, but I didn't know it had gotten so bad. I want to scold her for not telling me sooner, but I'm also well-aware I've been earning back her trust, and I should be grateful she's telling me at all.

Those hazel eyes of hers are wide and pleading, almost as if she has something else to confess. No, confess isn't the right word as I don't think she's done anything that could be considered "bad." And so what if she had? It would likely be something minor that she can't stop fixating on and perhaps offering to spank her as punishment would help her let it go.

She rolls her lips between her teeth and there are very few things she could ask me for that I wouldn't give her. Almost nothing, come to that.

"It's been a long time since I felt broken, but this is making me believe it. Maybe because I'm only a couple of weeks away from my ECT and all of this is happening when I'm on the downslope. Whatever it is, it's reminding me of how I was always too much for my father, how I always need too much, and I…I'm a grown goddamn woman. I am a capable human being but I can't do this. It's too much and I hate myself for it being too much. What is wrong with me? Why am I like this? Why are you here?"

She's crying now, voice ragged and tear-choked. It's as though someone's scraping their nails over my heart, ripping it to shreds. I've seen her like this before and it hurt me just as much then, but I wasn't in a position to take her in my arms and hold her close. At least I can do that. I'm not sure which part of me will be most helpful now, whether she wants her daddy, Lowry the relatively sensible man, or Doctor Campbell who can put into effect all the things I know about depression and anxiety—hers in particular. And whether what she wants would line up with what she actually needs, because God knows those aren't always the same thing.

"You're not broken, Star. Not any more than someone who needs glasses because they're nearsighted, not any more than a person who needs chemo because they've got cancer, not any more than someone who broke their leg on the ski slope. I think you're right that it's not helping that you're at the two-thirds mark of your ECT cycle. That's probably letting your depression yell at you a lot louder and enabling this anxiety to hit you harder than it would right after a treatment. You'll feel better in a couple of weeks; you know you will. If you don't think you can wait that long, call Doctor Gendron. We can get her on the phone right now if you like."

Course I don't know whether Starla's discussed our relationship with Lacey, but it doesn't matter now, does it? I'd do anything to help her, even if it's incurring Lacey's not inconsiderable wrath. Starla comes first.

This seems like a good time to give her my vote of confidence in her abilities instead of simply letting her spill her guts like at her father's house. I believe in her and would trust her with my life. I have no doubt she'll make good choices when it comes to Patrick Enterprises.

"I can't say I know much about business—you're the expert on that of the two of us, for sure—but I do know you. You're intelligent and conscientious, and you have good enough sense to surround yourself with people who are the same and who can give you good advice. If you think selling some of your shares to this Garrett fellow is your best choice, then it's probably true. Your father wasn't right about everything, you know."

I have a long list of things he was wrong about or could have done better, frankly. Which I ought to crumple and toss in my mental rubbish bin because he's gone now.

"I'm here because I care about you, very much, and you're absolutely brilliant. I feel fortunate to be here. I hurt when you're hurting, but that's not your fault, and I think we've pretty well seen that wherever you are is where I'd most like to be."

~

STARLA

He's the sweetest. The steadiest. And so very smart. It's almost enough to make me believe him.

That's part of why depression is shitty, and I *know* that. But at the moment it's not enough. My rational brain is not enough to overcome that god-awful, lying part of my brain that says I am worthless, unlovable, and that I should quit taking up space. That I am a failure and I've disappointed everyone who's been there for me like Lowry and Doctor Gendron and my father and Holden and the list goes on… All of those people are waiting for a chance to escape, a chance to get the hell away from this black hole of a girl who needs to much, who sucks all the fun and energy and pleasure out of the world.

I'd convinced myself earlier that perhaps this was okay. That I was at least making a solid decision, if not one that was perfect or that I was thrilled about. Not the worst.

And then seeing that little "YES" show up on that godforsaken pregnancy test and the one after that… I started to spiral. Hard and fast, and this is yet another thing I can't face because I can't handle it. I am weak and horrible and stupid, and how much more like my mother can I be, really?

I'd been a teenager when I found out my mother had killed herself. It was several years earlier that I'd done the math on my parents' wedding anniversary and my birthday, and since I wasn't a preemie in the NICU, yeah, they weren't married. Which fundamentally, who cares? What is the big fucking deal about children being born to parents who aren't married? Isn't all that matters is that they have a family who loves them and is able to raise them?

Sure, but when your father is one of the richest men in New England, and your mother is a gorgeous but mentally unstable woman who doesn't come from money and she happens to get knocked up? I'd like to think my parents were in love, that I was a product of love and not lust, but I don't remember them. I don't remember her, really. My father could have lied to me all this time about how much he loved my mother because he didn't want me to feel bad that he only married her because he's a stand-up guy and that's what good men are supposed to do when they get a woman pregnant.

I don't want Lowry to propose because I'm pregnant. I don't want him to stay with me if I'm pregnant because he feels obligated to. How much more can I heap on this man and not expect him to break? I am such a fucking burden it makes me want to…

No, I don't want to die. I don't want to kill myself. I don't, I really don't. I would tell anyone having the same thoughts as I am that it will get better. And I believe that with every atom of my rational brain. Too bad the goddamn depression monster is screaming over all of that. Which is why I couldn't, just couldn't, tell Lowry about her.

It doesn't make any sense at all, I know, and knowing me I'm probably wrong, but from the second I saw those three goddamn letters, I've thought this baby is a girl. Not even thought. Known. I can't explain it, it's not rational, but really, how much of what I think is? It's made me less likely to think about terminating this pregnancy for any reason except if my own mental health is circling the toilet, which might mean that neither of us would survive and what the hell good would that do anyone?

All of this adds up to me desperately wanting to tell Lowry about the baby, but also being absolutely terrified to. What would be worse, if he stayed or if he left? If he stays, will I always worry that it's because of the baby and he feels trapped? That wouldn't do anything to improve my mental health. What if that's why my mother killed herself? It's not as though I can ask her what the final straw was. And fuck all, what if it was me? Not good, not good at all.

And if he left…

Well, I know precisely what that's like. I'd be devastated. I don't think I could live through that again. Not after all this. Not after he gained my trust, coaxed me into handing over the deepest, most vulnerable parts of myself, letting me believe he valued and adored them. This meltdown is probably making him think twice about being with me. And adding a baby—a squalling package of need who's likely to grow up like me? No, I can't tell him. Can't. Yes, he'll find out eventually, but I don't need to tell him yet. Not yet. I'll get through this Garrett acquisition and be a slightly smaller disaster and then tell him. We can be rational people and discuss this rationally. And if he leaves…

I don't honestly know.

"Star?"

Right. I've been sitting here, lost in my dark thoughts. The least I can do is say something, anything.

"Yeah?"

"I hate to do this, but I need to use the bathroom. I won't be long, promise. Can I get you something while I'm up? Tea?

Whisky? Tuna and Doritos or some other vile concoction? Anything?"

The idea of one of Lowry's hot toddies makes my brain happy but my stomach miserable. Though I do appreciate having a few moments to collect myself, to strengthen my resolve, basically get any of my shit together at all.

"Tea, please."

"Course. I'll be right back, love."

Love. I'd be lying if I said I didn't notice the absence of that word when he was telling me why he was here. Would it have made a difference if he'd said it? I can't imagine it would've had much of an effect, but the lack certainly didn't ease any of my doubts.

And so I'll sit here with my asshole depression brain shouting lies I can't silence, the rational part of my mind being cowed by anxiety, and hell, fucking hell, doubting everything in the world as the man I love walks away from me.

CHAPTER 34

 tarla

"THANK you for squeezing me in, I know you're busy."

"Thank you for calling. I'd always rather have you call than not, you know that."

I do. Makes it a titch easier to do the thing, but not a ton. Which is why I look down at my nails—still with their fancy paint job from my meeting with Garrett—instead of volunteering more to Doctor Gendron about why precisely I'm here.

"So, what's up?"

She's so good about giving me an extra prod when I need it.

"I told you about the anxiety on the phone. It's maybe the worst I've ever had, and you know that's not nothing. And I feel like with all the shit that's going on with my father's company—"

"You know it's yours now, right?"

"Fuck all, do I ever," I mutter.

"I'm not pointing that out to add more pressure. I'm pointing it out because you're doing extraordinarily well given the pressure cooker you're in. I'm very proud of you, and I'm very proud that you're asking for help when you feel like you need it."

Her kind words make my eyes sting and my sinuses burn because she is one of the people I respect and trust most on the planet. She wouldn't lie to me. She's never spoon-fed me sugar when things are going to hell, which is why I listen when she says things are going well.

My only response is "yeah, okay," because it's still hard for me to take a compliment, no matter who it's coming from.

"So, anyway, there's all that, on top of my job, and yesterday I found out…"

Oh, not looking forward to telling her I'm pregnant. Partially because I haven't told her I'm seeing anyone, never mind who it is I've been seeing. She's going to have some questions. But she can't help me if I don't tell her. I know from a quick internet search that ECT is really safe in pregnancy, that sometimes people switch to ECT instead of meds for that reason. But I don't know much more than that. I sure as fuck don't have a medical degree. My father may have been able to get me into med school, but I'd probably still be finishing given how long it took me to finish my undergrad degree.

"I'm pregnant. Like not far along I don't think, but yeah."

I wait for the judgment, for the "how could you," but aside from an extra blink it doesn't come.

"I can understand how that would exacerbate your stress. And that could very well be contributing to your nausea. Anxiety may still be part of it, but it's hard to say. Have you decided what you're going to do about the pregnancy?"

She's the best. No judgment, no assumptions. Acting as though any decision I make is completely fine, and maybe it would be, with her.

"No."

"Do you know who the father is?"

God love Doctor Gendron and her lack of slut-shaming. But in fact, "I do."

She nods, and I wonder if she knows. How would she know? I haven't told her and Lowry wouldn't, especially not without talking to me about it first. I've been careful not to look for Lowry when I'm at Harbinson for my regular appointments and to not give more than a polite nod when we've passed in the halls. But Doctor Gendron isn't oblivious. Sometimes more observant than I'd like her to be, but honestly, usually precisely the right amount.

"Don't be mad."

She pulls a face. "Who's mad? I'm not mad."

"Just don't freak out."

Doctor Gendron places what I can only assume is a flippant hand over her heart. "On my honor, I promise not to freak out."

I still really don't want to tell her, because despite her word, I don't believe her. And I don't want to make things weird for Lowry. It's a talent I have—making it weird.

"It's Lowry. We've been, um, seeing each other. It's not like we just fucked. I mean, we do, obviously, but not like one time by mistake. Like a lot."

Oh my god, making it so very weird. I take a breath and start over, trying not to talk about how Lowry and I fuck every chance we get.

"What I'm trying to say is that we're in a relationship and have been for a while. I think… No, I know I love him. And I think he might love me too? But I'm not sure. I'm a hard person to love."

I burn with shame when I say that. It's not something I'm proud of, and it's not something I like to admit, but deep in my heart of hearts I believe that's true. Which sucks. Big time.

"You're not. That's your depression talking. And I'm not mad. I'm not thrilled about it, but I'm not surprised, and I'm not going to censure him for it. Have you told him?"

I bite my lip. Hard.

"Not yet."

"It's obviously up to you, and I should probably keep my mouth shut as such, but I'll go as far to say I think you should. And that's it. The rest is..." She shrugs. "ECT is incredibly safe during pregnancy, as I'm sure you've already looked up online. I can give you a bunch of studies saying so if you'd like to review them, and we can go over the details of what would be different if you choose to continue the pregnancy. If you choose to terminate the pregnancy, we could help you make arrangements for that. I know it can feel overwhelming. I've got to tell you that there's the possibility of pregnancy exacerbating your depression to the point that it's dangerous for you and the fetus. If that happens, I'm not going to be shy about advocating for you to have an abortion. I hope it doesn't come to that, but should it, you're my number one concern."

I appreciate Doctor Gendron's neutrality, not using the word *baby*, but the thing is, I already think of her as "she," so she's already a baby to me. I nod, though, because if things get worse, a lot worse, and we can't fix it? I won't be able to manage a pregnancy, never mind another human being, especially one that can't help itself at all. Whether I like it or not—which I don't—abortion is a thing I need to keep on the table. Especially if Lowry enjoys being my daddy but has no interest in being a child's father.

LOWRY

Last night with Starla was rough. She had some tea and agreed that she'd call Lacey first thing this morning. And then she begged me pretty please to fuck her.

It was mind-blowing as always, but she felt fragile to me in a way she doesn't usually, and distant. Not so distant that I didn't feel she was fully consenting, but she was holding back from me. I suppose if she's feeling as though she might blow apart, it makes sense she might withdraw a bit to hold herself together. But I didn't like it. Don't. Perhaps she'll feel better this evening after speaking with Lacey. I hope so because it was heartrending to hold her listless body over a fitful night for her and a sleepless one for me.

Considering all that, it's been a long day but not half bad. I asked a patient of mine to consider ECT today and it scared her —don't blame her at all—but she said she'd think about it and that's more than I thought I would get. She reminds me of Starla some, actually, which maybe inclines me to fondness more than I would be otherwise. But if ECT could do for her what it's done for Star... God, I hope she'll let us try. I'd do just about anything to get her to try. Maybe Starla would speak with her when she's more back to normal? It's worth an ask.

While the day had started out sunny and was still when I took my afternoon workout, the sky's gone grey and thin drizzle is starting to turn to fat drops plunking down from the sky. Good thing I've got my umbrella; I'm not in a hurry to get drenched on my way to the car. I promised myself I'd stop at home to check mail and water plants and such. It's possible I've been neglecting my apartment a bit since I'm at Starla's so often. Had to ask my neighbor Mrs. Rodriguez if she wouldn't mind dropping by to water the plants on occasion. Might've flushed when I did.

Would Starla consider moving? To live with me? Not into my current bachelor pad which has the personality of a gallon of beige paint, but somewhere new we'd both like. I'd moved in with Maeve before we married—that had seemed inevitable but not something particularly exciting, whereas the prospect of officially living with Starla is... Let's just say that despite the rain pelting down, there's sunshine in my heart. I don't know what exactly it is about her, but even thinking about Star, despite the dark spot she's in at the moment—

"Excuse me, Doctor Campbell?"

There's a bloke—younger than me but older than Starla—wearing a suit and trench coat and toting an umbrella, yeah, but still looking as though he's irritated because he didn't give the sky permission to open up so how dare it? I don't care for this type of person because every damn thing is about them, even the weather.

When I've given him my attention, he turns his displeasure on me. Not one of my patients, but could be a relative. This wouldn't be the first time I've been accosted in a parking lot.

"Doctor Lowry Campbell?"

"Yes. My hours are over for the day, though. If you'd like to make an appointment, please call my office and they can help you. I've got a card if you'd like. But otherwise, I'm actually on my way, so—"

He shakes his head, thin lips spreading into a grimace as if he's offended by my suggestion that he might need the services of a psychiatrist. "I don't need a shrink, doc. I'm actually not here about your professional life at all."

"Given that I've no idea who the fuck you are, seems odd you'd be here about my personal life."

All the muscles in my back and shoulders have gone taut, and the tension spreads up to my neck. I might need Starla to work her fingers into the nape of my neck and farther down when I get in. Depending on what sort of day she's had, of course. She might need me more than I need her and caring for her is its own satisfaction.

"I'm a business associate of Starla Patrick's."

A primal sort of growl forms in my chest and what I'd like to do is rip this man's arms off and beat him with them. Yell from the depths of my soul for him to get Starla's name out of his mouth.

"Still not sure what you want with me."

He grips my arm through my coat, and oh, this arsehole is

asking for it. I won't let him provoke me into action, though. That may be what he's after and I'm not going to give him the satisfaction.

"I'm on the board of directors for Patrick Enterprises. Starla's got some major decisions coming up and I'm not going to beat around the bush, here, Doctor Campbell. We don't have a great deal of confidence in her."

He must sense the rage coming to a boil under my skin because he drops his hand and holds up his palms as if to placate me. It's going to take a lot more than that to settle my displeasure. There are very few people on this earth I have more confidence in than Starla, so already his judgment is flawed in my opinion.

Before I can tell him exactly where he can shove his ridiculous assessment of Star, he cuts in. "I mean, I think we're all impressed with how she's been able to manage her very serious mental health issues, and she's certainly competent at running her little side business."

If this man had written a script with the goal of getting me to punch him in the face, he couldn't have done a better job. My fingers curl into my palms, and the keys I've got in one hand dig into my flesh. Her *side* business? Does this man have no idea how much time and energy Starla pours into her consulting business? How incredible she is and how many people she's helped? The kind of sensitivity and perseverance it takes to do her job well?

If anything is a side business, it's serving on the board of Patrick Enterprises. She doesn't like it, I don't think it's healthy for her, and if this jack hole is any indication of what the rest of the board members are like, I can see why it stresses her out and why she'd like to be rid of the responsibility.

"We're more concerned about her relationship with you, to be honest."

What the bloody bollocks is he on about?

FOR HER OWN GOOD

"With me? And it doesn't seem right, for you to know who I am, and for me to not have the pleasure of your name."

"Tad Harding." He holds out a hand that I don't take because this is not a friendly conversation. It's not even polite. Dropping his hand, he regards me with a look that reeks of his knowledge that he's hit a nerve. "And yes, Starla's relationship with you. It's awfully convenient, don't you think, that someone who had a quite intimate relationship with Starla as a minor, who disappeared fifteen years ago, shows up right around when she's come into being the wealthiest woman in New England? And charms his way into her bed?"

Bile churns in my stomach, and it feels as though all the blood drains from my face. I hope I'm not turning green, but it feels that way. "You think I'm taking advantage of Starla?"

The idea is sickening. I despise the idea of anyone taking advantage of her, but for it to be me? When all I've ever tried to do is protect her, even if I had to immolate myself to do it? I stayed away from her for far longer than I wanted to, and all to satisfy myself that I wouldn't be taking advantage of her.

No wonder nausea is overtaking me. I wish we were closer to my car so I could put a hand on it to steady myself.

Harding shrugs. "You do have a history of marrying women who are far wealthier than you. Maeve Maxwell's worth a pretty penny. Why wouldn't you do the same with a girl—and let's face it, she would've been a girl when you got to know her—"

Would serve this dickhead right if I punched him in the throat. But that wouldn't help anyone. I've got to keep my cool. For my sake, for Starla's. This is ridiculous.

"Yes, my ex-wife came from money, but if you've done as much research as you'd like me to believe you have, you know I left that marriage not much wealthier than I came into it. Maeve and I had a rock-solid prenup which I did nothing to dispute when we divorced, and should my relationship with Starla progress to that point, I'd expect the same. I'm not after her money."

Harding shrugs as though it doesn't matter to him either way, though he's clearly devoted some resources to finding out this information. I'll have to call Maeve later, see if he contacted her and apologize if so. No need for her to get dragged into this mess, especially since I'm unsure of how big of a mess it might be. At least he doesn't seem to know anything about Starla having met with Jerome Garrett. Or perhaps he does and this is his last-ditch effort to keep that from happening?

"Maybe you are, maybe you aren't. To be quite honest, I don't really care. If Starla wants to buy herself a daddy, what does it matter to me?"

The riot in my stomach is worse than when the Black and Whites played at home and lost. How does this tosser know anything about that?

"My point is that it's not going to look good to the board, and I can make it look worse. I can plant seeds of doubt about her capabilities, about her intellect, her sanity. She is regularly suicidal, isn't she?"

This man is lucky I love Starla and my job so much. If it weren't for the prospect of losing Starla or my license, my fist would be scattering Tad's teeth all over the pavement and sending some down his throat as well. I was never much for fisticuffs as a boy, but my brothers got into some scrapes I felt obligated to get them out of, Saint Lowry be damned.

"That's grounds for involuntary commitment, isn't it? Being a threat to oneself?" Tad strokes a finger across his chin, acting pensive. "Perhaps Starla isn't in any position to be making decisions about her own person, never mind a multibillion dollar corporation..."

"She's—" I want to leap to Starla's defense but my mouth snaps shut because I'm not going to inadvertently give him any more ammunition than he already has. Though I so desperately want to tell this arsehole that she isn't currently suicidal, nor has she been for some time. Even if she were, she has a long history of seeking help when she needs it, the latest example being checking herself into Harbinson for a bit when her father passed. No one with any integrity would advocate for Starla to be committed, but Tad seems to be coming up short on any of that.

His mouth curls into an ugly smirk. "It's actually quite disgusting of you to take advantage of such a vulnerable woman, Doctor Campbell. And you should know better than anyone else exactly how vulnerable she is. I don't think the medical board would feel kindly toward you if they were to find out."

"I don't take kindly to threats, Mr. Harding."

"And I don't take kindly to a corporate empire falling into shambles because a washed-up pervert wants to live a life of luxury. I know con men like you. You'll drag Starla's name and her father's business through the mud before you give up what you want. You'll ruin her. She'll be the laughingstock of the corporate world, Patrick Enterprises stock will tank because no one will have confidence in a company held primarily by a woman so easily swayed. It won't just be her, it'll be the thousands of people employed by Patrick Enterprises who will suffer. I'm guessing if you're willing to take advantage of a mentally unstable woman that you won't give much of a shit about that, but I had to throw it out there, just in case you do have a conscience."

"I've heard enough, Mr. Harding. Don't you ever come to my place of employment again. Come to think of it, don't ever talk to me again, period. My relationship with Starla is none of your business."

I don't wait for him to find more of my buttons to push, and instead stride toward my car while my heart races in the pouring rain.

Once shut in my car, I pull my phone from my pocket. I don't want to call Starla, but I feel as though I ought to. This is her life, her father's legacy after all. But on the other hand, I don't want to add any more nonsense to her plate which is clearly overfull. Whatever it is, I should call her.

Except that when I click my screen on, there's a text from her:

Saw Dr. G this afternoon, she wrote me a scrip for the anxiety and to help me sleep. I'm taking one now, I'll be out soon. You can come over if you want but I'm going to be a rag doll for the next twelve hours at least and I've got a board meeting in the morning.

There are days—many of them—that I would head to Starla's house anyhow. Hell, I'd sleep on the couch, but she'd be mad if she woke before I did and she realized it. I'd want to be there in case she needed me. Or to make her breakfast in the morning so she wouldn't be pouring cereal into a bowl and picking it out with her fingers because she doesn't even put milk on it—God forbid she consume anything with real nutritional value. Infuriating woman.

So, instead of calling Starla, I ring up the other person who might have a clue in the world of how to handle this. Course she doesn't answer when I truly need her advice, so I leave a voicemail.

"Maeve, it's Lowry. Call me back as soon as you have a minute, aye? It's important."

I don't mean to, but that will surely send her into a panic. It will be a fraction of the agitation that's gripping me. I feel as though I'm in a tailspin with my skull shaken about, scrambling my brains. I won't be the reason Starla loses control over Patrick Enterprises. Not after what she's told me about how the only recent approval her father gave her is about his goddamn business. She could live with parting with it voluntarily, but I'm not sure she'd ever forgive me if our relationship were the reason she lost control of her father's legacy.

CHAPTER 35

tarla

EVERYONE'S HEARD of morning sickness before, but for some reason it's hard to believe what a misery it is until you're waking up to it and hurling over the side of your bed. Not pleasant. It might all be over soon. Who's to say. I don't disagree with Doctor Gendron about keeping close tabs on my state of mind but it's not something I enjoy ruminating about. At least I have a bowl over here because I still felt sick after taking the meds Doctor Gendron prescribed.

In the meantime, I need to get up and make myself presentable for today's board meeting. I never like them, but today will be particularly unpleasant because I'm going to tell them about Jerome Garrett.

I don't think anyone's going to like that, but Tad especially will be seeing red when I make my announcement. Also, unlike the past several months, I haven't heard from Tad recently. I'd hoped he'd wised up and threw in the towel, but if nothing else, the man is persistent, so that doesn't seem like him. Probably more likely that he's up to some shit, but I don't have the bandwidth to think about what that might be with everything else going on.

After I finish my first-thing puke, I head into the bathroom and rinse out my mouth before doing anything else. I had best not to have to deal with vomiting the entire time I'm pregnant.

Which is a thought I've never had. And not a thought I can afford to dwell on now. Not while getting ready to deal with the wolves and the sharks and all the other vicious carnivores I'm up against today. I want to talk to Lowry, but I won't be a baby about this. I'm going to be a responsible adult. I'll text my boyfriend/daddy *after* my horrible meeting so he can tell me what a strong, smart, pretty girl I am. Because adulting. I should totes be in charge of the fate of a multibillion-dollar international corporation.

The shower heats up quickly, thank goodness, because I need a distraction. Washing my hair works, but when I soap up my body... I may be imagining things, because it really ought to be early to tell, but my midsection feels different to me already. Firmer, with more of a curve. But that's clearly my mind playing tricks on me. It's far too early for that. Far, far too early.

～

LOWRY

It startles me that Denny is in the driver's seat when Maeve picks me up at O'Hare, same terminal where she dropped me off nine months ago. She didn't say he'd stopped being her chauffeur when they'd started sleeping together, but it seems...unethical, somehow?

Not that I'll bring that up, given that I'm the one dating a woman who was a patient of mine when she was a minor and now she calls me *daddy*.

I only brought a carry-on, not knowing how long I'll be staying, and Denny gestures for it as he pops the trunk. Does this feel as odd to him as it does to me? But I'm not sure what to do aside from letting the man do his job so I hand over the roller board with a "thanks."

He opens the door to the passenger side back seat and I slide in next to my ex-wife and the woman he's currently sleeping with. It's an odd arrangement to me, but it's none of my business, if they're satisfied with it. Hell, even if they're not. I've got myself deep enough in my own shit, I don't need to be taking a flying leap into anyone else's.

Maeve greets me with a peck on my cheek and a chafe of my arm.

"Don't get me wrong, I'm glad to see you, but I'm not quite sure to whom or what I owe the pleasure of your company. You were pretty agitated on the phone and aside from your accent making you almost unintelligible—"

I grunt and she laughs.

"—I still wasn't sure what's going on aside from it having something to do with Starla. Did you break up?"

"No. I mean…no. Although she might do more than break up with me when she finds out where I am."

"Didn't you tell her?"

Yes, it's the same "you daft arsehole" look that Maeve's been giving me nearly since we met. And it's deserved.

"I did not. I didn't tell her because I need for this right tosser Tad Harding to think we've split up until this thing with her father's company is sorted. The only way he's going to believe that is if I make it look as though I've left, like he scared me off. And I didn't tell her about Tad because she's got a lot on her mind right now and if I told her about this sleekit reprobate sniffing around, it'd be too much."

Maeve raises one of her sculpted brows, unconvinced that I'm not making a royal hash of this. To be fair, neither am I, but I can't think of any other way.

"It's not just that, though. This Tad bloke has threatened Starla with some very ugly things. I'm certain no ethical person would take part, but it's..." It's none of Maeve's business why Starla has such an abject devotion to this thing that's not good for her and she hates, nor why my involvement with Star might contribute to her being forced out of the decision-making process for Patrick Enterprises. So I shake my head. "I take Starla's safety and happiness very seriously and if I came out here instead of staying there with her, you've got to believe I felt like— I *feel* like there's no other way, like I have no choice. Not for her to come through this whole, anyway. Maybe while I'm here, you could help me understand the actual risk. You know I've never had much of a head for business."

"Do I ever." She pats my hand fondly, knowing how grateful I am that all of my jobs have handled accounts for me and that I'd never start my own practice out of sheer terror of the finances of it. Yes, you can hire people for such things, but it makes me want to gag thinking about it. Course Starla's good at those things. Perhaps she'd help me?

Though I'm playing a dangerous game, coming out here. If all goes to plan, Maeve can give me some sound advice to help douse my sizzling nerves, it will look as though Starla and I are no longer together, and Tad won't be able to use me as leverage.

I don't know that Starla would ever forgive me for being the reason she lost control of Patrick Enterprises. It's one thing to do it in a deliberate way that still doesn't feel good, another entirely for it to be snatched out of her control, and I can't be responsible for that. Once this Garrett deal is settled—hopefully that will happen quickly—I'll go back to Boston and be the rock my little girl needs me to be as she reconciles what her father wanted with the person she actually is. If however, it does not...

Starla could believe I've abandoned her. Again. Which I haven't, I wouldn't, I... Curse these fucking choices I have to make when there isn't a good option. Only bad ones, only things that are going to hurt my darling girl. She perhaps won't see it this way, especially not right now, but she will. She has to.

I have some doubts about how she feels about me—namely whether she would want a future with me—but I know with absolute certainty how much her father's business means to her, how much *he* meant to her. I cannot be to blame for her taking on the heavy mantle of her father's disappointment yet again, I can't see her forgiving me for that should it come to pass. While I don't think she should let a dead man guide her decisions, it sure as hell isn't up to me, either. She'll make her choices and I will help her deal with the fallout if she'll let me.

STARLA

I'd like to claim I don't know what I ever saw in Tad, but that would be a lie. He's handsome, older, and so sure of himself— those are the things I liked. Shouldn't come as a surprise to anyone. Also, he didn't ask too much of me, and my father seemed to approve. God knows I like approval. Thirst for it, crave it.

Indeed, I may have texted Lowry on the way here to get a shot of that before my meeting started, but he didn't respond. Maybe he has an early patient? He's usually super on the ball about getting back to me unless he's with a patient. He hadn't mentioned it to me, but it's not as though he accounts for every second of every day to me. Nor do I expect him to. I just... Maybe hormones are making me paranoid. Perfect.

Enough fretting about Lowry. I ought to be fretting about the meeting that's about to start. And Tad. Ugh, Tad. Yeah, I really did think I was...maybe not in love with him exactly, nothing close to the way I feel about Lowry, but I definitely had romantic and sexual feelings toward him.

Now I look at his smug face across the large boardroom table and want to mash it into the platter of muffins and bagels no one will touch, because he's a condescending Machiavellian dickwad. At least I don't have to deal with him often, and if things go as I hope, soon I'll have to deal with him only rarely. Only on occasions when Jerome needs me to make an appearance to shore up our partnership and present concrete evidence of our united front.

The meeting is called to order, and I'm so anxious I want to vomit. Or is that the morning sickness? Whatever it is, I really wish my body would have a fucking *useful* reaction instead of feeling like I'm going to hurl. I mean, shouldn't this be all fight or flight? Not fight or having an involuntary personal protein spill? How is that *helpful*? Dammit.

I clear my throat, hoping nothing comes with it, but I'm safe.

Everyone at the table is looking at me expectantly, and I summon a vision of Lowry, telling me I'm making a good choice. For me, for my father's legacy, for all of the people who rely on Patrick Enterprises for their livelihood. I am smart, I am capable, and it's okay for me to let this go, at least a bit so I'm not crushed under the weight of the responsibilities I'd have to assume if I decided to run this company for the long term. I don't want to, I wouldn't be good at it. In selling a portion of my shares to Jerome Garrett, I'm making a decision that ensures the long-term prosperity of Patrick Enterprises but also removes a level of responsibility that would be—hell, *is*—detrimental to my mental health.

"I know everyone has been waiting to see what I'll do as the newly minted holder of the controlling interest in Patrick Enterprises. After much thought and much discussion with various parties, I've come to a decision."

Breathe, Starla. Just breathe. Because passing out face-first into a tray full of pastries does not inspire confidence.

"Provided that all of the reports return as expected from my lawyers and advisors, I will be selling slightly less than half of my shares to Jerome Garrett of Garrett Industries."

There's a collective murmur in the room and the way everyone turns to one another in shock and confusion starts my anxiety spiraling, which conveniently tangles with my depression to make me doubt every decision I've ever made. That's great. But I dredge up my rational brain to try to beat back all of my fears and all the voices yelling terrible things at me. I just have to hold them off for long enough to get through this meeting and then I can have another meltdown.

Would Lowry be willing to skip his workout today and let me cry on his shoulder instead? Maybe meet me at his place so he could do something to make me forget all of this for an hour or so? Center me in my body instead of being all tied up and twisted in my brain? When he's spanking me, everything is so clear.

"Given the two percent of the stock he already holds, this sale will result in myself holding twenty-six percent of Patrick Enterprises, which still makes me the largest shareholder. Mr. Garrett will then hold twenty-five percent of Patrick Enterprises. After negotiations with Mr. Garrett, we've identified common goals for Patrick Enterprises and plan to vote as a bloc when matters come to the board. Which means that between Mr. Garrett and myself, we will maintain control of Patrick Enterprises. Mr. Garrett will be more involved in regular decision-making, however I will be apprised of any major changes and I will meet with him regularly to ensure that he is steering the Patrick Enterprises ship on a course that my father would have approved of."

The murmur has grown to a dull roar and my face is burning, but I press on because this is the informed, educated decision I have made and I won't be made to feel as though I'm small Starla

Patrick who used to play under the boardroom table who should only be in charge of my paper and crayons, perhaps a doll.

"This sale doesn't require the board's approval, I'm fully within my rights to make this decision unilaterally. I'm informing you as a courtesy, and as I said before, this sale will only happen provided I can settle an agreement to my satisfaction with Mr. Garrett. My lawyers are currently reviewing the contract and should be done by this evening. Should Mr. Garrett renege on the tenets we have discussed, the sale will not go through. I'm not taking any questions at the moment, but please send any concerns you have to my attorneys. I'll circulate the agreement to the board as soon as the details have been finalized."

I feel as though I'm going to die, but other than that, everything's fine. Yep, totally fine. Given that no one's thrown anything or set the place on fire, I'd say that went pretty well. Now if only I could guarantee that I'm not going to start hyperventilating at any second.

Stealing a glance at my phone to see if there's a little blue blinking light to tell me there's a text—hopefully from Lowry—I miss Tad rising to his feet at the other end of the table that's still a cluster of serious people in expensive suits making incredulous noises. But he gets my attention with a clap of his hands, same as he gets everyone else's.

"I'd like to bring a few matters to the board's attention."

Preternatural dread creeps down my spine. I don't have a good feeling about this. And from the way Tad is looking at me, I shouldn't.

"Ms. Patrick's announcement is as surprising to me as it is to the rest of you. Especially given how Jameson Patrick felt about Jerome Garrett. To say they were on unfriendly terms is an understatement."

He levels me with a look meant to be stern, meant to shame me and reach that little part of me that gets hit hardest by disapproval. Except that Tad's approval doesn't mean jack shit to me anymore. I don't believe he ever wanted what was best for me, nor do I believe that handing him the reins to Patrick Enterprises would be the right decision. He may have played the lapdog and yes-man to my father, but I don't think he'd stay faithful to my father's vision on his own.

"As the person who holds a controlling interest in Patrick Enterprises, any decision Ms. Patrick makes will have a profound impact on the prospects of this company and its shareholders. We have a fiduciary duty to ensure that anyone making these types of decisions is fit."

Fit? Oh my fucking god, this little rat bastard. Death is too good for this fucker. I will show him precisely how *fit* I am by throwing a goddamn chair.

"I happen to know that Starla Patrick has some interesting fetishes in the bedroom."

I'd thought blinding rage was an expression. That and seeing red. I knew what they meant of course, but not how they felt. Spending so much of my life being emotionally numb on some level hadn't prepared me for when I got hit with all of these more vivid, visceral feelings. I've learned over time how to manage most of them even if it takes me a while to process them, but now I'm taking fury straight in the face.

How dare he? And how could I have been so wrong about him? I knew he was a dickhead, but I didn't think he'd go this far. Weren't these the things he'd told me Jerome Garrett would pull because he was a slimeball? And all this time, it was Tad who was planning to throw my dirty laundry all over my father's board-room. Lower than Salacious B. Crumb, this motherfucker.

Lillian Johnson appears to feel the same way, her blond eyebrow raised and the corners of her mouth turned down. "I'm assuming you know this from your time as Ms. Patrick's significant other, which would mean you also enjoy these same things as part of your sex life. So I'm not sure what you think you're going to accomplish with this stunt. It reeks of sexism, and I won't tolerate it, never mind consider it when making business decisions."

Thank heaven for Lillian. She scared me to death as a kid because she looked at me like I was some kind of vermin, but as I've grown up, I've come to understand she just doesn't enjoy children. Which doesn't make her a bad person, and I appreciate her efforts to encourage my father to make Patrick Enterprises a better and more equitable place for women. So yeah, thank goodness for her unabashed feminism because while I'm doing my best to maintain a bored, disinterested expression, my fingers are clutching my pen hard and it will be a minor miracle if it doesn't snap in half.

Tad puts on that faux-apologetic look of his, and sucks his teeth. What a fucker.

"You can understand I was in a bit of an awkward position. I was dating the boss's daughter for god's sake, so if she wanted to call me *daddy* and have me spank her… I'm not proud of it, and it wouldn't be something I would engage in otherwise, but you've got to keep Starla happy. Everyone knows that."

Lillian looks almost bored as she glowers at him. "Why are you bringing this up now? It's obviously been true for quite some time and you've never mentioned it before."

"I would've shrugged it off, honestly. Not my thing, but I doubt anyone's getting hurt so what does it matter? Except that when you put that into the context of Starla dating a gentleman named Lowry Campbell, it gets more concerning."

Lillian sighs heavily and taps her very expensive pen on the tabletop. "Can we get to the issue at hand? I don't need to spend any more of my precious time troubling myself with who Ms. Patrick dates or what she does on her own time. It's never been an issue before, and the fact that it's an issue now is redolent of misogyny. You're testing my patience. So make your point or shut the hell up, Tad."

The corners of Tad's mouth turn up, smiling as though he

were waiting for this moment, and perhaps he has been. My own stomach curdles, not so much on my own behalf, but on Lowry's. This is going to be wildly unfair to the man who has loved me with everything he has and has been almost achingly perfect, lack of returning my last text notwithstanding.

"Doctor Lowry Campbell is a psychiatrist. He was, when Ms. Patrick was a child, *her* psychiatrist for a period of four years. At which point he took a job in Chicago where he lived for the past fifteen years, and married a woman named Maeve Maxwell. Does that ring a bell for anyone?"

"The oatmeal heiress?"

Tad points at the man who volunteered this guess with an enthusiastic finger. "Yes, precisely the one. So, apparently, things didn't work out with *that* heiress, so Doctor Campbell leaves Chicago approximately nine months ago and comes back to Boston where he quickly becomes involved with…you guessed it, Starla Patrick."

I'm hoping for Lillian to dismiss this entire dog and pony show as a ridiculous waste of time. *Can we all move on now, please?* But she doesn't. No, she brings that pen to her lips, pensive.

"What Ms. Patrick does in the bedroom on her own time is none of our concern as long as it doesn't affect the business and I'm not buying your argument that it does. Taken alone, I would tell you to jump off the Pru, Tad."

I don't like the way she's phrased this. Yes, she loathes Tad— because who doesn't—but she's not outright dismissing his preposterous accusations against Lowry, against me. Never has Lowry tried to influence my business decisions, and if he had, I wouldn't have listened. If anything, he recuses himself because he's aware his knowledge about the corporate world is inferior to mine. To think I would give him my ear or let him take advantage of my clout or my money is absurd. How insulting.

"However?" Tad's brows are halfway up his forehead and I can tell he's waiting to pounce on the verdict Lillian's about to hand down.

"However...Doctor Campbell reappearing in your life right now is extraordinarily convenient timing. Your father passed recently, you're vulnerable, and you already have a predilection for, well, men of a certain type. He's older, he's already been in a position of authority over you, and he's established a level of trust with you that renders you vulnerable to his manipulations. I hate to say it, but Tad might have a point."

CHAPTER 36

$\mathcal{S}$tarla

THAT WAS AN UNQUALIFIED DISASTER. Possibly the most humiliated I have ever been, and definitely the angriest. The board meeting had to be called after the riot that erupted when Lillian fucking Johnson—who I had sort of counted on to have my back at least about the Lowry thing if not the Jerome Garrett thing—totally fucked me over. Goddammit. Goddammit.

I text Holden on my way out of the meeting: *If everything's in order, pull the trigger on the Garrett deal.*

Three seconds later, as I knew it would, my phone buzzes and despite having zero desire to talk to anyone with my brain exploding like the Death Star has just fired on it, I answer. And before I can say anything, Holden's voice is in my ear.

"Are you sure?"

He means well. I know he does. It's a huge decision and weighty for many reasons, but I've made up my mind and I'm tired of questioning myself, stewing over every little thing. Or every massive thing like this. I don't feel awesome about this decision. In fact, I feel pretty crap about it. But I also believe it's the best choice for myself and Patrick Enterprises and that's going to have to be good enough.

"Yes, do it. Just fucking do it."

Then I hang up and start trying to reach Lowry. Five maddening minutes later, I'm in a car on my way to his place because I've been texting and calling and even got desperate and tried to email him but nothing. Now I'm worried. Is he sick? Is he hurt or something bad happened to his family in Scotland and he didn't tell me because he didn't want me to fret? Except I'm goddamn fretting to the extent that I didn't trust myself to drive and I didn't have the patience for Holden to come pick me up, so here I am, checking my phone incessantly in the back of a Toyota Camry. Not a bad car, but the pickup is for shit and makes me want to yell at the driver. Because that would help, obviously.

At long last we reach Lowry's building, and I barely say thank you before I'm heading inside, waving to the doorman as I pass at slightly less than a run, and pressing the button in the elevator—repeatedly, because again, that will clearly make it go faster—and then riding up to his hall, a ball of impending nervous breakdown. I suppose running to Lowry doesn't help my case regarding being an independent woman whose boyfriend doesn't have any say in her business dealings.

Except that I fucking need him. Not to tell me what to do about my business, but to hold me and tell me everything's going to be okay, assure me that I have excellent judgment and that I'm not a horrible person nor an abject failure. And perhaps—as seems paramount to everyone who's on the board of Patrick Industries—that my mind can be trusted. The worst thing is that I can't even tell them I've never questioned my brain's abilities because I have.

I'm not going to cry. I'm not going to cry in a fucking elevator. It's not fair but I'm kinda mad at Lowry for not getting back to me. If he had, I could've asked him to come to my place, wouldn't have had to bother coming here and I could've had some privacy for fuck's sake. And I don't even have a key to his place so I'm standing in front of his door and wishing to fuck I'd asked for one. He would've given me one, I know for sure.

I knock and listen, but I'm met with silence. Where could he be? Was there an emergency with one of his patients? But surely he could've found a minute to shoot me a text and tell me that? He knows how I get, he knows I've been having a hard time, and I can't imagine he would ever do something to intentionally distress me. He wouldn't, especially knowing my brain has been in such hardcore betrayal mode that I asked Doctor Gendron for an extra appointment. I see her every week, so I don't make extra appointments without a damn good reason.

Even though it seems utterly fruitless, I knock again and press my ear to the door. Still nothing and I am way too close to having a tantrum right here in the hallway for comfort. I am a grown goddamn woman, I should be able to handle myself through this and not being able to see my boyfriend shouldn't send me into a tailspin. Except the thing is, he's not my boyfriend. He's my daddy and I could really use his help right now. The comfort of his body and his words, and the knowledge that he's one of the people who know me best on this earth and if he says I am competent and trustworthy then I am because he wouldn't lie. He's told me before when my mind is lying to me. He'd tell me if I wasn't in any condition to be making decisions or if the choices I was making were bad ones.

I need for him to say it. Loudly, repeatedly, until I believe him.

"Goddammit, Lowry, where are you?"

I jump back when someone answers.

"He's gone, dear. Left for Chicago late last night."

It is completely mortifying that Mrs. Rodriguez, the elderly woman who lives with her family down the hall, has seen me literally bang my head against the wall. And...Chicago? What the actual fuck?

Maybe something happened to Maeve? But he's been gone since last night and...

"I'm sorry to bother you, Mrs. Rodriguez. Are you sure he left?"

"Oh yes," she says, taking a key from her pocket. "He left in a hurry but asked me to water his plants while he's away. I've been doing it a couple of times a week anyway since he's been spending some of his nights...elsewhere."

She doesn't say it cruelly or with disgust, but with that knowing old lady look that tells me she approves of the Scottish doctor having a love interest who he's been having sexy sleepovers with. She's probably been asking him when he's going to marry me and have babies, for the love of god.

Which is when it hits me. *Baby.* He came over after I'd taken the test, when the sticks were sitting in the trash, and Lowry's an observant person. What if he saw...oh my god, what if he knows and that's why he...

I have to clap my hand over my mouth because I am too close —far too close—to vomiting for comfort.

That's it, isn't it? He saw the pregnancy tests in the trash and didn't want to deal. Didn't want to deal with a baby, something that would tie him to me forever, didn't think he could stomach dealing with not only my issues but whatever ones she might inherit as well. Too much. I've always been too much. Maybe he thought he could handle me—he was handling me, with aplomb, I'd say—but not anything else. God knows a baby throws a wrench into everything.

I wouldn't have thought he'd have left without a word, and if he's gone to Chicago—back to Maeve? He wouldn't. Except I wouldn't have thought he'd be capable of abandoning a pregnant woman either, but here we are. Maybe this has something to do with his deep-seated fear about being like his uncle and he bolted? Why didn't he fucking *talk* to me? He had enough time to ask Mrs. Rodriguez to water his goddamn plants, but he couldn't be arsed to say a single fucking word to me?

"Dear, are you all right? You look like you need to sit down. Can I—"

"No, Mrs. Rodriguez, I'm—" I'm choking on a sob is what I'm doing because my entire world is falling apart. Everything is upside down. I'm getting into business with Jerome Garrett who I should believe is the worst of the worst, I'm turning my back on my father's protégé—although after that performance today, I can't imagine my father would object—and the man I thought loved me has left.

Except, that's what Lowry does, isn't it? Makes me trust him, makes me love him, coaxes me into complacency and into dumping all of my vulnerability into his lap, and then he fucking up and leaves. This is a pattern and I can't believe I fell for this again.

"I'm fine," I finish, and she clearly doesn't believe me. Is looking at me like I'm a wounded fawn not worth saving because I'm so badly mangled. "There was a, uh, miscommunication. I'm sure we'll talk later. Have a good evening."

I bite my lip as hard as possible once I reach the elevator and punch the button for the lobby. Not going to cry. Not going to cry. I am not going to shed any more tears over Lowry Harrison Campbell. Not in front of his building where I summon another car to take me home. Not in the back seat where I sit in silence, not even bothering to check my phone now that I know why he's gone. Not on my way to my apartment and not even once I've locked my door and then collapsed on my couch.

Numbness is stealing over me and I welcome it. I used to fight

407

it because I knew what it meant, but it's so much easier to be unfeeling right now. So I let it envelop me, surround all my feelings, and wrap them up in mist where they disappear.

I'd thought this day couldn't get any worse. I was wrong. So very, very wrong. But who cares anymore? Not I.

CHAPTER 37

 owry

THIS IS my second night in Chicago. I've been haunting Maeve's house and I'm sure Denny wishes I would go the fuck away. I've got to be interfering, but Maeve claims I'm not.

I don't want to stay here. I want to go back to Starla, claim my rightful place as her daddy and look after her. Cuddle her, spank her, hold her, challenge her, but mostly love her.

I may have lost the privilege, though, because the calls and the texts and the emails have stopped, stopped less than twenty-four hours after I left, actually, and haven't resumed. I thought I'd be back in Boston by now or at the very least on a plane, but I'm not. I want some sort of sign, some sort of clarity and I've got none. Even Maeve's wisdom hasn't been able to shore up my reasoning. I'm a goddamn disaster.

I've been trying not to panic over what will happen to Patrick Enterprises, though distraction is a sizable job. At least Maeve's gotten me some awfully good whisky and I've spent a good portion of last night and today drunk off my arse.

My God, am I a rubbish human being. Maeve won't say so, but I know she must think so and is simply taking pity on me because of how pathetic I am. Which is very pathetic. And very Scottish, what with the whisky and the grunting, and I wish there were some moors for me to prowl about. God, I'm a misery. A human plague who has had far too much to drink and ought to go to bed but I haven't slept since I arrived and it might be morning again already? Awfully hard to say.

Yes, there've been some nights when I haven't been with Starla since we started… I don't know what to call it. Fucking seems vulgar, relationship seems vague. Whatever it was, I felt complete for the first time in my life. Twisted up into knots, aye, but also as though I couldn't expect anything else out of my whole entire life because everything I wanted had been handed to me in a Starla-shaped package. I simply adore that woman, and now I may have tossed it all in the trash in an effort to protect her. In an effort, let's be honest, to protect myself. Perhaps I ought to call? Try to explain?

But I suspect I've been a right tosser with no more sense in my head than all my brothers put together, which is still less than a thimble-full. I could've talked to her, told her that Tad had accosted me in the parking lot, threatening her, threatening me, threatening us. Except I was so determined not to trouble her, not to add any more to her heavy load, not to have her blame me for the loss of that final hope at her father's approval that I took it upon myself to try to save her when I know full well she's smarter than I am. In general, yes, but particularly where business—whatever the hell that means—is concerned.

There's a soft knock at my door and I nearly throw the bottle at it, but that would be a waste of the whisky I haven't drained out of this bottle. Yet. I will, I surely will.

I make, I don't know, some kind of noise that apparently lets

Maeve know I assent to her coming in? Or perhaps she's sick of having a soused Scotsman in her house and doesn't give a goddamn what I want. Which would be fair. Completely fair.

In she comes at any rate, looking like she pities me but also like I'm close to being a nuisance, which is not a corner of the matrix any man cares to occupy.

"There's something I think you ought to see. Are you too drunk to watch TV?"

"Is that even a thing, hen? Can ye be too drunk to watch TV?"

"If it is, I think you might be it."

That's…insulting. Or perhaps caring. Can't decide which. Probably because I'm rather soused.

"What's on TV, then? In the middle of the night?"

Her fine mouth pinches as though she can't decide whether to tell me or not, but eventually decides this can't get much worse and spits it out.

"It's six in the morning in Boston, you degenerate. There's been an announcement about Patrick Enterprises, all the financial channels are covering it and it's going to rock the markets when they open in a few hours. Shall I turn it on?"

Starla's on TV? No, surely Maeve would've said. She said an announcement about Patrick Enterprises. But from where I sit, that's just as good. An avatar, a proxy for the woman I love who might never speak to me again because I'm a complete numpty.

"Yes, please."

Maeve takes up the remote from the nightstand—issa bit odd to be staying in the guest room of a house that used to be yours, aye?—and flips to some high-up channel where a fancy-looking man and a fancier-looking woman are talking about…something.

And then I hear it: Patrick Enterprises. I know her. It. As Starla would say, whatevs. The point is, that means something. I try to focus through the whisky haze, and hear the fancy lady say, "In a move sure to rock the business world, Patrick Enterprises heiress Starla Patrick has sold a large portion of her shares to her late father, Jameson Patrick's, archrival, Jerome Garrett. The sale was announced moments ago, and I'm sure I'm not the only one eagerly awaiting the details of the transaction. This is one of the more surprising sales of the past decade."

She did it. Starla sold a fair portion of her father's business to Jerome Garrett, much as she said she would. Much as she wanted to. I knew she could, and if she were truly determined, would, but...it's still a bit of a shock to see the whole thing on TV. Nothing I ever do makes the evening news. Which is just as well. But Jesus Christ, Starla is important. Foolishly enough, I don't think I'd grasped the magnitude of the situation until now. The pressure she must've been under, and adding to that an attack on a very personal, incredibly tender part of herself...

Guilt swamps me. Whatever cells in my body that haven't been flooded with alcohol are now swollen with remorse. My strong and extremely capable yet also delicate girl, and I left her alone. Without another soul to rely on in the world, I abandoned her. Again. In an effort to not be the reason she lost the last shred of pride she'd gleaned from her father, but... Jesus, I'm terrible. And yet I have the same urge I had when her father died.

"Maeve, be a love and get me on a plane?"

FAIR ENOUGH, Starla's not answering calls, texts, anything else. She probably hates me and right about now, I'm hating myself. For a multitude of reasons, including the fact that I've had enough whisky in the past twenty-four hours to make an elephant intoxicated, and I've got the pounding headache to show for it.

I head straight to Starla's from Logan, fully prepared to be turned away. Except that when I reach her studio door, it swings open and I nearly fall over from the wind.

I've met Holden before, in passing, and while he's looked at me as though I were some sort of suspicious character, never has he looked at me as though he wanted to slit my throat. He is now.

"Ah, yes. Is Starla in?"

I attempt to peek around him, but he steps into my line of sight.

"No. She's not. Even if she were, I wouldn't tell you, you piece of shit."

"Tell me how you really feel," I joke, but the granite-faced man in front of me isn't having a bit of it. And why should he? Indeed, he crosses his arms over his slim chest.

"How dare you show up here, acting like everything's fine? Do you have any idea what she's been through in the past couple of days?"

I open my mouth to answer, but he cuts me off before I can.

"You really fucking don't, but I do. She lost or gave up some of the most important things in her life. And where the fuck were you, doc? Where the fuck were you? Because you sure as fuck weren't here watching her become a shell of herself. You left her. How could you do that? Not just as her partner, but like, as a physician? A human being? 'Is Starla in?'" Ah, his Lowry impression is notably better than Starla's. "No, she isn't. And you can fuck right off if you think I'm going to tell you where she is because you don't deserve to be the shit on her shoes."

"That was always true. But the thing is... Well, I don't actually want to say it to you before I say it to her. I will apologize, profusely, fall on my knees if I must, and I suspect will have to. I don't have a problem with that at all. If you have a sword, can I borrow it? Because I'll fall on that too. I left for a reason, but...I don't know. It seemed right at the time when I was in a panic, but I can't honestly say if it was right anymore. But here's the thing: Much as I shouldn't have made that decision for Starla, do you really think you should have final say over whether I should be able to apologize to her or not?"

That's a sneaky argument, it is, and perhaps Holden will fall for it, or perhaps he won't and I'll have to bide my time and find some other opportunity to talk to Starla. Not at her home because I don't want to make her feel unsafe, not at Harbinson because…

Harbinson.

That's where she is. It's her ECT day. And if I hadn't been drowning in the bottom of a bottle, I would've realized it. Lacey isn't my biggest fan right now as I claimed an emergency to take an undetermined leave of absence, but I hope she'll accept my apology as well and not have me escorted off clinic grounds if Holden allows me to go with him. I know he brings Starla to and from her appointments, and I have a surge of jealousy at the intimacy of it. But this is not about me. It's about the people I've hurt and alienated. I owe apologies to basically all the important people in my life. So much for Saint Lowry. Most of all, I owe an explanation and an apology to Starla.

"Please, Holden. I'm begging you. I…I would give my life for her. I would give anything for her. Let me apologize and then, swear on my gran's grave, I'll respect her decision. Just, please. For what it's worth, I think if she can forgive me, I might be able to make her happy."

He half looks like he wants to throttle me and half as though he wants to believe me. I send every wish I have up to heaven and hope that the God I forsook so long ago will hear me one last time.

owry

STARLA'S LASHES tremble and flutter, the first signs that she's coming up out of the anesthesia. Unlike some of my patients, she always had a fairly easy time of it and I have no reason to think anything's changed since then. I hope she would've told me. She's told me so much else.

And yet, here I am, having betrayed her yet again—because that is how she'll see it, and how I'm seeing it as well—and it's a wonder she ever saw fit to share anything with me at all. But if she gives me another chance I will spend every day of my life convincing her I am trustworthy, deserving of the faith she's always put in me. If she'll have me, anyway, and there's no guarantee. But God, I hope she will.

Partly for my own sake, and partly so Starla won't fire Holden. I'd feel terrible about that, but he knew the risks when he agreed to my scheme. He must agree that I am in fact a good choice. That I love Star more than I love breathing, and that I am worthy of at least a shot. Or perhaps he simply agrees that it's up to Starla to give me the final "shove off, you fucking fuck."

My fingers itch to take Starla's hand in mine, so she knows she's not alone as she wakes. It's no different than I've ever felt. She told me once that waking up after ECT was like swimming toward the surface of the water with no promise of when you'd break the surface. And to think she's put herself in that position every six weeks for the past eighteen years or so. Her bravery and fortitude are unfathomable to me.

I'd like to extend a hand, and promise that she's close, that she can make it. But if she's too tired to kick and thrash or pull through the water with her arms, that's fine, I'll wait for her. As long as it takes.

Her eyes move beneath her lids and her fingers twitch.

I hope I haven't made a mistake by coming here, but I couldn't bring myself to wait any longer, to shirk my responsibility to care for her for one more instant. She does look somewhat vulnerable beneath the bleached hospital linens, but she also looks sturdy, as though when she wakes up she'll be ready to take on the world. This is but a temporary setback. Which I suppose it is; a recharging of her battery, or perhaps more accurately, flipping her switch to off and then back on again. Not anything as serious as a factory reset.

The tips of her fingers grasp at the cotton of the blanket and she rolls her head to the side. It's selfish, but I hope she'll be with me soon. The way more of her is engaging in small movements makes me think yes.

STARLA

I have woken up in this room—or one of the three identical rooms that serve this purpose—many, many times. There have sometimes been nurses, my father, or Holden. Sometimes, though not often, a doctor. Sometimes even Lowry. When he was my doctor. Not since then has he been here because I didn't want him to be, and now, though I would desperately want to, I wouldn't let him be here even if he asked.

Come to think of it, I'm not sure if I'll see him again ever. Perhaps in another fifteen years because that's how this works? He waits until I'm good and in love with him, and then he leaves. It's cruel. And my brain, though it should be on good behavior now, is being an asshole. Like, more than usual.

It's tricking me into thinking I can smell him. It's not strong like it is when he's held me in his arms or when he's been on top of me, inside me, levering up on his elbows so he can take in the expression on my face or with his nose buried somewhere in my neck or my hair. No, it's more like when he's spent the night at my apartment and gotten up before I wake to get to work.

The lingering scent always made me smile because it felt as though he'd left a part of himself behind to stand guard over me even though he couldn't be there in the flesh. This, though? This is mean. Makes me ache for a thing that's been dangled in front of me, that I've been allowed to embrace and grow comfortable with, feel as though it's in fact a part of me, and then yanked away.

He's gone, and that's how things are. I ought to get used to it. And him being gone, I have some decisions to make about my life. Yes, mine, because apparently it's not going to be ours. I'd thought maybe... Doesn't matter what I thought. The reality is that Lowry is too haunted by old ghosts who should seek out someone who actually deserves it, and I am not reason enough to stay. I didn't even get the chance to tell him that I was unsure. Because I sure as hell can't raise a child by myself. I'm not sure if I can raise one with help, even all the help I could afford.

But if it were his, if he wanted to be a father—and he'd be an exceptionally wonderful father, I know—then I would do it for him. I believe in him so fully, I think he'd be able to shepherd me through that as well. Rather *had* believed.

Moot. I'll need to make decisions about this for myself. And though I'd like to think that this is indeed a choice, is it? Conceivably—if the pregnancy itself doesn't aggravate my depression to a place of danger, at any rate—I could have this child by myself. If anyone has the resources to pull that off, it's me. But for all the money I have, I'm still me, and I can't buy mental health. Is single parenthood even an option for me? I'd like to think so, but I can't imagine that actually being true.

Sometimes I wish I could stay here for a while when I wake up. Not the short window of observation I usually have to make sure nothing's gone awry, but something longer that might feel like actual rest. Today won't be that day, though.

I've got to get up, get back, and face the prospect of a life devoid of Lowry again. Perhaps I'll feign sleep a bit longer because if I don't open my eyes to see he isn't there and in fact it's only Holden sitting with an ankle perched on a knee while he swipes through his phone on the far side of the room, if I simply take a deep breath and let my brain trick itself into having a few more minutes of breathing in the subtle scent of him, then I won't have to face this.

But there is no more time to wallow, no more time to keep my eyelids shut against the world. It's time to face this day, and indeed, the rest of my life.

My eyelids feel closer to lead than feathers as I blink them open, and it doesn't seem like a terrible idea after all to rest a bit. Except that...

My brain may very well be an asshole, but it's not a delusional asshole. It's not only Lowry's scent that's present, but Lowry as well.

I've got ninety-nine problems, but hallucinating's never been one of them. So, nothing in my previous experience would explain why Lowry—face drawn and his facial hair a bit more grown out than usual but still handsome as ever—is in the chair that's always been to the side of the beds here, but which I've never woken to someone sitting in. My father was always pacing by the door, speaking in hushed, hurried tones, and Holden sits politely but distantly in the chair that's in the far corner.

I sit up like a jackknife and am swamped immediately by nausea. I know better, but I can't—

"Starla, shh. It's me. Would you lie back, please? I don't want you making yourself sick. I'll go if you want me to, but please."

His voice is gentle, soft, and coaxing, as though he thinks he might scare me. I'm not scared, but I am confused and not in the "searching my mind for information that's no longer there" way that I sometimes experience after I've had a treatment.

It's not so much what he's saying right now that gets me to cooperate as all the things he's said to me before. He's built a foundation which is, yes, cracked down to the core in some places, but I still find that in some things, I'm content to listen to his judgment.

I close my eyes, let his warm hands and firm grasp on my shoulders steer me back until my head hits the pillow again and I take long, deep breaths that help clear the feeling that I'm about to puke.

It's perhaps not wise, but I reach out anyhow, and it's not even a second before Lowry is slipping his hand into mine—warm and dry in distinct contrast to my cold and clammy palm. And then there are blunt fingers brushing away the fine strands at my hair-line, now matted there with sweat. That didn't take much.

"I'm sorry. I didn't mean to give you a fright. I guess you still — I didn't realize— I should've known— I'm sorry."

I can't reassure him at the moment, and I don't think that's actually on me to do. I'll take the comfort of his hands, though.

After a few minutes of breathing, when my roiling stomach has settled and I'm no longer actively sweating, I open my eyes again and don't snatch my hand back. I should. I know I should, but I can't quite figure out how to make my hand obey.

"What are you doing here?"

"I came to apologize. I'm sorry. You deserve more than that, and I'll give you whatever you'd like, whatever you need from me. I shouldn't have left the way I did. I just didn't feel as though I had any other choice. I couldn't..."

He makes a disgusted noise and I give him the benefit of the doubt and assume it's directed toward himself. Many people I would not because instead of filling the well of goodwill, they've drained it instead, never bothering to top it off. But Lowry? I'm angrier at him than I've been at anyone else in my existence, but I also can't let go and dismiss all of the good things he's done, all the ways he's loved me. I look at our hands, fingers entwined, and follow them in time to see Lowry dip his head to my knuckles and lay a kiss there. It's achingly sweet even as I want to visit violence upon his body.

It's difficult to wrap my head around all of my feelings, but I manage to choose the one that is the most sensitive. "I wish you would've talked to me. Nothing is set in stone. I don't know what I'm going to do. I'm really angry at you for leaving, but I also understand how hard this must be for you."

The crease between his ginger brows deepens, and he cocks his head. "Hard for me? I mean, yes, leaving was like ripping my heart out of my chest. But I wasn't going to be any good to you. I would've hurt you, lost you something that was so close to your heart and I couldn't stand the idea of hurting you so deeply. It may have been bloody stupid but I swear I was doing it for your own good. I left so I could protect you."

Protect me? How on earth would abandoning me when he found out I was pregnant be protecting me? So I could make the decision about whether to keep it without him? How can he not know that I value his opinion above all others and that this is nearly as much his decision as it is mine? How could he not realize that whether he stays or not would have a profound impact on whether I would even consider keeping this baby? He's not making any sense.

"I don't…"

The hand he's not holding drifts to my belly, and though it's far too early to feel anything, I swear I do. Perhaps not anything physical, exactly, but a…connection of some sort. That's a little woo-woo for me, but I can't explain it any other way.

"Didn't you leave because I'm pregnant?" Pregnant seems a little less final, a bit less personal and intimate than *having a baby*. "I thought you saw the test in the trash and freaked, and I get it, I do, because of your uncle, and I get how it could be overwhelming and scary and poke at those icky spots we all have, but I was really hoping…I was really hoping we could figure this out together because I know it's hard for you, but it's—"

Goddammit. I didn't want to cry. I wanted to be a reasonable, logical person who could enter—if not leave—this conversation like an adult, like a grown-ass woman, and here I am blubbering like an overly sensitive baby walrus. Goddammit. My voice cracks into a sob and Lowry's face is blurry beyond the tears crowding my eyes. They're going to spill any second but perhaps I can finish my sentence first.

"It's nearly impossible for me. I'm so scared and I don't know what to do because I can barely take care of myself and manage my business and throwing a baby in there—I don't know. And my mom—what if I turn out to be like her? What if I leave my baby alone? What if my depression lies so very hard it convinces me she's better off without me? What if she would be because I've got this pretty well under control and have for quite some time, but I wasn't planning on adding a baby. Probably not ever, and—How? How could you leave me like that?"

So, I'm oh-for-two in the not-having-a-breakdown score. Great.

Lowry presses tissues into my hands, and I blow my nose and

wipe my eyes. I told myself I wasn't going to yell at him, that I wasn't going to panic, but here we are. When I've tidied myself up as best I can, I look at him, tissues still crumpled in my hands. The nausea is back, but this time it's panic-induced, I'm pretty sure.

"Starla, love." He pets my hair, strokes my cheek with the back of his knuckles. Looks at me with those kind blue eyes. "You're pregnant?"

"Yes?"

He doesn't look afraid. Or haunted. If anything, I'd describe his expression as hopeful.

"I thought you knew. I thought that's why you left. I thought—"

He hushes me, wraps a hand around mine, and leans in to kiss my forehead. He murmurs against my skin, his lips brushing where he just planted a kiss. "I didn't know. I didn't know. I'm so sorry you thought that's why I'd left. I'd never leave because you were pregnant. Jesus, Star, not ever."

"Then why'd you leave? It hurt so much."

Like being stabbed in the precise place where I'd been stabbed before. Like a bruise being layered on top of a bruise that was already there, and not by a careful top who knew what they were doing and wanted to hurt but not harm. No, this bruise went so deep, it hit bone.

Lowry shakes his head and then lays his forehead on our joined hands before kissing my knuckles and looking up at me, a supplicant.

"Tad Harding came to me."

My breath leaves my body all in a rush. Not as though I've forced it out myself, but as if it's been sucked by a vacuum. "Tad?"

"Aye. He said…he said my showing up when I did was rather suspicious and made the board doubt your capabilities. Our being in a relationship made people wonder if I was taking advantage of you. I'm not proud of it, but I let that get under my skin because it's something I'd scratched at myself. Not because you're weak, but because that's been a fear I've had. He poked at my worst parts, and I hate the fact that you can probably identify with that, but he seems like the kind of arsehole who uses that tactic as much as possible, so I'd be surprised if he never turned it on you.

"And I…I'd always known how much your father meant to you, but I hadn't known you felt that overseeing his company was somehow a way to redeem yourself in his eyes, which is just… Fucking hell, Star, if he couldn't see how incredible you are and didn't make you feel loved and like he was proud of you every day then I can't say I have a high opinion of the man. That's not the point, though. I couldn't stomach contributing to you feeling like any less than the marvel you are."

Lowry blows a breath through his nose and shakes his head, bowing it again.

"Being the cause of you losing something you wanted so desperately, it sent me reeling. I can't say I was making rational choices. All I could think of was to run, get out of here where my presence could hurt you. I didn't think enough about how my *absence* would hurt you, partly because Tad is… Christ, he's awful. He threatened to have you committed."

Any air I'd managed to breathe back into my lungs leaves again, this time through something that feels like a horse kick to my chest, which would explain why my voice comes out as a croak. "What?"

"It's ridiculous, and it wouldn't work. No one who isn't total shit at their job would ever consider it and Lacey knows better, would fight tooth and nail not to let that happen and so would I and anyone else on staff here. But the threat of it…I thought of how that would make you feel, how it would make the board see you. If he made it public, how ugly and disgusting it could get. If I'd had more time and less rage, I might've thought of a better way to handle it, but all I could think was that I had to get away from you, needed for them to think I wasn't a party to your decisions and that I wasn't influencing you. How I could do that if I wasn't here, if I'd..."

His skin has gone from its usual faintly ruddy cast to grey.

"If I'd left you again. Made me sick to do it, but I thought it would be easier in the short term, until you figured out what you wanted to do with Patrick Enterprises and got the gears turning well enough no one could stop it. I didn't want to be the reason you lost something so important to you."

He shuts his eyes tight before opening them again, and pins me with the intensity of his gaze.

"The truth of it is that I love you, Starla Elizabeth Patrick. I love you with everything I have, with everything I ever will have, and I should've told you sooner."

He loves me? I mean, I could've perhaps guessed that. Hell, I even went so far to tell Doctor Gendron I think he might. But once you've had voices whispering in your ear for twenty-odd years that you're unlovable, not worth anyone's time or attention, and then too damaged or too much trouble to be worth caring for, well. It makes those words far more difficult to believe. Even if I do...

That's when the tears start to fall in earnest. I don't tend to cry a lot so maybe it's the hormones, or maybe it's that I'm overwhelmed with the emotional roller coaster I've been on for the past several months. For someone who's spent so much of their life feeling somewhere around numb, all of this is a lot. Just, a lot.

"Star, love, why are you crying? Is it really so bad? Would you rather I take it back?"

Under the teasing rhythm of his words, there's a note of panic, and I try to stamp it out by banging a fist on his solid chest.

"No, you son of a bantha. I'm mad I might not remember this. How dare you tell me this now? You know my memory is shit right after treatments."

He makes a gruff noise and mutters something I can't quite make out, but then he's off his feet and scooping me up before settling onto the hospital bed with me in his lap, cradling my head against his shoulder where I weep. He rocks me and pets my hair—pets, not pats because there's a goddamn distinction—and murmurs to me, the soft tones of whatever nonsense he's speaking soothing. When some of the storm's blown out, he takes my chin between his thumb and knuckle until I'm looking at him, tear-streaked cheeks, red nose and all.

"Did I make you sick by picking you up?"

I shake my head.

"Good. I didn't think until after I'd done it, so I'm sorry. I couldn't…"

He tightens his grip on my flank where his other hand is resting.

"I'm sorry I cocked this up. I've been thinking it so long, you'd think I'd've had a better plan. But here we are. I promise you, though, you don't have to worry about forgetting. I'll tell you every day. Because every day I've loved you—it'll be far easier to say the words out loud than to keep swallowing them. I love you, Star. Always have, even when I shouldn't have. Always will, because I don't know how not to love you."

"You fucker. I hope you have that memorized because you're going to have to say it over and over."

"I will, don't you worry. You don't have to worry about anything anymore. I know you will, but you should know I'll be right there beside you and I hope you have enough faith in me to believe I'll help whenever I can. Of course, you'll need to smack me upside the head sometimes too. You need to give yourself more credit. I have just enough good sense to love you. Probably not much more than that, though."

"Shush, you. You're not perfect but you're pretty darn close. Fine upstanding man you are, Doctor Lowry Campbell. Fine enough that I trust you when I haven't trusted anyone else. You handle me like I'm precious, which is sometimes a lot to take, but it's… I love it. And that being true, I've got to tell you something."

I look down at my hands, feeling a bit disconnected from them. So I look back at Lowry. "I was in a really bad place when you left. Like went past devastated and all the way to feeling numb. I'm not telling you this to make you feel bad. I mean, I obviously found the wherewithal to deal with it, show up for my appointment and push the sale of my shares through because intellectually I knew it would help even if emotionally I felt like nothing could. I'm telling you because… I don't know. Maybe I shouldn't be, but I need you to know it still happens sometimes, that swamping numbness. It's not and probably won't ever be a hundred percent under control and if you can't stick around for that…"

He makes a choked noise and holds me tighter. "I'm sorry, Star. So sorry. I should've thought, I should've known, and I failed you. I did. There's no way to deny it and I won't because I fucked it up. I can give you my most heartfelt apologies, tell you I am so, so sorry. And I can say I'm glad you're telling me now. It's not fun to hear, it hurts my heart, but it's important for me to know. I always want to know, even if it's scary. Especially if it's scary. That's what—"

He stops himself short and I hear the hitch in his breath.

"That's what I'm here for."

"Were you going to say that's what my daddy's here for? Because I kind of wish you would have."

He barks a startled laugh and clutches me, kisses the top of my head and rocks me a bit. Makes my eyes water.

"I wanted to. Didn't think I deserved to. I'd do anything to earn back the privilege if you'll give me the chance."

Maybe I'm foolish, and perhaps I'm inviting more heartache, but I want him. Can't in fact imagine what my life would be like without him.

"And if I do, give you another chance…would you want to be

a father or would that be too much for you? I don't want to put that on you because I know—"

Lowry takes my chin in a firm grip as he leans away. "When you said it first, I did—I got that squeeze of panic. Certainty that I'm not fit to be a father, that I've got that monstrous blood coursing through my veins. But then I heard you telling me that was nonsense. And I believe you. Not because I want to exactly, but because I believe in you. So I have to say that it's up to you, but I think I'd like to be a dad. Like to think I wouldn't be a total cock-up about it. I mean, obviously, I'd need you around to make sure, but…"

His gaze roams my face, concentrating on my red, puffy eyes.

"But it sounds like you're not so certain. Do you not want to have a baby? Or did you not want to have a baby with me?"

Tension shapes his jaw, though he's doing his best to hide it. Perhaps he's forgotten that as closely as he studied me for all those years, I studied him too.

"You're about the only person I'd even consider having a baby with, but…"

I swallow and look down, embarrassed to be still clutching the grody tissues. I'm supposed to be a mom, how? Although I suppose holding disgusting things is a core parental duty, so maybe I'll be all right.

"But what?"

Blinking more rising tears out of the way, I force myself to look at him.

"But you know about my mother. As much as you're afraid of being like your uncle, I'm terrified of being like her. And when you left me…"

The overwhelming feeling of sick rises in my throat.

"Hey, listen to me. You're not like your mother. Your mother's condition was untreated, unmedicated, she insisted there was nothing wrong. You know better. You have faithfully and conscientiously taken care of yourself, and look at all you've done. You have a wonderful life, one that you protect by slaying demons all the damn time. I didn't know your mother, but from what your father said about her...she seemed more likely to dance with her demons than fight.

"And regardless of whether you want me romantically or not, I'm not going to leave you to raise a child by yourself if you want to have the baby. I wouldn't dream of it. Not because I don't think you're capable, but because that's a lot for anyone to handle. And I might be wrong, but it hasn't ever seemed to me that you were desperate to have children. It's hard enough to deal with children when you desperately want them, and I would imagine it's harder when you aren't completely sure."

"And you don't think dealing with two of us would be too much? If she ends up like me?"

His jaw flexes and his brows nearly meet in the middle. I've said something wrong. He's really considering what it would be like now, and it's hit home that it would be miserable. I should've kept my mouth shut and let Saint Lowry sacrifice himself.

"First, I don't think of it as 'dealing' with you. I'm sorry people have made you feel that way and I wasn't loud enough about how wonderful you are to drown the rest of the voices out. It's a privilege to know you. Yes, you have your struggles, but so do we all, and you're more conscientious about yours than most anyone I know. And you still find it in you to take care of other people, use all you know to help others who have some of the same difficulties. You've spent untold hours listening and learning so you can help people who are different from you too. You're brilliant, love, and not just anyone could build the business you have. I wish there were a million more people like you; the world would be a better place if there were."

For fuck's sake. I didn't go fishing for compliments, but the way he's looking at me, and talking...I should climb in a boat with a can of worms and toss my line in the compliment pond every goddamn day. The sweet things he's saying are food for my soul. I feel nourished and treasured.

Will his words always be enough to silence the ones that depression whispers to me? No, of course not. That's not how things work. But that's why I have my ECT. It's like a bomb that takes out most of the threat, and Lowry could be a sniper, taking down the small doubts that crop up one by one. But he's not magic. For all of the wonderful things about him, he's not a wizard, and it wouldn't be fair to treat him as if he is one.

"Second—" Oh my, he's not done yet. "Second, you've done all the hard work already. If she inherits your depression, we're not starting from ground zero. She'll be different for sure, but we wouldn't be flailing around in the dark, grasping at anything. You've shone a light on how your depression works and that will be helpful. We'll recognize the signs because you went through it all. We'll be able to offer help sooner and I think your dad, as much as he loved you, also bought into the stigma of getting help for mental health. We don't have that barrier. Also, you keep saying 'she.' Are you certain it's a girl? I thought it would be too soon to know."

Mmm, yes, that's a little embarrassing. "I don't *know* know. Like, it hasn't been confirmed by science or anything, but I…I can't explain it. I just know. From the second I found out, I've thought of her as, well, *her*."

He smiles at me, a turning up of the corner of his mouth. Slightly lopsided but none the less handsome for that. This man, he kills me.

"All right then. She. Her. I'd count myself lucky to have you both. If that's an option."

I think, foolish or not, it is.

"Do you… When we have the baby, *if* we have the baby, do you think…"

I bite my lip because I hate to ask, but it matters. Not that I'll change my mind about wanting to be with him, but it might take some more negotiating our precise relationship, where I'm getting which of my needs.

"Do you think I can still be your little girl? Even when we have our own little girl?"

"Oh, is that what you were worried about, love? I don't think you need to. I can be someone's father and still be your daddy. Now that I've had a taste of what we can be like together, I don't think I could give it up. We'll have to see how we feel because things can change, but yes, I have no intention of giving up my little girl. You're too sweet. I think if I bit you, sunk my teeth into your flesh, I'd end up with a face slick with juice, like I'd bitten into a perfectly ripe peach."

I have to giggle, and when he looks at me, a question in those blue eyes, I flush. "I, um, don't know if you'd get a mouthful of peach juice if you bit me, but maybe if you…"

There's a flash in his eyes, and he knows what I'm saying. Of course, he'll want to hear it anyway. Make me blush and stutter and get me slick and swollen between my legs.

"If I what, sweetheart? Hmm?"

"If you licked me."

"Like this?"

His tongue dances over the side of my neck, from my shoulder to my earlobe where he nips and sucks.

Just like that I'm jelly in his arms, soft and pliable while being squirmy with need.

"No, Daddy," I whisper, and he bites, sending a bolt of desire straight from where he's mouthing my body to where I'd like him to be. "I want you to lick my pussy. Please, Daddy?"

He fairly growls in that sweet spot between ear and jaw.

"I'll do more than that, little girl. I'm going to tie you up with your legs spread wide open for me and you're going to come half a dozen times, only the first time with my mouth. I'm going to lick at that sweet little pussy of yours until my mouth is covered with you, until you come all over my face. And that will be just the beginning."

I squeak because dear god, there is nothing I'd like better, but I really ought to not be getting so aroused here of all places. And god, what if Dr. Gendron comes in? Or one of my nurses? This is a rather, um, compromising position, for the both of us.

"Yes, please, Daddy. Take me home already. Please."

"I will. As soon as you get checked out and they say you're good to go. You seem fine, but I'm not going to risk my little girl. What kind of daddy would I be if I didn't take care of you?"

"Not a good one, and you're the best."

I give him one of my little smiles. Not that it's small, because it's not. It's one of those completely free, adoring, full of worship and trust and yes, love, which reminds me. I'm kind of awful.

"Daddy?"

"Yeah, sweetheart?"

"I love you. I should've said it before and I hope you haven't been wondering if I don't love you back. Because I do. Bunches and bunches."

I slip my arms around his neck and bury my face in his neck because if I think about precisely how much I love him, I might start to cry again. It's…a lot. More than feels safe, to be honest. But he's not going to let anything bad happen to me. He's going to protect me and keep me safe, and I'll do my best to return the favor.

I know from the way he holds me so tight against him that he knows how much I love him and he's doing his best to take it all in, to hold it, but it's going to overflow because that's how full of it I am. It cannot be contained. And spilling all over the place doesn't feel so scary anymore.

EPILOGUE

$\mathcal{L}$owry

THE SUN IS BEATING DOWN on this perfect spring day. No, not beating. Definitely more like beaming. As though it's rather pleased with how everything has turned out and is bestowing its glory upon us to tell us so. I happen to agree.

I do have to shade my eyes to see down the lengthy driveway, but then I see her. Hair flying behind her helmet, pedaling like mad with a goofy smile on her face as her streamers blow back. Glorious.

"Look, Ava," I say, pointing in Starla's direction. I had the good sense to put a sun hat on her, so unlike me, she doesn't have to squint to see down the ribbon of pavement. "Here comes Mummy on her bike. When you're a little older, we'll teach you how to ride a bike. Would you like that, jelly bean?"

She holds out her chubby fists, reaching for Starla even from this far away. I am most definitely a second-class citizen in Ava's big blue eyes. Maybe because she sees me more I'm old news? I cut down to half-time at Harbinson when Ava was born eight months ago while Star took a few months leave and didn't take on new consulting clients but meets with Jerome regularly. Keeps her busy, happy, feeling capable and satisfied, and she still spends plenty of time with our daughter.

Ava loves me, I'm sure, falls asleep in my arms most nights as I read her stories or sing, and she's got the sweetest baby gurgles when I reach into her crib to pick her up in the mornings. But she adores her mother. Will choose Star every time if she's got a choice. I don't blame her. I'd choose Starla over most anyone else too.

Finally Star comes to a stop in front of us, her cheeks pink with the exertion of riding up and down, up and down the drive. It's hilly out here at her father's house. Which I really ought to start thinking of as ours since we moved in over six months ago. It's an enormous place, we don't occupy even a third of it, but with the way Star looks at Ava, I wouldn't be surprised if given a few years another bedroom or two are occupied.

"That was fun! I think I'm getting faster, what do you think?"

"I think you're right. And Ava agrees. Don't you?"

Ava is trying to wriggle out of my arms and into her mother's. Starla takes pity on her and puts the kickstand down on her bike to take the tiny girl into her arms, perching her on her hip like she's carried babies all her life.

"Bah," Ava says, which I'll assume is her concurrence. And then shoves her fist almost entirely in her mouth to gnaw on it. Poor thing's teething and she hasn't been happy about it.

Starla smiles down at the little mischief-maker. "How old does she have to be to ride in a bike seat? Or in one of those little trailers? I think she'd like that."

Starla's started what we call the baby sway, which must be hardwired into our brains somewhere because unless you're extraordinarily awkward with infants, everyone does it when they pick up a baby.

"I bet she would, the little speedster. At least then we'd know where she was. She scooted into the closet again today, couldn't find her for a couple of minutes."

"Oh, Ava! Did you scare Papa to death? You know he doesn't like it when you wander off. He likes to know where his girls are at all times. Take pity on the man. You shouldn't be giving him heart attacks until you're sixteen and driving."

Oh, dear God, she's going to be a menace on the roads if her early mobility is any indication. She can't walk yet but it's not far off and already she's climbing on things, crawling under things, generally making it difficult to keep an eye on her. At least one of them is well-behaved.

"Take pity indeed." I have to scratch my jaw because while my impulse is to clutch my chest, Star worries when I do. I've tried explaining it to her—it's not that I'm ill or having some sort of cardiac episode. It's that my heart is so damn full when I look at the two of them it feels swollen, as though I couldn't possibly fit any more love inside and if I tried, it would likely burst. "If you're done training for the Tour de France, shall we have some breakfast? Pancakes? Eggs?"

"Omelet, please. With those diced potatoes and onions. Ava liked those yesterday, didn't you? Just big enough to get in your chubby little hand and smash into your hair, huh?"

So true.

Inside, I set to work in the kitchen, chopping the veggies, mixing up the eggs, heating the pan. It's a pleasure to cook in and an even bigger pleasure knowing there's someone to clean up after me. I tend to make a bit of a mess in the kitchen, but I think my enthusiasm makes the food taste better. Besides, Corinne complains if we don't give her anything to do. She'll be here in bit to make lunch and put together Ava's dinner.

Starla leans up against the counter while Ava beats a wooden spoon and a spatula together. She's got no rhythm to speak of, but she clearly delights herself. While the baby is occupied, Starla looks up at me from under her lashes and gets a certain kind of expression on her face. A look I like very much and makes my stomach tighten because I know what it means. Especially as she rolls her lips between her teeth before she speaks as she's doing now.

"Roseline is coming tonight."

"Is she, then?"

I know damn well she is. I've been looking forward to it all week.

"Yes." Star sticks her tongue out at me and I have to purse my lips to keep from laughing. "I'd ask if you've planned anything, but apparently you forgot."

"Ah, I wouldn't say I forgot…"

I spoon some of the egg mixture into the pan, enjoying how the bacon grease makes it sizzle.

"So you did make plans."

"Aye, I may have. Hopefully I got the tickets for the right night."

Starla perks up and Ava turns at being jostled. Not distracted from her kitchen drum kit for long, she snags a whisk from a container on the counter and drops the spoon on the floor.

"Tickets? For what?"

I shrug and poke at the edge of the omelet for doneness. Time to add the cheese. My chest starts to quake as I sprinkle the cheddar over the eggs because Starla is glaring at me expectantly.

"Lowry."

"Hmm?"

"You're the worst. Tickets? I need to know where we're going so I can dress appropriately."

"Don't worry about that, I've picked out your clothes already."

I have. A brand-new dress that I think she'll like because it looks like a grown-up dress but has a subtle print that makes it somewhat less grown-up. And will go perfectly with the movie we're seeing tonight. Downtown, so we can go to a fancy dinner first, and we'll stay over at Starla's old studio. She mostly uses it as a distraction-free office these days, but it comes in handy as a pied-à-terre as well. Christ, we're spoiled. And I do intend to spoil her tonight. She's been working so hard with her consulting clients, spending a lot of time with Ava, serving on the board of the nonprofit we started to help marginalized kids access high-quality mental health care, and keeping an eye on Jerome Garrett's stewardship of Patrick Enterprises. She could really use a night of mindless enjoyment—which I'm all too happy to give to her.

I fold the omelet closed and slide it out onto a plate I've kept warm in the oven because it's already got the potatoes on it.

"Careful, it's hot."

"You ought to be careful," she grumbles as she accepts it, trading her late breakfast for a glower.

"Oh? I think perhaps you're the one who ought to be careful. You know what happens to girls who forget their manners."

I raise my brows and dip my chin to give her that stern look she enjoys so much, and my breath catches when she rolls her lips between her teeth. Roseline can't get here soon enough.

STARLA

The movie was really good. I knew it would be, I've been looking forward to it for weeks and while I didn't think he'd forget, I was still a little surprised. A late show on a Sunday, so there weren't many kids there and we sat in the back so he could whisper things to me. So very wicked, that man is. As was his hand, edging up my thigh until his fingertips were under the hem of my dress. Not anything wildly inappropriate, but risqué enough that by the time we're heading up in the elevator in my building, I'm already slick between my thighs.

Partly because of the way he keeps touching me and talking to me, and my dress also isn't helping matters any.

The dress he picked out for me. I think he enjoys that more than he thought he would—dressing me up like a little doll for him to play with. He tries to pick things that will make me happy, yes, but he can be quite wicked about it as well. Exhibit A: the off-the-shoulder number I've got on tonight.

Close-fitting bodice and a fluffy knee-length skirt—with a petticoat underneath because the pouffier the better—it's an innocent white, with what look like specks and swirls of color from a distance. But we know better. Unicorns and dinosaurs and narwhals, oh my.

I'm standing in front of him, his hands firmly gripping my waist as he bends down to take advantage of my exposed neck and shoulders, kissing that especially prominent vertebra where the cervical and thoracic spine meet, sinking his teeth into my traps, and running his tongue up my neck to nip at my ear.

"What do you think, Star? Were you a good girl or a naughty girl tonight?"

Sometimes this has to do with my actual behavior, but more often it's his way of asking how I'd like to play; how I'm feeling, what I need.

Right now I need his approval like I need the air I breathe, but I also feel the need to earn it and not have it handed to me.

The elevator comes to a stop and the doors slip open with a ding. His hands no longer at my waist, he takes up my fingers and twines them between his own to lead me down the hallway.

The studio looks much the way it did when I lived here and in some ways, I breathe easier here than I do out in Chestnut Hill. No ghosts here to haunt me, no feeling that if something were to happen to Lowry I would be entirely in over my head. But we've also made it *our* home. Where we'll raise Ava, sweet and troublesome child. Maybe one or two more. We'll see. For now, I have Lowry all to myself and I plan to take full advantage.

Once we're inside the studio, the door shut and locked behind us, Lowry presses my back against the wall and slides his hands from my waist to my thighs and then under my skirt. In between kisses, he says, "You didn't answer my question, little girl. Have you been naughty or nice?"

"I've been good, Daddy. But I'd like to…I need…"

He stops kissing me long enough to lean back and look at me, study my expression.

"Would you perhaps like to be pushed a bit?"

I sigh in relief. It seems so easy when he says it, as though it was so obvious. Perhaps it is, but even though I love my life and it's overflowing with happiness and luxury, it exhausts me. There are always at least a couple of days a week when I come home from a day full of clients and phone calls and meetings and all I want is for Lowry to feed me dinner and put me to bed. Lovely, obliging man that he is, he does.

"Yes, please. Push me. Or maybe pull? Coax me. Encourage me. I want to do something difficult, but I need your help."

"Always."

He kisses me again, this time more deeply, his lips moving against mine until I yield to him and he licks into my mouth, exploring me, consuming me. There's something about being kissed this way. It assures me of his…not exactly possession, since Lowry doesn't own me, but of being his. His responsibility, that he will carry and shelter and cherish me. It lets me unwind, inhale more deeply, let my shoulders drop because he's going to care for me.

I can't help but invite him closer, wrapping a leg around him, which he takes advantage of to grasp my thigh and hitch it up farther to rest nearly at his waist. Apparently it's not good enough because he grabs my other thigh and I squeak as he hefts me up, pressing his hips between my legs, and yes. Yes. I wrap my limbs around him, wanting to be as close as possible, needing the warmth and strength of his body. I don't think I'll ever get my fill of him.

Gripping my ass, he carries me across the room and drops me on the bed, following so he's still nestled between my thighs. I'm already squirming, already eager for him, but he won't give me satisfaction yet. Not unless this is one of those nights were he forces orgasm after orgasm from my body until I'm a wrung-out and quivering mess, at which point he tells me I can give him one more and I do. I always do. That would be fine.

But tonight he runs his nose alongside mine, presses kisses to the corners of my mouth and my eyes, nuzzles at me until I'm a pliant puddle.

"How would you feel," he murmurs while he teases my ear with lips and tongue and teeth, "about me fucking your arse?"

Oh. *Oh*.

"I…"

The prospect is exciting but also intimidating and I want to but I'm nervous and… All of that is precisely why he's proposed this. It's exactly the kind of thing I want. And if it weren't, I have my safeword. I have but to utter "penguin" and he knows to stop. Otherwise I can cry and scream and beg to my heart's content but it doesn't change a thing because Daddy knows best. And isn't that wonderful? To be given the gift of not having to ask for what I want, indeed, even protest that I don't but getting the thing anyway. Perhaps not for everyone, but god, do I love it.

I let the wide-eyed shyness—the teeth-sinking-into-lower-lip, the looking-at-him-through-my-lashes, the squirming—take over.

"I don't know, Daddy. I'm nervous. Will it…will it hurt?"

"Oh, sweet girl. It might hurt a little, but if it hurts too much we'll stop. You know I'd never hurt my little girl on purpose. And besides, we've been getting you ready for this, yes?"

I nod, recalling all the nights after Ava's gone to sleep when he's worked his fingers inside me, or pressed a plug deep and made me keep it in until after he's spanked and fucked me thoroughly. Or sometimes plugged me before we go out so I spend the evening feeling full and empty at the same time, needing and wanting him, and suffering through his sidelong smirks because he knows precisely what he's done to me.

There's something about him touching me there, patiently and carefully working his way inside my asshole that just... I don't know how to explain it. It's one of the fastest, most effective ways to make me feel small, vulnerable, at his mercy.

"So we'll try because I've been wanting to stuff my cock inside your tight little hole for such a long time, and if it's too much, we'll stop. But I know you can handle it. I know you and your body so well, I know what you can take and I assure you that you can take me inside you there. And why's that?"

"Because Daddy knows best."

"Aye, that's right."

Saying the words makes me sink deeper into our game, deeper into his hold.

"First, though, I think you need to be turned over my knee. Not for punishment, just because I say so."

He oh-so-very-rarely actually disciplines me and it's always for something I've specifically asked him to hold me accountable for. Sometimes we play that he's punishing me, but not today. Tonight he wants to spank my bottom because he wants to. Just the idea of it makes my whole body suffuse with warmth, and desire pools in my breasts and my pelvis, making me wet and needy for him. All the yes, please.

Lowry levers off me and sits at the edge of the bed, patting his lap, and I don't hesitate to drape myself over his thick, sturdy thighs and clutch the pillow he's offered me. He doesn't waste any time but folds my skirt over my back, followed by my petticoat, and makes a delightful, satisfied noise when he's bared my underwear. Pure white with lacy frills, they're adorable and have been doing their work of making me feel small and pretty and a little naughty since I put them on.

It's only a second before he's running a hand over the ruffles that cover my cheeks.

"You have some very pretty panties on tonight, little girl. I like them very much. They won't stay on for your whole spanking because I want to feel your bottom and see it turn red, but we'll start with them on since they're so very sweet. Just like you."

Not that he needs me to say it as he hasn't asked me a question, but I say it all the same because I like how the words feel coming out of my mouth, the path they wear in my brain, the message they send to my body, and how it makes me feel between my legs. "Yes, Daddy."

He rubs and kneads at me for a while and it's funny to feel appreciated for something I have so little control over, but I do. Admired. Makes me preen, and, pleased, rest my head on the pillow while he touches me, his caresses getting rougher until yes, he's started to spank me. It's different this way, with the force of his hand buffered by the ruffles. Softer and more diffuse, more about the pressure than the sting because there isn't any. Just the thud of his slightly cupped palm and fingers meeting my butt over and over again. It's hypnotic.

I settle into the rhythm, the familiar path he covers from the bottom of my thighs to below my hipbones. It's like taking a bath in the most pleasantly warm water, makes me want to stretch out like a cat. Except then his fingers hook into the waistband and down the pretty panties go, settling beneath my cheeks for maximum playful humiliation.

Lowry makes one of a wide variety of Scottish grunts I've

come to know and love. This one seems to be a mild and not-actually-displeased dissatisfaction.

"After all that and your bottom's not only not red, it's not even pink. Luckily, we can fix that easily enough."

And he sets about doing just that. Not hitting me any harder, but without the layers of fabric in between, the impact is so much more significant, and I like his skin on my skin. Feeling the way his fingers trail the slightest bit before he's raising his hand and bringing it down again, the delightful *thwack* of palm hitting ass, and I could listen to that for a very, very long time.

Turns out I do because he's being extremely thorough, working me over until I suspect I'm glowing a lovely shade of pink, no doubt with spots verging on red.

"There. That's better," he observes, almost to himself, but he's saying it out loud for me. "Nicely done, princess."

Praise, I will take it, soak in it, let it wash over me because I've been so very good and he's pleased with me. I'm not at all surprised when I hear the sound of a drawer opening and then the snick of a cap. There's not much of a gap between that and his slick finger gliding down my cleft and over my asshole. Jesus. I've gotten a little less...squirmy about this, but I'm still a bit embarrassed about how much I enjoy it and perhaps that's part of the fun for both of us.

He takes his sweet time stroking and pressing before he adds more lube and legit pushes a finger inside me. Slowly, slowly, murmuring praise and encouragement as he goes, along with some extremely filthy things that make me squirm.

A quick, hard spank gets my attention and makes me stop trying to get the contact with my clit I really wanted, but it doesn't make me sorry, not at all.

"Don't be a naughty little thing. Are you really so impatient for me to stuff my cock in your arse, little girl? I thought you'd want me to take my time, get you all relaxed and stretched and ready to take me, but I'd be happy to take you right now."

He won't, I know he won't, he's saying this to give me that glowing ball of embarrassment in my belly that somehow works its way to my pussy and, on the way, turns into desperation and desire.

"No, Daddy. Please, I'll be good, I promise."

And I try, I really do try, but it's hard when he works in a second finger and fucks me with them. I've started moaning a little, making small, increasingly desperate noises.

"That's it, Star. You like it when Daddy finger-fucks your tight little hole, don't you? Just imagine how much better it's going to feel when you're stuffed full of my cock. You like being filled up, don't you, little girl?"

"Yes, Daddy." A little plaintive because yes, I do, and I want him to and he's got me nearing the delirium that will allow me to beg for it shamelessly. I'm already soaked between my legs and I want more. Want to be fucked, want him to take what he wants while still making me feel good, because my daddy always does.

This isn't the first time he's added a third finger, but it still feels like a stretch, still makes me feel full and pried open.

"Come on, Star. Relax for me. This is going to make it so much easier for me to work my way inside you. Don't you want to be a good girl for Daddy while I stretch your hole? You can take it, love. That's right."

I feel pinned in a way that's complete and filthy and overwhelming with the movement of his fingers inside me. He's pressing a hand into the small of my back, but there's no need. I'm not going anywhere. I don't think I could, but more so, I don't want to. Ever.

∾

LOWRY

God, she's lovely—upturned bottom in my lap, with three of my fingers pressed into the most private part of her body and knowing she'll let me have more. I've earned it. It took a while, and occasionally she'll be skittish with me when she's especially nervous, but she always comes round and it's my goal in life to never make her worry about me leaving ever again. The platinum band on my ring finger glints from where my hand is spread over the small of her back.

I wouldn't have cared if she didn't want to get married, but I do enjoy it. I am hers and she is mine and all that good stuff. My sweet little thing who isn't going to be able to contain herself for much longer, so I ought to get down to business.

"You know you said you'd been a good girl but I don't think you can say that anymore, my squirmy little princess. I think you've had enough of this, though, because I want to feel your climax with my cock in your arse."

She squeaks and it's the most delightful sound—utterly brilliant that I can feel it with my fingers buried inside her like this.

As carefully and gently as I pushed my fingers into her, I slide them out and rub the still-pink skin of her bottom.

"I'm going to wash up. Before I do, you're going to take off all your clothes except these frilly panties. You're to keep them right where they are."

Starla groans as I lightly pinch along her panties where arse meets thigh.

"Up you get."

It's sweetly awkward how she has to climb off me with her underwear hobbling her a bit and she stands there, face nearly as red as her bottom and then pulls her dress over her head, unfastens her bra and drops it to the ground. She's just so pretty I hate to leave her for even a second, but needs must. I pile two pillows in the middle of the bed and gesture to them. "Over you go, bottoms up."

She mewls again, looking at me with those big, pouty hazel eyes, but she enjoys the embarrassment, yes, she does. And her body responds so nicely to it as well, making her cunt slick and wet and welcoming. Doing as I've asked, she drapes herself over the pillows and it's a lovely sight.

"Now stay right there and don't misbehave. I'll know if you've rubbed yourself off on those pillows like a naughty, horny girl. Don't you dare."

Would I really? Who knows. Should she get a guilty look on her face or tell me—which she likely would—yes, but otherwise, probably not.

Upon my return, she's lying quietly, face turned away, but a slight shift of her hips and the curl of her toes tells me she's not entirely at peace.

I climb on the bed and there's a hitch in her breath as I kneel behind her. Probably because she can feel I'm as naked as she is, having stripped off in the bathroom. Sometimes when we do role-play—badly behaved girl gets sent to the principal's office is one of her favorites—I'll keep my clothes mostly on, but tonight I want to feel her skin on mine and reassure her with the warmth of my body.

The pale expanse of her back and hips is before me, so I take the opportunity to glide my hands over her flesh. Not too light—since the point is not to make her shiver and tremble—but firm and constant.

"Are you ready for me, love? I'll go slow."

Her voice is small when she says, "Yes, Daddy."

"You need to relax. Breathe. If it's too much, say so and we'll stop. I know you're a brave, strong girl but you've got nothing to prove to me here. If it hurts, we stop. This is supposed to make you feel good, and I'll be as patient as you need me to be."

Some of the tension in her shoulders unravels beneath my hands and she breathes as I've told her to, deeply and fully.

"Okay, Daddy. I'm ready."

I doubt her a bit since there's a tinge of stubborn in her tone but it'll do. I wasn't lying about being patient, but I *would* be lying if I said my head weren't about to burst with lust. There is only so long a man can go on about fucking his wife's gorgeous arse before he loses all his senses. I'm nearly there.

Luckily, I left a condom on the bedside table, so I unwrap it, and roll the latex over my length, wincing because Christ, I'm hard. And then I lube up, coating my throbbing dick well before I edge even closer to Starla to settle my erection between her cheeks and use my slicked-up cock to rub over her tight hole, which makes her buck beneath me.

Sweet little thing, doesn't take much to rile her up.

"You feel like heaven, Star. Even like this. Can't wait till I'm buried in you to the hilt. Would you like that, sweetheart? For me to be balls deep inside your tight arsehole and fuck you until you come? Think you could do it, filthy girl? Reach your climax from having me pound my cock into your hot, slick hole, maybe while I spank you to bring the color back to your bottom while I do?"

The dirty talk always gets her motor running, and hard. She presses her hips back against me, begging with her body, and I goad her.

"Come on, little girl. Don't whine about it. Tell me what you want. I could do this all night. Or maybe squeeze your arse cheeks tight around my cock and fuck you like that until I come. I'd rather be inside you, but..."

She makes a noise of squeaky indignation.

"No, Daddy, please."

"'No, Daddy,' 'Please, Daddy'? Which one is it? Tell me what you want. I want to hear you beg. Just a little. Come on, then."

Her chest constricts on a desperate laugh and she shakes her head. I give her a few beats to work up the nerve and she doesn't disappoint me.

"Please, Daddy. I need you. I want you to…to…" A frustrated little cry escapes her lips as she thrusts back at me again.

"Ah. Not until you say it."

"Please, Daddy, stuff your big fat cock in my ass and fuck me hard. I want to feel stretched wide open for you. Please, Daddy, fill me up."

"There you go. What a good girl you are, doing as Daddy asks. And now you'll get what you asked for."

I take my cock in hand to get the proper angle and then I begin to apply pressure. Star is tight, so very tight, and hot. Yes, the lube helps and she's not resisting, but good Lord. I work my way in, easing forward and pulling back to let the lube coat the inside of her arse to smooth my way and soon enough, here we are.

It's perhaps a bit of a caveman thing to say, but I love the way her tight hole looks stretched tight round my cock. I've rarely seen anything sexier. It doesn't hurt that she's been following my every word, breathing and relaxing to let me in.

"Tell me how it feels, little girl, to have your daddy buried in your freshly spanked arse."

"Oh, god. It feels good, Daddy. So good. So filthy and good and I, I want…I want more, please. Fuck me harder, Daddy, please. Spank my bottom while you fuck my ass."

Who am I to refuse that? The only way I would is if I passed out from being too turned on. Christ. She's asked to be fucked but I still start out slow because I won't hurt her. I won't. Pretty soon, though, I'm gripping her waist with one hand, giving her bottom forehands and backhands with the other as I fuck into her.

Her noises make me delirious; the desperation, the pleasure, the surrender to her bodily sensations instead of being so stuck in her head. Yes, this is what I wanted to give her tonight. What I want to do for her whenever she needs it for the rest of our lives. It's not so long of hard rutting before I'm about to spend and I don't think I can wait much longer.

"Come on, little girl. Come for Daddy. I want to feel your muscles clench my cock, I want your arsehole to milk the come right out of me."

Her fingers scrabble against the sheets and her hips meet mine as she rocks back against me, driving me deeper than I ever thought possible. It turns into a hard pumping, ever faster pistoning, and then I feel it. Hear it.

"Oh, Daddy. Fuck, yes, please, more. I'm coming, Daddy. Please, please, please."

Her chant devolves into a series of gasps and grunts and pleas as I grip both her hips and ride it out, letting myself blow now that she's got hers. There's a supernova behind my tightly closed eyelids and I shout. Not anything articulate because every ounce of energy I have is being used to survive the intensity of our climaxes.

At long last, Starla's slowing and I'm so exhausted I could collapse on top of her. Instead, I roll to the side and strip off the condom with a conveniently placed tissue. Even those three seconds are too long for me to be away from her and I take her into my arms as though I've been pining for her for years, famished for the touch and taste and smell of her.

Sated, she snuggles closer, burying her face into my chest and snaking a leg between mine. She feels perfect to me, how we fit together, limbs tangled, breath coming in sync. It overwhelms me sometimes, the depth of my love for her. And whether she knows it or not, she gives me as much as I give her. I squeeze her tight and kiss the top of her head, my sweet and filthy, darling and dirty little princess.

"Star?"

"Yes, Daddy?"

"I love you, my precious little girl."

"I love you too, Daddy."

Simple, perhaps, but I don't think there are words for what I feel for this woman, for what she has given me, what we've become to each other, so these well-worn phrases will have to do. I'll cherish her for as long as I'm allowed, my shining Star.

THANK you for reading *For Her Own Good*, I hope you enjoyed Shep and Erin's story. If you want more elegant superfilth, you'll want to one click *Taming His Teacher*. Turn the page for an excerpt!

TAMING HIS TEACHER

ERIN

I'm back at Hawthorn Hill, the only place I've ever really called home. Is it weird that it's an all-boys boarding school and I'm only four years older than some of my students? Yes. And what makes it worse is Zach Shepherd. He's my student, but he's also my biggest crush. To let anything happen with him would be career suicide but to stay away from him might shatter my heart.

SHEP

Three years after I graduated, I'm back on the Hill, this time as a member of the faculty. Some things have changed but I still think Erin Brewster is the prettiest woman I've ever seen. I want to be with her more than anything, and I've picked up a trick or two while I've been gone. Maybe with my new skills, I'll have Erin begging to be held after class...

Thanksgiving break is coming to an end. The boys will be filtering in in a few hours with hair just cut and suitcases of freshly washed clothes, maybe with a new video game or some gadget I won't understand the point of. For now, the dorm my tiny attic apartment is in is empty and I intend to enjoy.

I'd had Thanksgiving with a few friends in Somerville. They're all in grad school or law school or med school. I'm the odd one out with an actual job. They'd expressed envy over the fact that I earn a paycheck, but I placated their egos by insinuating how little I get paid.

Teaching at a boarding school has its advantages: room and board are provided, the benefits are good, and the strength of community is unparalleled. Rolling in dough is not one of them. It had been fun to see everyone and catch up, gossip about our classmates. It was good to not be alone in that in-between space: the not-quite-adult I have to be with my colleagues and not-quite-adolescent I'm not allowed to be with my students. But I'm an introvert at heart and it was a distinct relief to climb into my car at the end of the night and drive back to my own apartment instead of crashing on a futon.

But in the stillness of the empty dorm, the silence is oppressive. I've finished the book I've been savoring—one that's incredibly hot in a way I should be perturbed by liking because it's hovering so close to the edge of being not okay. Followed by taking a bath in my too-small tub to wash away the slickness of my arousal and the subsequent orgasm I'd rubbed myself to while imagining all of those invasive and intimate and hotly shameful things happening to me.

Once I'd gotten that out of my system (and put the book in the freezer), I'd watched a few movies while eating leftover Halloween candy and folding heaps of overdue laundry. I'm looking forward to the boys coming back, settling into the familiar routine that fills my waking hours. It gives me confidence to get through the day. In the meantime, my body is bouncing, full of energy. The athletic facilities are locked, won't open again until morning, so I've got one alternative: Dance Party.

I'm already decked out in my *Flashdance* best: cropped leggings, a tank top and a sweatshirt I'd cut the neck off. It's a short trip to turn on my laptop, hook it up to the speakers and crank up my eighties mix. Soon I'm rocking out hard, busting out my best moves. For a white girl, I'm not too bad, thanks to the hip hop classes I'd taken to blow off steam and take up time in college.

After a good twenty minutes of shaking what my momma gave me—one of the only things she gave me—I'm sweating. They've turned the heat on in the dorms though this fall's been unseasonably warm and my apartment's sweltering. I shove open the window that's been painted a dozen times, the last coat still sticky from when it was painted over this summer, and open my door to let the cross-breeze in.

My head is clearing while I'm doing my best Molly Ringwald impression when there's a knock at my door. Or, more accurately, my doorframe. I'm startled into a shriek and clap my hands over my mouth, turning to see who my intruder is.

Shep.

My face flames and I hold up a finger to tell him to wait. We won't be able to hear each other over Deniece Williams. Never mind I need a minute to collect myself. How long was he standing there? This is humiliating. Although it could've been worse. I could've been going to Funkytown. Or whipping it. Or it could have been someone other than Shep. Shep's not going to do an impression of me in the dining hall and he's not going to bust my chops about my sick dance moves in class. My mortification settles into a low burn of embarrassment. Shep will keep my secrets.

"Mr. Shepherd. I thought you boys weren't due back until four."

He's standing there in jeans and one of the light fleeces all the kids seem to wear when they're not required to be in dress code, hands shoved deep in his pockets. He stubs an Adidas-clad toe into the dingy carpet of the hallway and looks down.

"My dad has to work tomorrow. He wanted to get home early."

Right. His eyes find mine and his gaze makes me flush hotter. It's not a leer like I get from some of the boys, especially the ones who don't have me in class, but it is an observation. A study. I have a flashback to Shep's drawings in the art show and all the wrong areas in my body tighten when I picture him sketching me. I drag the cuff of my sweatshirt over my forehead to wipe away the sweat and shove some escaped tendrils of hair behind my ears. *Don't remember me like this.* My thoughts stutter as I try not to imagine how I *would* like Shep to draw me. A rational thought would be great, but my head doesn't seem willing to supply one. I'm grateful when Shep does.

"I told Mr. Foster before I left I'd have to come back early. I guess he forgot. Dorm's locked."

"Of course. I'll get my key." *Jeez, Erin, why did you think he was showing up at your door? To seduce you?* I hurry to the rack on the wall where I keep my keys, find the extra set to Ford, and shove my feet into a worn pair of flip-flops. "Let's go."

Shep eyes me closely. "It's kinda cold out there, Miss Brewster."

I wave a hand. "It's not far. Besides, I need to cool off."

He tilts his head in a way that makes me want to run back to my bedroom and grab my warmest parka, but I've made my call. I shut the door to my apartment and scrawl a note on my white board to say I'll be back in five in case there are other early arrivals who come looking for me. Then I traipse down the stairs, Shep's heavy footsteps following mine.

I do my best not to look back at him and try to make small talk about his vacation as we cross the small quad. Shep's not a big talker anyway, but his one-word answers tell me home is not the greatest place in the world. It's possible he'd rather be here, feels more at ease on campus than he does with his family. He wouldn't be the only one. The Hill is the only place on earth where I can plant my feet on the ground.

By the time we reach the front door where a worn duffel and his familiar backpack are waiting, I'm shivering. My stubbornness has turned out to be foolishness. I use one hand to rub my arm while my shaking fingers attempt to get the key into the lock.

It's not that cold outside, but in my overheated state and sweat-drenched clothing, I'm freezing. My toes are thin and shivery, like they'd snap off if I stubbed my toe. The lock thunks open and I pull the door to let Shep in.

"Leave a note on Mr. Foster's door to let him know you're back, okay? See you in the morning."

I turn to skitter across the frozen tundra to Oliver, hugging my arms against my chest and trying to rub warmth into my biceps. I'm stopped by a warm hand on my shoulder. "Miss Brewster, take my coat."

Shep is stripping out of the fleece, revealing a hint of plaid boxers peeking out over the waistband of his jeans and a tantalizing strip of skin and a dust of hair trailing... *No, no, no no no!* I clench my eyes tight to get the picture of my fingers running over that skin, the ripple of muscle, out of my head. I open them to Shep holding out his fleece, a rugby shirt settled on his frame, mercifully hiding any more skin I might covet.

I hesitate. This seems inappropriate even if I weren't having the thoughts I'm having, and I am. I'm a second from waving him off.

"Erin."

His voice is a command. It's almost the tone I've heard him use on the soccer field with his teammates, but there's a different edge. One that makes my knees weak and, heaven help me, everything south of my waist tighten and throb. I should scold him for using my name but my synapses are too busy sending signals to other parts of my body to get the words out.

"Take my coat. Please. You're freezing. I don't want you making yourself sick." My lips part, revealing chattering teeth, and I reach for the coat. The expression on his face softens when I take it. He's back to being one of my students. "Can't have you missing class. There's too much to cover. I'll never pass the AP if we don't get through it all."

I yank the fleece over my head, warm from his body and smelling of his clean, Ivory-soap scent. A lot of the boys wear expensive colognes. They smell like luxe department stores. Not Shep. His aroma is drug-store toiletries made irresistible by the fragrance of him layered underneath. I tug the zipper all the way up my throat and realize I'm swimming in it. I have to push up the sleeves so I can see my hands. I look like a toddler in my father's clothes.

"Thank you. I'll have this back to you tomorrow."

He nods and bends to pick up his bags, slinging the backpack over his shoulder.

"Thanks, Miss Brewster."

"Of course. See you tomorrow."

I huddle inside the warmth of his coat, trying to deny the pleasure of being surrounded by him, and hurry across the quad. I look back before I open the door to Oliver. Shep is standing with the door open, waiting for me to go inside. Not until I swing the door open does he heft his duffel bag and go inside himself.

Click to read *Taming His Teacher* now!

THANK YOU!

- If you'd like to know when my next book is available, you can sign up for my new release mailing list at tamsenparker.com or follow me on social media (see the full list on my About the Author page).
- Reviews help readers discover books. I appreciate all reviews and the time it takes to share your thoughts.
- You've just read *For Her Own Good*. Turn the page for a full listing of my books. Thanks so much for reading, and I hope you'll keep in touch!

ALSO BY TAMSEN PARKER

The After Hours Series

Alpha in the Sheets

Bound in the Streets

Reclaiming His Wife

For His Eyes Only

A Heart to Keep

Insidious

The Snow and Ice Games Series

Love on the Tracks

Seduction on the Slopes

On the Edge of Scandal

Fire on the Ice

On the Brink of Passion

The License to Love Series

Thrown Off Track

The Inside Track

Hot on Her Tracks (Release Date TBD)

Camp Firefly Falls

In Her Court

Love, All

Standalone Novels

Taming His Teacher

His Custody (Re-releasing Fall 2019)

For Her Own Good

If I Loved You Less

Short Stories and Novellas

Needs

(Originally published in the Winter Rain anthology)

Looking for a Complication

(Originally published in the For the First Time anthology)

Dedication of a Lifetime

(Originally published in the Rogue Affair anthology)

Craving Flight

Anthologies

Rogue Desire

Rogue Affair

Rogue Hearts

Rogue Ever After

Best Women's Erotica of the Year Volume Four

ABOUT THE AUTHOR

Tamsen Parker is a USA Today bestselling romance writer, with books in the erotic romance, hot contemporary, sports, and now sweet subgenres, and writes about f/f, m/f, and m/m couples falling for each other. *The Lesbian Review* named both IF I LOVED YOU LESS and FIRE ON THE ICE to their Top 15 Books of 2018, and IN HER COURT as one of the Top 10 Audiobooks of 2018. Her novella CRAVING FLIGHT was named to the Best of 2015 lists of *Heroes and Heartbreakers, Smexy Books, Romance Novel News,* and *Dear Author. Heroes and Heartbreakers* called her After Hours series "bewitching, humorous, erotically intense and emotional."

facebook.com/tamsenparker

twitter.com/tamsenparker

instagram.com/authortamsenparker

bookbub.com/authors/tamsen-parker

pinterest.com/tamsenparker

ACKNOWLEDGMENTS

As those of you who follow me on social media know—because I referred to this as The Book That Won't Die—For Her Own Good has been A LOT. It's intensely personal in a lot of ways and writing it forced me to grapple with some really hard topics. It's a lot longer than I was anticipating which threw off my whole carefully orchestrated schedule but I needed to let Lowry and Starla tell their story, their whole story. I would not have made it without my squad, my team, and for them I am forever grateful.

AJ, Misha, and Jill kept me going when I felt like quitting. They listened to epic amounts of whining and angst and basically are the best friends a girl could ask for.

My Becca Bird's enthusiasm kept me going—she's been begging for this book since I uttered the words "ex-psychiatrist daddy kink."

Christa Désir, my editor, worked her usual magic with a sensitive and deft touch while still challenging me to make the best book possible and questioning my bullshit. Idk, she's magic.

Manuela Velasco from Tessera Editorial, my copy editor, was everything you would expect from one of Christa's mentees.

Thorough, consistent, compassionate, and, unlike me, knows where to put commas.

Lori Jackson, my cover designer, gave me the most swoon-worthy Lowry I could have dreamed of, and has the incredible ability to make things perfect based off my feedback which generally goes something like "Idk, it just doesn't look right?"

And as always to the readers and reviewers who spend their time and resources on my books when you have so many choices, thank you for spending your precious time with me and my words. I am so thankful for all of you.

Printed in Great Britain
by Amazon